THE DESCENDANTS

JADE ALTERS

SHARED BY THE FOUR

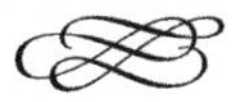

❀ Created with Vellum

Acknowledgment

I just want to thank all of those readers who have had the patience to follow me through the ups and downs of my journey.

I know I am far from perfect, but I will continue to work hard for my fans.

Love,
Jade

SELENA

"Shoot. Stupid lock!" I took a deep breath, turning my key with what my roommate had once called a 'loose wrist' because the damn lock was tricky as hell. "C'mon, c'mon!"

I was all dressed up and ready to head to the Asher Quinn opening at Room 6 in Chinatown but, of course, I'd left my lipstick in my dorm. I wasn't too precise about my makeup usually, but I knew how these things always went. I'd show up looking on point, ready to loosen up with some complimentary wine, and leave half my lipstick on the rim of one of those plastic cups like they give you on airplanes, just in time for a cute guy (who I had no time to date anyway) to see me looking less than flawless. My logic was, if I'm going to be running into hot guys I'll never talk to again, I might as well leave them with a lasting impression.

"Aha!" I all but fell into the dorm, catching myself quickly, and stomped over to my bed to grab the cheap drugstore version of my favorite MAC color off the pillow. Once back in the hallway, I packed the lipstick away in my clutch and took a deep breath. The shoes were new but they were pretty comfy for strappy heels. I'd nabbed them for a steal in the Garment District. I was wearing all skin-hugging black except for a mustard swing skirt. I called the outfit one of my Gallery Opening Ensembles. A small part of the reason I was majoring in Art History was to wear cool outfits to gallery openings. A *small* part. The larger part was because I dreamed of writing books about art, getting my Masters someday, and maybe teaching. Sometimes I fantasized about living in some mysterious huge house that looked out on some other country (I'd never decided which) and writing books about artists and art history, perhaps in the company of some beautiful man, assuming I ever met one worth spending any time with. So far, I was more interested in art than men, especially college guys. They always seemed to want to talk about themselves and I found them boring.

Having gathered myself, I made my way to the stairs and out onto the USC campus, shoving my hands into the pockets of my snug moto jacket. I was excited, and smiled to myself, humming as I walked. I'd had my head stuck in my books all day, writing papers on autopilot, and worrying about midterms. When I wasn't studying, I was reading. I'd barely seen the light of day lately outside of hustling from class to my dorm and back, guzzling coffee each way. It was nice to go out on the town. I was also giddy about this particular gallery opening.

Asher Quinn!

I'd been so busy with my schoolwork that I hardly had time to follow the world of contemporary art, but I paid attention somewhat by following a few blogs and arts news sites. Asher Quinn was one of my favorite contemporary artists and like any of my favorites, I had a difficult time summing up something academic sounding when I spoke about him. Of course, I could talk about his sense of form and design all day but, to me, great art is beyond words. All I knew was that Asher Quinn's paintings made me feel *alive*, and wasn't that what art was about? They were usually huge and bright, the color seeming to jump right off the canvas, or rather the screen. I had only ever seen Asher Quinn's magic on my crappy laptop. If he was that exciting in two dimensions, God knew how explosive his work would be in real life. I couldn't wait to find out.

It wasn't very late but the campus seemed quieter and darker than usual for a Friday night. Still, I felt relatively safe. When I'd left home in Green Bay for Los Angeles, my mother had been worried about me going off to such a big city alone, especially once she realized how close USC was to downtown. Campus could be tougher than downtown though, so I tried to walk like I was tough, like I knew Krav Maga or something. Which I don't...but I *could*. I kept my back straight and took big, hard steps, clutching my keys in my hand. It was not something I thought about constantly anymore but I'd managed to cultivate a pretty good 'don't fuck with me' stride. It helped that I was fairly tall, about as tall as the average guy. I had long, dark hair and big brown eyes on a heart-shaped face. Sometimes I stood in front of the mirror and made mean faces to use on people who might try to mess with me. But I usually looked ridiculous and ended up making myself laugh.

Despite that…

The steps were quiet, deliberately stealthy, but I heard them. The hairs on the back of my neck were standing up. I had been humming to myself but now I stopped, clenching my fists in my pockets. I whipped around, expecting to see somebody. I was hoping my intuition was wrong. I hoped I'd see some student out having a smoke who only seemed creepy in the unusual quiet of the night. But there was nobody. Great. A ninja was following me.

"Anyone out there?" I said, feeling like an idiot. "I know Krav Maga, ya know!" I shook my head. "My intuition is bullshit." I walked on, my mood now a little tainted by that spooky feeling that still wasn't going away. I focused on the sound of my own footsteps and the puff of my breath. I had my keys in my right fist. If somebody *was* following me I could make Wolverine claws out of the keys and stab an eye out probably-

Tap tap.

Footsteps again. I heard a cough that had enough of a voice in it that I recognized it and stopped, throwing my head back, and rolling my eyes. This was getting so old.

Goddammit.

"Aiden!" I said. I turned just in time to see an all too familiar figure jumping behind a big bulletin board papered with fliers. "Aiden! Come out, will you? It's not funny."

I heard a laugh that made me want to kill a man or two and then Aiden was strolling out from behind the bulletin board like he hadn't just been acting like a total creeper.

"Jesus, Aiden." I took a breath, trying to shake off that spooky feeling. Aiden was in a few of my classes. He kept asking me out. He didn't want to hear 'no' either. It was annoying.

"I was just messing with you," Aiden said, grinning. Aiden was pale, blond, and handsome enough, although he had a kind of cocky grin that was supposed to be charming and came off obnoxious, at least to me. Every time I rejected him, he seemed to take it as a challenge. If I said no, he thought I was just playing hard to get. He didn't seem to understand that I was never going to say yes.

"Yeah, every woman loves getting followed while she's walking alone at night," I said dryly. "Funny joke. You should do stand-up." I spun around, intent on getting to the gallery opening and away from Aiden...but Aiden wasn't getting the message - as usual.

"So, where you going?" Aiden skipped ahead, walking backward in front of me so that I was forced to look at him. "You look great, by the way."

"Nowhere," I muttered. "And I really don't give a shit if you think I look great."

"C'mon." He gave me a look like he was sorry and we were old pals. "Honestly, you shouldn't walk around here by yourself at night. Unless you really do know Krav Maga. And you don't."

"Maybe I do," I cracked.

"Let me walk you?" Aiden said. "You headed to your car or...?"

I didn't have a car. It was a sore subject; living in Los Angeles without a car. But between student loans and a few scholarships, I was barely making it. I couldn't afford insurance and gas on top of that. At least the public transit was pretty good downtown, and these days I didn't spend much time off campus anyway.

"I'm just going to the library!" I blurted out. I felt stupid making that up. I should've just demanded he leave me alone. If I told him I was lying now, it was a *thing*. Though I certainly wasn't about to tell him where I was really going. The last thing I wanted was annoying Aiden showing up and ruining my night of Asher Quinn.

"Well, I'll walk you then," Aiden said.

Great. Now I had to actually go to the library and hope he gave up like some messed up game of stalker chicken. I screwed up my face and snarled, "Wonderful."

Luckily, the library was close by and still open for students working on their papers late into the night. Or anyway, I told myself that it was lucky while thinking about how I only had the rest of the year to go before I never had to see annoying Aiden again. But *first,* I had to finish my paper on contemporary surrealism compared to neo-surrealism. I was trying to figure out a way to work in Asher Quinn who had a toe in the surrealist school though he was typically classified as an abstract expressionist.

"So, when are we going out?" Aiden had his obnoxious grin on again.

"Busy," I said, scowling.

"Pfft! You're not *that* busy," Aiden said. "I know for a fact that when you're not studying, you're just reading all day. Your roommate told me."

Oh fantastic, I thought. He was pumping my roommate for info.

"That's part of me being busy," I said, smiling tightly. "And don't ask my roommate about me. It's freaking me out." At the library I stopped at the door and threw out my hands. "Hey, we're here. Okay, bye."

Aiden tossed me a nod as if he was saying goodbye but he didn't actually move. I sighed heavily and went inside, wandering into the art history section like I usually did. I picked out a random book and sat close enough to the window that I could see Aiden.

It took a solid fifteen minutes before Aiden finally left. I was pissed. Screw Aiden for making me run late to an opening by one of my favorite painters. Also, screw my roommate for telling him anything about me. *Nice* one, Nancy. I wanted to listen to some music as I made my way to catch the shuttle to the Metro into Chinatown but I was still a little spooked, and thought I should stay alert. Instead I started thinking about how Asher Quinn's *Castle Series* was a good entry into talking about his surrealist tendency. Those paintings were the least abstract; surreal depictions of huge old houses in various states of decay. They made the viewer think of some fallen aristocracy; something ancient and grand that was fading into extinction. Yet, like all of Quinn's work, they were full of color and life. It was a weird juxtaposition. I promised myself, if I ever got a chance to talk to Asher Quinn, I'd ask him about it. Cheered by the very idea of talking to Asher Quinn, I smiled to myself, and hopped onto the shuffle just as it rolled to a stop in front of USC.

ASHER

I would never tell my brothers, but gallery openings always made me a little nervous. I am, by nature, a confident person. I mean for God's sake, I once hit on the Queen of Vampires at a vampire ball and they'll kill a shifter on sight if they're in the wrong mood, so I'm really not afraid of what people think of me. But when it comes to my art, deep down I can be a little sensitive. Even as I think it, I can hear Ben laughing at me and rolling his eyes and probably saying, "A *little* sensitive, huh?"

Alright, I can be quite sensitive about my work.

But Ben is also sensitive about his music and Carter feels strongly about his dance and if you make the wrong kind of comment about something Damien's just written he's likely to shift and run up into the Hollywood Hills and not be heard from for weeks. We are, all of us Quinns, quite devoted to our respective arts. Maybe that's what happens when you throw your passion into something after a terrible heartbreak. And our heartbreak was the deepest kind.

I clasped my hands behind my back and stood in front of *Red Wolf*. My exhibition was called *Wolf Series*. It was the most personal exhibition I'd done so far. It was so personal that my brothers and I had been hesitant to show it to anyone until Damien said we were all being stupid.

"Just step out of your little bubble and think about this logically for a minute," Damien had said. "You really expect a bunch of art critics to look at your paintings of wolves and think well, I guess Asher Quinn is a wolf shifter and a wizard?"

Yeah, probably not.

Still, critics would likely recognize the personal nature of the work. It was my job to be vague about *why* it was so personal. A magician•never reveals his secrets and an artist never reveals the meaning of his work. At least that was my philosophy.

"Oh, Mr. Quinn?" A young woman on staff at the gallery approached, looking a little intimidated, and smiled with bright red lips. "Henry Forsyth from *Art Now* would like a quick interview with you later? Do you think you'll have time-"

"Yes, fine," I snapped and quickly felt a bit guilty. I turned to smile at her in apology but she was already gone. The gallery had a buzzy feeling about it, staff all in black rushing around, putting on the final touches and laying out the wine and cheese.

"Somebody's nervous..." Ben's voice came in a sing-song like it so often did and I spun again, glowering at my (slightly) younger brother. Where I have the darkest hair of the Quinns that brushes my shoulders and eyes that are nearly black, Ben has a head of thick warm brown hair that he brushes into a kind of flume on top of his head. It's impressive really. His big soft brown eyes seemed even bigger behind his glasses tonight.

His glasses...

"Ben," I said darkly. "You're wearing glasses."

"Yeah yeah yeah." Ben waved a hand. "I know-

"How many times do we have to tell you-"

"I *know*-"

Carter's softer voice came from behind us. "Take your contacts out *before* you shift." Carter chuckled and punched Ben in the shoulder. "What's that, four pairs of contacts in the last three months?"

"Two!" Ben said. "Just two! Alright, three. It's hard to remember! Anyway, I think I'm going to switch back to glasses anyway. How come our clothes shift with us but not my contacts? Isn't there a spell around that?" He pushed up his glasses and his nose twitched. It was a funny little behavior that I think he'd picked up in his wolf form. "I get so excited when I'm about to..." He glanced around and seeing no one within earshot, quietly said, "shift."

"You were always like that," Carter said fondly. "Hyper puppy." Carter was the youngest of us, though considering we were all over a hundred years old, that hardly mattered. Yet I still thought of him as my baby brother. He was shorter than the rest of us and muscular yet lean which made sense for a professional ballet dancer. Unlike the rest of us, he was also blond and had blue eyes so pale and bright you might think he was magical even if you didn't know he was both a talented spellcaster and a shifter.

"Where do the contacts go when you shift?" Carter said. Carter looked rather debonair tonight, his blonde hair styled just so and his black suit fitting beautifully. He crossed his arms and smirked at Ben, his shaggier brother.

Ben sighed and ran a hand through his explosion of hair. "They fall out. Once one got kind of stuck in my wolf eye. Stung like a bitch."

Carter snorted a laugh at that and I frowned at Ben. "Are you wearing skinny jeans to my opening?"

"Carter," Ben said. "This is L.A., chill. It's not like Victorian times either. The queen isn't coming, ya know."

"You're missing a tag here." Damien was quiet, as was usual. His voice was so low it was easy to miss what he said, yet he was often the most thoughtful among us. He stalked forward and tapped the empty spot of wall next to *Green Wolf*. "See?"

My heart jumped into my throat. "WHAT KIND OF AMATEUR HOUR-"

"Asher!" Damien reached out to squeeze my hand. He looked at me hard, taking a deep breath, and I reflexively breathed with him. Damien is tall and broad like Ben and I, but he's thin and chiseled (his jaw could cut glass) because he thinks when he should be eating. Sporting dark maple hair and eyes as deeply green as fir needles, he was gorgeous in an ethereal way. I've always suspected Damien has some kind of power to calm people down by looking at them that the rest of us don't, but it's never been confirmed. "It's fine." He nodded at Ben. "Go find that Mara person and get the tag, will ya?"

"On it!" Ben chirped and spun away in his skinny jeans. He returned in less than a minute with the tag and stuck it to the wall with an expression of triumph.

It was typical of Ben, the second oldest and second in command to my Alpha. He could be infuriatingly devil-may-care but in a pinch, you wanted Ben on your side. And in battle, you definitely wanted Ben on your side. There was a reason he was my second, even if he did forget to take out his contacts before shifting and dressed too casually for my liking.

"Everything's cool, boss," Ben said. He came around behind me and rubbed my shoulders for a second which did somehow put me at ease. "Gonna be your best opening ever."

"You ready?" Damien gave me that steadying look of his and I nodded in spite of myself.

"Of course, I'm ready," I said.

Carter clapped his hands. "Let's do this!" He threw a little wave at two staff members waiting by the entrance and they nodded and turned to push the glass doors open. I was relieved to see a small crowd of people already rushing in, and the tensed up wolf within me relaxed as I heard the hum of oohs and aahs around me. The sharpened hearing of a wolf shifter can be both a blessing and a curse as my brothers and I could easily hear just about every conversation being had in the place. I saw Ben stifling a laugh as I made my way to the wine table, and wondered if he was listening to the same conversation I was as two bearded hipster types on the stairs tried to lump me in with Andy Warhol for some reason which made no sense at all.

I caught Ben's eye and spoke into his mind, the gift of speaking telepathically to each other was one we all shared.

Warhol? I said.

Didn't we meet him once? Ben said back.

Yes, he stiffed me on a dinner check.

Ben only shook his head at me and I shrugged, smirking. I poured myself a plastic cup of Cabernet and my hand shook for just a moment as I heard someone debating which *three* paintings to buy and gushing over the series. That was a nice surprise. Though I wasn't in art for the money (only a fool would be), it was always great to be appreciated. Anyway, us Quinns have more money than we could spend even if we lived another few hundred years. That's never been what the arts are about for us.

"Asher!" The gallery curator - a rail of a woman with a shock of silver hair - was waving me over to the smaller room off the main gallery and I threw back the rest of the wine, squeezing through a cluster of people so I could get to her over by *Orange Wolf*. "*...L.A. Weekly*," the curator nodded to yet another bearded hipster holding an iPhone out like a microphone and I smiled, attempting to look disarming, like Ben would.

"Asher Quinn." I shook his hand. "Pleasure to meet you."

The interview went alright...I think. Sometimes those things are a bit of a blur and I tend to get riled up when I talk about art - or spellcasting or shifting or my brothers and then I start clutching my hair until my scalp aches so that I won't shake the person I'm talking to by the shoulders. When the interview was over I started to head to the restroom in the back, intending to splash a little water on my face but I stopped short, standing in the middle of the crowd of people enjoying my exhibition.

A terribly strong feeling was pulling me back towards the main gallery. The feeling was so strong that a chill ran down my spine but I wasn't afraid. It took a lot to make me afraid. The closest thing I could compare the feeling to were times when I somehow knew my brothers were in danger without them reaching out to speak to my mind.

Do you feel that? I said to Damien. I thought he was upstairs but I wasn't sure.

Yes, Damien said. *What the hell is it?*

I'll find out. Tell the others to stay alert.

You got it, boss.

SELENA

It occurred to me as I strolled through the gallery that I might really get a chance to talk to Asher Quinn. I was hearing people say around me that Asher liked to talk to casual patrons, not just critics and people rich enough to invest in his work. There were plenty of casual patrons around too. I saw people of all ages enjoying *Wolf Series*, many who looked like they'd just walked in off the promenade to see what the fuss was about and now they all seemed enthralled. It made me happy to see his success.

Making my way back to the main room for yet another whole viewing of the series from start to finish, I stopped off at the wine table. The thing was, I didn't know what Asher Quinn looked like. I was racking my brain, but somehow reading about his work I'd never so much as glanced at a picture of him. At least, I didn't think I had. He was much older, wasn't he? His work seemed like the work of someone who had seen so much of life, it spoke of a great passion tempered by wisdom. I took a cup of merlot and ate a few pieces of brie and for the second time that night, as I thought about Asher Quinn, I had another strange feeling.

This time I didn't feel creeped out, rather, I felt like something very important was about to happen and I couldn't miss it. It felt urgent and seismic. I looked out over the crowd of people as if waiting for something. What I expected, I didn't know. But given how crappy my intuition had been tonight I tried to ignore it. I went back to the first painting, *Red Wolf*, and jostled my way into a good spot to view it just as some noteworthy critic started speaking on the other side of the room and a crowd rushed over to listen to him pontificate on the meaning of *Wolf Series*.

I heard something about *Wolf Series* being about the 'degradation of modern man' and snorted in derision.

"Gimme a break," I said to myself, taking another sip of merlot.

The one guy who hadn't followed the crowd to listen to the lecture was standing next to me, his hands clasped behind his back. Now he glanced at me, smiling, as if in agreement.

Everything stopped.

Just for a moment, the hum of conversation in the gallery was silenced, the rest of the gallery a blur around me, as everything seemed to focus in on this one man and my heart began to pound. I've never believed in love at first sight, and I wouldn't describe this that way. It was more like an intense instinctual feeling that this man was important *somehow*. Whatever the important thing was that I felt coming, it had to do with him. My heart thudded painfully and my hand holding the cup of wine shook so badly that I downed it all at once before I could spill it all over the floor. The man looking at me was dark-eyed and beautiful in some unconventional way; his face was not perfect with a long chin and crooked nose, but it was the kind of face that was a combination of elements that seemed to please without you knowing why, like some miracle of design. His long black hair gave him an air of drama too and only made his deep gaze more intense.

All of this lasted about two seconds as the man cast his dark eyes on me and then I breathed and everything seemed to go nearly back to normal except that my heart was still beating too loudly.

I turned back to the painting, thinking that I'd just been gaping like a wild-eyed loony at the guy and he probably thought I was nuts. I told myself that this was why I needed to go out more often and maybe make some more friends too. When I spent too much time studying by myself, I clearly started losing my grip on reality.

Red Wolf, I thought. I tried to focus on the painting. It was another surreal landscape that reminded me of *Castle Series*. But this work was painted in flaming oranges and reds and within was a massive red wolf running. You couldn't even see the wolf when you first looked at it, it was almost an illusion. I pursed my lips. The painting made me think of a wolf bounding through fire, an entire landscape made of fire, but that wasn't necessarily what it was. It was mysterious and powerful. A beast unchained, I thought. Was it running to or from something? Was the fire its power or its weakness?

"Do you like the painting?" The man said. He reached up and pushed a lock of black hair behind his ear and I was hypnotized again by the simple gesture. He had elegant hands. The thought made me blush. This was why I never dated. I had to pinch my wrist to break myself out of my trance and I clutched the empty cup of wine just to ground myself.

"Yes," I said, hardly able to speak.

Don't be an idiot.

I cleared my throat and said again, "Yes. It's my favorite of the series. If I *had* to pick one. If I was crazy rich, I'd snap it up in a heartbeat." Then I started rambling and I couldn't stop. "Quinn always paints with such passion, but I think this series is showing that passion more powerfully than anything else he's done. I mean… Okay, well, my theory is that these paintings are portraits. Everyone's saying how personal the works are, that's obvious. But I think the wolves are portraits. I don't know who *of*. Some of them are of the same person I *think*. And this one, if I had to guess, is a self-portrait."

I shut my mouth, my cheeks burning, but I refused to feel silly. It was a solid theory and I was going to write about it in my paper. My heart had not stopped pounding.

The guy was the one staring now, looking absolutely astonished.

"I'm…" He coughed, and held a hand to his mouth for a moment, watching me with those intense, dark eyes. "I'm glad you like it. I painted it."

It's a good thing those stupid wine cups at art galleries are made of plastic because I dropped mine when I gasped in surprise. Asher quickly bent down to pick it up, handing it back to me. It wasn't *just* that I had been spouting my little theory at Asher Quinn himself, it was that Asher Quinn was the cause of this strangely powerful feeling I couldn't name. It was also rather a shock that Asher Quinn was so young and handsome. I tried to tell myself that I had seen a picture of him somewhere after all and being such a fan, I was just flipping out a little. But I couldn't convince my racing heart of that.

"You're Asher Quinn," I said.

"Have been for a while," Asher said, smiling slightly. "And you are?"

Name, I thought. What the hell was my name?

"Selena Brock," I said, practically choking on it.

"Selena Brock." Asher nodded as if mulling it over. "Selena Brock. I like your theory, Selena Brock."

The way he said my name made me want to climb him like a tree but perhaps that was the wine.

"Oh my God, am I right about my theory?" I said, sputtering.

Asher only smiled and then we were staring at each other again, yet somehow it didn't feel weird. "I don't think an artist should definitively say what their work is intended to mean. Do you?"

"No," I said, and found myself smiling back. "They shouldn't. So, am I right?"

He laughed at that and it didn't make my heart pound any less.

ASHER

Selena Brock. I was racking my brain trying to think of where I'd met her. I must have met her before, I reasoned. That was the only explanation for this feeling. Yet even as I told myself that, I knew it made no sense. Stumbling into someone you might have met before would not at all explain this intensity of emotion, this feeling of connection as if she might be the most important person in the world to me. I had to focus too much energy on looking away so that I wouldn't get caught up in staring at her and make her uncomfortable. I squeezed my hands behind my back.

Selena was beautiful, but that was no explanation. I'd met countless beautiful women over my long lifetime. Selena had long, thick dark hair that fell in waves and a soft curl of bangs that fell over one eye, making her look just a little coquettish. She had big doe eyes and a full, wide mouth that promised a beaming grin. She was pretty. Adorable, I'd say. Yet the world is full of such women and men. Why then did I have an urge to have her immediately in my arms the longer I was in her presence? It was something other than pure lust.

Ash? I heard Carter in my head. *Are you okay?*

Do you feel this? I said, imagining that if he did, I wouldn't need to clarify any further.

Yeah, we're all feeling it.

Come over here.

"I...hope you're enjoying yourself," I said, desperate for some kind of normal talk while I waited for Carter to show up. It seemed vitally important that I keep her talking just so she wouldn't leave.

"Oh yes!" Selena grinned and I squeezed my hands harder. I was right, her grin was a thing to behold. "Um..."

"Ash?" I felt Carter coming before I saw him. That made sense. Sometimes when we're in a particularly sensitive or heightened state, we can feel each other coming. This feeling, whatever it was, met that criteria. He stopped short just behind me and I turned to him, dragging him forward by the cuff of his jacket. "What...?"

"Carter, this is Selena Brock," I said. "She had some interesting ideas about *Red Wolf.*"

Carter's eyes searched Selena's and I saw Selena giving him the same look back. Curious. Carter nodded and dropped his gaze, frowning, as he unbuttoned his top two buttons. He opened his jacket, flapping it for a moment as if he needed air.

"Oh," Carter said. He raised his eyes again, as if hesitant. I couldn't blame him. All this was a lot to take in. "Pleasure."

"Me, um..." Selena nodded. "Me too." At least it seemed to be affecting her the same way.

Somebody tapped me on the shoulder to tell me I'd made two sales and I barely heard them. The echo of footsteps on the shiny hardwood floor dimly registered. Outside the gallery a rock band was playing on the promenade, the lights of the gallery were bright, and the place was getting a little bit stuffy on this warm spring night. All of these were things I would be keenly aware of with my heightened senses as a wolf shifter anyway, but now every sense was aimed directly at Selena and my three brothers. The rest was a dullness I could not grab onto. It frightened and enchanted me.

"Ash, did we figure out what the hell...hell...hello there!" That was Ben, showing up with Damien.

The five of us now stood in a little circle, exchanging looks in turns - surprised, awe-struck, and baffled.

"My God," Damien said. "Um... I'm Damien Quinn." He politely shook her hand.

"It's nice to meet you," Selena murmured.

"We know her." Ben took off his glasses, squinted at Selena, and put them back on again. "We know her. Don't we? Don't we know her? I'm so sorry. I'm being very rude. I'm Benjamin Quinn." He stuck out his hand and Selena shook it.

"I'm Selena." She grinned at him in that way of hers that already seemed familiar and her eyelashes fluttered.

Ben nodded. "Of course."

"Of course...what?"

"I-I...I don't know."

Carter snorted at that and Damien said, "What is going *on*?"

"We have met," Selena said firmly, her eyebrows raised. "Haven't we?"

"No," Ben said. "I'd remember."

"I'd remember too," Carter said, and to Selena, he said, "I'm Carter Quinn, nice to meet you. Really, very nice to meet you."

"I didn't say you wouldn't remember," Ben said.

"I *know*, I'm just saying that I would."

"I mean, I think we *all* would."

"Guys." I rolled my eyes.

All at once my brothers started speaking in my head all at once.

Who is she?

We must know her!

Is she a shifter too?

Witch! She must be a witch. She's fucking with us.

Stop watching Buffy, *Ben.*

I haven't watched Buffy *in years!*

SHUT UP, YOU TWITS!

That was me. It's awful when they all start talking in my head at once. It made it difficult to keep one's composure. I glared at them all and looked back at Selena, trying not to appear insane.

"I have to speak to my brothers a moment," I said. "Would you... could you not... Do you have anything to do?"

"I'll be right here," Selena said. It really was comforting to know it wasn't just *us*. "I'm not going anywhere, my night just got really interesting."

I gave her a curt nod, hardly knowing just how to behave. "Thank you. We'll be just a minute."

I led my brothers towards the back of the gallery, blowing off a number of people who wanted to speak with me. When I saw the silver hair of the gallery curator walking by, I motioned her over.

"I'm comping *Red Wolf*," I said quietly into the curator's ear. I turned my head slightly and as inconspicuous as possible, I pointed to Selena. "To that woman. Selena Brock."

"I'm sorry, you're *comping* the painting?"

"*Red Wolf*. Yes."

"Um, Mr. Quinn, this is delicate but-"

"You'll get the commission," I assured her. "I'll pay it out of my own pocket. Her address will be on the sign-in. If not, find it. Get it to her. Free of charge."

"Okay. Will do."

"Thank you."

My brothers followed me right out the back door and into the alley behind the promenade where people went to smoke, but now it was mercifully empty. With a little distance from Selena, my heightened senses returned and I heard the distant sound of sirens, felt a cool draft coming out of the boutique next door, and smelled a batch of dumplings at one of the restaurants two blocks away. It was comforting to me and I took a breath, unbuttoning my jacket.

Concentrate, I said to myself. *Remember who you are.*

"Ash," Ben said. "Who is she?"

"I... Nobody." I shrugged. "I mean *not* nobody. Clearly. I'm sure I haven't met her before though. Have any of you?"

Everyone shook their heads but Carter muttered, "I could swear..."

"I've never felt anything like that before," Damien said quietly. Damien is seldom seen out of his long forest green overcoat but now he shook it off, folding it over his arm. He rubbed his neck and blinked rapidly. He still looked overly warm in his black button-down. "The connection I felt to her... And all of *you* with her."

"*Yeah,*" Carter said.

Benjamin's nose twitched again and he pinched his lips with his fingers before finally speaking. "Do you guys remember that thing about the clan mate of the Quinns..."

"I *knew* you were going to bring that up," Carter said.

"I mean... Tell me you're not all thinking it?"

"That was a myth," Damien said, but he didn't sound at all sure. "Something Granny Maura told the pups because it was a nice fairytale. If we were going to have a..." He blushed bright red as he spoke and I felt the warmth coming off of him in embarrassed little waves. "A *shared* mate who was intended for us... We would've met her already. Wouldn't we have?"

I trilled my lips, feeling at a loss, which I am not at all used to. "I don't know. I'm not... I haven't looked at the lore in a long time. Decades maybe. It's just been us for so long."

"A shared mate meant for the Quinns by the laws of fate," Ben said, smirking a little. "Kinky."

"Yeah, I always thought it was kind of a racy story for Granny to be telling us," Carter said, frowning now.

"Well, she kind of skipped over the sex part," Damien said.

"But maybe..." Ben threw up his hands. "Not a myth?"

Everyone looked at me and I couldn't help but agree. I couldn't think of any sort of spell powerful enough to make us feel this way so as to deceive or enchant us.

I nodded in agreement. "Maybe not. Okay... Well, perhaps we should try to get to know this woman? If *possible*. I don't want to freak her out. Every time I look at her..." My blood felt hot even now and for me, that was saying something. I run fiery in general.

Ben smirked at me. "How turned on are you right now?"

I flipped him off and the others tittered. I motioned for them to follow me back inside.

Things had been so calm for so long. There had been no big battles with any other shifter clans for decades. Sure, there was a disagreement here or there. There had been a tiff with a coyote clan last year that had taken us by surprise. We had not even known coyote shifters existed. Occasionally, we came across some pissy vampire or a witch who insisted she was supposed to marry Damien (witches loved Damien for some reason), but mostly we were on friendly terms with other magical sorts. Doubtless, it was our reputation as Quinns that went back hundreds of years. We were powerful but well behaved. We had no grand ambitions about taking over the world or opening hell dimensions. Truly, there were so few shifter clans left anymore, particularly wolves. We generally kept our heads down and focused on our artistic passions, going out for runs and long nights in the hills when our wolf's blood ran hot. Though when I thought too much about what our clan had lost, I could easily put myself in a dark place. By all rights, we should've had a huge clan of Quinns; hundreds of cousins and pups of every age who would grow up to find their own mates. But I'd given up on those dreams, at least for the foreseeable future. So the four of us kept to ourselves and our quiet yet successful lives and usually found it was enough to keep us out of trouble.

Or as Ben liked to put it in his annoyingly contemporary parlance: Don't start no shit, won't be no shit.

This question of a mate was a new wrinkle but I felt a sense of great excitement within me as we made our way back through the gallery to speak to Selena again. My skin felt a little bit tight, my teeth a little sharp. I had this electric feeling of suddenly wanting to shift and also to wrap the four of us around Selena and hope she would not want to be let go.

SELENA

I was somewhat relieved when Asher led his brothers away. That intense feeling that had come over me was powerful, but good... I thought it was good anyway. But the sensation was so overwhelming that it was difficult to hold a conversation or act like a normal person. The feeling subsided a bit once they were out of sight and I took a breath. Whatever this was, I wanted to know why I was feeling it. I wasn't going anywhere, but I took a walk around the main gallery, stretching my legs. I got myself a water at the wine table and when no one was looking I dabbed a few drops on my neck hoping it would wake me back up to reality. I don't think it worked.

All four of those brothers affected me equally. Just before they'd left I'd caught the scent of them individually and felt heady with it and - what did it even mean? Asher was wearing just a tiny bit of cologne but the others weren't. It wasn't the cologne I was smelling anyway, it was just the hint of their scent and the smell of their skin. They were, all of them, so attractive. And that connection had felt so powerful yet familiar...

I could hardly decide which of them I would want to make love to first.

Down, girl!

For God's sakes, they were brothers.

I dabbed a little bit more water on my neck and threw back the rest of the glass.

I still felt too warm and bit my lip, now wondering when those mysterious men would come back to overwhelm me again.

"Seriously," I said to myself. "Chill."

I poured myself some more water and took another lap and at *Red Wolf* I noticed a SOLD sign stuck to the tag. A little part of my heart broke. As silly it was, I'd already fantasized about taking it home. Not that I had much room for it in my little dorm. The painting was huge. It was also monstrously out of my price range. I was in school on student loans and some scholarship money, and sadly there was nothing there bookmarked for giant Asher Quinn paintings. Only rich people really bought stuff like that. I stood there in front of the painting for another couple of minutes trying to etch it into my brain since I would probably never see it again in person. I also decided that my theory about *Wolf Series* was right, even if Asher Quinn refused to tell me so.

I turned around slowly, spinning on the heel of my shoe, and that's when I saw Aiden on the stairs. My stomach dropped. He was trotting down from the second floor, looking around for someone. I wanted to believe it was a coincidence but I was too smart for that. Aiden was here for me. Something about it was just too much. It actually frightened me. He'd gone from annoying to stalker and it gave me a feeling as bad as my sudden feelings about the Quinn brothers were good.

I ducked my head, hiding my face a bit with my hand

because that's what people do in the movies. Maybe if I believed I was invisible to him, I would be. Because I had no intention leaving because of him. I suspected I looked a little more conspicuous than not. I made my way quickly toward the back of the gallery. Maybe I could escape out that way for a minute and he would leave, thinking I wasn't there. I was pretty sure there was an alley behind the promenade. I could sense him getting closer behind me and I hated how much I was suddenly so afraid of him. The way he'd waited outside the library as if to catch me out had been much more than an inconvenience.

My palms were sweaty. I don't like feeling helpless. At least I was with a crowd, that was reason enough to stay too, as much as I wanted to get away from him. It was safer here in a well lit, peopled place just in *case* he tried something. I couldn't bear the thought of leaving the Quinns. I needed to see that through, whatever it was.

I ducked low behind a little cluster of art-goers. I'd seen Aiden out of the corner of my eye and I wasn't sure if he'd seen me yet.

"Goddammit, where is that bitch," I heard him say. He was so close as I turned again just out of his reach. I double-backed to the front of the gallery, pretending to search for something in my purse.

Help help help, I thought. I felt cold all over. I was being chased and there was something terrifying about that.

My mother had told me to buy pepper spray, in fact, she kept threatening to send it to me whether I liked it or not and I'd insisted she wait and told her I'd buy it myself. But, of course, I hadn't.

I was really starting to regret not learning Krav Maga.

DAMIEN

A shared mate, destined to be bound to us by fate and the magics. The thought was both thrilling and exciting to me. We Quinn brothers have been on our own for so long. We know each other so well, it's hard to think that anyone else could understand the bond we share as shifters of the same blood. Wolf shifters are quite rare in this day and age and our family goes back thousands of years. The family lore is written in old tomes. Of course, now those ancient and infinitely valuable tomes are stacked up in the storage closet of our penthouse, probably hiding behind Asher's old Stairmaster.

On our way back into the gallery we were delayed by a reporter from *Los Angeles Magazine* who wanted to do a profile on Asher that included the rest of us. We were trying to schedule a time to talk, preferably *another* time when there wasn't a beautiful woman in the other room making us all feel as if we might have just found our true place in the world when an urgent call came to me that nearly had me shifting on the spot.

Help help help.

It wasn't her voice in my mind, more like an echo, but I knew it was this Selena Brock and I could smell her fear and feel her sense of frustration and helplessness. She needed us. We were clustered in a corner of the back gallery in front of *Green Wolf*, and I grabbed Carter by the shoulder.

"Do you feel that?" I said.

Ben spoke up before Carter could and said, "She needs us. Damien, with me. Let's find her. *Now*." He caught Asher's eye as he was speaking to the reporter and they exchanged one of their secret little signals that had to do with being the Alpha and the Second. Ben spun back around nodded firmly.

Selena had thankfully kept her word and the gallery wasn't very large. Ben and I crashed right into her as we turned a corner into the main gallery. She looked shaken but her eyes were bright as she gripped her purse in her hands. I could feel the tension coming off of her in waves. She seemed relieved to see us which instantly made me feel a bit better about the whole situation. It wasn't as if our help had been definitively asked for after all. I had no way of knowing if the little echo she'd sent into my head had been intentional.

"Selena," I said, narrowing my eyes. "Are you alright?"

"H-how'd you know…" She blinked at us.

"Hard to say," Ben said darkly. "But are you okay?"

Selena stepped forward and seemed to reach out to the both of us before stopping herself, looking shocked at her own actions. She shook her head. "Yes, no… I don't know. There's this guy following me from school. He's been following me *everywhere* and he's getting worse at hearing no. He just won't leave me alone!" She crossed her arms, curling in on herself just a little bit. Just minutes ago she had been standing up straight, looking like a woman you might not want to mess with. I didn't like this at all.

"Sonofabitch," Ben muttered.

"Where is he?" I said. "What's he look like?"

"He looks like a pasty-faced little toe-headed rat," Selena said, all but growling. She raised an eyebrow and turned her head and we followed her gaze to the staircase where Aiden was leaning against a wall. We caught his eye just as he spotted her, lighting up.

He really did look like a toe-headed rat. His outfit was also painfully out of date. He looked like some 90's prep from New England.

I turned my head and Benjamin was somehow already at the staircase, yanking Aiden down the bottom two steps by the collar and shoving him against the wall with enough force to mean business but without attracting too much attention.

Selena looked a little shocked but her lips curved into a smile as she murmured, "Nice."

"Be right back," I told her.

"Hey, asshole," Ben was saying, glaring through his wire-rim glasses at Aiden as he struggled and sputtered. "I want you to listen to me because I'm only saying this once. You're freaking out Selena and she doesn't want you around so cut it the fuck out or me, and my three brothers will kick your ass from here to the Valley - oh, and one of em' is bigger than me." Ben's good at the threatening thing. He can go from laidback musician and wiseass to hardass henchman in about two seconds. I suspected the glasses even helped. People never expected the guy with glasses to be tough. He tightened his grip a little and Aiden wheezed. "You got that, friend? Leave her *alone*."

I saw Aiden's eyes flash and all at once I felt a rush of magic emanating from him. He was a wizard and doubtless a malevolent one. I felt protective of Selena, but at that moment I was more worried about the threat to my brother. I gathered my power within and muttered a spell under my breath, feeling my hands heat up. It was dangerous and also less powerful without a wand but it worked well enough for these purposes. I shoved Ben out of the way and kept my eyes on Aiden's, gripping his collar and gritting my teeth as a terrible heat flowed through my fingers and scorched his nice white collar to black, a bit of smoke rising around his neck. It was enough to hurt him without hurting him so badly he needed a hospital and it didn't draw *too* much attention. By the time people noticed the smell of something burning, the little bit of smoke had vanished.

Aiden bared his teeth and shoved me back so hard I lost a couple steps and fell back against Ben, who caught me in his arms as we watched Aiden push his way through the crowd and out the door. It takes some doing to make me lose my feet. For a human, I'm strong, but I'm also a shifter *and* a wizard. There had been some power in that push, brute strength fueled by magic. Too much power. If there hadn't been people around I had a feeling it would've turned truly ugly.

Behind us, Selena was talking to a concerned looking Asher and Carter. I wasn't sure if she had seen me singe a guy's collar with my *hands* but she didn't look like she'd seen a magic spell for the first time either, though she was clearly a bit overwhelmed, all tensed up with her arms still crossed at her chest. I hoped we weren't going too far, only that feeling of connection between all of us came roaring back as I returned with Ben and we found ourselves all standing together again.

Despite her obvious discomfort, Selena said, "God, thank you for that. I really didn't want to leave."

"My pleasure," Ben said, tipping an imaginary hat.

Selena cleared her throat and shifted on her feet. She looked like she wanted to be standing there with us but had no idea what to do next. Maybe it helped that the rest of us didn't either.

Carter stepped forward and said, "Hey, would you like to get some air? Go on a walk real quick?"

"*Yes,*" Selena said, looking relieved. "Thank you."

Carter took her arm like a gentleman and led her to the door. He rolled his eyes when Ben tossed him an approving wink. I was too caught up in my own thoughts to be charmed by any of it. If Selena really was our mate, she was also being stalked by a pretty powerful wizard. That was a problem. A big one. I felt a surge of protectiveness for Selena that I'm sure my brothers were feeling too. Carter tossed one last look over his shoulder and we all knew what it meant without him needing to speak it into our minds.

Stay alert.

CARTER

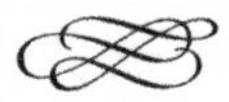

Sounds better than a dating app.

Honestly, that was my first thought when Ben had brought up the idea of the clan mate for the Quinns. A while back (by which I mean decades), Asher had decided that we could all date if we wanted to. Which doesn't seem like a thing somebody would decide for his brothers, except we aren't exactly normal brothers. A hundred years ago, when shifters were more common, we would've been assured of mates. But this wasn't a hundred years ago and Asher was afraid the rest of us were feeling lonely or lacking. The agreement had been, if you found somebody special enough, the brothers Quinn would figure out how to tell them, "Oh, by the way, we are wolf shifters and also wizards and also we're all over a hundred years old, not in our twenties."

At the time, we were all excited at the prospect of maybe finding somebody special enough to bring into the fold. After a few years of dating fail after dating fail, we were less excited. All of us tried dating (both women and men) to some extent, though Damien hardly at all. Every date we came across didn't seem like somebody we could ever share our lives with, and some of them were weirded out by how close we are as brothers. Perhaps if we'd explained that we weren't ordinary brothers, they would have understood, but no one had ever gotten that far.

I held the gallery door open for Selena and wondered if she was the type who might understand us. If she were truly our mate, did that guarantee her understanding? Did fate work that way? I had no idea. I've never gone into Quinn lore much myself. Ben and Damien were the lore nerds. I inwardly tried not to think about questions like that. When I thought too much about our family's lore I started thinking about our family and that way lay too much sadness. We didn't even know if Selena was our mate. As far as I knew, clans didn't have those anymore. Still, there was some reason we all felt this strong connection.

"It was getting a bit stuffy in there," I said now, as we stepped outside into the crisp night air of the promenade set back from the street and lined with small galleries. It was another busy Friday night downtown and the promenade on Chung King Road in the middle of Chinatown was bustling and alive with music, lit by bright red lanterns on strings, swayed by the breeze. I led Selena through the crowd with my hand on the small of her back, headed to a quieter courtyard, and she tossed me a smile. I felt a tingling in my fingers even at that simple touch.

"Stuffy as hell," Selena said. "Thanks."

I gestured to a stone bench that ran around a fountain in the courtyard and Selena nodded, and sat down. Things felt awkward and quiet suddenly, not least because I could feel that strong connection, that sense that we were fated to fall in love with each other and that I must protect her with my life...which is a strange thing to feel about someone you've just met. Yet, even on a good day and in normal circumstance, romance was not exactly my strength.

"Do you think Aiden is still out there somewhere?" Selena said, still looking vaguely worried.

I wished I had been close enough to catch a good whiff of his scent but as it was, I just didn't know and now I shrugged. "I don't know. Possible, I guess. I'll keep an eye out. I know my brothers will too."

"Maybe we should flirt," Selena said, and I couldn't tell if she was joking or not. "If he saw us, it might put him off. Or it might piss him off. I'm not sure. But as long as he's unhappy, I'm good."

"Ah..." I chuckled, uncertain of myself. This woman... "I'll do my best."

"So, what do you do anyway?" Selena said, smiling warmly. She was wearing a dark shade of lipstick and I suddenly imagined all of our faces decorated with lipstick kisses and stifled a smile.

"I'm a dancer," I said. "I'm with the California Dance Company. We tour a bit but generally we perform right down the block."

"Oh!" Selena said. "Yeah, I've heard of it. Ballet, right? That's amazing! I used to be obsessed with ballet when I was a kid. I even took lessons -"

"Did you?" My head snapped up with interest and holding her gaze for just that moment, I felt heat creeping up my throat and into my face. I was probably turning red. This is why I'm not good at romance. My brothers say I'm the prettiest of all of us, but what good does it do when I get so tongue-tied?

"Yeah!" Selena laughed, sounding perhaps a little nervous herself. Though I wondered if she was only putting it on in case Aiden was watching. She twirled a lock of hair around her finger and I had trouble not finding it adorable. "Until I was about thirteen? Puberty did a number on me and anyway, I didn't really have the discipline to stay with it. But I see it now…" She looked me up and down and I was not imagining the way her tongue snuck out to lick along her bottom lip. Just *that* made my cock swell a little bit and I swallowed. "You have the build of a dancer. You must be ripped."

"I'm short," I said with a snort.

"Short?" Selena tilted her head. "You might be an inch taller than me. What, like five foot eight? I don't think that's short. Not that it's bad to be short. But objectively..."

"The shortest of my brothers," I said by way of explanation. "Damien's the next tallest and he's got three inches on me. Asher and Ben are both six and change… and I'm the youngest." I shrugged. I had a tendency to fall back into self-deprecation when it came to comparing myself to my brothers. "Runt of the litter. They always try to protect me if there's a fight."

"You guys get in fights a lot?" Selena raised an eyebrow.

"Oh! Uh…" I was usually very good about keeping up appearances but I had this feeling of already being a little comfortable with Selena, as if she wouldn't be surprised that we'd once battled a coven in the Black Forest before going out for pints with an Austrian troll clan. "I mean, ya know...if somebody gets aggressive in a bar or...back in school." I smiled tightly.

We had last attended school in 1912. There had not been many brawls.

"Well, I think you're selling yourself…" She giggled and it sounded like music. "*Short*. For one thing, you have the prettiest eyes I've ever seen."

Of course, that made me immediately drop my gaze. "Oh, I don't…"

"No, really." She tipped my chin up so I had to look at her.

My wolfy senses were losing their little minds and I could pick out the notes of her perfume; freesia...narcissus...sandalwood... She was wearing Eternity or something similar. Whatever it was, it would smell even better if I were kissing her neck.

"Your eyes are so blue, they're nearly glowing," she said softly. "And your lashes are like paintbrushes, with those heavy lids..." Selena bit her lip and I felt the puff of her breath. Somehow my hand landed on her knee and her skirt was short, but she was wearing tights. I resisted the urge to tear right through those tights. "You must fight them off with a stick," Selena whispered.

She wasn't completely wrong. I had no shortage of interest, but I was awful at responding to it confidently, a dynamic which I now explained to Selena by saying, "Um..." I summed up all my nerve now and said, "You think I should kiss you? In case Aiden is watching?"

Selena's lips twitched in a manner I could only describe as mischievous and she whispered, "I think you should kiss me even if Aiden isn't watching."

I leaned in and felt myself begin to tremble so I gripped Selena's knee a little harder and hearing her intake of breath didn't make me any less aroused. I kissed her with every bit of restraint I possessed; a brush of our lips. The sensation of that alone was so electrifying that my eyes welled up and we stopped for a moment, our lips just barely touching.

"What *is* this?" Selena whispered.

"I-I could ex-explain but..."

"Not now," Selena said, and kissed my bottom lip, taking it in her mouth with a delicate little smack. It galvanized me. I reached up to cradle her cheek and tipped her mouth open a little more with my thumb. Her nose nuzzled mine as she tilted her head a little and I kissed her top lip, teasing her with my tongue. I had never trembled from a kiss before but the magics were speaking through me, singing to me that Selena was my mate, that she was mate to the four of us. Selena's hand tangled in my hair as her clever tongue met mine. I had enjoyed countless lovely kisses in my long time on earth but nothing compared to this, nothing came remotely close to this pleasure. I couldn't breathe, I could hardly think, and Selena whispered my name against my lips as if we were already making love. My cock was hard, throbbing with need in my tailored trousers and I pulled away, intending to stop, yet my lips somehow ended up at her throat.

"Please," Selena whispered. "Oh, please..."

I was right, her perfume did smell even better when I was mouthing at her neck, tongue kissing that wonderful nook under her ear. I could smell her skin and the blood within her and when I pulled aside the collar of her shirt and my teeth grazed her shoulder, her hand covered my crotch and I gasped and pulled away.

"Okay!" I said.

"Oh, I'm sorry!" Selena said, her eyes big and round as she yanked her hands away. "I just-"

"No, no," I said quickly. "Trust me, you were headed in a direction I liked but..." I gestured around us. Somehow the world had disappeared while we were making out but there were *people* around. Selena seemed to have forgotten that as much as I had for a minute there.

"God, we're in public," Selena said, catching her breath. She waved a hand in front of her face as if to cool herself down. "I mean I'm not against PDA but I'm no exhibitionist."

"Right," I said, still winded.

We looked at each other a beat too long and I felt myself leaning in again.

"Maybe we should go back in," Selena said, laughing like a bell again, and gently pushing me away.

"Good idea," I said, and sat back, rubbing my neck. "Damn."

Selena stood up, rather than risk falling into my arms again perhaps. But I still had a bit of a problem. "I'm gonna need a minute," I said darkly. "Maybe you should um...not look at me."

"Oh!" Selena covered her mouth and her nose scrunched up in the cutest way. "I'm so sorry."

"Please do not apologize," I said, chuckling at myself.

Selena turned around which gave me a perfect view of her curvaceous ass hugged by her short little mustard skirt blown around by the breeze. I groaned, slapping a hand over my eyes. I tried to think about something unsexy.

Chess. I thought about chess. Then I imagined Selena playing chess against all of us. I wondered if she could play it and if she was good and if she was competitive. Competitive women are so sexy to me. I wondered if such a thing as Strip Chess existed. If not we could certainly invent it...

"Damn," I muttered again.

"Are you okay?" she said behind me.

"Just a second," I said, sighing.

When I finally composed myself enough to function in public, I led Selena back to the gallery. I rested my hand at the small of her back again but this time everything felt even more charged than it had before and Selena kept sneaking me looks I couldn't quite read though they looked heated to me. Just before we slipped back inside the gallery she gently took my hand and squeezed it, giving me a soft smile.

The gallery was less crowded when we returned and even through the fog of intense feeling, Selena fell back into conversation with the four of us and we stood at the wine table nibbling cheese, and sipping cabernet. There was some unspoken understanding that none of us wanted to leave and there was a feeling between my brothers and I, not of competition, but of shared amazement. Ben kept making her laugh. Damien intermittently said something thoughtful that made her eyes bright as she countered with a smart reply. Asher engaged her on the subject of art until they were locked on each other and both speaking with passion about the subject. And I, I merely watched and gave her ice water when she seemed too warm and asked her how she was enjoying school. I felt, as always, that my contributions weren't as great as my brothers. I was used to feeling that way. But in my own small way I felt I was romancing Selena as much as the rest of them.

I had also been the first to kiss her and that little victory made my heart swoop with joy.

Her attention was fixed on the three of them as I mainly stood around silently, but during a quiet moment when my brothers' backs were turned, Selena leaned over and kissed my cheek and whispered, "I like you, Carter."

I had no idea what I had done to make her like me, but I hoped I could keep managing to do it.

We stood there in the gallery talking and drinking wine for hours until the gallery closed and then we stood out in the courtyard for another couple of hours until Selena was finally checking her watch. I couldn't help but feel a little embarrassed that we had kept her so absurdly late except that she had never said a word about wanting to leave and had seemed to be having a good time.

"I didn't mean to be out this late," she said, sounding a little regretful.

"I apologize if we've kept you," Asher said. "We just…"

"No, no!" She waved a hand. "I didn't want to leave at all. I just didn't expect this. How could I have?"

We all exchanged a look that said: *What now?*

Asher said, "Are you worried about Aiden?"

She was, it was clearly written on her face. "He lives in my building," she said. She frowned, picking at her fingernails. I catalogued that, wondering if it was something she did when she was especially worried. "He does follow me a lot. And he's been bothering my roommate and... Ugh."

I heard Damien in my head: *And he's a powerful wizard. I felt it, guys!*

Asher nodded in that decisive way of his. "If you're worried about going home alone," Asher said firmly, "please let one of us come with you. I realize how that sounds but-"

"Okay!" Selena said, and blushed a little. She was so charming when she blushed. "I mean...that's fine. I'd feel safer if it really isn't too much trouble for you. I do feel so safe with all of you. I don't know why."

I didn't have to ask my brothers what I already knew. Doubtless, we would shift and hang around near Selena's dorm just in case. But at some point I knew, we would have to tell Selena not only what we were but what Aiden was.

"I'll go!" Ben said, and the rest of us briefly shot him a glare. "Dibs!"

Selena burst out laughing. "Did you just call dibs on *me*?"

"I called dibs on securing your safety," Ben said loftily.

"Well, okay," Selena said, sending him a beatific smile. "Ben's got dibs then."

Telepathically Asher, Damien, and myself said in unison: *Lucky bastard.*

SELENA

I didn't know exactly what had gotten into me but I wanted more of it. My head was swimming. I'd had some wine but that wasn't why I felt drunk. I felt drunk on the Quinns and sucking face with Carter was only making all these crazy feelings more intense. The oddest part was the lack of competition between the brothers. All of them were flirting with me, engaging me, and seeking my attention. Yet there was no sense of them fighting over me. Even when Benjamin had called 'dibs' the others had seemed crestfallen but I'd definitely seen Asher toss Ben a wink as if encouraging him. I didn't understand any of it. If I thought about the situation objectively, I should've felt like a piece of meat but I didn't at all. I felt like we all belonged to each other, that I wanted them, all of them, in every way, and somehow...that was okay.

Ben drove us to my dorm in a very shiny, very fast car giving me plenty of opportunities to study him. I'm an art history major, and only an average artist myself. But I love to study a face. Ben had a subtly aquiline nose and a beautifully wide mouth with a cute dip in the middle. His soft, brown eyes were hooded and his hair was thick, brushed carelessly up and forward like it was splashing off his head. He also looked pretty sexy in glasses. I decided I liked his face.

"You're staring at me," Ben said, smiling over at me as he shifted gears.

"It's hard not to stare at you Quinns," I said, shifting in my seat.

Ben scoffed at that. "Oh, please. I'm not Asher or Carter, they got the looks. And Damien has that brooding writer thing going and the intense green eyes." He shrugged then, licking his lips. "Not that I'm complaining. I get by on my charm and endless wit, and chicks love the guitar." He smirked at me and I couldn't help but wonder how much of it was a bit of an act. "And the hair, of course."

We were at a stoplight so I had a chance to look at him hard. "You're gorgeous," I said. "I'm an art major, I know these things."

Ben look slightly taken aback by that and he ducked his head, as if bashful. "Back at you."

Just for something to do, I smoothed my skirt down and then frowned at my short, barren nails. Stupid nails. They made me a little self-conscious but I never had them done because I was just going to pick away at them anyhow.

As if reading my mind, Ben said, "You bite your nails?"

My mouth dropped but I couldn't help but smile. "How'd you-"

"I dunno. I noticed it before." He held a hand out for me to look at. "Me too."

I took his hand and inspected his nails, bitten right down to the quick, a couple looking like they might start bleeding at any time. But I was a little more distracted by his long, strong looking fingers, the vein that ran down his forearm. Why were men's forearms so sexy anyway? "I pick at mine," I said quietly. "Started when I was little when I was afraid of a teacher. Never could stop." I realized I was sort of playing with his fingers, softly stroking the nail bed of a particularly raw looking middle finger. "Ooh, your fingertips are so calloused." I turned his hand over and examined his thickened fingertips. I flashed on the image of those fingers inside of me and heat rushed up my neck.

"Guitar," Ben said quietly, and looked more serious than I'd seen him so far. "Anyway..."

I dropped his hand, feeling ridiculous. "Yeah, anyway..."

Ben had been so flirtatious and over the course of the night it'd become very clear that he was the funny one, the one who kept things light for the others, always quick with a smile. I wondered if that got tiring. As Ben pulled into the parking structure at school, I decided the night had become weird enough to ask him something like that. I licked my lips as he followed me to the walkway towards my dorm, the late night breeze making me shiver. Ben came up beside me, looking a little sheepish, his hands shoved in the pockets of his dark skinny jeans. He wore a gray cardigan over what looked like an overpriced t-shirt with some abstract graphic on it. He looked absolutely delicious.

"M'lady," Ben said grandly, as if shifting into a character. He took my hand and kissed my knuckles. "Allow me to carry your burden."

I laughed but handed over my purse. "Not much of a burden. It weighs about five ounces."

"Nevertheless," he said, tossing me a wink.

"Is it hard to be the fun brother?" I said as we ambled down the path to my dorm. Ben only raised an eyebrow and I said, "You know you're the funny one, right? You make everyone laugh. Asher was all worried about one of the critics for a minute while we were talking before and you had him laughing a second later. Is it ever..." I looked at him and he was frowning, looking down at his shoes as he walked. "Is it hard?"

"I like being the funny one," Ben said, shrugging.

"Oh, yeah. Sorry." I waved a hand. "I'm being so presumptuous. It's none of my business at all. I'm sorry."

"*But...*" Ben stopped walking so I did too and we faced each other as we stood there on the deserted path. "Asher's... Well, Asher's kind of in charge of us and we've been on our own a long time. Like...a *long* time. It hasn't always been easy and he can be a bit much on a good day so when he's...*being* a bit much, I cheer him up. It's kinda like I'm the second in command? So, I keep Asher on track, ya know? And Carter, he's super insecure and he gets down on himself so, I cheer Carter up. And Damien, well..." Ben snorted and pushed his glasses up the bridge of his nose. "Damien gets into dark moods. Real dark moods sometimes. So, I cheer Damien up too."

It was all so clear now.

"I get it," I said. "So, who cheers you up?"

Ben opened and closed his mouth and finally said, "Oh, I'm alright."

It was the least convincing thing I'd heard in ages.

"Oh, man," I said softly. "You're such a liar." I grabbed his hand in an attempt to drag him down the path. "C'mon, liar."

"I'm not lyin'," Ben mumbled. He sounded like a little kid and when his hand clasped mine I felt a swell of affection and couldn't bear to look at him.

We didn't talk as we walked up to my dorm but as I struggled with the key, Ben leaned on the wall just watching me. He reached over and tucked a lock of hair behind my ear and that affection swelled again.

"What about you?" Ben said.

I beat the door into submission and let him in, smiling

over my shoulder as I kicked off my heels and took off my jacket. "What about me?"

Ben stood in the middle of the messy dorm room, taking a look around, his hands back in his pockets. "You have siblings?" he asked as I rushed around, shoving clothes off my bed into a hamper, clearing off the counter at our tiny makeshift kitchenette.

"Nah." I was feeling warm and dug some bottled water out of our little fridge, tossing him one. I took a swig and hopped up onto one of our beaten up bar stools. "I wasn't exactly planned. I was more of a...let's say, happy surprise? And my dad ran off when I was a baby so it was just my mom and I."

"Hmm." Ben leaned on the counter, setting down my purse and facing me, nodding thoughtfully. "Bet you had a lot of friends though."

"Oh, well…" I swallowed some water. It was going to sound so much more depressing than I thought it had been although I guess, objectively, it had been a little depressing. "We lived in this weird town that was sort of industrial? We had this little apartment and there were like no kids around there. I had to bus out really far for school. And my mom had two jobs so she couldn't be around much. So…not really, I guess?"

I was trying to cover but I wasn't very convincing either. I couldn't even meet his eyes.

Ben tapped his finger on the counter and then reached over and tapped my hand. "Sounds lonely."

"Oh, I'm alright." I didn't smile and we looked at each other and something shifted between us.

"Touché." Ben nibbled on a fingernail and I wanted to either kiss him or just wrap the two of us in a blanket. "You tired?"

"Yes and no," I said. I wiped my mouth. I wasn't uncomfortable exactly. It was only that thus far, every time I found myself alone with a Quinn everything felt so...intense. The only thing more intense was being with all four at the same time. I hopped down off the stool and forgetting all notions of propriety, took off my shirt.

"Oh!" Ben whipped around, clearing his throat.

"Oh my God," I said, giggling into my hand. "I'm sorry, Ben. I wasn't even... I didn't even think about it."

"It's okay!" He waved a hand, facing away from me. "Go ahead." He shifted over to my desk and I saw him looking at the pictures on my corkboard which were mostly postcards advertising other gallery openings and little prints from art museums. But there were also some fliers of music festivals and concerts I'd been to. I kept an eye on him as I took off my skirt and peeled off my tights, changing into a t-shirt and the little pair of men's polka-dot boxers I liked to wear to bed. "You like...a lot of bands I like," Ben said. "Unless this is your roommate's stuff?"

"No," I said. "That's me."

"Hmm."

The door opened and I clapped a hand to my mouth. Somehow I'd just assumed my roommate, Nancy, would be sleeping at her boyfriend's.

This wasn't going to work at all. Her eyes bugged out when she saw Ben. "Holy shit!"

"Nancy!" I said, shoving her towards the door. "That's Ben! Hey, you have to go. Remember when we said -"

"Oh yeah, it's not a problem," Nancy said quickly, but she braced herself in the door, craning her neck to see Ben over my shoulder. Ben waved. "He is *cute*. Wow, is he cute!"

"I *know*."

"Good for you, girl! Get some!"

"Okay -"

"You *never* get laid!"

"Okay, Nancy -"

"No, I'm not saying you can't, you just never put yourself out there."

"Bye bye now."

"Okay, okay," Nancy sputtered as I started to close the door in her face. "There are extra condoms in my nightstand! Feel free!"

I stuck my head through the door so only she could hear me and whispered, "Thank you."

Nancy gave me a thumbs up and all but skipped down the hall. She really was kind of sweet. I just needed to talk to her about not answering Aiden's questions. When I turned around, shutting the door behind me, Ben was smirking. I wondered if he could possibly have heard that? He'd have to have super hearing.

"She's..."

"Nice!" Ben supplied.

"Yeah, she's nice." I bit my lip. "She's nice except you can't sleep in her bed. She'll know and she'll freak out. She has a thing about it."

"Oh, that's fine, I'll sleep on the floor." He was starting to take off his cardigan and the chivalry killed me.

"Oh, please," I said, pretending it was all very casual. "Sleep in the bed with me."

The bed in question was a tiny dorm twin. We'd be getting to know each other *very* well sleeping in it.

"No no no," Ben said, with a wave of his hand. He set his glasses on my desk and took off his shirt. I felt hot again, and squeezed my lips with my fingers. Ben was lean but muscular, broader than Carter, a dusting of dark hair on his chest leading down to some softly sculpted abs and the V of his hips just visible above his low-slung jeans. He had sort of a swimmer's body. "Seriously. The floor is fine. Trust me, I've slept worse places. Plus, I hate to tell you this, but I can't sleep in my clothes. Makes me itch like crazy." He started to unbutton his jeans, giving me a nod, and I turned around, playing with my hands.

"Okay," I said, more than a bit disappointed. "That's fine."

I found him a spare blanket and tossed him a pillow from my bed and he nodded his thanks before settling down on the floor between the dorm beds. He wore only a pair of black boxer-briefs. The sight made me vaguely light-headed.

I smiled, nervous, and turned out the lights before climbing into bed under the covers. We murmured good-nights and lay down to sleep but I could tell Ben wasn't any closer to sleep than I was. I could hear him breathing. I could practically feel the warmth radiating from his body even two feet away.

"Are you even sleepy?" Ben said.

"No."

"Hmm."

"You say that a lot," I said, and he chuckled. I turned over and leaned on my hand, finding him in the same position on the floor. "You're a musician, right?"

"Yep." It was dim in the room now but the moonlight through the window was bright enough for me to make out his soft smile. "I'm a singer-songwriter."

"Why don't you sing me something?" I said. "So I'll fall asleep."

"I don't have my guitar," he said, looking shy.

"Sing a lullaby," I said. "Don't need a guitar for that."

Ben chewed on his thumbnail and finally said, "Yeah, okay."

"Yay." I settled in nice and cozy and gazed down at Ben as he started to sing. He had an amazing range, deep and throaty one moment and going higher than I would've thought a guy like him would be able to the next. He was singing something in what sounded like Irish or Gaelic and though I didn't know the words, I found myself welling up, a lump stuck in my throat. When he was through he just sat there, steadily looking at me.

"I don't know what you were singing," I said, wiping my eyes and feeling a little silly. "But it was beautiful."

"It's an Irish lullaby," Ben said, his voice a little husky. I wondered if he was teary too. "It goes back in our family a long time. It's about a wolf who's separated from his pack. He can't find them anywhere no matter how long he howls. They don't hear him, they can't find him. He just keeps running over the whole earth, always looking for his brothers. Never finding them."

"That's so sad," I said, sniffing.

"Yeah, it used to scare the hell out of me when I was kid, to be honest."

"Why?" I said, chortling. "Are you a wolf?"

"Uh... Oh, I just mean... Like you said, it's so sad."

"Come here, please," I whispered, pulling back the sheets. Ben didn't argue this time and crawled into bed with me and we faced each other in the moonlight. "I gotta tell you something. I kissed Carter. Like, a lot. Like -"

"No, I know," Ben said. "I could tell. It's okay."

"It *is* okay, isn't it?" I said. "Why is it okay?"

"We're not...your ordinary brothers," Ben said. "Is it weird for you though?"

"No," I said, surprised at myself. "It should be but it's not."

"Good," Ben whispered. "Because if I don't kiss you, I think I might die."

"Ben," I said, before our lips met. Kissing Ben was just as electrifying as kissing Carter yet different. He smelled different, he felt different. I'd never felt anything so strongly for multiple men at the same time but I wanted all of them, I felt greedy with want. My hands went around his back and I ran my palms up that deliciously warm back and felt the curve of

his spine and the muscles that rippled there as he bit my bottom lip and then licked into my mouth, an arm coming around to grasp at my t-shirt. I hummed and threw my leg over his hip, desperate to get him closer.

"Jesus, Selena," Ben mumbled and went to work at my neck as I clutched at him. He was hard against me and I ground into him, smiling when I heard him whimpering helplessly, and faltering at the sensation of him swelling yet more. It had been a while for me but I didn't remember this part feeling so good. I wanted more, needed more. I leaned back and Ben looked mildly panicked for a second before I started taking my shirt off. He stared at my chest blankly for a moment, enough to start making me self-conscious.

Ben laughed at himself. "Sorry, you're just..." He shook his head. "You're just so beautiful. I can't think."

"Me either," I said, the words lost in another kiss as he pushed me back on the bed. He palmed my breast and I arched up into, hooking my legs over his, desperate to feel that hardness press into me. He ducked his head and his teeth grazed my nipple and just that had me crying out.

Closer, closer....

"Selena..." His hand, those long, beautiful fingers spanned my chest and worked their way down down to my panties and pressed there, insistent but not forceful. I held him closer and he kissed me again, our tongues curling around each other. "Selena...?" A finger snuck under the band of my panties and I clutched at his shoulders, nodding furiously.

"Please," I said. "Please, yes please..." Slowly, as if testing me, he slipped one long finger into my panties and found my clit with expert swiftness. He stroked me there, slowly, teasing, as I mindlessly mouthed at him, shaking with want, absently kissing him as I moaned and rode his finger. I could feel that rough callous and it drove me wild. "Condoms," I babbled. "Condoms, condoms..."

"Nancy's nightstand," Ben said, breathless, but he grinned against my cheek.

"I knew you heard!" I said, and Ben ducked his head to nibble at my breast, making me yelp before he rolled out of the bed all at once and stumbled over to Nancy's bed, throwing open the nightstand drawer. I lay on my back and raised my hands up behind my head, grasping the headboard, wanting to give him a show when he turned back around, my eyes big and innocent. I giggled, watching Ben fumble as he tore into a condom packet, and when he finally turned back towards me he went a bit googly-eyed. I went a bit googly-eyed myself seeing the sizeable bulge about to burst out of his boxer briefs.

Ben took off his briefs and then he half knelt on the bed to roll the condom over a big, hard cock that made me almost worried. I leaned over and bit his thigh, pinching his ass. "You're big," I said, biting my lip as I looked up at him.

"You okay?" Ben said, stroking my cheek, all concern.

"Yeah, just be careful."

"Of course I will."

I pulled him on top of me and just the sensation of his cock heavy against my stomach and then pressing against my entrance as we writhed and kissed made me see stars. But he was slow and gentle, slower even than he needed to be as he held himself above me and ever so gradually pushed himself inside me. I wrapped my arms and legs around him, breathless and wanting to be closer, closer than was possible. We were both trembling and that intense connection between the Quinns and I that had begun when I'd first spoken to Asher thrummed inside me and became something electric. I felt the Quinns' hearts bound to mine, their blood my blood as Ben pushed inside, filling me up, his eyes locked on mine.

"Oh my God," Ben breathed, and I wondered if he was feeling what I felt as a tear slid down his cheek. The sight of it stirred some feeling of power in me and I rolled us over, sitting up so I could ride him. I wasn't careful with myself and the girth of him made me ache but that was good too and I gasped, bracing my hands on his chest, so close to the edge I didn't want to move, that electric sense of connection and pleasure at him inside me making me shake like a leaf. I realized my eyes were shut and opened them, hesitant, to look down at Ben who stared up at me in awe, his hand snaking up my body to stroke my cheek. I hadn't realized I was crying too and I kissed his palm as I begin to move.

I might have woken up people in the next building over for how loudly I cried out, clasping Ben's hand in mine as he gripped my hip with his other hand and I rode him. There was no sense of rhythm. I couldn't concentrate on anything like that. I couldn't think of anything at all. There was just me and Ben and the Quinns' connection to me only increasing every sensation. When I came everything but Ben disappeared, the two of us so entwined, and I felt as if I were inside of him just as he was inside me. How long it went on, I didn't know, but we came down gradually until I was slumped on top of him, unwilling to let him pull out of me, and still feeling his pulse throughout my whole body.

"Selena," Ben whispered, and kissed me, pushing back the thick curtain of my hair. I relaxed on top of him, still trying to catch my breath, and he wrapped his arms around me.

"I'm going to fall in love with all of you," I said, resting my cheek on his heart. "Is that okay?"

"Yeah," Ben said. "That's okay."

BENJAMIN

I woke up wrapped in Selena's arms, her hugging me like a teddy bear. Her thick, dark hair was a complete disaster, falling over half of her face as she smiled in her sleep and I mirrored her, smiling to myself as I shifted to lie on my side. I reached up to tuck her hair behind her ear and her lips twitched. I felt like I'd been bathed in her scent and it made my wolf's blood boil.

"You're awake," I whispered, and kissed the tip of her nose.

"Nope," Selena murmured, and squeezed me a little tighter.

I kissed each of her cheeks and her forehead and returned to the tip of her nose and couldn't resist the crook of her neck and she sighed, her hand running up my back to squeeze the back of my neck. I leaned back and her eyes were open, bright and happy.

"Good morning," I said. I was interrupted when her alarm clock began buzzing abruptly and I jerked, yelping in surprise. Selena burst out laughing and climbed over me to hit the snooze. Her breasts were exactly at the level of my mouth and I couldn't help sitting up a little to lick at a nipple. Selena giggled and fell on top of me again, tangling a hand in my hair.

"Your hair is catastrophic," she said, laughing. "Like, more than usual would be my guess."

"Back at you," I said. She stuck out her tongue and I kissed her, morning breath be damned, but she made a face, pulling back.

"Toothpaste!" Selena said. "Come - do the walk of shame with me to the bathroom. You'll have to use your finger to brush your teeth though." She rolled out of bed and stretched, nude and unselfconscious and I took the opportunity to admire her curves, having an urge to bite her soft tummy. She wiggled her nose at me and grabbed a bathrobe from a hook on the wall. "Do you have to be somewhere right away?"

"Ah, no." I laughed a little derisively. "Us Quinns don't exactly work on a nine to five schedule." I stretched, groaning a little, and sat up. I reached for my glasses and leaned on my hands, not much covered by the rumpled up sheets and Selena bit her finger as she gazed at me.

"Sex hair and glasses all naked in the sheets." Selena was blushing and my heart thudded hard enough to ache. "You *are* a snack."

I blushed despite myself and wrinkled my nose. "What's that mean anyway? I never know what that means."

"*Ben*!" She rolled her eyes, cinching a ratty peach bathrobe around her. "What are you? A hundred years old?"

"Ah..." I tittered at that.

"C'mon." She nodded at the door. "Let's get rid of this morning breath so I can kiss you properly."

Selena brushed her teeth in the communal bathroom as I waited, feeling sheepish in the hallway clothed only in my jeans and receiving more than one appreciative wink by several young women and even a couple of guys. I nodded at them, smiling tightly, and when Selena returned sporting a messy ponytail, I sighed in relief.

She handed me the toothpaste and kissed me on the cheek. "We have a coffee maker in the room. I'll make a pot."

Minutes later, Selena was in my lap on the bed again, lazily kissing me.

"You know what's better than going to class," I mumbled. "Ditching class!"

She leaned back and I grinned, batting my eyes. "Oooh. You're a bad influence!"

"Always."

She smacked my shoulder and stood up. "I'm not ditching classes this pricey," she said, and poured us two mugs of coffee from the still percolating pot. "I'm *very* studious."

"I take it black with sugar," I said, and pursed my lips as she made it up. "Do you have classes with that asshole?" She handed me my coffee and frowned.

"Aiden," Selena said, her eyes narrowing over her mug. "Yeah, he's in half my classes. Two today. Pretty sure he did it on purpose."

The thought turned my blood cold. If Aiden had been just a regular guy who was also stalking Selena I would've said she needed to go to the campus police at the very least but...this was a wizard. The normal rules didn't apply.

"Can you change any of the classes?" I asked, taking a sip of coffee. "Drop them or something?"

"No way. Too late now. I'll just have to... I don't know, be careful. Should probably report him to campus police. Maybe buy that pepper spray my mother told me to get."

"Hmm." I rose, a fingertip somehow making it to my mouth as I tried to chew on nails that were already bitten to the nub. I had to do something. People were going to notice if a bunch of giant wolves were skulking around campus in broad daylight, but maybe… I noticed a ceramic sculpture of a hand on the window sill that held necklaces and bracelets and I pretended to be casually inspecting the jewelry. I found a gold necklace with an opal pendant. Perfect. Selena was busy getting dressed and since she wasn't looking I muttered a spell of protection under my breath, charming the necklace. It would be more powerful if I had a wand with me, but it would do well enough temporarily. I hoped. Selena was nearly dressed and I cleared my throat, holding up the necklace. "Hey, this is pretty. This must really bring out your eyes," I babbled. "Will you wear it today?"

"Okaaaay." Selena scowled, as if comically suspicious, but she took the necklace and put it on. It made me feel slightly better, but I was still a bit on edge knowing that some potentially unstable wizard wielding too much power was out there with his sights set on Selena. I was eager to talk to my brothers about what we should do next. But I didn't want to worry Selena anymore than she was already worried.

"Snazzy!" I said, leaning over to kiss her neck.

A sharp knock at the door made me jump and I nearly growled which all of us have a habit of doing when caught by surprise. Luckily, I didn't. I hardly needed another thing to explain without actually lying. Selena was dressed in jeans, a thin t-shirt, and a pretty scarf, somehow making just that seem cute. She trotted to the door and opened it without asking who it was and I breathed in. I didn't want to be *that* guy, the type telling her how she should do this and that for her own good (although Asher would and say it was for her own protection after all), but I couldn't help clenching my fists, ready to strike if needed.

"I have a delivery, ma'am?" The voice was male. I couldn't see him, but I didn't smell Aiden.

"Delivery?" Selena was saying. "Of what?"

"From the Room 6 Gallery?"

Selena opened the door wide and I heard her gasp. "No way."

"From Asher Quinn, ma'am," the guy said.

Red Wolf, I thought. *Of course.* I smiled to myself. Asher could be a bit much sometimes but he was nothing if not generous. I laughed to myself and scratched my head, playing with my out of control hair. "Don't know where you're going to put that thing."

"Me either!" Selena spun around, tears in her eyes. "I can't believe him!"

"Yeah, he's like that," I said fondly. I helped the delivery guy drag in the giant painting and the only place we could manage to fit it was behind Selena's bed. She had no way of actually displaying it properly at all and I couldn't help but imagine it hanging in a giant bedroom of Selena's own in the penthouse I lived in with my brothers. She could have that room we used as a gym if she wanted. Carter was the only one using that stuff anyway and really just the elliptical.

Selena, I couldn't help but think, could truly be our shared mate. If she was we would give ourselves to her as much as she could possibly want and be grateful for whatever she gave us in return. I imagined playing songs for her on our balcony as Damien rubbed her shoulders and added Asher rubbing her feet for good measure. Carter could give her a damn manicure if she wanted. We'd pamper her all day and thank her for it.

I wondered if she'd really been telling the truth when she'd said she would fall in love with us all.

"Ben?" Selena was waving a hand at me. "Ben? You with me?"

"Huh? Uh yeah." I slipped on my cardigan on and adjusted my glasses. Selena was packing up her backpack, and grabbing her phone. "Class time, huh? I'll walk you."

On the way to her class, Selena and I chatted about

nothing in particular yet it still felt meaningful. I wondered where the guys were but I also felt just a little bit selfish for time alone with Selena and so didn't speak into their minds. I was feeling a little bit guilty too that they might very well be hidden somewhere still shifted. There was no doubt they'd watched over Selena's dorm all night. Our wolf forms were large but we could stay out of sight when we wanted to. I needed to talk to Asher. I wasn't going to tell Selena about us or about Aiden's true self without his go ahead but I didn't like the deception one bit, not when I already felt so connected to her.

"Hey," I said, tugging on her scarf when we stopped in front of her class. "Um… Do you mind if I like keep an eye out for a while? For whatshisname?"

"Aiden."

"Yeah, whatshisname. I'm just worried. But I don't want to skulk around here if it's not okay with you." I smiled tightly. It really didn't excuse what we *weren't* telling her, but at least it was something.

"Skulk away," Selena said, grinning. She was wearing some kind of scented lip gloss. When she kissed me, it tasted like watermelon. "I think it's chivalrous."

"Well, chivalry is my middle name," I said, bouncing on my toes. "Okay, it's actually Cillian. But I'm thinking of changing it to Chivalry."

"You're so charming, it's gross," Selena said.

"Go to class, ya jerk."

"Okaaay." She kissed me one last time and all but danced through the door into class and I sighed, feeling dizzy with everything that was Selena.

SELENA

My Medieval Art class is a big one and the room is an auditorium so it's easy to miss people when you walk in. But I saw Aiden right away, sitting on the left side towards the front. My stomach dropped. I had an urge to go back and find Ben but I couldn't stand the thought of running to a guy to help me. Aiden was just a man after all. Also, there were plenty of people around. He wasn't going to pull anything here.

Even I could see that having to think this way was awful and not at all what I deserved.

I spun on my heel and quickly made my way to the opposite end of the auditorium, sitting towards the back on the right. Apparently, that wasn't far enough away. I pretended to be busy setting up my laptop, resolutely not looking up even as I saw him approaching out of the corner of my eye. As he neared I became more angry and also more afraid. I hated him for that. He was behind me, pretending to sit for class even though he'd left his things on the other side.

"Selena!" He hissed right next to my ear and I jumped. I

hadn't realized he was so close. "I *know* you're cheating on me!"

At that, my heart started pounding. Either he was messing with me or he was delusional. I really didn't like either option. I clenched my jaw and hunched over my laptop even though ignoring somebody who's bothering you really never works. If he wasn't delusional, I suspected that at this point he was just trying to wear me down. It would become worse and worse, then when he behaved better it would seem like kindness. The manipulation made my skin crawl.

"I saw you with those men, *slut*." He spat when he spoke and I felt it on my cheek. "You think you can make me look like a fool -"

"Fuck off!" I said, turning to face him. I shouted, not caring that I was making a scene. I looked him right in the eye and my words were sharp, echoing in the auditorium. "I'm not your girlfriend, asshole! I don't *want* you! I don't like you! Leave me the fuck alone or those friends of mine you met last night will fuck you up again and worse! Are you hearing me?!"

Aiden reared back a little, perhaps surprised at my ferocity. But I was done playing around and pretending he wasn't truly bothering me. The adrenaline rushing through me was making my hands shake but I felt good finally telling him off as I should have a long time ago.

"Hey!" A girl I vaguely knew who'd shared notes with me appeared next to my seat and glared down at Aiden behind me. "I heard that shit. Sounds like you're seriously harassing this girl. You want to leave her alone, asshole?"

"If I see you bothering her again, I'm reporting you to campus police!" Somebody in the back yelled.

"Yeah! Fuck off, dude!"

More voices chimed in, backing me up and I smiled back at them, thankful. Aiden's expression twisted into an ugly sneer and he jumped to his feet. He looked frighteningly angry.

"How about you all shut the hell up!" Aiden said. "She's my girlfriend! We're just fighting so mind your own business and stay the hell out of it!"

"I'm *not* his girlfriend!" I said, half laughing and half horrified. "He's been following me around and pumping my friends for info about me! He won't leave me alone! He's a goddamn stalker!"

"Bitch!" Aiden spat.

People actually booed him, shouting him down. He glared at the students and finally set his jaw, stomping back to his seat on the other side where somebody shoved his backpack into his arms. Then he was dashing away, perhaps too humiliated to stand staying for class. Everyone cheered as he made his way out and I bit my lip, feeling a sense of triumph.

The girl who'd originally backed me up ducked down next to me and said, "Good for you telling him off. What a creep."

"Thanks," I said. "Yeah, seriously. Thinks he can just have whatever he wants."

"Guys like that always do," she said, rolling her eyes. "Well, I'll keep an eye out for you, girl."

"Thanks, you're sweet." She gave me a little high five and finally the professor arrived. But it was difficult to concentrate. I was proud of myself for telling him off though. I liked to think of myself as tough enough but I wasn't always the greatest with confrontation. It was seemingly so much easier to go along and hide in the library instead of telling Aiden to go fuck himself. I wondered if a little bit of that Quinn strength had rubbed off on me and leaned on my hand, thinking of Carter's kiss and Ben in my arms, Asher's passion, and Damien's quiet intelligence. I couldn't wait to see them later and tell them what I'd done.

BENJAMIN

I heard the smackdown on Aiden happening once Selena started shouting and at the doorway I stopped myself, merely peaking in. She was handling herself just fine and there were people around. If Aiden tried anything serious I had a number of spells on hand I could try and barring that, I could always beat him senseless. I was hoping I would get the chance at this point. I was growling under my breath, I was so angry. But seeing Selena's fire directed at Aiden cheered me up. It was also nice to see her fellow students backing her up and good to know they were aware of the situation. It looked like Aiden might have more eyes on him than I'd thought. When he headed for the door, I hid around a corner, planning to follow him. But first I muttered a stealth spell.

Or rather, I started to mutter a stealth spell I hadn't used since that time Asher and I had fought a band of vampires (of course) in the middle of Central Park which had been difficult because there'd been a massive concert going on in the park at the time. But that had been back in the 70's. In fact,

I'd lost a really nice pair of velvet-trimmed bell-bottoms in that fight. You can't find anything like those nowadays.

This particular spell was in French. My French has always been weak. Aiden was out of the building by the time I remembered it, after smacking myself in the forehead a few times. I went after him, reflexively ducking behind pillars and trees on the campus just in case he had some means of deflecting my stealth spell. At one point, Aiden stopped and looked around. I suspected he could sense me but couldn't see me and it was probably pissing him off. If he knew I was standing all of three feet away, leaning casually against a brick wall, he would've been *very* pissed off.

Aiden whipped a wand out of his pocket as he hid in a shadow. Interesting. If he was using a wand on the regular he was either powerful and wanting to be more powerful *all* the time or not particularly powerful at all. But my read on Aiden was that he was fairly powerful and also young and stupid.

I watched Aiden mutter some variant of my stealth spell only he couldn't get it right and I stifled a laugh. It was amusing to watch him frustrated. He even kicked a trash can. He seemed to be trying to compose himself and I was about to cast something to disarm him for a while when I sensed one of my brothers coming, though I couldn't tell who. I stepped away from the wall to the stone pathway where Aiden was currently huffing and checking something on his phone. I focused my strength and made out Carter jogging to meet me, magic shimmering around him. I could only see him because he was my brother and probably because he wanted me too. I raised a hand to signal Carter to stay back as Aiden walked on and we let him get a little ahead of us.

Carter was looking mischievous when he found me. "You look...sated," he said, though he kept his eyes on Aiden.

"Huh." I shook my head. "I don't even know what to say, man. This girl, Carter. Seriously. She blew my mind."

"I knew it," Carter said. "We all kind of felt something. I had some wild dreams myself. Anyway, don't say anything, Ben. It was hard enough staying away last night. I just feel this pull all the time."

"Yeah." I was feeling it too now that he'd said so; a fierce urge to return to Selena.

"Anyway, Damien and Ash are shifted. They're close to Selena's class."

"I figured you guys would hang around."

"Of course," Carter said. "Who knows what this guy is capable of."

I tugged on his sleeve and nodded in Aiden's direction and we followed him across campus. In our spelled stealth mode, other students couldn't see us either but doubtless, they felt us pushing past them and we left some disturbed looking people in our wake as we hurried to keep our tail on Aiden. He was headed back to the dorm and I hoped he was going to his own room. I wanted to know how far he lived from Selena. It occurred to me that even with Selena's charmed necklace if this asshole wizard was powerful enough he might be able to spell past it. The thought gave me an urgent desire to return to her and make sure she was okay. I was about to send a question into Asher's mind when Carter grabbed my hand and squeezed it as we followed after Aiden into the dorm.

"They'll look after her," Carter said as if already reading my mind. "It's Asher."

"Right," I said. The intensity of feeling for this woman had me so turned around. "It's Asher."

As it turned out, Aiden lived just one floor above Selena, almost directly above her. Though him being anywhere in her building was too close to Selena for my liking. Carter and I huddled in the hallway near Aiden's door and I thought of the expression on Selena's face when I'd told her about the lullaby I'd been so afraid of as a child. I supposed I'd tried to tell her without telling her. She's seemed to understand the heart of it, even if she didn't know the details.

"Spell of repulsion," Carter whispered in my ear.

"We'll do that first. Then disorientation," I whispered back.

"And forgetfulness!"

"Yes!" I said. "We'll double up, yeah? On three?"

"Count off," Carter said in my ear, as we peeked through Aiden's door, left ajar, leaving us with a view of him angrily changing his shirt and grumbling to himself.

"One...two...three!"

Carter and I began muttering the spells in sync. It had been a few years since I'd spelled in sync with one of my brothers but it was sort of like riding a bike. Carter's eyes narrowed, as he kept his focus on Aiden, hissing the spell with decent pronunciation even as he spoke it so quietly. I felt the magic flowing through me and aimed through my hand pointed in Aiden's general direction. It was a method I'd always found more than effective, although my little brother had a showier way of doing things.

I was bopping my head along to the rhythm of the forgetfulness spell and couldn't help but glance at Carter as he waved his hand around, his fingers twisting up and tracing figures in the air. Typical Carter. Everything was a little performance. I made it through the spell but couldn't help giggling a little at how flashy Carter's spellcasting was.

"*What*?" Carter said.

"It's nothing."

"Hey, one more for disarmament?" Carter said.

I hissed through my teeth and pressed against the wall as

a group of students brushed past us. "That's a powerful one, he might feel that."

Carter just gave me a look and I shrugged. "Okay, bro." I shook my hands out which I'd always felt sort of juiced up with magic before a big spell. "Can't wait to see how flashy this one is," I said.

"What?" Carter scowled at me.

"Nothing." I smiled, all innocence. Aiden was rifling through a pile of papers on his desk. "On three."

"One," Carter said. "Two...three!"

Carter and I had barely begun the spell when Aiden, doubtless feeling the powerful magics being thrown at him, spun around, and I swear he could see us even in our stealth.

Carter reared back and hissed, "Shit!"

Aiden whipped a wand out of his waistband and fired something in our direction and I yanked my brother back. But I felt the force of the spell hit him like a bullet and he cried out, making my stomach turn. I summoned up my anger, pushing it into the force of my own magic and hissed a binding spell, throwing my hand out towards Aiden. That one had so much power in it I could see the magic shoot towards him like a bolt of lightning. Aiden seized up and fell to the floor. It would only keep him incapacitated for a short time so it wasn't exactly a long term solution but it would do for now. I glanced over at Carter, who was cradling his arm, his mouth twisted in pain. His stealth had dropped and I allowed mine to drop too and I bared my teeth as I stalked into the room, glaring down at Aiden who lay frozen on the floor, snarling at me. He looked like any other preppy sort of guy at USC; blonde, good looking, dressed in khakis and a nice button-up shirt.

I hated him.

"Stay away from Selena Brock," I said, rage making me

want to kick his face in even as I caught my breath. "This is your last warning, *boy*. Next time we *will* kill you."

I spun and threw my arm around Carter, helping him down the hall. Aiden seemed to have burned his arm and the thought that the entitled little asshole had hurt my kid brother made me see red. I brought Carter to an empty nook by the stairs and examined the burn. Half of his left arm was swollen and pink, some of the skin blistering. It looked more painful than Carter was letting on as he grit his teeth. I racked my brain for a healing spell.

"What's the one for burns?" I said. "I can only think of that Flemish one but I don't remember how it goes..." I started to recite it and Carter nodded along and finished the rest. "Right, right okay." I healed his arm the best I could. The burn was still quite pink but his ability to heal quickly as a shifter would take care of the rest. For good measure I cast a bit of cooling on his skin.

"I'm fine," Carter said. He was always a little touchy when he got hurt, as if the rest of us would think he was weak for experiencing pain. Burden of being the youngest, I supposed.

Attempting to lighten the mood as we headed down the stairs, I said, "It wasn't for lack of trying, man. I loved that show you put on."

"Ugh. Don't start," Carter said, with a groan. "It's just a *style*."

I waved my hand around, impersonating Carter's flamboyant method of casting. "No, I like it. I call it the Drunken Gandalf."

"You're a dick," Carter said.

"Love you too."

Outside, as we made our way back towards Selena's class, intending to meet up with Asher and Damien, Carter tilted his head, looking up at me.

"That binding spell was something else," he said. "Haven't

seen you throw a spell that hot without a wand in a long time."

"Well, I was pissed," I said, a little sheepish. "Nobody fucks with my little brother." Carter snorted at that and I threw an arm around him, squeezing his shoulder.

SELENA

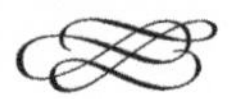

It was a little difficult to concentrate on the finer points of Medieval Art after that ugly confrontation with Aiden, even as triumphant as I'd felt when he'd stormed off in a huff. That victorious feeling I'd enjoyed wore off as I tried to focus on my notes and by the time class was over I felt crappy about the whole situation all over again. Even trying to recapture the memory of Ben's awestruck look as his hand snaked up my body to caress my cheek while I rode his body into bliss wasn't making me feel any better. By some kind of reflex I reached out within myself for that feeling of connection to the Quinn brothers but everything was a little dulled. My head felt a bit fuzzy too.

"Hey, Selena." It was that girl from before, the one who'd insisted on backing me up. She tossed me a thumbs up as I packed up my things at the end of class. "Don't forget. We're here for ya."

"Thanks," I mumbled. But now I could hardly remember what the big deal was.

As I made my way out of the building, the heat of embarrassment burned my cheeks. I felt sick. *What* had I been so upset about anyway? I clutched the straps of my backpack. I felt just a little bit sick, the sun too hot, my feet too heavy as I ambled across campus back to my dorm.

Wasn't Aiden just a guy who was interested in me? If anything, I should be flattered. Anyway, if I'd taken a date with him in the first place, he wouldn't be so upset. I was starting to feel guilty about the whole thing. He definitely had not deserved to be humiliated like that in front of everyone. I felt so small suddenly. I should be grateful that a catch like Aiden was into me, I should be thanking my lucky stars...

"Selena?"

I squinted, a little dizzy. Asher Quinn was looking at me funny. Damien was with him. I felt a stirring of that feeling for them but it was like reaching through fog. "Oh hey," I said softly.

I needed to go apologize to Aiden. I needed to find him right away and beg forgiveness -

"We just wanted to make sure you're alright?" Asher said. "I hope that's okay with you."

"Yeah, whatever," I said. I was sweating, the sun felt so hot on my skin. I wanted to get away from the Quinns suddenly. They only confused everything. Didn't I have enough problems? "Fine."

"Are you sure you're alright?" Damien said. He looked so concerned. It was *annoying*.

"Yeah, I'll be *fine*," I snapped. "I'm just not feeling so great so I'm going back to my dorm. Jesus."

"Are you ill?" Asher said. "Because..." He exchanged an alarmed look with Damien that I couldn't begin to figure out. "Um, can we walk you anyway? After what happened with Aiden, I just want to make sure..."

"We just want to make sure you're okay," Damien finished for him. "We'll walk you."

"No, don't *walk* me!" I said, feeling suddenly so aggravated. I wished they'd just disappear. "Just get out of my face! God! I can't think with you assholes in my face and I just need to… I need to.. I can't think!"

"Selena," Damien murmured. He stayed back and Asher's concentrated gaze was like a laser.

"Just go away! I'm fine! Just get away!" I backed away from them and then stomped off. I couldn't think of the last time I'd acted so rudely towards somebody who was trying to be helpful. But I felt childish suddenly. I felt like a misbehaving little girl.

Everything would be okay, I thought. I just needed to find Aiden and apologize and he would make everything alright.

Back in my dorm, I threw my backpack on my bed and all at once I felt a rush of such overwhelming confusion that it made my heart race in fear, panic overcoming me. My scarf felt as if it were choking me and I took it off, tossing it aside. I rubbed my face, tears welling up. I had been so sure that Aiden was at best really annoying and more likely an actual threat. The Quinns seemed convinced of it and though I'd only just met them I'd talked to them for hours and hours, I'd truly bonded to Ben. As crazy as it seemed, I felt I already knew and trusted them. That connection...where had it gone? Maybe I *was* crazy.

I paced around my room trying to sort myself out but my brain was racing. An insistent voice in my head told me to go talk to Aiden. He'd help me sort this out. I should apologize anyway for embarrassing him in front of anyone. Without any better ideas, I left my dorm, intending to find Aiden.

Instead, I found Asher in the hall. The confusion returned with a vengeance. I wanted him to help me but that insistent voice told me to ignore him and go find Aiden. I swallowed, feeling frozen, unable to move to go speak to Aiden and unable to do anything else.

Asher looked at me steadily with his intense dark eyes. "Selena," he said calmly. "What's going on? Forgive me, but you don't seem like yourself."

"I don't..." I shook my head, tears sliding down my face. "I don't know! I told Aiden off and I felt so good about it and now I just... It was stupid, it was stupid! He cares about me and I was so mean to him, I need to apologize! I've been awful! But I also... Nothing *feels* right! Asher!" I threw my arms around him, the fog clearing a bit with him so close. He was solid and warm and he rubbed my back as he spoke.

"Hey, you did not do one thing wrong," he said in my ear. "I think something's making you feel this way, making you confused and panicky."

I sniffed and leaned back. That made no sense. You couldn't *make* a person feel that way.

"I'll explain," Asher said. He smiled softly and rubbed a tear away with his thumb. "I promise. I'll explain everything. You want to go back to your room? Maybe have some water?"

I nodded and went back inside and watched Asher shut the door and lock it. He looked at me as if asking if that was okay and I nodded.

Asher Quinn was in my room. One of my favorite contemporary artists. I felt a joy in me about that and the connection between us quivered. Yet everything was still dulled and it was frustrating. In my room I sat at my desk, wiping my eyes. Asher found the fridge and handed me a bottle of water and a kleenex from a box on my dresser before sitting on the bed, still messy from the morning. I watched Asher's eyelashes flutter for a moment as he tipped his chin up in a peculiar way. It almost looked like he was sniffing the air. He smiled softly to himself and nodded.

I drank my water as he stared at me, muttering something under his breath, his hand raised slightly.

"What're you doing?" I said. When he was finished I took a breath. My mind felt clearer suddenly, the fog gone away as if blown by the wind. "Oh…"

"Feel better?" Asher said kindly, bracing his hands on his knees.

"Yeah, I do." All the dumbass thoughts I'd had about being a misbehaving little girl and wanting to apologize to Aiden now seemed beyond absurd and offensive to me and I groaned. "Ugh. That was *gross*. What was that?"

Asher nodded. "Yeah. Um, I know what it was. I have a lot to explain. It might not be easy for you to hear though or...believe."

I narrowed my eyes. Asher was beautiful with his dark scruff and his tall, impressive physique. He was a brilliant painter and I admired him and that was not to mention the feeling I'd had since first meeting him that I was somehow destined to be in his life. But also… what in the hell? "Okay."

"Right," Asher said, sighing. He was about to go on when the door blew open and Nancy walked in, stopping immediately when she saw Asher on the bed.

"Wow," Nancy said flatly.

I said, "Um."

"No!" Nancy put a hand up. She dashed over to her dresser, grabbing some clothes out of a drawer. "It's fine! I'll stay at Adam's again tonight! Or just for the next hour? Whatever! Text me!" She laughed and threw me a thumbs up. "Get it, girl."

"Okay," I said, blushing furiously. "Thanks, Nancy."

The door shut behind Nancy and I turned back to Asher who looked sort of proud of himself, smirking there on the bed. He laughed lightly, scratching his neck. "I don't know that you're going to like all this," he said, and rubbed at his temples for good measure

I crossed my arms and took another sip of water, feeling much more like myself. "Try me."

ASHER

"Okay," I said. Where to begin? Perhaps in order of priority. Selena was in more danger than she knew and she needed to understand why. "First of all, Aiden is a wizard."

Selena blinked at me, waited a beat, and said, "Uh, what's that now?"

"Aiden is a wizard," I said again, not breaking eye contact so that Selena would understand I was being serious. "And he cast a spell on you that made you doubt yourself, made you confused and all that. He probably did it before he confronted you in class and it took awhile to take effect is my guess but -"

"What do you mean a *wizard*?" Selena snapped. "Cast a spell? A *spell*? Like magic? Asher, are you insane?"

"No," I said softly. I rubbed the back of my neck, squeezing my eyes shut, gathering strength. It was difficult to guess how Selena might react. "Can I see your hand?"

Selena gave me a long look but she held out her hand, palm up. That was good. I supposed it meant she still trusted me. I took her hand gently in mine and spoke a simple floral spell, sending a gentle stream of magic through my other hand as I waved it over her palm. Selena watched, her mouth dropping open, as a tiny little bud of a flower appeared in her palm. It began to grow before her eyes, rich green leaves and pale pink petals springing out of it, petal after petal until a fully bloomed peony sat in her hand. She swallowed, staring at the flower and then up at me, trying to make sense of the impossible. She pulled her hand back and carefully inspected the flower as if that would provide her answers but it was real, the petals soft but solid. She bit her lip and set the flower carefully behind her on the desk.

"Magic," Selena whispered.

"Yeah," I said, shrugging. "Um, so we're wizards too. Myself and all my brothers. I know this is a lot but I need you to hear it so you know why Aiden is so dangerous. He's powerful but he's young and dumb. There's no telling how much damage he can cause. And he's targeted you."

"Oh," Selena breathed, trying to take it in. "Wonderful. And I thought my biggest problem would be student loans." I chuckled at that and watched her absorb the shock of this information. "So, what else can you do?"

That was a loaded question.

"Oh, lots of things," I said, sitting up straight. "Most of the spells I know by heart are rather utilitarian and generally everything's more powerful with a wand -"

"A *wand*?" Selena sputtered. "Oh, c'mon! There are seriously wands?"

"Sure." I grinned. "I don't use mine very much unless I know I'll need some juice. It's at home. I keep it in my underwear drawer."

Selena stared at me for a second and then snorted a laugh that turned into full blown helpless giggles. She fell forward, grabbing my arm. "Your underwear drawer?!"

"Well..." Her hair was all tousled, coming loose from her

ponytail, and her eyes were bright as she laughed, her glossed lips stretched wide. "Where would you keep it?"

She shook her head, wiping her eyes. "I don't know! I don't even know why that's so funny but it is!" She composed herself and sat back in her chair, shaking her head. She had a fond expression on her face and it was as if she were talking about people she'd known all her life. I wanted to memorize every expression and I couldn't wait to see every little tic and smile. "And where do your brothers keep their wands?"

I snorted at that, scratching my arm. "Carter keeps his with his old ballet slippers. Damien's is in his desk and..." I stroked my chin. "Ben's is..."

"In his guitar case, I bet," Selena said.

"You know, I think it is." I smiled at her. "How'd you know?"

"I guessed. But yours is the underwear drawer. Very interesting."

I felt scrutinized for a moment, but that was fair. I was restless though and got to my feet. "Is that a coffee maker? Do you mind if I make a pot?"

"Go ahead," Selena said. "But I'll need to see another spell."

I laughed at that and tried to think of something simple yet charming. I picked a plastic pen off of her desk and said, "Is this important to you?"

Selena eyed me warily. "No."

"Okay." I tossed the pen in the air and began speaking rapid French, wiggling my fingers, The pen didn't drop but spun in the air faster and faster, end over end, until finally it burst into bright blue sparks like fireworks, the embers falling to the carpet and turning to ash.

Selena looked like a kid at the circus. "Wow!"

"*Now* can I make coffee?" I said, smiling slyly.

"Sure," Selena said. "But...if you can do magic, why can't you just magically make coffee?"

"I mean, I *could*," I said. "If I remembered whatever spell makes coffee, I'm sure there is one. The thing is, magic takes some energy and focus. With that sort of thing, it's less work to just..."

"Make coffee," Selena said.

"Precisely," I said, dumping her old coffee grounds into the trash and replacing the filter.

"Have you guys put any spells on me?" Selena said.

I couldn't think of any and holding the coffee can in one hand, I looked her up and down. Selena was wearing a loose, thin peach t-shirt and jeans. She'd been wearing a scarf before but now I noticed a gold necklace with an opal pendant that seemed slightly formal for the rest of the outfit. And Ben had been with her the night before...

"Was it your idea to wear that necklace?" I said, measuring coffee into the filter.

"Oh...no," Selena said. "It wasn't actually. Ben wanted me to wear it."

"He probably put a spell of protection on it," I said. Historically, Ben liked spelling worn items when it came to loved ones. Spelling directly at people made him a little queasy unless it was for healing.

"Guess it didn't work very well," Selena said.

Selena's kitchenette had a tiny sink and I poured out the old coffee and filled up the pot again. "On the contrary, I'm guessing whatever Aiden put on you would've been much stronger if not for Ben's protection. But I'll bet he was conflicted about it. Ben hates lying." I flipped on the coffee maker and stretched, scratching my stomach. Selena seemed more comfortable and settled now and the connection between us felt warm like a blanket. It almost made me sleepy. I'm rarely sleepy. Even when I'm dropping off to sleep I wouldn't describe myself as sleepy.

"Well, I can understand not wanting to run out and tell everyone you're a wizard," Selena said. "And you just met me. Anyway, it makes a little more sense now. How'd you know Aiden's a wizard though?"

"Oh, we can feel it," I said easily. "Magic coming off of him in waves. Once you're attuned to it, you feel it right away. And he threw off Damien last night like he was nothing, that's hard to do. But there's more and it's…" I chuckled. "It's tricky. First, coffee." I poured us two cups, one with cream and sugar for Selena and made sure she'd had a few swallows before I started to explain the rest. I opened my mouth and closed it again. Telling a regular human about us was an exceedingly rare occasion. They had to be special and precious to us. Worthy of knowing. But if Selena truly was our shared mate…

"Go ahead, Asher," Selena said, reaching over to squeeze my arm. "I'm listening."

I felt that warm blanket of connection again and nodded. "My brothers and I, we're shifters."

Selena seemed to think about that for a moment and then said, "I don't know what that means."

She was funny even when she didn't mean to be funny and I snorted a laugh and took a sip of coffee, bracing myself. "Shifters are also animals. They can turn into their particular animal forms at will. My brothers and I are wolf shifters. We're like a pack. The Quinn clan. Wolves." I shrugged, pursed my lips, and downed the rest of my coffee before setting the mug on Selena's desk.

"You're a wolf," Selena said, sounding all too casual. "Okay. But...what?"

"We shift into wolves," I said again. "All of us. We have some enhanced strength, sense of smell, speed… Do you want me to show you?" I stood up and spread my hands, stepping back a little to appear as non-threatening as possible.

"You're gonna show me how you turn into a wolf?" Selena said, laughing a little. "Yeah okay, magic is one thing but…"

I figured it was better to just get it over with and I allowed the human part of me to simply fall away as the wolf came rising up, my body shifting all at once from man to beast. When I was very young, it hurt terribly but over time one's human body becomes used to it. Now it just feels like a very good stretch. My wolf form was slightly over three feet tall on all fours, the biggest of the Quinn clan. My coloring was deep gray, flecked with silver, also the darkest of my brothers. I sat back on my haunches, regarding Selena.

She looked pretty freaked out.

She screamed into her hand, holding it to her mouth. I hated the sight of her being afraid of me and falling into animal behavior I bowed, lowering my head to my front paws, and whimpering as I raised my eyes.

"Uh...ah…Asher?" Selena said weakly.

I whined at that and inched forward and to her credit, Selena didn't move or rear back. I waited until I could feel her tension ease and then nuzzled her knee, whining in hopes of a pet.

"Okay, okay," Selena muttered. "Okay, wow. Well, you're very pretty. And huge."

I wagged my tail and she laughed in that sweet way of hers. She reached a hand out and I found myself eager with the emotional impatience of my wolf self. I wanted her to pat me on the head. It was a certain kind of comfort that I hadn't felt in too long. She sighed, relaxing a little more and then her palm rested on my head, in that sweet spot right between my ears. I whined a little more and she stroked my fur. I nuzzled her knee with my nose and she giggled, scratching between my ears and then under my chin. It all felt delicious and I wagged my tail furiously.

"Oh man, you're pretty cute, huh?" Selena laughed and soon enough she was slipping down to the floor and reaching up with both hands to pet me and rub my belly. I licked at her cheek and she sank her hands in my thick fur and her arms came around to hug me.

See? I wanted to say. *I can be sweet too.*

I was as helpless as a child in her arms as she embraced me so sweetly and I couldn't help but paw at her, just gently, because my paws are enormous. She mumbled nonsensical little things as she stroked and scratched my back, complimenting my fur. I rested my head on her shoulder, lost to the comfort and affection.

"Asher Quinn is a wolf," Selena said, leaning back to shake her head. I licked her cheek one more time and she yelped and kissed the top of my head. "I knew the *Wolf Series* was a little too personal." She gave me a long look and said, "Can you change back now? I have more questions."

I shifted back into human form and found myself sitting on the floor, still feeling a little giddy with affection for Selena, that connection between us as powerful as ever. I could feel its pull on my brothers too and it made me feel closer to them.

"There's one thing you haven't explained," Selena said. She was sitting close to me now and she rested a hand on my knee, stroking softly as if I were the one who needed comfort. "What is it that connects us? When I met you and your brothers it was like I already knew you, like I was meant to never leave you and I don't want to. So what is *that?*"

"Right." I took her hand in mine, clasping our fingers together. "There is lore in the Quinn histories, legends, promises… There's an old myth in the family history that says a later Quinn generation would be given a mate, one who would be bonded to the clan. One person who we Quinns would give ourselves completely to, forever at their will. Or rather, we thought it was a myth. But given the way we feel and the way you seem to feel too, we think that person is you."

"So..." Selena looked serious and I couldn't tell if she was pleased or upset. "You mean I would belong to you? All four of you?"

"It's more like we'd belong to *you*," I said. I didn't need to ask my brothers if they felt as helplessly at Selena's mercy as I did. I could feel that it was true. "But you must understand," I went on. "This is all at your will. Fate and magics be damned; if you want no part of this -"

"I *do*," Selena said fiercely, and her arms snaked around my neck. "I want it. I want to belong to you and I want all of you to belong to me. Please, Asher, please tell me it's all true," she whispered, her lips brushing mine. Her scent engulfed me and her skin was cool as I ran my hands up her arms and wrapped them around her, dizzy with joy which was hardly a feeling to which I was accustomed.

Selena was on the taller side and her hips curved and her stomach was soft but she felt small in my too big hands that ran up her back, frustrated by the thin fabric of her t-shirt.

"It's true," I breathed. "If you want it. It's all yours. *We're* all yours. We'll give you anything you want, Selena."

"You, you," Selena murmured. "I want all of you." She kissed me and I shook, heady with desire. Her mouth tasted too good to be human somehow and I couldn't stop kissing her; soft, sweet little kisses as if testing her taste until, with a murmur of frustration, she nudged my mouth open and her tongue touched mine, the mere sensation making me shiver.

I am one hundred and twenty years-old and I have had

some compelling times in bedrooms, but Selena made me feel like virgin.

Selena's finger went to the buttons of my shirt and she began to undress me. I let my hand sneak up under her tee and smiled when she leaned forward and kissed my cheek then the crook of my neck as she pushed my shirt off my shoulders. My chest bare, she sat back and gazed on me, making me feel entirely naked. I reached up to slip the band from her hair, reveling in the way her long, dark locks fell around her shoulders.

"You painted *Red Wolf*," Selena said, nodding back at the painting shoved behind the bed for lack of space. I'd almost forgotten it was there.

"Yes," I said, taken aback. Did she really want to talk about my art career right now? My cock was already throbbing for all that was holy.

"*Red Wolf*," Selena said, "and all your work, it's filled with such *passion*." Selena raked her nails ran down my back and my blood heated. I tightened my grip on her. She leaned forward and mouthed at my neck, her breath hot on my skin. "Will you show that to me? Because I'm not lying, Asher. I want *you*. All of you." She took her shirt off and threw it behind her and keeping her eyes on me, she unhooked her bra and let it drop. "Show me. All of you," she whispered. I was overcome, a permission to unleash myself rising up like fire in my belly, and I wrapped my arm around her even as I pushed her to floor, my lips locked with hers.

Selena wrapped her legs around my back and arched up into me and I couldn't get enough as I gripped her shoulders too hard and nibbled my way down her neck. I felt her gasp when I bit her shoulder, my palm coming up to feel the pleasing swell of her breast.

"Yes," Selena said. "*Yes*, Asher."

We kicked off our shoes and scrambled a little, her hands

all over me, clawing at my broad chest and leaving marks on my shoulders. I had not expected this from Selena at all and I was drunk on it as her curvy body entwined with mine, the soft skin of her breasts cooling the heat of my body as I pressed against her, meeting her lips again. I sat back and growled as I unbuttoned her jeans, wanting to tear them right off her body. Instead I yanked them off and she mewled, dropping her arms on the floor, playing with her hair, nearly naked and seemingly helpless before me. Yet the knowledge that she wasn't helpless at all made me want her all the more. She was writhing a little now, arching off the floor again as if her body was calling to me. I ran my palms down the back of her legs, squeezing the generous flesh of her pale thighs, wanting to taste her but wanting so many things at once I hardly knew where to start.

"What do you want me to do?" Selena said, her voice rough and low. She palmed her own breast and I unbuttoned my trousers, painfully hard.

"Touch yourself," I said impulsively, hardly knowing my own cravings. "Until you're desperate for me."

Selena blushed scarlet and for a nightmarish moment I thought perhaps I'd read her all wrong and then she was smiling, her hand slowly reaching down to press at herself through her panties. I sat back and took off my trousers and her eyes went straight to the erection swelling my briefs. I crawled to hover over her and reached down to pinch a nipple. She cried out as she slipped her hand inside her panties and began to finger herself.

"I'm already desperate for you," she said breathlessly. "If...if you were wondering, Asher."

I fondled her breasts, impossibly aroused as she squirmed and pleasured herself for my benefit. "Don't come without me," I said. I pressed a finger to her lips and she bit it gently and her tongue curled around it and she began to suck.

"God, Selena..." I snuck another finger into her mouth and she sucked on both of them, her eyes glassy as she arched against her own hand. When my fingers were good and wet I traced her lips and ran them in a line down her throat and between her breasts. She scrambled to take off her underwear and pulled at mine.

"Asher, please. *Please.*" Selena gripped my shoulders and pulled me down, her legs wrapping around me. I was trembling with need but I pushed her hands back so her arms were over her head, her fingers clasped in mind as I entered her, and she convulsed around me, pulling me in yet closer with the strength of her thighs.

"There it is," Selena breathed, squeezing my hands. "I feel all of you."

Something between fear and love rose within me. I dimly recalled reading something about that in the lore, that one of the clan making love to the shared mate further bonded the clan together, and that she would feel all of us with her.

"Is it good?" I whispered, feeling her pulse around me, tears in my eyes for how close I felt to her.

"It's beautiful."

We found some rhythm, her pressing up into me as I thrusted into her and when my climax surged up within me I felt tears slide down my face and ducked down to bite her shoulder. I wasn't thinking but Selena only held me harder, shouting as I came inside her. I expected to come down from the strength of my orgasm but found I was still hard and Selena sat up, her palms sliding up my sweaty chest.

"Now from behind," she whispered in my ear.

Somehow we never made it to Selena's too small bed and even once we were sated, hours later, Selena only dragged her blankets down to the floor so we could sprawl out on top of them. She curled up against me, resting her cheek on my arm and drawing circles on my chest with her fingertip. My neck was sore from turning my head to look at her but I didn't want to look anywhere else.

"What about the rest of your family?" Selena said.

I stroked her long hair, letting it fall through my fingers, enchanted with the sight. "You've met them all."

"Parents?" Selena said.

The familiar ache returned as it always did when the subject of my parents came up. "They died when we were young," I said. "Back in Ireland."

"You're from Ireland?" She looked surprised at that. I kept forgetting how many things she didn't know. It already felt as if she'd always been with us. "None of you even have an accent."

"Long time ago," I said. "Like I said, we were young."

She chewed her lip, perhaps deciding whether to prod further. I half hoped she would and half hoped she wouldn't. "What happened?"

I took a breath and summoned my strength. I generally never spoke of my parents' deaths but I felt as if Selena had weakened my will and I didn't even mind it. "We grew up in a village called Belderrig near the ocean in a big...well, in a castle."

"You grew up in a castle?" Selena said.

"I mean it didn't really feel like a castle," I said. "It felt more like a big manor, I guess. And it was warm and our clan was much larger then. There were cousins and aunts and uncles and. It was a *real* clan. All shifters. My brothers and I would shift as pups and run all up and down the coast or all the way to Blanemore Forest. Our mother taught us magic and our father taught us the responsibilities of heading the clan. I was the oldest so... He was the Alpha and I was his oldest son so, it would fall to me to lead one day. And then..." Selena gazed up at me, seeming to know something terrible was coming.

"Who was it?" Selena said softly.

"Vampires," I said. Her eyes went wide about that but she didn't question it. "The war between shifters and vampires goes back a couple of thousand years but it's been pretty cold for the last century or so. The Quinns, in particular, had been campaigning for peace. We didn't see the point of war even though back then we thought all vampires were atrocities. This one particular sect did not want peace." I squeezed my eyes shut and heard the roar of fire. I opened them again and couldn't bear to look at Selena. "I was fifteen. God, Carter was only nine. We were coming back from Blanemore early in the morning, wasn't even dawn yet. We'd been there all night just running wild. It was cold but for once it wasn't raining. I remember just the way it smelled, like wet peat moss, and the way the seaspray felt on my fur as we ran down the beach to Belderrig. We smelled the smoke miles out but we didn't think anything of it. I don't know why. And we had to run much slower than usual because Carter was there. It was the first time he'd run out that far with the rest of us without our parents. I think he still blames himself for running so slow but we were just pups. We wouldn't have been able to stop them and then they would've killed Carter too if he hadn't been with us. By the time we got back, there was nobody left. Just smoke and flame. And they'd staked their claim so we had to take what we could and leave. Our parents had left us a great inheritance but the vampire sect was in our way. We wouldn't be able to get to it for years. So we just got by the best we could for a while. Had to keep on the move. The sect knew there were sons, so…"

"You got by?" Selena reached up to stroke my cheek. "What's that mean, exactly?"

"Well, sometimes we'd just live as wolves," I said. "Which can be easier when you have no money and you have to keep moving. But then we'd come across some other clan or run into trouble. Sometimes we starved. But then we got older, fought our way to our inheritance. Now we have more money than we can spend." I shrugged as if it were nothing.

"Well, what about the vampire sect?" Selena said. "Are they still after you?"

"No. When we were all of age and we were strong enough, we tracked them down." I reached for her hand and kissed her fingertips. "We killed them all. Every last one of them. Vampires don't fuck with us anymore."

Selena kissed me long and hard and said, "Good."

SELENA

"Um...mmm, ask me again?" I said, sighing. Ben was kissing the nape of my neck, making me melt while Damien was reading questions off of notecards and rubbing my feet occasionally. We were sprawled on my floor and I was supposed to be studying for midterms but it was difficult with the way my 'help' was distracting me.

Damien cleared his throat and said, "What era evolved into the Gothic period?"

That was easy. I knew it was easy but my head was swimming. Ben whispered in my ear but his eyes were on Damien. "If you get it right, Damien will give you a treat."

Damien blushed at that and said, "Shut up."

"He's shy," Ben said, nibbling on my ear.

I could feel Damien's nerves coming off of him in waves and I hated the thought that I might be making him uncomfortable at all. It had been his idea to help me study which *he* was. Ben was mostly distracting me. Although I hadn't exactly told him to stop.

"I'm not shy," Damien grumbled. "We're studying. Midterms."

He was right but Damien's deep green eyes and sharp, stubbled chin made it hard to think about midterms. The dorm was running warm and he'd peeled down to a slim gray t-shirt that kept riding up and showing his tight stomach. There was also the fact that I'd read a couple of short stories he'd written for a literary magazine and his writing turned me on as much as Asher's paintings.

I said, "How about if I get it right, I give *you* a treat?"

"Um..." Damien chuckled at that, which made me think he wanted me to make the first move.

"So shy," Ben whispered in my ear.

"Shut up," Damien murmured. Ben nudged Damien's leg with his foot and Damien rolled his eyes but he was smiling.

I rose to my knees and tugged at Damien's shirt. "Romanesque."

"That is correct," Damien said, his eyes glimmering. He sat up and knelt in front of me and I pulled him forward into a kiss. I felt I knew Damien the least of the Quinns but my connection to him was just as strong and his kiss just as electrifying. I curled my tongue around his, pulling him closer.

"I think I'll go pick up some snacks from the vending machines you two enjoy your...treat," Ben said, starting to get up. I was so wrapped up in Damien, I barely heard him leave. His hand was massaging my breast through my shirt and I had deciding he had the best tasting neck of all the brothers.

Things would've gotten much sweatier in another minute if my phone hadn't buzzed and I remembered that I was going to a study meet-up for my Aesthetics & Philosophy class.

"Shit," I mumbled, as Damien made out with my collarbone. "I have to go."

Damien whimpered helplessly. He sounded like a whiny puppy. It was out of character for him and it made me smile.

"Trust me," I murmured. "Already starting to regret it. But

- midterms." I tipped Damien's chin up and he kissed me once softly. "Aesthetics and Philosophy."

Ben returned with candy bars and frowned to see Damien getting ready to leave. "Wait, is it over? What about *my* treat?"

"I'll save your treat for later, Benjamin," I said, rolling my eyes.

"Midterms," Damien said. "We understand." He reached behind me, thwacking Ben in his flume of hair. "C'mon, you horn dog."

Ben tossed the candy bars on my desk and sighed. "Ya know, Asher knows all that Aesthetics and Philosophy stuff. You could study with him?"

"Yeah," I said. "Clearly I get a lot of studying done with you guys."

"Sorry," Damien said, looking sheepish. "I wanted to help.'

"That's okay," I said, kissing his cheek. "You're sweet."

"I wanted to help too!" Ben piped up. I spun around, raising an eyebrow. "I'm just bad at it."

"You tried," I said, and kissed him with a loud smack. "You guys better go. I'm liable to start tearing off my clothes at any second."

They both froze and gaped at me, blinking. "Don't wait for that happen!" I said, laughing. "Scram!"

"Okay," Ben said, grabbing his sweater. He pointed to the ceiling. "What about…?"

"He hasn't done anything since you guys put the spell whammy on him," I said. "But don't pretend there aren't gonna be a couple of giant wolves hanging around tonight just in case."

"Well...yeah," Damien said shrugging. "Although making sure one or two of us are here all the time is getting…"

"Complicated," Ben finished for him.

That gave me a bad feeling and I flushed. "Oh! Guys, you

don't need to do that at all, you know. Aiden hasn't done anything since then and if I suspected -"

"Nah nah." Ben waved a hand. "Selena, you're our mate. You know that now. Asher's not gonna let you go unguarded when we know there's a potential threat to you. It's just not gonna happen. We'll figure it out."

"Okay," I said, still feeling a little guilty.

Damien fixed me with one of his steady gazes. "Please don't worry about it, sweetheart. Just focus on your studies. We'll figure out the rest."

I nodded, leaving them with one more kiss each and saw them to the door, wishing Aiden would just leave school or, I don't know, keel over and die suddenly.

"Sweetheart?" Ben said, nudging Damien. "That's so cute."

"Shut up," Damien said.

I chuckled at their little interplay, closing the door behind them. I wished I could just go home with the Quinns. School had been so busy but a routine had developed of one Quinn or another meeting me in the morning or hanging out with me at some point during the day if only to have lunch. Where they hid as wolves while they guarded me during the night, I didn't know. But I slept soundly with the assurance that they were out there, just in case. My schedule, not to mention the Quinns', had been so jam packed, I hadn't gotten the chance to see their place. I'd heard it described as a 'lavish penthouse' downtown. But I'd had papers and tests and no chance to visit.

The next morning I went to Medieval Art class, my head with my studies but my heart with the Quinns. I was setting up my laptop near the front of the auditorium when I saw Aiden walk through the door. It was strange, but I hadn't even thought of him lately which only made me realize how much I'd had him on my mind before, in the worst way possible. Before, I'd gone to classes I knew Aiden would be attending with a sense of dread even if it was only in the back of my mind. Was he going to ask me out again and make me scramble to find a reason to say no when I didn't need to give a reason? Was he going to block my way or pepper me with questions I didn't feel comfortable answering?

I sat at my desk and and risked a look in Aiden's direction. He was staring straight ahead. I focused on class but a part of me waited for him to bother me and he didn't. When he walked out at the end of the lecture without a word, I felt a near thrill. Perhaps my new wizard-wolf boyfriends had knocked him into submission. I found myself grinning at the thought, my feet feeling light as I made my way out of class.

"Hey, beautiful!" That was Carter, appearing in front of the Arts building, and I tossed him a wave and took his hand, bringing him into a kiss. "How are you today? I just saw Aiden go by. He didn't give you any trouble, did he?"

"I'm wonderful now that you're here," I said, batting my eyes. He threw an arm around my waist as we walked. "No, not a peep from Aiden. I think he's finally gotten the message."

"Well, I hope so," Carter said, as we walked to my next class. "But you know we're gonna want to keep an eye out as long as he's around. The only problem is, with everyone's schedule..."

A ripple of anxiety coursed through me. I *was* too much trouble for them, no matter what Asher said. How presumptuous of me to think they could just keep watch at all hours when they had lives of their own. Of course, they had better things to do. I must've had my worry on my face because Carter stopped walking and turned to face me, tipping my chin up.

"Hey," Carter said. "Don't look so sad. I'm here with good news. Or, I hope so anyway."

"What's that?" I said, still feeling anxious.

"Well, Asher and, well *all* of us think it would just be easier if... " He took a breath. "I don't know why they sent me to ask, it's like they knew I'd be nervous about it..."

"Geez, Carter. What?"

"We wanted to know if you'd consider moving in," Carter said in a rush. "With us."

I should've worried about the speed of things, I supposed. But all I felt was giddiness at the very idea. I guess next to dating wizard brothers who could also turn into wolves, moving in quickly really didn't sound too shocking.

"Really?" I said. "Are you serious?"

"Well, yeah," Carter said, as if I was being ridiculous. "You're our mate. We were going to ask you eventually."

"I like being your mate," I said, kissing the corner of his mouth. "Of course, I'd love to."

Carter lit up at that. "That's great! You'd have your own room too, you know. We'll make all kinds of space for you and -"

"You make it sound like I'm doing you a favor," I said.

"That's how we look at it, silly," Carter said. And just for that, I kissed him again.

SELENA

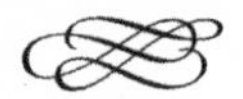

"I think I can carry *one* thing," I said, even as Benjamin grabbed my backpack. Asher took my hand, helping me out of his shiny, black Tesla. He kissed my knuckles as I stood. With the Quinns helping me, I'd packed up my dorm in no time. Now we were parked in their building's parking structure, our voices echoing as the guys shouldered my bags.

"Don't think of it, m'lady," Ben said, tossing me a wink.

"We are at your disposal." Asher wrapped an arm around my shoulders. "We have keys for you, a parking card. No alarm codes for the penthouse though. It's just spelled to hell. Very well protected."

"Yeah," Damien said gravely. "None of that weak hand stuff either"

"And you can borrow any of the cars whenever," Carter added.

"Oh!" Ben said. "No, we should buy her a car though. She's gotta have her own car."

"Well, I figured we would eventually," Carter said. "I just meant for now."

"*Don't* buy me a car!" I sputtered.

They all gaped at me. "But you don't have one," Asher said.

Ben shrugged. "Can't live in L.A. without a car. I think it's illegal."

I opened my mouth, unsure of whether I should go along with such an absurdly generous offer or not. Damien patted my shoulder, frowning at his brothers. "Guys, you're overwhelming her. One thing at a time."

"Thank you," I said, covering his hand with mine as we walked across the structure to the elevator. "I could actually go for a good burger more than a car about now anyway."

"Oooh, burgers!" That was Carter, his eyes big. "That does sound good. Asher makes a great burger."

"Accurate," Asher said, nodding. "I think we have some good beef around if Damien didn't eat it all. Damien gets into his moods and holes up writing for days and then gorges on meat. Still too thin though."

"I didn't eat it all," Damien said quickly as he pressed their floor. "This time."

"Huh." I leaned against Asher in the elevator. I'd worn a new pair of heels that day and they were hurting my feet. I rubbed my left leg with my right foot under my skirt and saw Damien's eyes follow the movement. "Didn't figure you guys for burger types."

"We're wolves," Ben said. "We love meat."

"Oh, right."

"I can cook," Asher said. "But it's Carter's turn for clean-up."

"Damn," Carter muttered. "I'm beat, Ash. Rehearsals."

"I'll cover you," Ben said, giving him a nudge.

"We could eat out," Damien said. "I wouldn't mind eating out."

I leaned towards Damien in the tight space of the elevator

and reached up to play with his hair. "You wouldn't, huh?" I said in his ear.

He blushed so intensely I could feel it. But the brother who Ben claimed was 'shy' turned his head and softly said, "I'd *love* it."

"Get a room!" Ben said, grinning. He pushed up his glasses and stuck his tongue out at us, seemingly gleeful, just as the elevators opened.

"I'm working on it, smartass," I cracked.

I'd expected something luxurious with the way the boys threw around the word 'penthouse' but even that didn't do their home justice. The Quinn residence was really the top three stories of a big brick building near Little Tokyo. The elevator opened into a spacious foyer. I'd expected modern design too but the floors were dark hardwood and the interiors were part exposed brick and part deep colored wallpapers in greens and woody browns, that is where a bookshelf didn't take up a wall. Most of the furniture was antique. Even as huge as it was, the first word I thought of was 'homey' as Asher led me into a parlor where a spiral staircase led to a circular balcony on the second story. Floor to ceiling windows looked out on the city and I forgot to breathe for a second, trying to get my head around the idea that I would be living in such a place. Me, a girl who had slept on a couch in a crappy apartment for three years as a kid.

I strolled by an antique looking globe and gave it a spin. The place actually did look like wizards might live in it. Cool, young wizards anyway. "How many rooms does this place have?"

Carter stroked his chin. "Well, we each have a bedroom and then I have a dance studio, Ash has a studio, Ben has a music room, and there's a library, and now you have the room where Damien's office was."

I whirled around to look at Damien who stood sheepishly

leaning on a blue velvet chaise. "I'm putting you out of your office?"

"No no." He waved a hand. "I don't need an office. We have a library too. I'll be writing in there. We're absolutely spoiled with space."

"Well, that was sweet of you," I said, kicking his shoe.

Damien nodded, shoving his hands in his pockets and locking his elbows. He looked like a nervous teenager on a date.

"I'm gonna get started on dinner," Asher said, clapping his hands. "Damien, maybe you could give Selena the grand tour?"

"Excellent idea," I said, taking his hand.

The tour took longer than it should have, even considering the size of the place. I had to sit down a few times when I became dizzy trying to get around this new reality. Fortunately, the Quinns had a series of fancy antique side chairs at convenient points in the penthouse, perfect for an overwhelmed mate trying to catch her breath. Damien showed me my room last and I could tell they'd had it remodeled a bit to suit me. *Red Wolf* hung on the wall, now properly displayed, and the interior design was a little more bohemian than the common rooms of the house. My stuff took up hardly any space but they'd supplied me with art books packed into a huge shelf next to the windows that looked out on downtown. They'd set up a little reading nook of big comfy floor cushions on the plush carpet. There were even prints of posters for concerts of my favorite bands on the wall and I knew that was Ben's touch.

Outside, the city at night looked like an ocean of stars and I swallowed the lump in my throat. "It's exactly what I would have wished for," I said, my voice breaking. "If I could pick anywhere to live in the city." I felt Damien come up behind me and I turned a little to take his hands so he would wrap his arms around my waist. He sighed and kissed my neck and I reached back to ruffle his dark hair.

"We wanted to make a home for you that you'd like," Damien said, and I shut my eyes as he pressed kisses to my throat. "I've never seen my brothers like this and I've never felt like this either. We just sit around trying to think of ways to make you happy."

I turned around in the circle of his arms and kissed him softly. "You really don't have to try." We got caught up in kissing and I'd been thinking about Damien since that moment in the dorm with Ben but then his stomach rumbled I pulled away and giggled.

"I guess I am hungry," Damien said, blushing.

"I'd make another joke about eating out," I said. "But I'm guessing burgers are more filling for now."

"For *now*," Damien agreed, and I tugged him forward one more time and moaned a little when he bit my lip. He smiled, pulling away. I seemed to be working on relieving his nerves and that pleased me. "Oh, hang on." He reached into his pocket and pressed something cool and metal into my hand. "We made you this ring. Well, we spelled the ring. For protection, I mean. We didn't make it. It's an heirloom, goes back to the first Quinn mate in the tenth century."

"The *tenth* century," I said gasping. I opened my palm and gaped at the intricate band of gold with a neat oval of emerald at its center. My hands shook as Damien took my hand and slipped the ring on my finger. "Damien, what if I lose it? What if something happens to it?"

"Don't worry." He kissed my hand. "It's enchanted. It's really hard to lose enchanted things. They have a way of making their way back to you. We spelled this ring to repel unwanted men."

"As long as it's only *unwanted* men," I said. "Or I'll be very lonely." I mumbled the last few words into his mouth but I was a little weak with hunger too and reluctantly took a step back. "God, it's like I'm on Spanish Fly. Let's go see if dinner's ready, huh?"

"After you, sweetheart," Damien said, gesturing to the door.

I smiled, feeling almost bashful. There was something so old-fashioned about the endearment. "I like when you call me sweetheart," I said.

"Then I always will," Damien said, as we made our way out.

I was half through my second burger at dinner when Asher proposed a toast. I found myself hungrier than usual and wondered if there was some kind of magic working on me as the Quinns' new mate. I would've been almost embarrassed by how much I was eating except that the boys kept pushing food in my direction and themselves ate with such gusto, not at all acting as if I shouldn't be eating exactly the same way.

"A toast to our mate," Asher said, looking a little glassy-eyed. "And to a future of shared love, shared desire, and shared lives."

I swallowed the lump in my throat and murmured, "Cheers." Carter must've seen me looking teary because he squeezed my knee under the table.

"I never thought we'd have a mate," Damien said, shaking his head. "Much less one so...astonishing. Of course, I haven't looked at the lore in fifty years or so, maybe it was more detailed than I remember."

I choked on my arugula and aioli topped burger and swallowed with difficulty, wiping my lips with my napkin. Thinking I must've misheard, I chuckled and said, "I'm sorry, how many years?"

"Fifty," Damien said, shrugging.

Asher looked a little pale suddenly and said, "Uh oh."

"What?"

"Asher," Ben said darky. "You told her how old we are, right?"

My eyes went wide and I threw back the rest of my wine, bracing myself. Wizards, wolves...they could be five hundred for all I knew. I didn't know how magic worked. Or were they immortal like vampires?

"I may have forgotten to mention that," Asher said, stroking his chin. "It's easy to forget about that type of thing."

"So - how old *are* you?" I said.

"I'm one hundred and twenty," Asher said. "Carter's the youngest, of course. He's one hundred and fourteen."

"You whippersnapper," I said dryly to Carter. The others tittered and I motioned Ben for more wine. "Alright. Well, I never thought I had a thing for older men but you learn something new everyday."

"We don't live forever or anything," Carter said as he poured me some more wine. "We just drink a potion that slows aging. By a lot. We're hoping you're willing to drink it too."

"Sure, why not?" I said, as he handed me back my glass. "Plastic surgery's way out of my budget anyway."

After dinner, I went on another walk around the place just to familiarize myself with the space and avoid getting lost. With great reluctance, I went back to my room after that to study for a while. I knew if I wasn't careful I'd let myself get so caught up in the Quinns that I would lose focus on my studies, and I'd sacrificed too much and worked too hard for that. The boys seemed to understand and left me to myself. At least it was more comfy to study at my giant window in my cozy boho nook than my old dorm room. After a few hours of Aesthetics and Philosophy I put away my textbooks for the night and lay back, stretching on that big plush carpet and looking out at the glimmering night skyline. I was hoping Damien would somehow know I was finished for the night and come find me. Of course, I could just text him. Asher had told me he suspected that eventually I would develop the ability to telepathically speak to them but until then, I supposed there was going to be a lot of texting from room to room. Still though, I wanted Damien to find me and somehow know that I was ready and wanted him. Just the thought of it had me absently stroking my bare thigh under my skirt.

I didn't have to wait long.

The knock at the door was so quiet, I was lucky to hear it. "Please, come in!" I called out.

Damien appeared, beautiful and all in black, shutting the door behind him and leaning there a moment. "Am I interrupting?" He said.

"No, I was hoping you'd come find me," I said. I stretched my arms over my head, trying to look a bit seductive sprawled there on the floor, my hair splayed around me. "Please, come here."

Damien walked over and sank to his knees by my feet. "I want to make you feel good," he said, his voice husky. "I want you to let me take care of you."

"Please do," I said, and though I felt a bit princessy I lay there, waiting for him to pleasure me.

Damien gently removed my shoes, neatly putting them aside. He crawled forward and pushed my shirt up, helping me take it off. I'd taken off my bra already while studying and Damien kissed me deeply before lowering his head to work at one nipple with his mouth. His hands were cool as they slid over my skin and pushed my skirt up around my waist. I threw my head back as he nibbled at my breast, rubbing circles into the other. He kept raising his eyes to see my reaction and I nodded, feeling stupid as my mouth hung open. All at once he sat up again and slowly pulled my skirt down and slid it off my feet. I was naked before him and my nipples hardened as the cool air hit them. I shivered and Damien didn't speak as he took my right foot in his hand softly kissing my ankle, working his way down my leg with agonizing slowness.

"I've been thinking about this since that first night," Damien said. "How I would taste every inch of you. How you would feel in my mouth, how my tongue would learn you."

"God, Damien," I whispered, biting hard on my lip. I wanted his mouth and he was barely at my knee, kissing behind it. Now he seemed to be examining the top of my thigh with great interest. He ran his hands along the back of my legs, seeming to know exactly where to touch me, and crawled back up to hover over me, smirking.

"You seem a little impatient about something," Damien said. He ran his thumb along my bottom lip and my tongue snuck out to taste it. "Is there something you'd like?"

"You know, I thought you were the nice one," I said, practically moaning as I spoke because he was licking my throat now, a hand at my hip and sliding down temptingly low. "But you're mean. You're a mean, mean man."

Damien kissed his way bit by bit from my collarbone, down between my breasts that rose and fell as I breathed, and across the curve of my stomach. "I'll be nice then," he murmured.

I had always been a little self-conscious about spreading my legs, especially while completely naked. Something about it felt undignified somehow under bright lights, as if I were at the doctor's. But Damien gently nudged my thighs apart and brought my legs up until I was wide open before him, feeling painfully vulnerable. But the nerves only lasted for a moment before his arm came around one of my thighs, holding it in place as he spread me open with his other hand, and his tongue licked into me. I shuddered, gasping, and he smiled up at me before licking again; teasing and all too brief. I hadn't realized how wet I was until he was lapping me up and I trembled as he pushed one finger inside while his tongue went to work on my clit. I closed my eyes and I could feel that shared connection to other Quinns inside me as Damien made me moan and writhe. The more noise I made, the more it seemed to spur him on. He seemed to be truly enjoying it as much as I was as his broad tongue tasted me, licking at my clit with sometimes wild abandon only to slow again just as I thought I was about to fall off the edge. I couldn't feel the floor under me. I didn't know anything but Damien's mouth until he finally took mercy on me and quickened his pace while thrusting his finger in and out of me until I was screaming, arching off the floor. I might've been levitating for all I knew, sparks flashing in my eyes as I shook with the pleasure of it. Damien, the bastard, did not let up but continued to taste me until I wept and reflexively closed my thighs to him, too sensitive to bear anymore.

"Sorry," Damien said, looking mischievous as he lay down beside me. I sighed happily and rolled on my side to face him as he wrapped an arm around me. "Asher once told me I have an oral fixation. I chew up my pens all the time when I write."

"I really don't think you have anything to apologize for," I said. "But if you ever want to exercise that fixation again, I'll be right here." I shivered against him and Damien grabbed a thick, fluffy throw from behind a pillow and covered me up but it wasn't long before I was pressing my body to his for the next round.

BENJAMIN

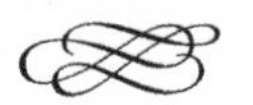

All five of us were in a near constant state of euphoria. Aiden had been quiet and Selena was settling in at the penthouse. When she wasn't busy or tired from school and the rest of us weren't working, she was in one of our laps or one of our rooms. I felt a little sorry for Carter, too swamped with rehearsals and dance to get himself alone with Selena for a night. But Selena always seemed aware of all four of us all the time and left sweet little notes for Carter to find on his way out (I didn't see them but Carter had told me about them with a secretive smile on his face). Sometimes Selena would surprise us when we least expected it.

One morning I went to our shared bathroom to brush my teeth and found Selena sitting on the counter, lazily combing her long, dark hair in nothing but her underwear and a lacy little cami. I was glad I'd put my glasses on when I'd rolled out of bed.

"Good morning to you too," I'd said, pretending to tip my hat.

"Good morning," Selena said, and set her brush down,

leaning back on her hands. She kept her eyes on me as I brushed and spit, a bare foot now traveling up my leg."Having a nice morning?"

"I sure am," I mumbled, and tossed my toothbrush aside, stepping in between her legs to take her in my arms.

On a Friday night not long after Selena moved in, we decided to take her to the ballet to see Carter dance. I was wearing my best suit and waiting with Asher and Damien in the parlor. I leaned against Damien, hanging on his shoulder as he showed me all the pics of Selena on his phone. We wanted to take her on a clothes shopping spree when we got the chance.

Asher's eyes were screwed on the spiral staircase as if willing her to come down. "You don't think she would be offended?" He said. "As if we're saying her clothes aren't good enough? I wouldn't want her to think that."

Damien and I glanced at each other and smirked. "You're cute, Ash," I said, straightening my glasses.

He glowered at us and fixed his tie for the tenth time. "How so?"

Damien said exactly what I was thinking. "It's just nice that you're as flustered as the rest of us."

"I'm not flustered," Asher grumbled.

"Okay," I muttered, and Damien snickered.

With impeccable timing, Selena came down the stairs; a vision draped in burgundy silk, a beaded bag looped around her wrist. Her hair was piled on top of her head and long, softly curling tendrils framed her heart-shaped face.

Asher stared at her. "You look... You look..." He coughed. "Um..."

Selena pressed her palms to his chest and kissed him. "Thank you, lovely might be the word you're looking for my love."

"Not flustered at all," Damien said.

Selena smiled slyly at us, sharing our joke and took each of our elbows. I felt like a king with our mate on my arm and even more so later as we made our entrance at the theater. Heads turned to look at us as we walked in and I kissed Selena's cheek. More heads turned when Selena kissed Damien on the mouth before he went to find our seats, and just as quickly kissed Asher on the mouth before he went to get cocktails. She spun around to face me. I could swear she was glowing.

"You're going to create a stir," I said, but I set my hands at her waist anyway.

"Sorry," Selena said, not sounding sorry at all. She fiddled with my tie, pretending to straighten it when it didn't need straightening. "It's hard to keep my hands off of you boys."

"I guess we'll have to manage then," I said, and we would have started making out in the middle of the formally dressed crowd if Asher hadn't returned with our drinks.

There was mild disagreement over who Selena would sit between which really came down to Damien and me as Asher generally won any disagreement by default. I pouted but as the overture began I cast puppy eyes upon Damien and asked if I could switch for intermission.

"Alright," Damien whispered. "But only if you read the short story I just finished. It's awful and I need feedback."

"Everything you write is brilliant," I whispered back. He grinned bashfully at that and I saw Selena smile at the exchange.

The ballet began and when Carter danced onstage in his skintight costume and his tights I heard Selena's intake of breath and that was before Carter really began to move. I stifled a chuckle. But it was fair. Selena hadn't even seen Carter practice yet. It was easy to forget the flawless dancer's body he hid under his jeans. Asher might have been the strongest by brute force, but Carter had more muscles than the rest of us even knew about. The show was *Don Quixote* and Carter was the lead. His body seemed endlessly fluid as he leapt and spun and lifted his lady in the air.

"He's *beautiful*!" Selena said, clearly impressed.

I felt proud for my brother and nodded. "That he is." I enjoyed Carter's dancing yet I could hardly wait until it was over and we could spend some time together, all of us. I leaned on Damien's shoulder, feeling warmed by our happiness, the connection between all five of us like a hot bath.

And then Carter fell.

By now, I knew Carter's moves in *Don Quixote* almost as well as he did. It was not the first time he'd danced it and I'd watched him rehearse plenty. This was the last big jump before the intermission. Carter leapt into the air with his typical breathtaking grace and then abruptly, he lost position in mid-air and plummeted straight down, landing on his ankle. My heart stopped for a moment and Damien gripped my arm painfully.

"Oh!" Selena clapped a hand to her mouth.

Asher had shot from his seat and members of the audience were grumbling for him to sit down even as the curtain drew for intermission. "Something's wrong," Asher said, and grabbed me by the collar. "Ben, come. And you two as well. *Shit*. I'll kill him. I'll *kill* him!"

It did not take a genius to realize he was talking about Aiden and not Carter.

We shuffled our way to the aisle just as everyone else was also getting up. Selena found my hand and squeezed it tight and I was grateful. She must've seen the fear in my face.

"Carter doesn't fall," I said darkly. "It's almost impossible. He's been dancing for decades and besides that, our talents are enhanced by our magic ability. Carter does *not* fall."

"You think it was Aiden," Selena said, almost running to keep up with us as we headed backstage.

"Of course, it was Aiden," Asher growled. "I'm going to rip his heart out with my teeth!"

"Chill, big bro," I said, patting his back as we rushed down the aisle. "Let's find out what happened first."

"It was definitely Aiden," Carter said not a minute later.

Well, that sealed it.

We were huddled around him in the chaos of backstage. He was pretending it was nothing for the benefit of the medical aides who would have otherwise wrapped his foot but I knew that was because Asher would probably heal it.

"I felt it," Carter said. "Even before the jump. Felt the spell coming right at me. And after I fell I could smell him. He must be here somewhere."

"Are you sure you could smell him?" I said. "I don't smell anything."

"I don't anymore," Carter said, his brows knit with worry. "Must've taken off."

"Let me see your ankle." Asher gently covered Carter's ankle with his hands and without hesitating he spouted some healing spell I'd never even heard before. Carter looked visibly relieved.

"I have to finish the show," Carter said. "But I'll find you afterwards."

"I swear to God, I'll murder that son of a bitch," Asher said, spitting his words.

"Be careful," Carter said. "Please stay safe, Selena."

Selena kissed Carter and squeezed his hand. "I'll be fine. You are phenomenal, by the way. We'll see you later."

It was a sweet moment but I saw Carter mouth, "Get her out of here!" to Damien when Selena turned away. Which I'd assumed was part of whatever plan we didn't have yet.

The plan we didn't have was quickly thwarted when we discovered that all the doors were locked. The intermission for *Don Quixote* is short, so the audience was already returning to their seats just as we were dashing through the lobby to the front doors which we found sealed although they didn't even appear to be bolted. Nobody seemed to take notice of us either as we tried every door. Asher tried to break the spell and I saw his jaw clench painfully.

"We can break it together," I said, and reached up to squeeze the nape of his neck. "C'mon. We got this, boss."

Asher nodded and we thrust our hands towards the door, hissing a spell that unlatched locks. It was a tricky one but no bother for me to remember. We'd used it a thousand times. It took a few tries but eventually the doors gave and we rushed out into the cool night air, looking around for Aiden on the plaza in front of the theater as if he would just be waiting there for us. The wind blew spray from a fountain nearby and it chilled my over warmed skin. I pushed my hair back and blindly followed Asher and the rest of them to the parking garage.

I felt the kind of dread I'd only felt a couple of times before in my life; once just before we'd found our home destroyed by the vampire sect and once when I'd lost track of my brothers and wandered for months looking for them on my own. Selena caught my eye and I tried to draw strength from her, but she was not smiling.

SELENA

Asher seemed to know what he was doing so I clutched Damien for dear life and followed him to the car, walking as quickly as I could in heels. I hated to admit even to myself how afraid I was but the sight of Carter falling to the stage, and the way Asher had tensed up beside me kept replaying itself in my mind. The Quinns seemed so strong to me. The thought that an obnoxious little asshole like Aiden could hurt them was disturbing. Asher had warned me that Aiden was powerful and more dangerous for being both entitled and young, but it seemed more real now. It was terrifying but not surprising that Aiden could potentially hurt *me*. But the idea that he could hurt *them* was a shock.

I had my arm hooked through Damien's elbow as we ran down the stairs of the theater 's parking structure and dimly made out Asher and Ben arguing over potential spells they could use on Aiden if they found him once they took me home. My enchanted ring was heavy on my finger. I knew that it could repel unwanted men but it couldn't help my guys. I hated the thought of staying home, helpless while they were out there possibly getting hurt. I began wondering if my power as a mate gave me enough sway to insist on going with them or if I would just get in the way as we walked out to our parking level. Our footsteps were echoing loudly in the empty lot when all at once everything went black and I gasped, stumbling and hanging onto Damien for support.

For a moment I thought all the lights in the parking structure had gone out and only a second later realized I truly couldn't see *anything,* not even my hand in front of my face.

"Asher!" My heart was pounding. Suddenly I was as scared as I'd ever been in my life. "Damien..."

"Selena?" That was Damien beside me. "What's the matter?"

We stopped walking and I whipped my head around as if I might see suddenly if I looked in the right place. "I can't see! Damien, I can't see! I can't see anything!"

I think Damien must have waved a hand in front of my face because I heard him more distantly saying to Asher, "He's blinded her." His voice sounded frighteningly flat. My mind was already racing. What if they couldn't undo it? What if I was blinded for life? What if I could never see an Asher Quinn painting again or look into Ben's big brown eyes?

I heard a noise like a huge dog growling and ready to kill and then Ben was saying, "Whoa, okay. Asher, stay calm. Let's get Selena home and then we'll go find Aiden and fucking kill him. Sound good?"

I heard another low growl and Damien quietly saying, "Look at me. Look at me, Ash. We got this."

"Okay," Asher said then. "Sounds good." But his voice sounded different; hard and cold. That was the voice of the man who'd killed the vampire sect that murdered his parents.

Ben's voice was suddenly in my ear, quiet but insistent. "We'll reverse it. Baby, it's okay. I swear, we'll fix this. Let's just get you home."

He kissed my temple and I let them lead me to the car. I was petrified but trying not to show it. It helped that Ben rubbed my back and Damien squeezed my hand, muttering calming things as we piled into Asher's backseat.

The car wouldn't start.

"Son of a bitch," Asher hissed.

Damien said, "There's no magic here. It's not a spell..."

Ben said, "Check the engine." He kept rubbing my back and I was trying very hard not to cry. I heard car doors open and close and echoing footsteps.

"He took the goddamn battery!" Asher said. The hood shut with a jolt and I jerked in Ben's arms. "I can't fix this with a spell right now!"

"Okay," Damien said, resolutely calm. "Okay, we'll walk home. It's really not far from here."

That was true. The Music Center where Carter danced was at most a mile from the penthouse, centered in the downtown area. But the thought of walking there *blinded* with Aiden out there somewhere and able to hurt me was the stuff of nightmares.

"I don't want to walk home like this," I said, sniffing. "Please..." I heard Ben sigh and then it was too quiet. But I could feel their worried eyes on me anyway.

"We could try..." Ben's voice faded out. I heard him discussing spells with Asher and Damien.

"What if it doesn't work?" Damien said softly.

"What if we don't try it," Ben said, "and then something happens to us and she's helpless in some alley -"

"Do whatever it is you're talking about!" I said, my voice too sharp in the quiet of the garage.

"It might hurt, a lot," Damien said.

"I don't care," I snapped.

"Okay." That was Ben, stroking my hair, and they helped me out of the car. I felt them surrounding me and then three pairs of hands covered my eyes. I expected some long drawn out ritual but this was short and sharp. I had no idea what language they were speaking. Then all once I felt as if my eyes were on fire. I screamed and someone hugged me tight. I felt hot tears on my face.

"It's okay, sweetheart."

"I'm so sorry, baby. I'm so sorry."

"We've got you, Selena, my love." That was Asher.

The pain was all consuming and it only lasted for about a minute yet it felt like forever. But when it was over it was entirely over. The pain vanished abruptly and I opened my eyes, tentatively blinking. Ben had wept, his eyes red and swollen. Damien looked as calm as ever. Asher looked like he wanted to quite literally tear Aiden limb from limb.

"I'm fine," I said, clenching my fists. I was still shaky but I was determined.

"Then let's go," Asher said, taking my hand. "We'll stick to backstreets. Stay stealthy."

ASHER

I was angrier than I could ever remember being. If Damien and Ben hadn't calmed me, I might have shifted right away and run off to sniff Aiden out. Given enough motivation I could track somebody from a few miles away. Yet if I stopped to think, I could see that someone of Aiden's apparent power might be able to disguise even his scent. That was assuming he knew we were shifters. He might have figured it out just as we'd sensed his magic.

I took long breaths as we made our way down a deserted alley in the direction of the penthouse. I was clenching my fist so hard I was about to draw blood, my nails digging into my palm.

The man had hurt my little brother *twice* and was a dangerous threat to our mate. It made me see red. As it was, I thought I might be able to run a little farther ahead without putting the others in danger, if I was careful.

I nodded at Ben beside me. "I'm gonna shift," I said. "Sniff things out a little. Check for traps. He might have guessed we'd head this way."

"Don't go too far," Ben said, his expression grim. Ben

had his serious face on. He could slip in and out of it, seemingly at will. "Stay in range." That to meant to stay close enough that they'd hear me if I howled or sniff me out. I nodded and took one look back at Selena and Damien, just in case something happened, and then I began to jog ahead. I let the human part of me drop away and felt that satisfying stretch as I shifted and fell to all fours, loping down the alley. The downtown backstreets were already a traffic of odors and now they were a riot and I sorted them out one by one as I ran, trying to discern whether Aiden was there somewhere. Was he hiding? Was he lying in wait until he could strike and try to take my beloved away? I growled as I ran, the cool evening air pleasant on my fur.

I caught a whiff of a scent that I thought smelled potentially like Aiden and I stopped for a moment, glancing over my shoulder back at Selena and my brothers. I told myself to be careful and took off again, giving chase to the scent. The temptation to find the man hurting my loved ones was too great. It always had been. At fifteen, upon finding my massacred home, I'd wanted to go off and hunt down the vampires who had done it right away. I had been blinded by rage. It was doubly insulting that they had burned our home. Vampires can be killed by fire. For them to burn someone else is akin to spitting on a grave. Ben had talked sense into me. It was the first time I'd ever seen him so serious. He was thirteen and gawky, still hardly able to run very far without falling over his own paws, which he hadn't quite grown into yet. And if it hadn't been for him, I surely would've been killed too and left my brothers alone.

But I wasn't thinking rationally of that now as I chased Aiden's scent. I was thinking that Aiden was only one man, powerful or not. And we were four. We would find him and we would kill him.

When the ground gave out from under me I thought: *You fool.*

The trap was an old one. It's so primitive that it is literally just called a Hole Trap. I'd put out feelers for traps but Aiden must've cloaked it somehow. It was an invisible hole in the ground that I'd stepped right into. Now I was half stuck in the ground, painfully caught around my shoulders with my paws sticking up and tight against me. I couldn't move my legs at all, I could only wag my tail. Worse, I had taken a few too many turns, caught up in chasing that smell. I didn't know where the others were.

I'm going to kill him!

I growled and snapped at nothing, losing myself to the wolf for precious seconds. When I calmed down I shifted back into human form thinking I might escape. But in my human skin, the trap was more painful. The hole was so tight around me I thought it might be gradually breaking bones and I couldn't breathe properly, wheezing instead, my lungs unable to get enough air. I could easily die here, slowly and painfully. Alone. I focused on spells, closing my eyes to focus. It shouldn't be hard to break a Hole Trap. But I knew before trying that it wasn't going to work. If his magic was strong enough to remain hidden from me, it was strong enough to resist my counters. I muttered spell after spell, allowing the magic to course through my fingers. Nothing worked and I ended up feeling drained of energy, my head now throbbing with the effort of the spellcasting. I decided to shift back if only because the Hole Trap was actually less confining in my wolf form and found that I couldn't. I took a breath and concentrated, imagining my human form dropping away and searching for my other self, my wolf self. I waited for my wolf self to rise up with me and overtake the human but nothing happened.

I tried again and again but I couldn't shift.

Damien! Where are you? I can't shift.

I sent my thoughts out but I couldn't feel them reaching my brothers.

Ben, are you there?

I waited for some response, anything at all. I could tell my thoughts weren't going out to them and it was as if I'd forgotten how to speak to them. But I hadn't. It was Aiden blocking me somehow.

I couldn't smell my brothers or Selena. I couldn't hear them and they didn't know where I was.

I was alone and powerless. And I was enraged.

DAMIEN

We turned another corner and found ourselves in an alley behind a glassy office building. Asher had run too far ahead and I couldn't even smell him. I was always aware of my brothers' scents. If he was anywhere near us I should've been able to pick him right out among the various stenches of downtown L.A. Ben was walking ahead, careful, and occasionally looking back at us. His gaze was too serious over the rim of his glasses. For once, I wanted him to crack a joke at an inappropriate time. That would mean things were okay.

Selena clasped her hand in mine. "Maybe he found Aiden?" she said quietly.

"If he did, he shouldn't fight him alone," I said.

"ASHER!" Ben's call echoed in the empty alley, answered only by a distant siren.

"We should've taken Carter with us," I said.

"Why's that?" Ben said over his shoulder.

"He's picking us off one by one," I said. "He's trying to separate us from Selena."

We'd seen it before. The best way to attack the Quinns was to separate us from each other. We needed to try to stay together if possible. I wondered what could have taken Asher so far away and shuddered to think about it. Although, it might have been his anger making him act against his own better judgment. If Ben or I had been there to calm him down...

"ASHER!" Ben called again. He sighed and turned to face us. He took off his glasses and slipped them in his pocket. "I'm going to shift."

"Don't run ahead," I said quickly.

"I think he's on the next block that away," Ben said, pointing east. "I could swear it..."

"Ben," Selena said. "Didn't you hear what he just said? Aiden's picking you guys off. Don't go running away. We should stick together."

"I know." He scratched his head. I could see him thinking. "Look, we're close to home. It's not like it's a strange place. We know these streets. If we do get separated, just get home."

"Ben, no! Asher's not talking to us," I said, tapping my head. I was sure if something had happened, Asher would let us know telepathically. And if nothing had happened, then where the hell was he? "Something's *wrong*."

"I'm not leaving him out there," Ben snapped. "He might just be on Aiden's track, you know how he gets. And if he is, he needs the back-up. I'm second, Damien. I gotta be there for him. You stay with Selena. I'm gonna try to stay close, but you heard what I said. Now do it." Ah, the serious Ben. I hated him sometimes. Ben shifted into the familiar chestnut colored wolf I knew so well. He trotted up to Selena and nudged her hand with his nose.

"Please be careful," Selena said, scratching him between the ears.

Ben gave her hand a little lick and then he turned away and trotted off. He stayed within my line of sight for a bit and I hurried Selena along to the street, hoping against hope that Asher would suddenly appear, that the ballet would end soon and Carter would pop up out of nowhere. I could focus on the task at hand as much as any of my brothers but things like this bothered me for weeks and months afterwards. I would have nightmares about it, I knew. And then I would think of our family again; the smoking castle as the four of us ran in from the shore...

I was starting to panic, my heart racing as I thought of all the worst case scenarios. What if Aiden killed all my brothers and then killed Selena? What if they were terribly hurt? What if he killed me? Or everyone but Asher? Or Carter? Those two would blame themselves their whole lives if anything happened to the rest of us. They might not survive it. I had a little flask of a calming potion in my pocket and I took it out now, taking a healthy swig. I'd taught myself some useful potions a few decades ago. But the one that could calm my anxious blood I used the most.

Ben disappeared into shadow behind a streetlight. I heard the soft tops of his paws as he trotted and when I looked back he was gone.

"Ben!" I called out. "BEN!"

It was as if some power was picking them out of the air. My blood ran cold and I took another sip of potion. If we did make it through this, I was going to strongly consider kicking Ben's ass. I couldn't kick Asher's, but I could give it a good shot.

Selena looked pale and petrified behind me and I nudged her, smiling softly as we crossed the street into the next labyrinth of alleys in and around the towering office buildings and hotels of downtown. "Would you like a sip of this? It will calm you."

"God, yes," Selena muttered, and nodded gratefully as she took the flask. She took a long swallow and handed it back. "Thanks, Damien."

"We're gonna get through this," I said, trying to speak the truth of it through my eyes.

"If you really thought that, you wouldn't have taken a calming potion just now," Selena said.

"Yeah, I'm scared," I admitted. "I get nuts when I'm scared. Doesn't mean we're not gonna get through this."

"I hope so,' Selena said, and tapped the flask. "Because I have better uses for your mouth than this."

I snorted at that. "Minx."

"You betcha."

I sniffed the air. I couldn't smell anyone. I sent thoughts out, calling to my brothers and heard nothing.

"I'm going to shift," I said.

"Not you too!"

"I'm not going anywhere," I said, turning to face Selena. "I promise. I'm just going to shift to get a better scent. See if they can hear me. I won't run."

"*Please...*"

"I won't," I said. I brought Selena's hands up between mine and kissed her fingers. "I won't leave you alone, Selena. I swear it."

"Okay," she said, but she looked a little teary.

I nodded and shifted into my wolf form. I concentrated as hard as I could, sniffing and sending out my thoughts as loudly as possible.

ASHER! WHERE ARE YOU? BENJAMIN!

Nothing. I couldn't even hear Carter. I leaned into Selena for support, pressing my muzzle to her thigh and felt her sigh as she petted me. I didn't move, determined not to disappear like my brother's had. I tried calling out to them a few more times. As a last resort, I howled as long and loudly as I could.

Nothing.

I shifted back and I must've looked sick with fear because Selena hugged me and I held her tight. "We'll make it through this," she whispered. "Just don't leave me."

BENJAMIN

I've had nightmares about being trapped before. For a long time after our family was killed, I had the same nightmare over and over; I was chained to a wall in some nameless dungeon and somehow I knew that somewhere out there my brothers were hurt and needing my help. In the dream, I thought that if I was really strong I'd rip my own arm off or something to be able to get to them. But I couldn't and it made me feel weak even when I woke up and everything was fine.

It was as if Aiden had seen inside my soul. Maybe not, maybe it was just a coincidence.

The trap was like that of a bear trap. Sharp little teeth were shut tight around my leg. I was still the wolf and I was ashamed of how I shivered with fear. I'd been in worse scrapes than this. But that was before Selena. I had even more to lose now than I had before. I felt like if we should lose Selena now, it would break the spirits that had survived even our family's destruction.

If I was strong, I would chew my own foot off.

Instead, I whimpered.

I didn't know where I was. Somehow I'd become turned around. I didn't even remember running here to this dank, dark lot behind a decaying building. A dumpster full of putrid garbage was near enough to make me gag and there was no good light. Nobody would see me from the street. The awful smell might disguise my scent.

If I was strong, I would chew my own foot off. If I truly loved Selena and my brothers, I would chew my own foot off.

I tried spells and nothing worked.

I was summoning up the nerve to chew my own foot off when abruptly, I shifted into human form.

If I was already feeling disoriented, now I was truly confused. I had not dropped my human form. I was stronger as a wolf. For an instant after shifting, I could not feel the pain of the trap, but now as a human, I felt the knife-sharp claws of the thing biting into my human leg and if it had hurt as a wolf, as a human I thought I would die. I began to shake uncontrollably and looked down to see blood soaking through my trousers. My ankle was hot with the feel of blood gushing into my sock and shoe.

I muttered any remotely helpful spell I could think of but I was scattered and dizzy with pain. I could think of nothing and nothing I did remember worked anyhow. I couldn't shift back into my wolf form and I couldn't hear my brothers in my mind nor speak to them nor smell them.

I felt like the wolf in the lullaby that had always terrified me when I was young. What if I were left alone without Asher to lead, without Damien's steadying hand, and without Carter's heart? What if brilliant, beautiful, kind Selena were to be hurt or killed by Aiden and I could not stop it? I would be a lone wolf wandering the earth, forever seeking that lost love.

For lack of any better ideas, I threw back my head and howled my agony and fear as loudly as I could, praying my brothers might hear it. Howling as a human felt like an impotent act but for an instant it made me feel better.

CARTER

I danced badly. Actually, from the point of view of ninety percent of the audience, I probably danced beautifully. But I was not flawless like usual. I could feel myself slipping, my form imperfect, my jumps just a little bit listless. I nearly fell again in the second act without any magical sabotage, so distracted was I with worry for my brothers. I kept waiting for some kind of signal. I fully expected Asher or Ben to speak some warning or update into my mind, even if they did know I was performing. But there was nothing. When I tried to speak to them, I could feel that my messages weren't going through. The thought was so terrifying that I knew my dance was suffering.

At the beginning of the third act, my ankle began to throb. Asher had healed it, I had watched him. Yet the pain was awful. Backstage, I had to lean on a pillar for support. I could hardly walk, I could hardly dance. I took one deep breath after another, trying to ignore the pressure of the performance, my fear for Selena and my brothers weighing on me. This was surely all in my head. Asher had healed me. There was nothing wrong with my ankle.

When I tried to walk on it again, I cried out from the pain and almost collapsed. I hardly made it to my dressing room.

It was hard not to think back to when our family had been killed. For years, I could think of nothing but how if I had not been with my brothers at the time, they would've gotten home sooner. They might have stopped it. I knew now, if they were killed by Aiden, I would not survive it.

I was sweating for how hard my ankle throbbed and it was making my head hurt too. I caught sight of myself in the mirror and hardly recognized the pale, haggard person looking back at me.

"Carter..." That was the stage manager, stopping by my dressing room. He found me just as I was crumbling into a chair and gripped my shoulder. "Is it that from the fall before? Are you ill?"

"I...I guess," I said shakily. "I don't know, I can't walk. My understudy will need to finish -"

"Yes, of course."

It was difficult not to feel ashamed. I had never needed to call in an understudy in my life. Yet now I wished I had gone with my brothers rather than finishing the show. Which made no sense, I supposed, given that now I couldn't even walk. I had no desirable choice here.

A medic stopped by my dressing room to see to my ankle and declared nothing wrong with it. Fantastic. Now I looked insane as well as being helpless.

I had an overwhelming urge to go find my brothers and when the medical aide left, I packed my things into my duffle and limped outside as well as I could manage.

I couldn't smell anyone and that was frightening. I thought I might do better in wolf form and I let my human self drop, feeling myself shift into the comforting body of the wolf only to find the pain exponentially increased. I whimpered and screamed, crumbling to the ground in the alley behind the backstage. My mind was a riot it hurt so badly. When I did manage to gather my thoughts, I concentrated and shifted back.

No wolf form for me.

My ankle still hurt like hell but I could at least withstand it in human form. But I had no idea what to do. I had no clue where my brothers or Selena were or if they were in danger. I checked my phone and saw no messages. Wanting to break down into helpless tears, I sank to the ground in the alley and thought I might as well wait and see if they came back to get me. I could hardly walk as it was and if Aiden found me alone like this, I'd be a sitting duck. At least this way if he came, I could slip back inside the theater and be among other people. He might hold back in mixed company.

It was all I had and feeling powerless, I pressed my palms to my eyes and began to cry for what I might lose.

DAMIEN

I was turned around and that was frightening because we'd lived in Los Angeles for about thirty years. Every street seemed the same. I thought we should have been headed towards the few blocks of pricey lofts where our penthouse was but I couldn't see our familiar brick building with the deco archways over the big windows anywhere. I felt as if Selena and I had passed the same Chinese restaurant three times yet I was sure I'd tried different directions. My phone was getting no reception.

Selena seemed concerned as if catching on to my confusion. I tried to calm myself and told her I thought we were headed the right way but I was sure we were lost.

I took out my phone for the tenth time and tried to find us on a map once again and this time nothing made sense to me. The apps all looked the same and now I couldn't remember which one was for maps. Worse, I couldn't remember my address. I was panicking, that was all. I took a swallow of my calming potion but this time it didn't help at all.

"Stop a second," I muttered to Selena. She had her gaze

fixed on me and that was not making me less nervous but now she stood in front of me and rubbed my shoulders.

"It's okay, Damien," she said firmly. "We'll get through this. Right?"

"Right…" I took a breath again and blinked, looking down the street. What street was this again?

A bright blue sign said Flower St.

Flower St...where was Flower St.?

Nothing here looked right or familiar and the scents all seemed strange.

What is my address?

"I just have to think," I mumbled and shut my eyes.

Think...think...Flower St...find...

I opened my eyes, feeling vague and fuzzy. I shoved my hands in my pockets and walked out of the shadowy alley to a brightly lit sidewalk, squinting down the block. I just needed to get somewhere warm and think things through. If I could just find some place to gather my thoughts for a minute…

"Damien! Where are you going?" A dark haired woman came trotting after me. She pointed over her shoulder. "I thought we were going this way down Flower? I'm sure it's this way. Am I nuts?"

I blinked at the woman. She was beautiful but she was talking at me like she knew me. It gave me a creepy feeling and I smiled tightly, turning away to walk on.

"Damien!" She ran after me. "What the hell? Are you okay? Ben went that way, shouldn't we…?"

"Who are you?" I snapped. "I don't know you. If I knew you, I think I'd remember."

Her already big doe eyes got bigger and she whispered, "What?"

She knew my name but she might have just learned it somewhere. If I could just remember what I'd been intending to do. I had been walking along. I'd wanted to find my brothers. My brothers were somewhere... Weren't they? Was it a dream? Everything felt muddled and surreal. I wondered if I'd been drugged. I wondered if this beautiful woman in the fancy dress had something to do with it and I had a strong urge to get away from her.

"Leave me alone," I said, staring at her hard. "Leave me the fuck alone."

"Damien! It's Aiden! He's messing with your head! Please, it's me, Selena! Selena! Your mate! Please, Damien!" She grabbed my arm and I threw her off so she slipped and fell back against a streetlight, gaping at me. She clapped her hands to her mouth as if holding back a scream.

"Leave me alone, witch," I said slowly. "Or I'll *make* you leave me alone." I turned up the collar of my coat and walked away, hearing her crying behind me.

My brothers. I had to find my brothers. Back in Belderrig with mother and father... Everything would be fine if I could find my brothers...

SELENA

All this is my fault.

They're all gone.

I was alone. A stoplight was glaring down on me, the red light blurred by my tears and I sniffed, stepping into shadows to compose myself. Damien had disappeared. When I looked down the street, I couldn't see him anymore. I trotted down the sidewalk, a little awkward in my heels, and my steps echoed in the quiet night. He was nowhere to be seen in any direction. Maybe he had shifted again and run off in his wolf form.

He was gone. They were, all of them, just gone.

I rubbed my ring and turned back in the direction Damien and I had been walking before he'd seemingly lost his mind out of nowhere. All I had to do was find the penthouse. I had a key and unless somebody messed with the magics protecting the house, I would be able to get in.

But I didn't want to go home, I thought fiercely, even as I headed in that direction. I wanted to go find my men and help them. Not that I had the slightest idea *how* to help them. Maybe Aiden would offer a trade, I thought to myself, hurrying down the alley in the direction of the penthouse. Maybe he would let me trade myself for the safety of the Quinns. I would gladly make that trade if it was possible. Buoyed by the possibility, I held my head up and walked a little firmer. The Quinns would be heartbroken. I knew they loved me even if we hadn't known each other long, I could feel my connection to them even now. I was their mate and they were mine. If I died, they would mourn me. Although for their sake, it might be preferable. I knew that if Aiden merely took me away, Asher and his brothers wouldn't stop until they found me again.

Somewhere, I thought, Ben was alone and scared. Maybe all of them were. The thought of it broke my heart, but Ben in particular. I heard the melody of that lullaby in my head. What if something happened and Carter blamed himself? What if Damien had no one to bring him out of his dark periods? What if Asher had no one to lead and love?

I was crying again and I cleared my throat, wiping my eyes. There was no time for that now.

East on Flower to Washington, I told myself.

I heard the echo of footsteps from somewhere and whipped around. I thought I heard a distant howl.

"Asher!" I called. No one answered me and I called again. "Benjamin! Damien! Anyone!"

I kept calling as I walked on. I had no wolf shifter's sense of smell to guide me but I attempted to reach out with my heart, for whatever that was worth. Surely, this bond between me and the Quinns was good for something?

Please hear me, boys. Please find each other.

"Asher!"

A car skidded by and I almost jumped out of my skin but it was no one. Then the street was as quiet as a tomb again. There had to be some magic to that quiet. Downtown Los Angeles was never like this. It wasn't even midnight yet.

Please hear me. Please please please be okay.

"Hello, sweetheart."

I heard the voice behind me and for one heartbreaking moment, I thought it was Damien. But, of course, the voice was all wrong. I turned, my heart pounding, and saw Aiden step out of a shadow. He seemed larger somehow, only subtly. He had an eerie glow about him too, the red stoplight now flickering behind him like the power was starting to go out. Somewhere across the street, windows shattered. Aiden seemed to not quite be touching the ground and I felt the hairs on my arms standing up. There was power emanating from him. It was as if he were bursting with it.

Somehow I kept my cool well enough, though I was clenching my fists beside me. Impulsively, I turned to run even as I knew it would do no good and sure enough my feet stuck like glue to the ground. I looked down at them and as I raised my foot, my heels seems to melt and become like black glue seeping into the cruddy sidewalk. Then all at once they turned back to normal. When I picked up my foot again, it once more turned to goo.

I opened my mouth to scream and no sound came out. I shut my eyes wishing it all away.

"Are they dead?" I said flatly.

Aiden laughed.

"What did you do to them?" I said, my voice quavering.

"They're alive," Aiden said, shrugging. "Far as I know. I'm sure they'll *wish* they were dead soon."

Aiden had always been good looking in a really conventional way but now his skin seemed somehow wrong. I thought for a moment that it was the power within him threatening to break right through his skin but there was something off about the way he smirked, one side of his mouth curling up too much, the other too far down. He walked up to me slowly, as if he had all the time in the world.

I couldn't move and he came close enough to kiss me. His breath smelled weirdly metallic. I wondered if that was some side effect of magical power.

"All you had to do was go out with me," he said, tipping my chin up. "What is it with girls who think they're so much better than a guy who just wants to go out with them? As if I'm not worth your time? You conceited *bitch*!" I jumped and his shout echoed. His face twisted up in a parody of a real person. I couldn't breathe. There was something very wrong with him.

"You know, the young guys these days," Aiden said, suddenly taking a step back and tossing his head, "they think this is new. But it's always been like this. Stuck up girls who just need to be taught a lesson."

These days, I thought. I watched as his eye twitched and then he scratched at his forehead until it was bloody.

"This shit's getting old," he muttered, and with that he peeled off his face.

I screamed and again it came out more like a wheeze. Aiden's true face was bright red and veiny with blood vessels bursting over his sagging, grizzled cheeks. He was covered in liver spots and scaly patches of skin. There was a pustule leaking under his eye. He looked about a thousand years old, like he might have drunk a bad mix of the Quinns' life preserving potion. He dropped his apparent mask on the ground and took a deep breath, rubbing his real face with his hands. He looked no better when he was done.

He appeared impossibly old but he was strong and he grabbed my arm so hard it felt as if he were trying to rip it out of the socket. My feet moved now as he dragged me down the sidewalk and through a door into an abandoned building.

"It's really sweet," he said, his nails breaking my skin, "how the Quinns have got you so snowed. You pretend to be this sweet, sensitive artist, this brooding wolf, and some slut will tear off her clothes wanting to fuck you."

"I can't stop you," I said, and spat at him. "But I'll never love you."

The building he'd dragged me into was an old, empty warehouse, and he shoved me to a filthy floor that smelled like a dumpster. I hit the ground and something slimy clung to my hands, making me retch.

You think crazy things when you're sure you're about to die. My first thought was: *I'm going to ruin this nice dress they bought me.*

Go figure.

"The Quinns think they're so old and powerful," Aiden said, laughing. He was wearing a blue designer suit and now he pulled a stick out of his back pocket and it took me a moment to realize it was a wand. "They're children. I knew the vampires who killed their parents before they were even sired."

"How old are you?" I said, gasping a little. I stayed on the disgusting ground, if only to remain a little farther away from him.

Aiden laughed, almost sounding sad. "I don't remember."

"You could have anyone," I said. "Why me?"

Aiden snorted at that and then he stared at me for one baffled moment before he burst into laughter. "Christ, woman! Do you think it has anything to do with you? I have my sources. The *Quinns*, one of the last old shifter families… what's left of them anyway. I knew they had a mate coming. Finally. Some scant reward for all their heartache. Awww." He put on a pretense of crying. "Those poor little puppies. You know how powerful you are? Of course not. You don't know shit. I need you for myself. It's all energy transference, you see!" He grinned as if we were having a friendly conversation. "Of course, I'll have to keep it rather one-sided in our case..."

"Our case," I murmured.

"Oh, I'm gonna fuck that power right out of you," Aiden said. "I mean it was all very romantic. You give power to them, they give power to you... You would've become a shifter, you know? Then you could have had their little puppies. Bring wolf shifters back from near extinction. It's a nice story, but I'd really rather be crazy powerful and fuck you in my dungeon if it's all the same to you. I mean even if it's *not* all the same to you, I'm going to do it anyway so -"

"Can't you just kill me?" I said. I hadn't realized I was crying.

"Oh, sorry baby, sweetheart, darling girl," Aiden said, sticking out his bottom lip. "Doesn't work that way." He leaned down and grabbed me by the front of my dress, yanking me to my feet. Up close he was even more repellent. His nose seemed too bulbous as if there might be something growing inside of it. "And please...don't get used to it too quickly. Because I really enjoy teaching girls a lesson."

"You're so...evil." It was a silly thing to say yet it was all I could think of in the moment.

Aiden laughed again. "Oh, you're going to be entertaining. I always knew you would be. And when I bring you to submission over and over again I'll have your Quinns tortured while they watch -"

"*No.*"

"Actually *yeah*. Don't worry. I'll kill them eventually, and then you'll be mine."

"I'll never be yours," I hissed, and my stomach heaved.

"Oh honey." Aiden shook his head. "You say that like I haven't done this before. Now kiss me, baby." Aiden opened his mouth and something like a dying snake that I suppose was his tongue came slithering out. I gagged and turned my head away but found that I was unable to move much beyond that.

I've never really followed sports but I do know the phrase 'Hail Mary pass'. The hopeless attempt at a saving play.

I shut my eyes and thought with all the strength within me: *QUINNS! HELP ME! AIDEN HAS ME! MY LOVES, PLEASE HELP ME!*

ASHER

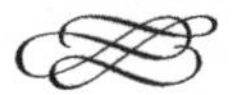

The hole was so tight around me that I passed out for a while, having wheezed myself into hyperventilating. It made me feel more helpless and I snarled and snapped, feeling half feral with anger even in my human form.

When I passed out, I dreamed. I dreamed of the five of us starting a family in a new castle. I was so dizzily in love with Selena, I had not had time to think about the possibility of children someday. It hadn't come up in conversation with my brothers. It would certainly be something I needed to ask Selena about before even beginning to think of it. But still, a part of me couldn't help but ask; *what if*? What if Selena gave us pups and were able to rebuild our clan? In my dream, I imagined us living somewhere outside the city. It would be some great house where we could raise our children to run in the woods and create art all day. Selena had told me she wanted to write books about art history and someday perhaps the definitive book about my work. Who better? I dreamed of it; Selena laughing and rolling her eyes as Quinn pups nipped at her feet. I dreamed of Damien helping her with writing a book, Ben and Carter watching the children..

When I came to, I was still trapped and I could not smell or hear my brothers in my mind. I wanted to scream but could not breathe well enough to manage it.

Again, I began to struggle inside the hole, even as I knew it was futile. I thought perhaps a will strengthened by love would be enough yet nothing would give and the harder I pushed the more I felt my bones were about to crumble instead. If I were broken, I wouldn't be able to do much rescuing.

Brothers, hear me, I prayed, putting all the force of my strength into the thought, clinging to our connection with desperate hope. I sent my thoughts out to Selena even though we had no telepathic connection. *Selena, hear me*!

All at once, a thought that wasn't mine came upon me with such force that it knocked the wind out of me. It was not one of my brothers as they were much quieter. My head began to throb. It felt as if somebody who didn't know their strength had just punched me in the stomach and brought me to my knees yet the voice was familiar and I could have wept for joy at hearing it in my head.

QUINNS! HELP ME! AIDEN HAS ME! MY LOVES, PLEASE HELP ME!

Somehow Selena was not only already able to speak to our minds, but able to do so with incredible power. I had thought it might happen though there had not been a shared mate in so long, it was difficult to find such details even in the lore. I didn't know how or why, I was only grateful. The strength of her signal was so great that I could lock onto it like a beacon pointing me towards her. I could feel it in the air and in my mind. I took a breath and grasped onto that power, hoping I could perhaps borrow a bit of it to help myself out of the trap. I felt the bond between us throb and convulse like a muscle and I howled - the sound of it strange in my human voice - as I burst out of the trap and took off running. I tried to shift but found I still wasn't able to though I could run faster than I ever had before, the ground under me seeming to carry me along with impossible speed towards Selena and, I hoped, to my brothers.

The air was sharp and cool on my skin and I felt it keenly as if I were somehow still a wolf even if I hadn't shifted. I could feel myself getting closer to Selena with every step as I pumped my arms and attempted to send my thoughts to her.

I hear you, Selena! I'm coming, my love!

I turned a corner tightly, so fast that I nearly fell over, and a car headed right towards me didn't phase me. I was going too fast to change direction and simply leapt, running up the hood and down the other side, jumping down to the ground and picking up my speed again as I heard the driver shout behind me. I could smell her now as I closed in towards a dark, old abandoned building up ahead. I clenched my fists hard enough to threaten bone as I focused on my wolf self, shoving away any magical impediment. Love, I thought. Love can strengthen me. If this bond with my mate was enough to reach me, perhaps it was enough to make me shift.

Selena, help me. Send me your power.

There was not much chance she had known what she was doing when she'd spoken to my mind but I ran at full speed towards her and the villain I could now smell as strongly as a rotten fish and hoped for a miracle.

SELENA

Aiden's awful tongue licked at my neck and his metallic breath made me want to puke. I had the strangest sensation of my thoughts going out to the boys. I could sense them hearing me. It was like stumbling upon someone else inside your head, almost like a remembered dream.

Asher! Ben! Damien! Carter! Can you hear me?!

I heard a distant howl so faint I wondered if I'd imagined it, but I saw Aiden's eyes flash and the repulsive teasing with his tongue stopped as his head whipped around to scowl at the door. If the boys were coming for me, I thought, I might be able to help them if I kept Aiden distracted. Now he turned his head again and sneered at me, yanking me towards him, fisting my dress.

"Are you a shifter?" I said it fearfully but I really didn't care about the answer. I thought I might keep him talking.

"I'm not some disgusting *cur*," Aiden hissed. "I bet you'd like me better if I were though, wouldn't you? You know we had a name for you in the very old days..."

I heard Ben in my mind suddenly: *Selena, we can hear you. Send us thoughts as hard as you can, it gives us power.*

I kept my eyes on Aiden, attempting to give nothing away but it was amazing to me that he couldn't hear what was so loud and clear in my mind. He was too busy grinning, his rotten teeth making me ill. That snakey tongue came out to lick at my ear again.

I concentrated all my strength as I had before. I shut my eyes and images flashed in my head: Ben smiling softly at me in bed, Asher naked and looking down at me with such awe, Damien's uncharacteristically mischievous smirk when he flirted, and Carter's first kiss. Love, I thought. Perhaps there was power in the love and connection between us.

HEAR ME, MY LOVES. I'M TRYING TO SEND YOU ALL THE POWER I CAN.

"*Canis madames,* they called them." Aiden was whispering in my ear, his hot breath acrid. A piece of skin slid off of his face. "A whore of dogs!" He threw back his head and laughed. It sounded like the grinding of metal. "I'll have you show me all the things they taught you, dog whore!" He twirled his wand and a bed appeared in the empty warehouse. It looked particularly out of place all made up in silver silks and big luxurious pillows. I gagged and Aiden's lip curled as my stomach heaved and I coughed up a bit of saliva at his feet.

ASHER! BEN! CARTER! DAMIEN! MY QUINNS, I LOVE YOU! IF YOU DON'T FIND ME IN TIME, I LOVE YOU!

I wondered if there was any way I could make Aiden kill me if needed. I wasn't about to live in some dungeon as his sex slave to be tortured and brutalized forever.

I opened my eyes and stared at him hard, forcing myself to look in his dead yellow eyes even as I shook with the force that sent out my thoughts to the Quinns.

"They're not dogs," I said slowly. "They're *wolves*. And *men*. But I'd rather fuck a dog than you any day."

Aiden backhanded me and the sharp pain of it took me by surprise. He shoved me towards the bed and I twisted to keep my eyes on him, just as a noise crashed outside.

My boys.

Aiden whirled around, pointing his wand, and I shouted, "NO!" I could feel them close and I shut my eyes and screamed bloody murder, sending my thoughts with all the power I could muster. I could feel it come rippling out of me, bursting through the wall of silence that Aiden had cast upon my screams. I could even see it, the air around me sparking. Aiden turned to gape at me, horrified.

Every window in the warehouse shattered and a dark gray wolf flecked with silver came bounding through the cascading glass. Asher! Aiden shot a spell and I tackled him, throwing him to the floor, but Asher was hit and whatever it was threw him to the ground.

"Asher!" I clapped my hands to my face and saw Aiden's delighted grimace just as another wolf came leaping from behind me through a shattered window. With a roar, the dark brown wolf tackled Aiden to the ground, its huge teeth bared and its ears flat as it tore at him. Aiden rolled away just as two other wolves came running in from the same window, charging at him. I backed away and I was terrified at the sight. Even if I hated Aiden and hoped he would be killed, it was horrible to see wolves going after a person. They hadn't even done much damage until the smallest wolf, who I assumed was Carter, tore at Aiden's hand and he screamed as it was torn away from his arm, the mangled thing hanging off the bone as he writhed on the ground. Then I saw Carter's real target; the wand Aiden had held. I dove for the wand, dangerous enough if only because I was diving into a pile of riled up, bloody-toothed wolves. I managed to grab the wand and immediately thinking it was the easiest solution, I snapped it in two. I rolled over on my back and crab walked backwards, my eyes on Aiden as he scrambled, shielding his face from the attacking wolves. I saw him grab a piece of wood on the floor and couldn't fathom what it meant until he was brandishing it like another wand and aiming it at the wolves as he climbed to his feet. The Quinns were growling, ready to murder, but they stopped, forming a circle around him.

"Do you get it now?" Aiden said quietly. "I have more power than you mutts could ever dream."

ASHER

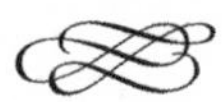

Damien was missing. I flexed my muscles, feeling the body of my wolf self as if to make sure I was still alive. The Ireland winter had turned harsh and food was scarce. I took as little of it as I could get away with and left the bulk for my brothers. But here we were in some unnamed forest and it was getting on toward dark and Damien was missing. I let Ben and Carter get ahead of me. I didn't like these strange woods. They looked too much like Blanemore. I felt as if at any moment we were going to burst out of them and find ourselves on the beach of Belderrig only to run and run and run and discover that fire...

I had sent Damien my thoughts and felt them reach my brother with no response.

Carter kept glancing over his shoulder, his worried dark eyes too big and young. He was whimpering. He couldn't seem to help but whimper when he shifted now. He was too small and too scared to stay shifted for so many days on end but it was easier to stay warm and safe as a wolf. I trotted ahead and nudged Ben who nudged Carter. We stopped and leaned against a mossy stump. Ben went to work grooming Carter, licking his face all spattered with mud and rain and a little bit of blood from the afternoon's rabbit.

Carter closed his eyes and hung his head and Ben licked at him, gently nuzzling, sniffing at him out of habit. I well knew it wasn't so much about the grooming as the care. Carter still wanted his mother.

Did you see where Damien went? I asked Ben.

He was headed towards that creek, Ben replied. He said he was thirsty.

It started to rain and I shivered. I should not have been cold in my wolf form. I should be plenty warm enough. The rain poured down and I trotted ahead again and sniffed for Damien, the middle one; the one who seemed to take things the hardest but didn't have the excuse of being the youngest. I looked back at Ben, casting him a significant stare.

Should we wait here? Ben said.

I could feel everyone's anxiety. Damien had gone off by himself and that wasn't inherently dangerous, only we hadn't been apart for more than a few minutes since our parents had been killed and we'd been on the run.

No, I said. Let's go find our brother.

I had wanted to hunt down the vampire sect and tear them apart with my own teeth until Ben had talked sense into me. We were just too small, too young. Our younger brothers needed us. Carter was nine and Damien was eleven. They still needed looking after.

Sometimes I was so filled with rage I couldn't speak and the others left me alone then.

Now Carter and Ben followed me as I tracked Damien's scent down the creek to a little cove inside the hollowed trunk of a big gnarled tree. The scent stopped there but no Damien. I sniffed at the ground, ignoring the rain pouring down on me, making me shudder to the bone even as thick as my fur was. We were all too thin.

We found Damien in his human body, hugging his knees, curled up by a boulder and looking out on the creek. He was crying.

I spoke into his mind. Damien, why aren't you shifted?

It hurts, Damien said. It hurts when I shift too long and my head aches and I get so tired I can't run anymore. I don't know why. I'm sorry, Asher! I'm sorry!

As a wolf, Damien was nearly full grown. He only betrayed his age with his less experienced way of fighting or when he was playful. But he had not been playful since the castle had burned and he had not had to fight much yet. It was too easy to forget how young he was. Carter still looked like a pup and was small even for his age. Damien looked much older but inside he was a child.

I regarded my brother. It was a frightening thought if Damien couldn't stay shifted. It was so much easier to live as wolves when there was no money. But I had heard of shifters having trouble turning after a traumatic event. The emotions could muddle things, especially for young wolves.

"Your brothers will need you as a leader," my father had told me once. "That doesn't just mean fighting."

I had not known what he meant at the time. Now I did, and I knew Damien was mourning. I didn't know what I could say to make him feel any better. We were all in deep mourning but we were also running and staying shifted much of the time. We didn't talk much.

My father had also told me that some things needed to be spoken aloud.

I shifted back into my human body and hugged myself. I felt so fragile as a human without a nice thick layer of fur and without my big teeth. But some things needed to be spoken aloud. I sat my still growing, too thin, and gawky body down next to Damien and sighed. Carter and Ben stayed shifted, sitting at our feet as if waiting for instructions.

"There's nothing to be sorry for, Damien," I said. We watched the rain splash drop by drop into the creek and I wondered if it would flood over. "You're sad. Sometimes it's hard to stay shifted when you're sad." I slid my gaze over to Damien who was shud-

dering from the cold, his teeth chattering. "Let's get inside this tree," I said. "We can get out of the rain."

Damien followed me and the four of us huddled inside the tree and I put an arm around my brother.

"I didn't mind the rain really," Damien said softly. "It made me feel something that's not sad."

"I miss them too," I whispered, and watched as Ben shifted and crawled over to sit on Damien's other side. The lump in my throat was difficult to swallow and my eyes stung with tears.

"I miss them too," Ben said. "Carter, come here, lad."

Carter shifted into his little boy body. He was little for his age to begin with but he looked far too small now as a human, his baby blue eyes gazing on us, worried, as a raindrop slid down his pale cheek. He crawled over to curl up between Ben and I.

"I miss them too," Carter said, wiping his nose.

I tried to somehow stretch my arms around all of them. "Well...we'll miss them together. And we'll stay together. And...and we'll fight for each other. No matter what, lads. Boy or wolf. Whatever happens, we remain together. I love you, brothers."

When it became very cold Ben and Carter and I shifted again and curled up around Damien to keep him warm.

We can't fight him with magic, I thought.

"Come at me, dogs," Aiden said, licking his lips with a gross serpent of a tongue. He was wielding a wooden stick as if it were a wand. If it were me wielding that stick, it would be a silly delusion. But I suspected Aiden could actually brandish his magic with whatever happened to be lying around and it would still be exponentially more powerful than doing it by hand.

Of course we had all left our own wands at home.

My epiphany was abrupt and so clearly accurate that I thought I might faint from the relief.

He's weak to us as wolves, I said to my brothers. *Maybe to shifters. He's vulnerable. That's why he trapped us and kept us from shifting.*

We were poised to strike, frozen in a stand-off with Aiden. Selena was crouched on the floor behind us, the moonlight through the window casting her in an eerie glow. I hated the thought of her seeing us tear a man apart or, if it all went wrong, Aiden killing us in front of her eyes. Spelling is more difficult as a wolf and my spells are sometimes not as strong but I sent a spell for blinding at Selena as Aiden stood there, smugly staring at us. The magic hit Selena and she reared back. I saw her shake it off as if it were a bit of dust in her eye.

If she could do that and not know it, she was going to become exceptionally powerful.

It was just as well. Blinding her after Aiden had done the same thing was kind of a dick move. I could almost hear Ben in my head telling me so.

She seemed to catch on and glared at me. "How does that help?"

If I had been human, I would have shrugged. Our little exchange seemed to throw Aiden off for a second but he spelled a shield of protection around himself, all the while wagging his awful tongue at us.

Selena, can you hear me?

YES!

Her thoughts were so loud it was painful.

Can you block his spells?

Selena backed up a little and kept her eyes on Aiden. I saw the magic crackling in the air, an agitated expression on Aiden's face. She was stopping him, likely without even knowing how she was doing it. They were frozen in a stand-off and Aiden looked a little afraid, sweat pouring down his grizzled brow. Selena's fists were clenched, her eyes big and her jaw tight.

Take him now! I said to my brothers. *You know what to do, brothers! Hard and fast!*

Selena, this is going to be ugly.

Just kill him!

I would have laughed but instead, I darted forward and went straight for Aiden's flank. Aiden screamed and his shield went back up, throwing me back. Selena hollered in frustration and the shield went away again just as Ben dove for his leg. The shield kept appearing and disappearing as Selena fought his magic off with the strength of her own power enhanced by our connection. I could feel our bond with her fueling her fight and it made me want to weep. We circled him and saw the shield drop completely, all of us charging forward at once. I watched Carter leap towards him. Even as a wolf, he had the grace of a dancer, and he caught Aiden's already mangled arm and tore at it once more. Aiden screamed and I bit his flank again just as Damien took his ankle between his jaws. I felt his magic pulling me. Even in the moment it occurred to me that if he was powerful enough to fight us all off in such a state, he couldn't be allowed to attain yet more power. He would take over the world. I felt his spell pulling my insides apart and Selena screamed. Her own power was pure in form, not even cast in the shape of a spell and the force of it sparked in the air dropping embers to the ground, still burning as they rested on the ground.

We had to withdraw once more as I tasted blood in my mouth. We were so close yet he was still able to fight us, even with one hand hanging gruesomely from his wrist. Ben had been thrown back by some spell and staggered to his feet. Damien's ear was torn. He would wear us down if we weren't careful. If he would just drop his shield for one moment, we could finish him. His leg was gushing blood and he staggered back. I saw intestines hanging from his stomach where I'd ripped into him, but still, he lived.

Selena cried out and she crumpled to the ground, clawing at her throat, suddenly choking. He was killing her. Or no, I thought, he was trying to knock her out so she couldn't block his spells.

In the chaos of the fight, I only noticed the big luxurious bed sitting incongruously in the middle of the floor and the thought of what Aiden would use it for filled me with a rage I hadn't felt in a century, not since my parents had been killed. I felt as if I were somehow growing bigger, my blood pumping hot as the anger boiled within me. He could do that to my mate? To any woman? I would shred his insides with my teeth and spit them out. I would grind his bones to dust.

I charged forward with no thought to my self-preservation and the action distracted Aiden enough that Selena could breath for a moment.

"Aiden!" Selena shouted. "I love you!"

ASHER

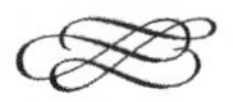

Everything stopped. In my hysteria, blinded by rage, I thought for the briefest moment that Selena was telling the truth. Just as quickly I realized that she was distracting Aiden who was now still, only breathing and bleeding there in the dim warehouse as Selena's shout echoed.

I love you!

I love you!

I wondered how delusional Aiden could be. Thinking he might fall for something so unbelievable seemed like a stretch. But then Selena had been dealing with him much longer than we had. The moment of quiet as we all waited for whatever came next seemed to slow impossibly yet it was probably not more than two seconds altogether. I was leaping to attack Aiden. I could smell Selena so sharply; her fear, her love, her fury. I could smell my brothers too. Apart from the stench of Aiden and the building, it was a heady blend, as if we'd all been grown and curated specifically to complement each other. Selena was half crouched on the ground, her burgundy gown splayed out around her. Her dark hair was half fallen from its updo and stray hairs blew around her face in the moonlight. Her cheeks were covered with tears yet I could see the fierceness in her dark eyes as her chest heaved from effort or nerves.

Selena, my love.

The shield dropped entirely, no sparks lit the air around Aiden. He was without protection even as I charged at him and now I knocked him to the ground and my brothers and I wasted no time. I went right for his throat, tearing into his blood and sinew with every bit of strength I possessed. Aiden screamed as Damien ripped an entire arm off. I heard Selena groan behind us and hoped she was hiding her eyes as bones snapped and Aiden's screams were muted as Ben ate right through his stomach, chomping through his ribs to find the trophy of his heart. The four of us fought each other briefly for the still pumping muscle though it tasted sour and dead to my tongue. We tore it into four but did not eat it. Such a decayed thing would poison us, I thought.

Aiden was dead.

But riled up wolves on the attack aren't generally quick to calm back down and by the time we were done, there was not much left of him. With Aiden's final breath, the bed had vanished. All his spells were broken. Selena didn't stop us and it wasn't until the only sounds were a gentle rain that had begun to fall outside and the snapping of Aiden's toes between Carter's teeth before we finally stopped. My brothers and I stood quietly for a moment, observing the mess of gore we had left. Behind us, Selena stood stoically, her rapid breath betraying her.

"I think you got him," Selena said shakily.

She did not flinch and again I felt the swell of love for her within me. I shifted into human form and grimaced at the sensation of Aiden's dried blood caked around my mouth. I rubbed my hands on the trousers and nodded at my brothers who all shifted back and stood, catching their breath.

Ben took a deep breath and stretched. His normally big and perfectly coiffed hair was a mess and I saw a bit of spleen and too much blood matting it together. He stretched and wiped his mouth on his sleeve. "We gotta get rid of this body. Or what's left of it."

Carter coughed and a pinky toe came out of his mouth. He glanced at Selena who looked a bit green at that and dropped it on the floor. I rubbed my eyes, one eyelid too sticky with God knew what.

"Okay," I said, my voice hoarse. I cleared my throat and babbled the first useful spell I could think of, creating a giant hole in the floor beneath Aiden. We watched him sink into the darkness and the four of us stretched out our hands, muttering a spell to turn him into nothing more than dust. When we were done there was nothing left at all, not even the smell of the kill.

I watched Ben and Carter slink over to Selena and wrap her in a gentle hug. The sight made my heart swell and Damien came up behind me as the floor closed over Aiden's scant remains. He threw an arm around my shoulders and leaned his head on mine. I shut my eyes, comforted by my brother's affection.

"Boy or wolf, we remain together," Damien said softly. "Us and our mate."

"I love you, brother," I murmured.

"I love you too, brother."

SELENA

"Who's the fastest runner?" Asher was rubbing his eyes as we stood on the sidewalk looking like a group of people who had just left a formal party at a slaughterhouse. It was raining and we huddled under an awning, Ben with his arm around my shoulders as I leaned my head against his. Asher had healed our scrapes and the minor wounds the boys had suffered. Now we hung around outside, in a bit of a daze.

"It's me," Ben muttered in my ear. "But I don't feel like doing whatever he's going to ask me to do."

I snorted at that and felt Ben's smile. Carter said, "What is it?"

"Somebody shift," Asher said. "And pick up one of the cars from the penthouse, come pick us up."

Damien squinted. "Why didn't we do that before?" I'd never seen Damien looking disheveled but his hair was a mess, and he was half drenched as he paced in and out of the rain, his hands shoved in his pockets. He still seemed riled up.

"Probably would've ended the same way," Carter said. "I'll go."

"Good man," Asher said with a sigh. We watched Carter shift and run off down the street.

I wanted a long hot bath and I was starving for some food.

Asher stepped out into the pouring rain and threw back his head, letting himself get soaked. His shirt clung to his muscled chest and though I should've been tired or at least in no mood, it was giving me all kinds of ideas.

Ben must've caught on to my gaze because he kissed my neck and said, "You're a naughty minx."

"So are you," I said, and wrapped my arm around his waist.

"Oh, yes."

"We couldn't have done any of that without you," Damien said, spinning around on the heel of his shoe. He pushed his wet hair back and smiled at me. "You're ferocious, Selena."

"Of course, she is!" Asher shouted from the middle of the street. "She's our mate!"

"I'm so hungry," I said, sighing. And then without quite thinking about it, I said, "Oh, but you guys just ate."

Damien burst into laughter and Ben and I watched, staring, as he hunched over, holding his knees, laughing so hard he was helpless with it. I'd never seen him laugh like that and from the looks of Ben and Asher, as they turned to stare at their brother, it was not very in character for him. I let go of Ben and sauntered over to Damien, grinning as I awkwardly hugged his hunching form. He stood up to embrace me, his eyes leaking, and he hugged me tightly, still giggling in my ear.

"You're something else, Selena," Damien said.

"Do you want Chinese?" Ben said, bouncing on his toes. "Steak? Italian? Sushi?"

"Yes," I said and felt the rumble of Damien's fresh laughter. I decided my new job was making him do that as often as possible.

Asher was singing. It was something in Irish though it sounded more cheerful than Ben's lullaby. I watched him hop around puddles in the street before he jogged over and kissed me on the cheek. Ben laughed and threw an arm around him. Everyone seemed so happy and I tried to stifle a cry, finding a terrible lump in my throat, but it wouldn't be moved and I broke, ducking my head as tears came.

"Oh, sweetheart," Damien said. "What's the matter?"

They all crowded around me and I bit my lip. "Nothing at all, my beautiful boys. I'm just happy I found you."

Carter returned like a flash, tires squealing as he revved the engine of his own shiny blue sports car. We piled inside and in the back seat I practically sat in Damien's lap and Ben played with my hair as Carter drove us all home while arguing with Asher about what to feed me.

We had made it, I thought to myself. We'd really made it and now we would never be parted. Just me and my boys for as long as we could manage to go on, though now for the first time, I started to imagine what little puppy Carters and Bens and Ashers and Damiens would be like. I imagined a nice big house full of laughter and pups nipping at my heels, surrounded always by the love of my Quinns. What a life that would be.

At home, Ben made a big production of carrying me up to the penthouse in his arms which made me roll my eyes. I wasn't even hurt or tired, but it seemed to entertain him. He carried me even in the elevator, humming softly the whole time, and Asher absently reached over to rub my calf.

Ben set me down inside the penthouse as Asher flicked on the lights. I sniffed the air.

Meat. I needed meat!

I kicked off my heels and ran for the Quinn's absurdly fancy kitchen; all silver and granite countertops and exposed shelving. Their fridge was huge and usually pretty well stocked (unless Damien had just gone on a bender). I threw open the door and all but growled, grabbing a couple packages of raw steak and tearing into them at the counter. I didn't even really think about it as I gobbled down the raw meat though it did occur to me for a moment that I'd never craved raw meat before. Still though, the idea of a nice big Chinese food feast also sounded perfect about now.

The boys were watching me, mouths agape, as they ambled into the kitchen.

"She's becoming a shifter," Carter said in wonder.

"Am I?" I said, my mouth full of steak.

Asher's face split into a grin and he clapped his hands. "Of course! Fantastic!" He dashed to my side and threw a piece of steak into his mouth before kissing my packed cheeks. "Our girl!"

"Can we still get Chinese food though?" I said, grabbing a package of pink ground beef from the fridge.

"Anything you want, my love," Asher said, wrapping his arms around me.

I ate like a fiend. The Quinns seemed equal parts impressed and amused by it. There was something liberating about unselfconsciously ripping into some meat. I felt like I was accessing some primal urge unleashed by my beloved mates. We ate our fill and took our time with the feast. I felt like some decadent figure from the Middle Ages as Ben hand fed me grapes and Damien poured me more wine. Then Ben played us a song on his guitar. He sang us a comical song from the old days of shifters about a wolf who was fooled by a chicken. In all honesty, I had no idea what the point of the song was. But Ben was hilarious when he sang it.

When Ben had sung us a few songs, Damien got up and

read us some poem he'd been working on. He was nervous as anything, considering himself more of a fiction writer. But his brothers were so supportive, it made me choke up. When he was finished everyone applauded and I jumped up and threw my arms around him. There was something so beautiful to me about being surrounded by these men who loved the arts. Carter's dance, Asher's paintings, Damien's writing, and Ben's music. I was happy to drown myself in the brilliance and beauty of the Quinns and their attention on me felt like the radiance of the sun.

I thought I was full of meat, but Damien cajoled me into dessert while the others were clearing up dinner. I told him I could only stand something small and he took me out to the balcony and fed me dark chocolate and champagne, or at least he tried to while I pestered him with questions about his poems.

He looked sheepish about it as he poured a little more champagne into my glass. "You don't have to act interested in all that, Selena. I know you're more into Asher's art or Ben's songs than- okay, ow."

I'd swatted him in the ear and he cracked an apologetic smile at me as I glowered back at him. "I never pretend to be interested in something a guy is doing when I'm not. Understand, Damien Quinn? I love you and I know you love me. I'm not trying to make you feel better. But I'm genuinely interested." I leaned in and kissed him, teasing him until he kissed me back with more intention. "I'm interested in everything you do, Damien. Believe me?"

"I believe you," he whispered.

"Good." I kissed him one last time and said, "And now I need a bath. I am well fed but I feel very grimy."

Damien chuckled and kissed the tip of my nose. "I believe Carter would love a chance to help you out with that."

"Oh!" I brightened at that. I'd been more than a little eager to get some time alone with Carter. I blushed at my own enthusiasm and said, "That sounds quite nice."

"Go into the master bath," Damien said, nodding back at the penthouse. "I'll send him to you."

"You Quinns are so helpful," I said, pecking a kiss to his forehead. "Thank you, darling."

The Quinns' huge master bathroom was a lesson in luxury. I turned the gold plated knobs on the jacuzzi style tub to get the hot water going. The marble was cool under my feet and I wiggled my toes. I pursed my lips, looking for bubble bath or something that smelled pretty and wondered if that was too "girly" for a bunch of wolves.

There was a soft knock at the door and I answered to find Carter looking almost apprehensive. He'd changed into a robe and I suppose it wouldn't have mattered what he was wearing. I was impatient to get him naked as soon as possible.

"You don't have to knock," I said, leaning against the door. "I was waiting for you."

"I'm a gentleman," Carter said, shrugging.

"You sure are." I tugged him forward by the belt of his robe and he kicked the door closed behind him. "I haven't gotten to spend much time with you." I kissed him slowly but with increasing hunger and he rested his forehead against mine. I saw a soft little smile on his face that was almost sad.

"I know," he said quietly. "But listen, Selena. It's okay if you feel closer to the others. I'm happy just to be near you, to be honest-"

"Ugh!" I squeezed my eyes shut because his words had brought tears up almost before I could process them. I cleared my throat, shaking my head. "You Quinns and your insecurities." I kissed him hard again, cradling his face in my hands. "I love *all* of you. It's not like...I have some fixed amount of love to split up. It's like falling in love with all of you has made be able to love more and more... Please, Carter. Please never doubt my love for you. *Please.*" My voice shook and he embraced me, rubbing my back.

"Okay," he whispered. "I'm sorry, sweetheart. I'll never doubt you again. I promise." He kissed me, taking the lead this time, holding me tight against him. He kissed the couple tears that slid down my face and frowned. "I didn't mean to make you cry our first night together."

"No no," I said, shaking my head. "I'm just... I get overwhelmed with how I feel about all of you sometimes. But it's okay. It's *good.*"

"Okay," he said, nodding. "So...bath?"

"Yes, please," I said, grinning now. "Although, I couldn't find any bubble bath. I was wondering-"

"Ah!" Carter smiled, looking mischievous. He stepped out of my arms and went to the line of marble sinks on the side of the bathroom. "I have my own private stock actually." He knelt down and pulled a few plastic bottle out of a cabinet. "I love a bubble bath and the guys like to tease me about it."

I clapped my hands. "Their loss," I said, giggling. "A tub full of Carter Quinn and bubbles. This night gets better all the time."

Carter laughed and held up the lavender bottle, raising an eyebrow. I nodded eagerly and he poured some into the tub, bubbles quickly forming as the hot water continued to run. "Yeah," Carter said. "I love all that kinda stuff. Lotions and soaps and body oils and things. I guess it's from having to take care of my body really carefully."

"Yeah, good job with that, by the way," I said, and came around to hug him from behind.

When the bath was nice and bubbly, Carter turned around in the circle of my arms and kissed my neck, softly and teasing. His fingers curled around the straps of my silk dress and he let them fall off my shoulders so that it fell neatly to the floor. His hands ran up my back and gently unhooked my strapless bra and I let it fall.

"God, you're beautiful," Carter whispered. I pulled at the belt cinching his robe and snuck my hand in side, marveling at the flawlessly sculpted chest, all rippling little muscles that led to a blonde happy trail and a swelling cock.

"Back at you," I breathed, and pushed his robe of his shoulders.

I shimmied out of my panties and Carter helped me into the bath. The hot water and the calming scent of lavender felt like the best kind of balm but I clung to Carter, straddling his lap where he sat on the ledge seat in their huge tub.

"Tell me the truth," I said, wrapping my arms around his neck. "Does it kill Asher just a little bit that you kissed me before he did?"

"You know we don't get jealous between ourselves like that," Carter said, sounding a little haughty as his fingers lightly traced my arms and he leaned forward to brush a kiss to my lips. "It's not in our nature. We're above it." I raised an eyebrow and Carter laughed. "Of course, it does. But just a *little* bit."

"I knew it," I whispered, and kissed him again. We kissed lazily, as if we had all the time in the world. His erection pressed into my belly and I pressed against it just enough to make him moan into my mouth, though it was torturing me as much as it was him.

"I'm glad it was you who kissed me first," I said, and kissed his chin and his cheek and the corner of his mouth. "It's like this special thing we have between us."

"Thank you, Selena," Carter said, looking a little shy. "That means a lot."

I nuzzled his nose with mine. "I never told you how beautiful you are dancing," I said. "It was wonderful to see you." I kissed him long and deep and the thrill of our connection, the power that came pouring through me, made me shiver. "The way you move, the things you do with that body..." I sucked on his bottom lip and gasped as he pressed his cock teasingly at my entrance. "This perfect body."

"Gee, I think you're trying to seduce me, Selena Brock." Carter said, and kissed his way along my jaw.

I massaged the back of his neck and watched my own hands slide down his chest, under the water where I stroked his cock, making him gasp. "I know it's not official or anything," I said softly. "But I'd like to be known as Selena Quinn."

Carter clutched my ass and lifted me in the water before slowly guiding himself inside me and I cried out a little, hugging him closer to me. "Selena Quinn," he whispered into my ear, and I trembled at the pleasing fullness of him. "I love you, Selena Quinn."

"I love you too, Carter," I said, looking in his eyes as I moved with him. I wanted all of them to know how much I loved them individually and together. I had fallen in love with The Quinns yet I had also fallen in love with Carter, Asher, Ben, and Damien. I couldn't imagine a world where I had to choose just one of them. I felt like I needed them all so much, I was greedy with need and want. I felt like my heart had grown knowing them so that I would be strong enough to love them all properly.

I felt the connection that was always there between all five of us and magic coursing through me. I could feel that power growing inside me. I would be a wolf, I thought. The reassurance of that was thrilling.

"Do you feel that?" I whispered.

"Your magic," Carter breathed. "I feel it. It's amazing, Selena. Make me feel it."

I found myself able to hold onto that power and send it through my body and Carter moaned in my ear and thrusted harder. I bounced on top of him, pulling him into a heated kiss. The water bubbled around us and the walls shook a little and I could feel that it was the power of my growing magic joined with the Quinns. I gasped Carter's name and he reached down to finger my clit and it threw me over the edge as I clutched his back, my nails digging into those perfect muscles. Electric pleasure coursed through me and I screamed, the walls creaking as if they might burst, when I felt the pulsing of his cock as he came inside me. I clenched around him, taking all that he had to give me until we returned to earth. I sagged against him finally and mouthed at his neck, hesitant to let him pull out of me, wanting to stay in the comfort of this bath with lovely Carter forever. We sat there for a bit and then reluctantly, I unseated myself and bobbed in the water, still catching my breath, my wrists locked around Carter's neck.

"Your power is phenomenal," Carter said, smirking at me. "I felt it. You're something else. I thought you were about to blow something up."

"Is it always going to be like that?" I said, slightly concerned. "I don't want to like accidentally throw a hex because I came too hard."

"We'll teach you how to control it," Carter said, kissing my cheek. "Although I'm guessing some of us wouldn't mind seeing you come that hard." That made me flustered too and I splashed Carter, getting him with a clump of bubbles right to the nose.

Carter was all sweetness and tenderness then, washing my hair, soaping me up and rinsing me off. When we started to prune, we finally got out of the bath and he dressed me in one of their big, thick terry cloth robes.

"I'll see you later," Carter said, and left me with one last soft kiss before winking at me and sending me back to my room.

In my bedroom, I found Asher pacing and Ben leaning on my bookcase and playing with his phone. The difference in their postures was such a perfect representation of the two brothers, that I stifled a laugh.

"Boys?" I said, swanning in and playing with the belt of my robe. "Can I help you?"

Ben looked up quickly, smirking. "Oh, we just wanted to make sure your magic orgasm didn't destroy the place? Jesus, Selena! The walls were shaking!"

My cheeks burned and I swatted his shoulder. "Well, I can't help it! I don't know how!"

"We're going to teach you how to control it," Asher said and leaned on me, resting a hand at my back. "And that's not why we're here." He shot Ben a look and said, "Don't be a dick."

"I was just kidding," Ben said, adjusting his glasses.

"I know you were, sweetie," I said, kissing him on the cheek. "It's fine."

"I do have some magic type business to discuss though," Asher said.

"I don't," Ben said, holding up his phone. "I'm just sending you a really important Spotify playlist." I rolled my eyes at Ben and we exchanged a smile.

Asher took my hand and turned it over to display the ring they had given me. "I think we should take off the spell that repulses other men. Just because, I don't like unnecessary spells when I don't have to use them. And then we'll cast the spell of binding destiny."

"Wow," Ben said, raising an eyebrow. "Kicking it old school."

"What's the spell of binding destiny?" I said.

Ben said, "Damien told me all about that. It was used in the old golden age of shifter clans. It's for clan marriages to destined mates. Since there hasn't been a mate quite like you in generations, it probably makes sense that we cast it. Damien thinks we're meant too."

"I should tell you," Asher said, "it's more powerful than a mere marriage. We'll be bound to you by the ties of blood and magic. That means that connection we have between us will *never* break."

"I don't want it to!" I said quickly. The thought chilled me. "I didn't even know it could break. I want to be with you all forever. Also, I want that potion thing that keeps me from aging so I'm not ninety when you guys still look twenty-five."

"We can do that," Asher said laughing, and kissed me on the nose. I slipped an arm around his waist, hoping he wasn't planning on leaving. As much as Carter had sated me, I felt the urge to keep Asher in my room tonight. I looked in his eyes and he met my gaze. We couldn't seem to get our eyes off each other.

Ben clearly read the energy between us and said, "I think I'll leave you two alone for a while, huh?"

He started to leave and I poked him in the back so that he spun around on his heel again. "I'll see you in the morning, won't I? Let's have breakfast together, just you and I? Can we?"

Ben beamed at me and pressed his thumb to my chin in a sweet gesture of affection. "Count on it, sweet cheeks."

Ben closed the door behind him and I whirled around to face Asher. "You're looking serious," I said, stepping up close to him. He'd showered in one of the other bathrooms and his hair was still wet. He smelled fresh and clean and looked comfy in sweatpants and a t-shirt. It was rare to see Asher so casual. "I liked seeing you all giddy after that fight." I kissed his chin. "It looks good on you."

Asher pressed his palms to my cheeks and his eyes skated over to my face. "Trust me," he whispered. "I'm giddy. You make me so happy. And you make my brothers happy which makes me even happier."

"Come make love to me," I said, and my fingers snuck up under his tee shirt, playing with the little hairs I found there.

"I'm gonna make love to you slowly and softly," Asher said, moving my robe aside to press a kiss to my collarbone. "Because I don't want to the roof to cave in when you come."

I giggled at that and pushed Asher towards my bed. "Well, I can't guarantee that, regardless of the speed."

In bed, I let Asher take over. Ever so slowly he untied my robe and pushed it open, sliding his hand down the length of my body as I lay back atop the duvet. I felt more naked than I ever had in my life as his artist's eyes took in every inch of me, following with a kiss to every spot he touched. His mouth made a slow but scalding journey from my neck and the curves of my shoulders to my breasts. But I could feel his hardness through his sweats pressing against my hip.

"Asher," I whispered, making his way downwards.

"Not yet," he said, smiling slyly. He teased me with his tongue and his fingers, light licks and flicks to my clit before he circled. I pressed into his hand and the bastard laughed at me, one hand holding me firm to the bed as he explored me, his hot breath and the gentle press of his thumb making me buck and moan.

"Asher, please please *please*," I begged, after what felt like an eternity of torture under his attentions.

"Okay, my love," Asher said, nibbling on my thigh. He sat back and took off his shirt and I raised my arms above my head, grabbing the headboard, grounding myself in the grip as I squeezed my thighs together, wet and wanting.

Asher's cock was tenting his sweats and he shoved them down now, his erection heavy as it bobbed. I licked my lips at the sight of its leaking head and rubbed my legs together, writhing in the sheets.

The roof will collapse, I thought, feeling a little dizzy.

Asher crawled up my body and as he entered me, I clamped my legs around him, abruptly arching into him, no longer wanting things slow and gentle. Asher yelled into my shoulder, probably surprised by the sudden shift in intensity, and he thrusted into me, the bed now shaking under us as magic coursed through me and the electricity of my connection to the Quinns made me shudder beneath its alpha.

"Mine," Asher breathed, thrusting into me. He felt impossibly big but my thighs gripped his body, wanting him yet deeper. "You're ours and you're mine too," he whispered, and bit my neck as he pulsed inside me so that I screamed as the windows rattled and the bookshelf shook.

"Yours," I cried out. "I'm theirs and yours too."

We came together, merged into one being, and it felt like it went on for ages, as I trembled under Asher and he pressed into me, filling me.

"Stay here," I said softly, and curled up against him, when we'd come down. "Sleep with me."

"Whatever you like, my love," Asher said, kissing me once more. "Whatever you want."

The ceremony of binding destiny, I discovered, was sort of *like* a wedding. I took that as a decent excuse for the Quinns to buy me a new dress. On a Friday evening, under a full moon, I put on a silver gown and spent too much time on my hair and at the bottom of the spiral staircase, I met my grooms. They made a sight, all of them snazzy in their perfectly tailored tuxedos. I'd teased Ben about potentially wearing skinny jeans but even he had dressed for the occasion. He'd charmed a harp to play Celtic music for us and floating candles lit the parlor. They had fashioned for themselves gold rings with the old signet of their clan that was also the shape of the stone in my ring.

Asher cast a spell in Gaelic. It was paragraphs long and had taken him ages to memorize it. Apparently a spell of binding destiny was very complicated to cast yet I couldn't help but smile watching his brow furrow as he concentrated. When it came to the part about tying us together for eternity, that was my cue. I closed my eyes and focused on the magic I knew was within me. They'd trained me for this moment the last few weeks. Luckily, school was out, or I might have really struggled. Apparently, my power was wild and didn't like to be tamed. But Asher had comforted me; there was plenty of time to learn. I was also close to shifting, at least that's what Damien said. It certainly explained my bloodthirst for raw meat and my growing desire to just run and run through downtown and up into the hills, to run for days alongside my mates until I had only enough energy to make love to each of them and fall asleep. But I hadn't shifted yet and it had given me an itchy feeling under my skin. I wanted to be a wolf just like my boys, and someday I wanted to give them little pups.

As we finished the spell, the magic between us was so great that it threw us all across the room and I landed on the chaise. Our fingers were slightly singed around our rings but apparently that meant it had worked. We were bound forever and I couldn't have been happier. I got to my feet, beaming, and intending to kiss whoever was closest, but just then my stomach lurched. It didn't feel as if I were sick but more like I was about to plunge down a very high drop on a rollercoaster. My muscles felt as if they were flexing too hard and I wanted to stretch. That itchy feeling intensified and my eyes ached. I opened my mouth and a growl came out as the boys surrounded me.

"She's shifting," Asher said, awestruck. "How beautiful."

"That's our girl," Ben said. "Shift!"

"You can do it, Selena!" Carter said.

"Feel your human form drop away," Damien said, rubbing my arm. "Let the wolf come out. Let it run!"

I closed my eyes and concentrated on letting my human form fall and give way to the wolf and whispered, "Here I go," as the Quinns encircled me.

EPILOGUE

Selena

Four years later...

I had dreamed happily, though I couldn't remember exactly what the dream was about. The blankets had been kicked away in the middle of the night and I was naked, though warm, Ben spooned up behind me, my Quinn for the night. Every time I woke up nowadays, I thought to myself that I had never been more comfortable. Though finding the will to remove myself from a Quinn was another story.

"We slept in," Ben murmured behind me, and I felt him kiss me between my shoulders, his hair tickling my neck.

"It's okay," I mumbled. "It's Sunday."

It was pouring rain outside the thick windows of the castle and I frowned, stretching, Ben groaning in protest when I moved. I had promised the little ones we'd go running out to the forest today but I wasn't sure we should go if it was so cold. I closed my eyes and thought about showing the boys how to make s'mores in the fireplace. Somehow the Quinns had lived on the earth for over a hundred years and never tried a s'more.

"But I don't like marshmallows," Ben said, and climbed on top of me, grinning. His hair was all tousled and I reached up to play with it.

"How did you hear that?" I said, sticking out my tongue. Though I really knew better than to ask. I'd become a powerful witch and shifter but I had quite a time learning to control my powers, sometimes my thoughts went firing off into my men's minds without me intending it.

"Your mind is loud," he mumbled, and leaned down to kiss my neck, before I pushed him over into the blankets.

"Can you hear how hungry I am then?" I said, rolling out of giant four-poster bed and shivering as I grabbed a robe hanging off one post. "And Carter's making pancakes. He promised Finn."

"I don't wanna get up," Ben whined.

"Too bad," I said, cinching my robe. I padded over to my vanity. My feet were freezing on the stone floor, but I'd lost my slippers somehow during a particularly rambunctious lovemaking session with Ben the night before. "You know the pups are going to be up already."

I pinned my hair up and went to the arched windows that looked out on Belderrig. It had surprised me when I'd asked my mates where they would live if they could live anywhere in the world and Asher had said Belderrig and the others had agreed with him. I had thought the last place they would want to be was in the home they had lost so brutally all those years ago. But their hearts had healed and grown bigger since then. We'd rebuilt and remodeled their castle where it needed it and I'd found myself excited to move to Ireland. Our home was surrounded by a seemingly endless and lush green forest and it was close enough to the beach to walk.

Ben rolled out of bed and I snorted, watching him buck naked and on all fours on the floor as he rooted around under the bed to find his pajama pants. He pulled them on and put on his glasses. "Damien has a story for you to read. He told me. He's nervous about it. But he needs your feedback"

"Yeah, of course," I said, and grabbed my favorite lotion that Carter had bought for me and lathered up my hands. "And you have some new songs, yes?"

Ben adjusted his glasses, looking uncharacteristically shy. "I don't know if they're ready -"

"They're ready," I said sternly. "They're gorgeous. Will you play them before dinner?"

"Okaaay." He said softly, chewing on his thumbnail.

"You look cold." I found his t-shirt on the floor and threw it at him. "C'mon! Let's go eat."

Down in the absurdly huge kitchen with its woodfire stove and marble counters, we found Carter and Asher already making pancakes and I kissed them each on the cheek as they muttered happily sleepy good mornings.

"Have you decided yet?" I said to Carter, giving him a significant look as he flipped pancakes.

"About what?" He said, all innocence.

"Carter!" The four of us all said at once.

"Are you taking the tour?" I said. "Or what?"

He had been offered the lead in the London Ballet Company which included a world tour and he'd been on the fence for months.

"I'll be away a lot," he said. But I knew him too well by now. He wanted it.

I stood behind him at the stove and wrapped my arms around his waist. "We'll come and meet you places," I said, and kissed his cheek. "Don't you want to make love to me in Paris?"

A slow smile crept across his face. "I wouldn't say no."

"As it happens," Asher said, as he put on coffee, "I'll have an opening in Paris just as you'd be touring there. Kismet."

"There you go!" I said, grinning at Asher. "It's perfect."

"And what about you?" Asher said, looking at me all too pointedly.

"*Moi*?" I said.

"You're finished, aren't you?" Ben said. He stared at me and then they were all staring at me, just waiting.

Technically, my book, meant to be the definitive work on the career of Asher Quinn, *was* done. I was just a little bit nervous about it as my agent was telling me about various high profile periodicals that wanted to interview me and write about Asher. I felt like I'd been preparing for exactly this for years. But still...somehow bonding myself to four wolf shifter wizards seemed less intimidating. I was also working on my Masters in Art History so there was my thesis to contend with too. So much to do.

"It's sort of...almost finished," I lied.

"Ha!" Ben clapped his hands. "I bet it's brilliant!"

"I can't wait to read it," Asher said, giving me a wink.

Just then little Finn ran in and went straight to Asher, hugging his leg before he clamped onto mine. "Mommy!" Finn cried. "Daddies!"

Asher swept Finn up into his arms and kissed his forehead. "Good morning, my little pup. Where's your sister?"

"Piano!" Finn chirped. "Nelly is playing piano!"

"Chip off the old block!" Ben declared just before grabbing me around the waist and throwing me over his shoulder. I feigned protest and swatted his butt as he carried down to the parlor where little Nelly, still not yet three and already showing signs of Damien's quiet determination, was pounding on the baby grand. Asher followed, carrying Finn over his shoulder as he giggled in delight.

Ben set me down on a chaise and Asher dropped Finn into my lap. I hugged him tight and he giggled when I gave his neck a raspberry.

"I was going to take them running in the woods," I said, "but it's raining so hard."

"My pups can take a little rain," Asher said. He tossed Finn a wink.

Finn shrieked and shifted right in my lap, his wolfy tongue licking my face. I laughed and scratched him between his ears.

"See?" Asher said. "He's so excited. Really, Selena, it's good to take them running when they're little pups, get them acclimated. We'll watch them closely."

The thought of it made my wolf's blood run warm. I did enjoy running in the rain myself, especially in the woods. "Alright," I said. "Does that sound good, my darlings?"

Finn wagged his tail and Nelly answered by shifting and jumping down to wag her tail too and tapping her paws on the floor.

"After the pancakes!" Carter declared, hollering from the kitchen down the hall. I snorted. They were always listening in on each other's minds nowadays. Though it did make parenting a lot easier. I picked up Nelly in my arms, still shifted and happy to lick my nose and took her back to the kitchen as the others followed.

Breakfast in the castle was the loudest meal of the day and it usually involved Ben leading a sing-a-long of whatever came to mind. Today it was some boisterous pub tune about a sinking ship. He leaned on the counter, conducting like a composer and something about the serious expression on his face had me helpless with laughter. Asher had Finn in his arms, holding him up to the stove as Carter helped him flip a pancake. Nelly tugged on my robe with her teeth. She was still fooling around in her wolf form and I picked her up, burying my face in her warm fur.

I was surprised at my desire to have more pups but ever since I'd become a full shifter, I'd wanted dearly to rebuild the Quinn clan. I wanted to have lots of pups who would find mates someday and fill up the castle with cousins and aunts and uncles.

"One pup at a time!" Asher had said, astonished by my gusto.

After breakfast, we cleaned up and dressed. Soon enough we were tromping out to the stone courtyard outside the front doors of the castle. I couldn't tell if Carter or Finn was more excited about stomping in puddles, their paws already muddy.

"Now, Finn and Nelly," I said, attempting to get their attention, "stay close to us, sweeties!"

We all shifted and feeling energized, I bounded over to Finn and splashed in the puddle. Finn bowed on his front paws, showing submission, and I wagged my tail. We played around in the mud in front of the castle for a bit until Asher started herding us into a line and then he stood in front of us, the largest of the Quinn wolves, beautiful in his dark gray and silver flecked coat. He reared back on his hind paws for a moment and then turned and began to run and the rest of us took off after him.

I ran alongside my boys, the five of us keeping pace with our slower pups and the wind and rain whipping through our fur as we bounded towards the woods with no thought in our minds but how happy we were to be with each other.

AFTERWORD

A Final Note from Jade:

I hope you enjoyed this story. Well, the good news is that there's more to come. If you want to be the first to hear about my new releases, promotions and giveaways, I urge you to join my Exclusive Reader's Club:

[Yes. Sign me up, please!]

I love supporting my readers and I want to be able to provide more to you, you can also join me on Facebook **here**.

ALSO BY JADE ALTERS

Magic & Mates

The Sharing Spell

Fated Shifter Mates :

Mated to Team Shadow

Mated to the Clan

Mated to the Pack

Mated to the Pride

In the Heat of the Pack :

Protected by the Pack

Claimed by the Pack

DESIRED BY FOUR

Acknowledgment

Thank you for following me on my journey. This book goes out to those who continue to read my stories and to those who have inspired me to keep going.

Love,
Jade

This book is a work of fiction. Any resemblance to persons, living or dead, or places, events or locations is purely coincidental.

Created with Vellum

ELLIE

I threw out the last of the takeout from my early dinner, carefully wiping the crumbs on my desk into the little trash bin underneath. I logged off my computer, grabbed my keys and my phone, shouldered my purse, and took one last look around my office before turning out the light and locking up behind me. I was the last one out at Wilhelm Realty, as I was most evenings. I tended to work late and I'd been teased before for my, perhaps, excessive thoroughness. But I'd also made Realtor of the Month five times and that had come with some nice bonuses. I stopped by the restroom in the lobby on the way out to fix my hair, rinse out my mouth, and apply some lip balm.

There is not much out of place about me at any given time.

I unfastened my sleek, dark ponytail worn low on my head and combed out my hair before fastening it neatly again. I checked my teeth again for any crumbs. I took the well-loved tube of Pomegranate Burt's Bees from my purse and put on a couple of good coats. It was spring in Boulder, Colorado, and the cool, dry hair played havoc with my lips and skin. As usual, I'd applied some light make up that morning; a BB cream, a neutral shadow, mascara, and my balm. But I wasn't going anywhere now that required makeup and didn't refresh before leaving the restroom, turning out the floor lights, and stepping out into the crisp and breezy April night to lock the front doors of the office on Pearl Street behind me.

"Woo!" A cold gust of wind made me shiver and I cinched my coat a little more snugly around me as I crossed Pearl Street, headed toward the parking structure. I nodded hello at the gate guy who always made a point of asking me about Indiana, my Welsh Corgi. When I pulled my blue Accord out of the lot, I turned left instead of right. For once I wouldn't be going straight home or to a happy hour with the girls, or to another disappointing date. No, tonight I was going to finally take action in order to avoid more of those disappointing dates. This had been a long time coming, but as I navigated the lightly populated streets of downtown Boulder on a Thursday night and headed towards Settler's Park, it felt like the right decision.

"Do I want caffeine?" I murmured, chewing on my lip as I eyed the Starbucks two blocks up ahead. I would be out a bit late and needed to stay alert, which surely justified buying myself chai latte. Even at seven o'clock at night. "Yes, I do want caffeine." Giving in, I circled the block and found some street parking.

The sun wasn't fully set yet anyway, and it would need to be fully dark out for my purposes. I hung around for a few minutes at Starbucks, sipping my drink, and playing around on Instagram while listening to music. When it was good and dark, I headed back out and made my way down Pearl and straight into Settler's Park. I slowed down, humming along to Stevie Nicks, as I carefully turned into the winding road up into the woods. It was a little bit eerie out in the park this late but then that was sort of the point, I supposed. And it wasn't as if I was actually scared. I can handle myself pretty well generally.

I hit the thick of the woods where things were almost dangerously dark and completely deserted and pulled over to park. I pictured how I would look to somebody passing by; a woman alone in the woods at night. I probably looked like I was about to bury a body. I tittered at myself just thinking about it. In the car, I grabbed my sneakers from the backseat and switched them for my heels. In the trunk, I found my two reusable grocery bags with all my supplies. I flicked on the safety flashlight on my keychain and checked just one more time to make sure I had everything. Satisfied, I took a breath, shut the trunk, and headed into the woods.

Tonight, things were finally going to change. I was taking my future back into my own hands.

I hated dating. Or I guess I should say, I hated what dating usually was. I had tried it for years and it never got any easier. I'd constructed carefully thought out dating profiles, written to show me in the best light while remaining authentic with my best face on display. It was always the same; an onslaught of guys who just wanted sex, a whole bunch of guys who ostensibly wanted to go on a date but were completely unappealing, and then maybe two guys who seemed like they might not be nightmares. Then I'd go out with the non-nightmares and there was just no...spark. The last time I'd felt anything like a spark was with an insurance examiner named David and the relationship had lasted three months before I'd realized I'd been working really hard to make myself feel a spark and that I was exhausted. It's amazing what you can talk yourself into sometimes.

The last date I'd gone on was with some wine buyer for a tasting bar in town. I admit, I was sucked in because he'd been very attractive. Then I went out with him and he had nothing to say. As in, he didn't ask me any questions and he didn't offer up any information. He seemed to be happy with sharing complete silence during nearly the entire date and while I think being able to share a silence once in a while with someone is a good sign that you're comfortable with them, it was the strangest date I'd ever been on and I'd ghosted him when he texted afterward. I don't need constant clever conversation, but I do need to be able to talk to somebody for Pete's sake.

Suddenly, I'd looked around and realized that dating was kind of an insane proposition. You find some random person you think is physically attractive and who you don't immediately dislike and spend a few hours together with the expectation of romantic interest. No pressure there!

So, I'd decided to opt out. No more dating for me. I'd been told to be patient again and again but after so many years of being patient, it seemed like a new strategy was in order. Because the truth was, I *wanted* a partner. I'd built myself a nice career, I had friends and family. I considered myself generally pretty autonomous. But I couldn't lie to myself either. I wanted passionate love. People have never thought of me as romantic. I'd always been down-to-business, practical, no-nonsense. Those traits described me well. But that didn't mean I didn't want to be swept off my feet or to feel I was the center of somebody's world and to make them the center of mine. It didn't mean I didn't want to wake up beside a lover and feel the warm delight of them wrapping me in their arms.

So, new strategy. And since I happened to be a pretty well-trained witch, I figured magic was the way to shortcut dating. I don't often use magic. It's something that I've always thought I could take or leave and I'd never been deeply involved in the magical world. It runs in the family. My mother was a witch and she raised me and my sister in the art. Our line goes back centuries. It's something I have respect for and I'm proud of the legacy, but I'd never wanted to center my life around it. Every once in a while though, it did come in handy. I'd put a few spells on houses I was trying to sell before and gotten some good results out of it. I once hexed the postal carrier because he kept leaving mail in the mud. He was chased by wasps for three blocks. To be fair, I *had* warned him.

My new strategy to 'dating' was a three-hundred-year-old spell that had commonly and traditionally been used to find women husbands back when that had been a matter of survival. I'd tweaked it a little bit. There were other similar spells but this one seemed to catch the best results from everything I'd read. Yet it was also a little too focussed on *just* catching the husband. But I didn't want to just catch a husband. I wanted a soulmate, a great love. This spell, as I'd redesigned it, worked on the assumption that my guy, my great love, was out there somewhere. All I had to do was find him. It was a matter of fate.

I kept my little safety flashlight on and traipsed down a narrow trail through the woods. There was a particular spot that faced the moon and had a nice big boulder that I thought would be good for brewing. A boulder is usually good for brewing. There's often just enough crystallization going on to absorb the spell and throw it back on you, you just have to be careful you're not brewing around some volatile crystal that could seriously mess you up. But an igneous rock is generally safe.

I whistled to myself as I set out a blanket and set down my cauldron. The cauldron was my mother's. She'd passed it down to me before retiring to Florida with my dad. My younger sister got our grandmother's cauldron. We also have our own. Every decently raised witch gets their own cauldron around the age of twelve. But I liked to use my mother's for luck.

I set out my mini-lantern, flicked it on, and went to work. Some of the ingredients had been difficult to find. It had been a little while since I'd tried my hand at spelling. This one called for aged blood. I'd cut my arm months before and let it sit in a jar out of sight just in case of prying guests.

I muttered to myself as I mixed the base; sulphur, sand from my home, feathers from a blessed bird… I burned sage and recited an old protection spell to keep the area safe while I was working. I lit a fire under the cauldron and brought up the spell on my iPhone. I began to recite the two paragraph spell, watching the position of the clouds around the moon carefully. This was an important night for the spell. The moon was waning but the sky was mainly clear. The moon couldn't be covered while I enacted the spell, it had to 'see' me.

"Bring me my fated one," I said quietly, shuddering at a cold gust of wind. "Bring me my soulmate, gods. One fire of love. Tie me to my love and let the tether remain unbroken."

I poured in two jars full of goat's blood, then the bit of my own blood I'd saved, along with a pitcher of lavender milk. The cauldron roiled and the wind picked up. I could feel the power of the spell in my veins and it made my heart pound. That was a good sign and I knelt on the blanket, spouting the spell as I stirred the potion while it bubbled and foamed.

"Bring me my fated one," I said louder. My hair came unclasped from my ponytail and whipped around my face and the trees rustled so hard I was sure they were speaking to me. Too bad I didn't know how to speak tree. "Bring me my soulmate, gods! One fire of love!" The fire under the cauldron flamed up around the cauldron for a second, singing my blanket, and my heart leapt, but I stayed where I was even as the wind blew pine needles and dirt at my face. "Tie me to my love and let the tether remain unbroken!"

Smoke began to spiral up from the cauldron and I smiled, feeling the almost orgasmic power of a successful spell thrumming through me. I raised my hands over my head and closed my eyes, trusting the magics not to kill me.

"Bring me my fated one! Bring me my soulmate, gods! One fire of love! Tie me to my love and let the tether remain unbroken!"

When I could feel the power of the spell peaking, I grabbed the mug I'd brought with me, dunked it into the cauldron and drank up the cup full before I could think about how gross it would taste.

And it did taste pretty gross. But I held it down, still reciting the spell at full volume as the spiralling smoke rose up into the trees and formed a heart before fading into the wind.

It had definitely worked. And I felt a bit giddy with the assurance that soon I would be finding my one true love. As self-made and strong as I consider myself to be, I wanted someone to laugh with who could challenge me and support me as much as I would for them.

Now, I was going to get him. I just had to keep my eyes peeled for the signs.

I felt the slow release as the spell came down and began packing my things away. A potion once catalyzed by a spell is harmless and I dumped the cauldron out into the dirt before packing it in a garbage bag to clean later. Finally, I stood with my packed up tote bags and flashed my safety light around to make sure I hadn't littered or left anything behind and when I was satisfied, I hiked back to the car.

On the drive home, I felt better than I had in a long while. It was a satisfying sensation to know I'd taken my future in my own hands rather than leaving it to chance or some stupid dating app. I cranked up the radio, singing along to Steve Nicks' 'Sorcerer' which felt strangely prescient.

At home, Indiana did his little happy tap dance when I walked in the door and I fed him before changing into my pyjamas and grabbing the last of the Mint Milanos, ready to settle in for whatever my friends were telling me to watch on Netflix.

For some reason, when I sat on my couch, I always sat on the right side, with Indiana curled up next to me. It was weird because I had a big couch. It was as if I were waiting for someone to come along and take their seat.

And soon now, somebody finally would.

ELLIE

The next morning, I woke up excited. I was singing 'Sorcerer' to myself as I scooped granola into my Greek yogurt, swinging my hips a little as I applied my BB cream. I hadn't felt so giddy and positive in ages and never for anything so legitimately exciting. I suppose it might be different for somebody who doesn't understand the true power of a well-cast spell. But I do. The only potential danger or risk is that your interpretation might be different than how magic will interpret your casting. It's sort of a 'Monkey's Paw' situation. But I was careful about such things and confident that I'd cast it so that I wouldn't be surprised by any weird twists. The spell was meant to find you someone you'd love who would love you back. I wasn't worried that I was going to get seduced by some evil wizard or something. Because I was pretty sure I wouldn't fall for an evil wizard. Magic, in my experience, was benevolent as long as your intentions were benevolent.

"Indiana, baby!" I sang out. Indiana came tap dancing over to the kitchen as I slipped in my second earring, and I squatted down to scratch him behind the ears before spooning the rest of a can of dog food into his bowl. "Be good, sweetie."

I found myself looking around for potential soulmates before I'd even left my building. It was a little ridiculous. My guy was out there somewhere and I'd know when I felt pulled towards him. That was what I had to keep my senses alerted to. I trusted the fates.

I tend to think of myself as an observant person when I'm walking around in the world. But I don't often size men up as I walked past them unless they were particularly striking. Now all of a sudden, every man was a possible love interest. I found myself judging every man I saw. The guy carrying a tray of coffee as he crossed the street in front of my car had nice hair and good taste in suits but he wore a sour look on his face so I dimly hoped it wasn't him. The guy who pulled up next to me in a Lexus, singing along to Journey and bobbing his head was cute, I decided. I wouldn't mind if it was him. The guy waiting by the entrance of the parking garage talked too loud on his blue tooth but he also had a pretty smile so that was a toss-up.

At work, I had a few phone calls from nervous sellers. Their houses were all in a particularly nice neighborhood and the market was hot, so they required a lot of personal attention and it kept me busy all morning and into lunch.

I kept waiting to feel the pull towards my inevitable soulmate. At one point, I thought I was feeling it as Andy, one of my co-workers, hovered outside my office. Andy was cute in a nerdy sort of way, and he glanced over at me once before taking a call on his phone. But it turned out that 'pull' was just my stomach rumbling because I'd worked through my usual lunch hour.

At two, I finally grabbed my purse, intending to eat at the deli across the street and down a few blocks. My stroll was leisurely as I sized up man after man. I knew very well it was pretty useless to accept or dismiss the very idea of dating a person just by judging them in less than a second and only based on their appearance at the moment. That was the whole modern dating thing I'd rejected in the first place. I'd been swiping left and right for a few years. I had to stop thinking in those terms now and leave it to the pull.

"Trust the fates," I muttered to myself as I walked into Lovebird's Deli. I got in line, intending to order my usual chicken Caesar sandwich. The guy in front of me glanced over his shoulder at me. He looked like a construction worker type in coveralls with the top pulled down and wrapped around his waist. He wore a white tank top that clung to his impressive and sweaty muscles. There was a little bit of dirt or dust, smudged here and there. His hair was sort of adorably tousled. He looked at me and the corner of his mouth turned up for the briefest moment before he turned back. He was sexy. I squinted and tried to sense some kind of pull within me.

No, nothing. Just low blood sugar.

I ordered my chicken Caesar and an iced tea and took my drink and my little number on its metal stand to a free table to wait for my lunch. The construction guy was sitting at the table just opposite me with some roast beef and he kept glancing over, his expression a combination of wonder and intrigue. I started to get excited. Maybe this was it. My food came and I found myself eating a little bit more carefully, trying to look appealing. But I don't think I needed to try much. The guy couldn't seem to keep his eyes off me. They were intense eyes too, a deep green that eventually fixed on me without straying.

I'm an attractive woman, conventionally speaking. It's not as if I get approached constantly but I don't generally want for male attention, and like most women, I'm annoyed by too much of it. But I couldn't remember ever having been focused on like this. It might have creeped me out a little bit usually, but now I had the fates on my side.

This must be it, I thought. The spell was bringing me my soulmate. One fire of love, no waiting. Summing up my nerve, I raised my eyes to meet his and did not blink. I tried to look as smoldering as he was. I decided to be bold and make a move. So, I got up and went to the condiment bar near his table. I took some napkins and a packet of sweetener for my iced tea that I didn't really need and as smoothly as I could manage, I slid my eyes over to him. He was sitting facing me and his gaze was fixed on me like I was the only person in the world. I met his eyes again and smiled just enough before going back to my table and sitting down.

A minute later he was coming to talk to me. My heart raced and my fingertips tingled as he slowly and deliberately made his way to my table. I wondered what he was like. Did he like documentaries like me? Was he a dog person? Was he a decent kisser?

"Hey," he said, running a hand through his hair as he paused by my table. I was done with my sandwich now and sat sipping my iced tea. I raised my eyes to him, hoping my makeup was in place. "I don't mean to bother you but I was sitting over there and… There's just something about you. I had to come over and talk to you. Is that alright?" His voice was gravelly like he'd just rolled out of bed, and there was a little twang to it. I pegged him for a Midwestern boy.

"That's alright," I said, nodding. "Have a seat."

The midwestern guy sat and leaned forward on his elbows. His legs were kind of long and his knees bumped mine under the table. "I'm Dixon," he said, in that gravelly voice of his. He stuck out his hand and I shook it.

"Ellie," I said. "Crawford. Nice to meet you."

"Nice to meet you too, Ellie," Dixon said. His eyelids lowered just a little bit. His biceps bulged a little as he shifted around. He smelled like soap and sweat and I breathed in. Everything about him was sexy, including the smile now slowly crossing his face. I kept waiting to feel that pull towards him, compliments of the fates, but it wasn't really happening. I told myself to be patient. Maybe that stuff would come a little later. I had to trust in my own spell. Besides, talking to a sexy looking man like this one wasn't exactly a chore. "You having a good day, Ellie?"

"Pretty good day," I said, Feeling a little bit nervous, I crossed my arms, pinching my skin just a little bit. The guy was very attractive, sure, but I really hate looking flustered. "And you?"

"Getting better by the second," he said, grinning fully.

I licked my lips and sat up a little straighter. "So you just had to talk to me, huh?"

"That's right," Dixon said. His eyes skimmed over me and I felt just a little bit naked. "Never felt anything like it before. Just had to make sure you didn't get away before I spoke to you. Have you ever felt anything like that?"

"I don't think so," I said, sounding much too breathy. I cleared my throat, blushing a little. I felt ridiculous but then, it's not every day you meet your soulmate. And this could be the one. I downed the rest of my iced tea and dabbed my lips with the napkin, wishing I could calm myself down a bit.

"You have the most beautiful brown eyes I've ever seen," Dixon said, fixing his gaze on me again. "Looking right into me."

I blinked at him. From any other guy, it would just sound like a line. But coming from a possible soulmate, I felt flattered. "Oh," I said. "Thank you."

He must have read my reaction as hesitation because now he raised his hands in surrender and leaned back a little. "I know, I know," he said. "I'm coming on too strong. It's not as if we know anything about each other."

"No, I guess not," I said. "But I wouldn't mind knowing more."

"Is that a fact?" Dixon said, and his eyes twinkled so brightly, it was as if he'd plugged them in.

"That's a fact," I said, chuckling a little.

"So, what's your favorite movie?" Dixon said, leaning on his hand.

"Oh!" I laughed. "I have no idea. I hate picking favorites."

"Well, there you go," Dixon said. He chuckled warmly. "Now I know something about you. You hate picking favorites. I am intrigued. Ask me something."

"Are you allergic to dogs?" I said, genuinely on the edge of my seat to hear the answer.

Dixon reeled a little, his eyes big. "Oh God, no. That would be awful." He shrugged then, looking sheepish. "I don't have one myself. I work construction and they keep me pretty busy. But I love dogs. Do you have one?"

"Welsh Corgi," I said. "His name is Indiana."

Dixon snorted at that and smiled slyly. "Is that from *Indiana Jones and the Last Crusade*?" he asked. "As in, we-"

"Named the dog Indiana," I said, putting on my best Sean Connery. "I wouldn't say that's my favorite movie, but it's definitely up there. It was one of my favorites as a kid."

"A fine choice," Dixon said, nodding. "A fine choice. Listen, if you don't give me your number soon, I'm gonna have to beg for it. You don't want that, do you?"

"Hmm…" I tapped my chin, pretending to think about it.

Dixon clasped his hands as if in prayer and his brow furrowed like a sad puppy's. "Please?" He said. "Pretty please with sugar on top, Ellie Crawford?"

"Since you asked so nicely," I said, smirking just a little bit. I found a pen in my purse and wrote my number on a napkin, signing it with a flourish.

Dixon pocket the note, looking very proud of himself. "You know what, I think it's destiny we just met."

"Fate?" I said.

"Yeah," Dixon said. "Exactly." He took his phone from his pocket, grimacing when he saw the time, and he tapped the table. "Shoot, I'm late getting back."

"Yeah," I said, sighing. "I gotta get back too."

"What do you do?"

"Real estate agent," I said.

"Ah! I build em', you sell em." He reached out to shake my hand again. "Well, have a wonderful rest of your day, Ellie Crawford. I'll call you."

"See that you do," I said, hoping I sounded playful and cute. He grinned at that and kind nodded to himself, patting me on the shoulder before making his way out.

I finished up my lunch quickly and made way back to the office on cloud nine. I felt so much better now that I'd met him and it was such a relief not to have to worry about him being a creep or having some terrible deal breaker of a flaw. He'd felt it! He'd felt the pull towards me that the spell had cast and even if he hadn't known what it was, it had worked on him.

As I waited at a stoplight, I wondered why *I* hadn't felt the pull. I'd kept searching for that sensation within me, something that would tell me that this was definitely the one and...nothing. I wondered if maybe the spell had been just a little bit flawed? Or maybe it was harder for me to absorb those effects since I was a witch? Traditionally, this spell would have been cast by a witch on to somebody else. Maybe I did need to give it a little while.

Oh well, I thought and shrugged to myself as I slipped my earbuds in and turned on some music.

Dixon had felt the pull toward me.

That was the important thing.

I still had a few minutes left of my lunch. I'd told Dixon I was in a rush too just to be agreeable and not seem too desperate. Which was pretty silly in hindsight. But now I took my time as I walked back to work.

I was about to cross a street when I gasped at the sudden and intense compulsion I had to turn left and walk to the pharmacy one block over. The urge was so strong that my palms were starting to sweat as I stood there on Pearl Street. I had a feeling that were I to go anywhere other than the pharmacy right now, something dreadful would happen.

The longer I stood there, the worse I felt. Though I'm a pragmatic person, I tend to trust in magic and my own intuition. I follow hunches and I'm attentive to 'bad feelings'.

So, I turned left and headed toward the pharmacy. My skin felt too hot, even while the brisk air cooled it. Yet I immediately began to feel better as I walked. The sick sensation of coming dread if I failed to follow my instinct faded quickly.

But now I didn't know what I was supposed to do next. I wondered if this had something to do with Dixon.

I walked into the pharmacy, feeling hesitant.

Just then, my phone buzzed. I had a text message from the pharmacy that my prescription was ready.

Now, that was weird. Being raised a witch, I believed such strange coincidences were meaningful. I just wasn't sure of the meaning.

I'd had a bacterial infection a couple of months of back and the doctor had prescribed ongoing antibiotics for a few months just in case. But I couldn't remember dropping off the slip. I must have, I thought. Perhaps I'd been too distracted by planning my spell and just forgotten that I'd done it. Or just as likely, maybe the doctor had ended up calling it in for me. He was only a few blocks away. Still, it was pretty strange that I'd had that gut feeling to walk to the pharmacy before getting the text. Fates didn't usually alert you to such mundane things as a prescription refill. There must be more to it, I thought.

I picked up my prescription and paid the few bucks after insurance but I had a strange feeling as I ambled out of there. I felt like there was something I was supposed to be doing, someone I was supposed to see.

I kept an eye out for Dixon. Maybe he was in trouble?

I was so busy worrying about whether my new soulmate was in danger and the fates were trying to help me help him, that I forgot to pay attention to my own safety. I wasn't even aware of the light as I stepped off the curb and nearly got ploughed down by a car.

But suddenly there was a strong arm, curving around my waist and yanking me back as smoothly as if it had been choreographed. My heart pounded as the car that would have ploughed right into me sped by and I stood there on the pavement, catching my breath.

"Are you alright?" The voice was low and smooth, but I didn't hear the question the first few times the stranger said it. I blinked at him, feeling horribly foolish. I was never so distracted or flaky.

"Yes," I said, smiling sheepishly. "Oh God, thank you so much. I don't know where my head was. I could have been killed."

"I'm certainly glad you weren't." The stranger shuddered a little. He was tall, a little taller than Dixon, and he had warm brown skin and jet black hair buzzed short in a way that suited his squarish face. He looked a little bit like an action hero and there was a subtle kind of charisma about him that made me want to lean in closer.

"Well..." I felt flustered suddenly, and not on my game at all like when I'd spoken to Dixon. "Thanks to you." My cheeks were burning. It was a little ridiculous. Though I supposed I was just embarrassed. And objectively speaking, the man was incredibly attractive. His features looked sculpted and long, thick eyelashes framed brown eyes that glittered warmly as he smiled.

"Only too happy to help," he said, waving a hand. "I'm Mateo. Mateo Marquez. If you plan to keep stepping off curbs into traffic, I'm going to have to keep an eye on you."

That made me laugh and I tucked my hair behind my ear. Dimly I thought of Dixon. Dixon. It was hard to remember Dixon as this man fixed his gaze on me.

"I'm Ellie," I said. We didn't end up shaking hands. Instead, we awkwardly stared at each other as if waiting for something to happen. Somebody brushed against me and the simple movement broke that little spell. I laughed nervously and Mateo cleared his throat, his eyes flitted around. He seemed as off-kilter as I was.

"Alright," Mateo said, scratching his head and frowning. "I'm going to let you get back to it. Um…just be careful, please? I saved your life, that means you have to grant me that one wish."

I chuckled at that and nodded. "Will do. Thank you." I swallowed and our eyes met again. I felt pulled in, lost, welcomed… But Dixon… "Mateo," I said softly.

"Right," Mateo whispered and cleared his throat before seeming come back to himself. He spun on his heel with one last nod and walked away.

I turned away from him. I felt short of breath as if I'd run a long way and I knew it didn't all have to do with almost getting hit by a car.

I felt an inexplicable urge to look back at him that was so strong, I couldn't possibly deny it. When I looked back, Mateo was looking back at me from the end of the block. When our eyes met, he turned his head again. I blushed but simply turned away again and headed back to work.

I was confused and wondered if there was something more to the spell that I was missing. Dixon had definitely felt the pull. What he'd described had to be more than a coincidence.

I wondered if what I'd felt with the pharmacy and the man who'd saved me had just been a test. Very old fashioned spells used to have similar little tests of loyalty or will. I didn't think this one had, but maybe I'd missed it.

In any case, if it was a test to see if I was completely loyal to my new soulmate, I'd surely failed.

MATEO

Our house sits at the top of a drive on a hill in the north end of Boulder. It's a huge wood-sided thing that we built ourselves. It's got dark wood siding and huge thick glass windows that look up into the mountains on one side and over the city on the other. The best thing about the house is that the back lets out into the woods and it's not a populated area either. Our closest neighbors are a half-mile down the drive and we have this part of the woods to ourselves. We also have a custom-made back door that swings in and out. We only latch it at night when we're all accounted for. It makes casual shifting much easier (and more fun too) when we can just run down the hill from the woods at full speed and blow right into the house.

My cousins and I are private investigators and we work from home when we're not out in the field or meeting clients at our office in town. The day I met Ellie—that mysterious, beautiful woman who had seemed to call to my blood—I was coming back from lunch. I'd been working in the office that day, doing some easy money background checks in between meeting a couple of new clients.

I'm the oldest of my four cousins. Or rather, we're technically cousins...I think. I couldn't tell you how we're related as it's so distant. Javier once joked that I could probably provide more evidence for my relation to Cleopatra than the three of them. We own the PI business together, just like we live together and shift together. We do pretty much everything together. It's a good thing I can stand them. In fact, I love them all dearly.

That day, my youngest cousin Emiliano was home most of the afternoon doing the books. He's always had a head for numbers and called dibs on accounting as if the rest of us were actually going to fight him for it. Alejandro, the second oldest, was out in the field, doing some surveillance. He's the best at customer service and normally with a light workload, I would be in the field and he would be at the office. But it had been a little while since Alejandro had pounded the pavement working a case, so I'd sent him out that day instead. Meanwhile, Javier was out shopping for some odds and ends. Javier kind of gets stuck with everything else; cooking, cleaning, logistics, administration. But all four of us can handle ourselves capably as investigators.

At the end of the day, when I finally returned home, I waited for everyone in the dining room that looked out on the cliffside of our hill where there was a steep drop to the road below. I folded my hands on the table and Javier, without needing to ask, brought me coffee. He can always seem to tell when I'm deep in thought and need a little caffeine.

And I was definitely deep in thought. I couldn't stop thinking about that woman I'd pulled back from getting hit by the bus. I remember the exact curve of her high cheekbones, the elegance of her long neck, her bare legs under that skirt... Everything about her was pleasing to me. But it wasn't just superficial attraction. There'd been something else at work. Before that, I'd felt this strange compulsion to go to the pharmacy. I'd never felt anything like it before. I was walking back to the office on Pearl and I'd been nearly forced by an itchy and uncomfortable feeling to turn around and go to the pharmacy.

There was nothing for me there, and nothing I needed. I'd looked around, confused and bothered by my own actions. Just as I walked out of the place, I saw her walking in. She was wearing earbuds and seemed a million miles away even as her gaze flitted around the place. Then I had to wait outside, the same inexplicable need driving me to each action. I'd had a meeting with a client in five minutes. I should've been rushing back to our office. Until recently, we'd had an office on the fringes of town, but since taking this new place, our business had almost doubled.

I was about to text Alejandro then, sure that there was some strange magic at work. I wanted to ask him if he felt anything too. Then I saw her again. She carried herself with confidence and grace. How anybody does that in heels, I'll never know.

Then it was as if everything happened in slow motion. I noticed the few strands of dark hair that escaped her neat ponytail and the way the sun glinted off them as she turned her head. Her eyes weren't quite seeing, as if her mind was somewhere else as she walked. Then she was stepping off the curb and the car was speeding toward her.

I'd had the most awful feeling then as if my own life was in danger. Without hesitation, I'd darted forward and yanked her back. She'd yelped as she stumbled back into me.

Then she'd spoken to me. It was nothing special, nothing strange. Yet, I'd felt as if I were floating off the ground. I could hardly remember how to compose myself. I was lucky to make it out of there half coherent.

Now, I waited for my cousins because this was the kind

of thing it was necessary to share. As insignificant as it had seemed (though not insignificant to my own mind), I knew my cousins would want to know about it.

I leaned on my hand and Javier finally came out, a dish towel over his shoulder, his black, curly hair clipped to one side. He took cleanliness in the kitchen very seriously, though you wouldn't know that he took anything very seriously by his demeanour. Now he plopped down in front of me and gave me a funny look.

"You look like you're trying to play Sudoku in your head and you're losing," Javier cracked. "Chicken alfredo for dinner tonight. Heavy on the alfredo. What's up?"

"I'll tell you when the others get in," I muttered. "How was your day?"

"Thrilling," Javier said dryly. "There was a sale on those magic eraser things at Target. I cleaned up. I also reorganized Al's shitty filing system he keeps trying to use. Tell him to stop doing that?"

"I'll tell him," I said with a snort. "Ah, wait, there he is now. You tell him."

Alejandro breezed in. He's as tall as I am but leaner. He has a more serious look to him on first sight, but he's actually the friendliest. It doesn't hurt that he's got the refined bone structure of a total heart-throb. I'm the biggest and strongest, which is usually the case with the alpha of a pride. But Alejandro is who the ladies always gravitate to first.

"Ali!" Javier said as Alejandro sat down next to him, nodding hello at me. "Seriously, stop trying to get fancy with the filing. I can't find anything. And I always have to fix it."

"It's by date of case opening," Al said, shrugging. "What's so complicated about that?"

"Oh my God..." Javier rolled his eyes and cupped his hands around his mouth. "Dude, nobody remembers what date a case opened! You file by last name! Any dummy knows that!"

Al pursed his lips. "I remember when cases open."

"Yeah," I said with a snort. "Because you have a photographic memory and you enter all the initial data."

"I thought everyone would know," he mumbled. And then he sighed heavily. "Fine! Fine, I'll keep it alphabetical."

"Thank you," Javier said, spreading his hands. "Was that so hard?"

I was edgy in my seat, tapping my fingers on our big oval dining room table.

"Expense reports," Emiliano said from the doorway to the kitchen.

The rest of us turned to blink at him. "What about em'?" Javier said.

"Receipts," Emi said, glaring at us. "Could you please save, I don't know, a few of them at least? I don't know if you're all aware of this, but the IRS frowns on *guessing*."

"Will do," Al said, simply, and smiled as if that would make Emi crack.

"I think I've got a few hiding in my wallet," I admitted. "I'll dig them out for you later, Emi."

"Thank you," Emi said gravely as if all our lives depended on it.

Javier raised his eyebrows as Emi still hovered there. Emi has a long face and it fits his sometimes almost humourless ways. But people who don't know Emi like the rest of us do, miss out when they only label him as too serious. He's always the first at your side when you need him and he can be surprisingly affectionate when he really cares. Javier said, "Are you going to unclench now or...?"

Emi rolled his eyes and sat down next to me. "I'm starving." He nodded at Javier. "When's dinner?"

"The Alfredo isn't done alfredo-ing," Javier said. "And I made mint ice cream."

"You made mint ice cream?" I asked, surprised.

"Yeah, I did!" Javier said, smacking his fist on the table. "Because Emi bought me that ice cream maker for my birthday and you said I'd never use it! You doubted me-"

"Okay, okay-"

"Never doubt me!"

"I don't doubt you," I say dryly. "Now shut up, all of you. I gotta tell you all about this thing that happened today." I was edgy just thinking about the whole thing, and not knowing what it would mean. I rolled my neck and cracked my knuckles. When I get restless like this, it makes me want to shift and go running up beyond the woods late at night where there are long stretches of dirt road - deserted and waiting to be run so I can stretch those muscles. "This afternoon," I began, "after lunch-"

"Did you get a weird feeling?" Javier said. "Like you *had* to go down to Pearl Street Pharmacy? Because I felt it too."

"Me too," Emiliano said, nodding.

"Yep," Alejandro said, sighing. "I was miles away watching a motel for the Stossel case. But I felt it. I was damn close to turning right around and speeding to the pharmacy. And I have no idea why. Made me itchy as hell. Then it went away."

"Hmm." I stroked my chin. "I wonder if it went away after I spoke to her?"

"Who?" Javier said.

"Ellie," I said softly. Even her name was sweet on my lips and I'm not much of a romantic about things. "Her name was Ellie. She was this woman I saw nearly dart right out into the street. She was just distracted, I guess. Almost got clipped by a car. I yanked her back and..." I glanced around at my cousins. I couldn't think of a way to put this that wouldn't end in them mocking me. "She was enchanting," I said, rubbing my eyes. "Bewitching."

"Bewitching!" Javier said, clapping his hands. "Our Mateo has been bewitched? Is it possible?'

"Apparently, it *is* possible," I grumbled. "And you weren't there. I've never... I've never ever felt anything like it. The attraction... I think she felt it too. The way she looked at me. It was like..."

"Mateo got zapped by the love bug," Alejandro said, chuckling.

"Not a love bug," I said. "I talked to her for about two seconds. But there was...*something*. I'm telling you. I find it strange that we all felt that same pull to go to the pharmacy..."

"Yeah," Emi said. "That is odd."

"Alright," Javier said slowly. "Confession time. I saw her too. Actually...I did more than just feel the pull. I was just a few blocks away buying office supplies when I felt it. Tried to ignore the feeling, but when I did, my head started pounding. So I figured what the hell, jetted on over toward the office and I was pulling right up to the pharmacy when I saw her. I can't even explain it, man. It was a religious experience."

"See, you were bewitched too!" I said pointedly.

"Damn right, I was!" Javier said. "I mean...to me she looked like a goddess or something. Ethereal. Can't really explain it. And as soon as I saw her, I felt a little better. Felt okay to drive away. Which is probably good. Most women don't want men chasing them down the street because they have a *feeling*. Anyway, it must've been right before you saw her."

I started to answer when Javier suddenly clapped his hands and said, "Shoot! My chicken alfredo!" He jumped up and dashed to the kitchen and the three of us chatted about the strangeness of the experience and who the woman could possibly be.

We didn't really have guesses. She could've just been a very powerful witch. Sometimes they put out weird vibes without even meaning to. Or she could have been walking around *deliberately* enchanting men.

We all ate dinner and the topic moved to work and our clients- who ran the gamut from reasonable to absolutely batshit crazy. Javier was especially fond of an older rich lady who, over the course of three years, had hired us to surveil *three* different husbands. Only the first had actually had an affair. Though the others had also kept secrets from her. We all agreed she needed to give up on the idea of husbands and just enjoy her money, not that we thought Mrs. Studebaker would ever take our advice.

After dinner, we sat and drank coffee for a while, and then it was time to shift. Most nights we liked to take a night run; stretch our muscles and enjoy the woods. We always felt a little bit riled up just before a run and now we stripped off our shirts and hooted at each other before making our way outside. I led the way a little farther up into the woods, now dark and foreboding but for the dim light of the moon. I shifted, feeling the almost stinging but satisfying stretch of my muscles as the ground came up to meet me and my hands and feet became huge golden haired paws, my whiskers appearing, a thousand scents pleasantly assaulting my nose.

The Marquez pride goes back even further than the written out family tree scrawled across multiple parchments that we keep down in the wine cellar. They track my father's line all the way down. For as long as there have been shifters, there has been a Marquez pride of lions. Hundreds of years ago, when there were lions in Spain there was a Marquez pride. We evolved into pumas, but remained in Spain, until the only kind of that species were shifters.

Threw the naturalists for a loop, to be sure. That's as far as our records go and it still gives us hundreds of years of Marquez history.

My cousins and I had formed the pride as teenagers. Or rather, the pride had been formed for us by my parents who still live back in Spain in the Basque Country where I grew up. I have the purest Marquez bloodline of the four of us. The only evidence I do have of my relation to the three men I share my life with is that they are puma shifters from Spain, and the only remaining puma shifters are Marquez. But that's the weird nature of shifters sometimes. If there's a drop of Marquez in you, you're a puma.

And I'm the alpha. That means I lead. Now, I led them through the woods, scrambling over logs and, feeling playful, up a tree and then back down. Finally, we hit the dirt road that was my favorite and we ran full speed. Boulder's been good to us. There aren't any other shifters nearby that we know about which means there are no stupid fights over territory and the people here have an ingrained sense of respect for the wildlife. Even when we've been spotted, we've never been bothered.

We ran and fooled around for a good hour and a half and then I led my cousins back to the house just as it started to sprinkle outside. I shifted in the woods before I reached the house, and I felt good as I always did after a run. Yet I was still hung up on thoughts of this woman. I couldn't shake her loose from my mind. The others followed after me and we crowded into the kitchen to drink some water and catch our breath.

I grabbed my shirt off the floor and was about to head upstairs to shower when Emiliano nudged me as he fiddled with a water bottle cap. Emi said, "I've been thinking-"

"Don't strain yourself," Javier said, smirking.

"Haha. Anyway, I was thinking while we were out there,

how my grandmother used to talk about fated mates. Did you ever hear about that?"

I sighed, racking my brain. There was a lot of old lore in shifter world. Most of it was irrelevant these days. It was difficult to keep track of.

"Fated mates?" I said. "Maybe? I don't know. What is it?"

"It means a shifter is destined for their mate," Emi said slowly as if he was struggling to remember. "But I remember my grandmother telling me these little romance stories about shifter knights back in the day. How they'd see their lady love and feel this magic compulsion to go to her. Like a pull. So, ya know... This thing with this woman kinda reminds me of that."

Fated mates. The words made my blood race. It's only become more and more difficult to find a mate these days as a shifter. If there was any chance magic was going to enter into it and help me out, I wanted to know. It was something I never talked about, but I *did* want a mate. I wanted love, cubs, and all the rest of that mushy stuff. I just didn't like talking about it.

I tried not to let on how deeply I cared about it, yet as the alpha, it was definitely something we needed to look into, so I said, "Alright then. Let's go to the old texts."

The 'old texts' were a bunch of books that probably should've been in a fancy library somewhere, but instead, they were in boxes behind an antique dresser that Emiliano refused to give away in the basement. The oldest book of lore dated back to the fourteenth century and Javier coughed as Alejandro blew a thick layer of dust off the cover while we all crowded around him in the dining room.

If we were less assimilated shifters, I suppose we would've known more about our history. But since there are so few prides nowadays, I suppose we've tried to make a life for ourselves in the human world. I try not to forget where I came from at least, but there's a lot more responsibility as an alpha. It's easy to lose sight of the legacy on your shoulders. You tend to forget you're carrying it.

"Here we go," Emi said, as carefully turned the pages. "Fated mates..." He cleared his throat and began to read aloud. "From time to time, one of a pride may be fated to one. They may be of man or fae or beast or one other of Lucifer's children. The fates will cause a fever of the mind within that of the pride who is fated. It may be of such power as to deceive one into thinking he may die. Those mates once joined will be forever in union." Emi trilled his lips. "And then it talks about the ceremony of the binding... I dunno, there's a lot of stuff here..."

"Fever of the mind," I muttered. "That's what it felt like to me."

"Hang on..." Emi read, sounding increasingly astonished as he went on: "When a pride is joined together in harmony, when their lives are owed to each other, and fates smile on them or the magics bless them, one fated mate may join with the whole of the pride. One shared among them, bound to all by love."

"Shared among them," Javier said. "Does that mean..."

"One woman who'd be a mate to all of us," Alejandro said slowly.

The thought made my cheeks warm. Sharing something so intimate with the rest of them sounded...not terrible, but nothing I'd ever imagined before.

"Damn," Javier said. "I didn't even know that was a thing."

"Me either," I murmured.

We all kind of looked at each other a bit bashfully. We'd been together as a pride for about fifteen years. I thought of these three men as my closest friends and allies and I knew them better than I knew anyone else in the world. I trusted them with my life and they trusted me to lead them. But sharing a woman between us, one who we would all love as one... The thought wasn't terrible, it was just strange and new.

I knew as I saw the tentative and dazed expressions around me that we all had a whole lot to think about suddenly. I was suddenly certain that if there was such a thing as a *shared* fated mate, that perhaps that's what this woman was.

Now, I just had to find her again and see if I was right.

ELLIE

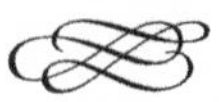

I was racked with nerves for the rest of the day and the next morning. I felt like a giddy young girl again, with the promise of love waiting on the horizon. It was true that when I'd talked to Dixon, he hadn't struck me right away as an obvious choice for my soulmate. But then, I'd hardly spoken to him. I tried to put that little worry out of my head. My mother had taught me to trust the fates and that's what I would do. They wouldn't steer me wrong. If Dixon was my destiny, then he must be great. I just had to get to know him better and soon enough the both of us would be head over heels.

The next afternoon, Dixon texted to ask me out.

Drinks & maybe more, he wrote. *We'll see.*

I bit my lip and squinted at the text because over analyzing text messages is what modern courting is all about. I couldn't tell if the 'maybe more' was referring to dinner or sex. If it was dinner, there was no problem. If it was sex, he was awfully presumptuous. He'd probably meant dinner.

I texted back and we made plans for the next night. He had some bar he wanted to take me to and seemed awfully excited about it. We chatted for a second over text, nothing exciting. He left me with a winky face emoji and I went back to work feeling like I was on the brink of something potentially special and new. It was a good feeling.

In the back of my head though, I kept thinking of the mysterious man who'd pulled me out of the street; the man with warm and glimmering eyes and the fierceness in them that I'd noticed even after less than a second of looking at him. I'd never really looked at a person's face and felt as if I could read so much about them just by a single glance. But Mateo had seemed that way.

"Stop thinking about Mateo," I mumbled, pinching the bridge of my nose. I'd just been texting Dixon mere seconds ago and here I was, thinking about another guy. I shook my head and focused on my computer screen. "Lunch," I said. That's right, I needed lunch and then I had to drive out to a showing. I sighed and stood to grab my purse.

On the way to the deli, I couldn't help but keep an eye out for Dixon. I couldn't help but keep an eye out for Mateo either, but I told myself that was only because he was mysterious.

I hadn't been on a date in a little while and I found myself nervous. Maybe especially because this was it: the *soulmate*. I wanted to look my best. I wore full makeup, eyeliner and everything. I blew out my hair and wore a little black dress that had been in the back of my closet since the last Wilhelm realty Christmas party. I decided to go for a dark but glossy lipstick and I wore my favorite earrings.

Dixon was supposed to pick me up at seven. At five til, I was jittery. I was careful not to cuddle Indiana, not wanting to get dog hair on my dress. I paced around the apartment in my heels, trying to break them in a little more.

At ten after, I was very jittery. At twenty minutes after, I was annoyed. No text. I absolutely hate it when guys are late. I texted Dixon which is always a gamble because if the person is driving, they shouldn't be texting.

On your way?

Dixon texted back: *Y*.

I assumed that meant yes. He finally arrived at 7:30 and I was so relieved, I forgot to be pissed. Dixon was dressed nicely, or anyway, just nice enough. I don't need a guy to dress to the nines though. He wore a button down and nice pants. He cleaned up pretty well. He had some sexy stubble going on that I wouldn't say no to.

"Sorry, I'm late," he said, shrugging apologetically.

"Traffic?" I said.

"Oh, ya know."

I frowned at that, having no idea what it meant. But not wanting to push the issue, I just nodded and let him take my arm and walk me to his car. The car was clean and fairly new. I always notice the state of a person's car. It's not as if a dirty car is a deal breaker, but I do think it says something about you. But Dixon's car was nice and there was no trash on the floor.

"You look great," Dixon said, glancing over at me with a smile.

"Thanks, likewise," I said. "So where are we going again?"

"It's called Double's," Dixon said. "Just this place where my friends and I hang out. I thought it would be fun to go there for a first date. Ya know, keep things loose? And you can meet my friends?"

"Oh!" I smiled agreeably. Hanging out with a dude's friend group seemed like a *terrible* first date to me unless there was a group date going on, but I could see he meant well anyway. "Sounds good, sure."

As bad as I thought the idea of hanging out with a guy's friends on the first date might be, the reality turned out to be much worse.

Part of the problem was the venue. Double's turned out to be a loud sports bar. I don't hate sports and sometimes if there's an exciting season of something, I might even pay attention. But I loathe sports bars. When we pulled up to the place, my stomach plummeted. I could see inside through the open countertop windows that looked out on the patio. The place was full of giant televisions all blaring a basketball game while music blasted at the same time. It was also packed.

I swallowed my irritation and told myself that someday, this date would be a funny story that Dixon and I would tell our kids. We'd talk about how much I'd hated the bar he took me too and how I'd actually worried that it meant we weren't supposed to be together. But in the end, everything had worked out fine.

Unfortunately, looking back on a thing is difficult when you're in the middle of it. We parked and got out of the car and Dixon led me inside. The place was even more packed than it looked from the outside. There was a very important Denver Nuggets game on (apparently) and most of the people there were wearing jerseys or team shirts or caps. People were yelling at the game, and hooting and laughing and being generally...loud and drunk.

It all set me on edge.

I was also horribly overdressed and I felt ridiculous in my little black dress.

"You good?" Dixon said, nodding at me as he led me to two free seats at an otherwise crowded long table. "My friends are shooting pool, when they come over, I'll introduce you."

Oh fantastic, I thought. *I cannot wait.*

Then it got worse.

"Hey, guys!" The voice came from a beaming server, a strikingly hot young woman in a tube top that said Double's with a logo that accentuated her breasts. Her skirt was practically non-existent. "What can I get for you to tonight?"

I ordered a vodka tonic out of habit. The server was gracious and it's not as if I blamed *her* for how horribly uncomfortable every bit of this made me.

Before she left the table, she said, "Be sure to catch the body shots dance! Starts in twenty! Body shots half off!"

"Thanks, sweetheart," Dixon said, as she made her way to the next table.

The thing is, there may well be a scenario in which I'd be comfortable doing a body shot.

This wasn't it.

I couldn't hide my discomfort either. At least, I wasn't even trying to. I'm sure it could be read on my face, especially when Dixon's friends came over all dressed in their team gear and didn't even make eye contact with me as Dixon introduced us, their eyes glued to the big screens. To add insult to injury, it was a commercial break.

I drank my vodka tonic and picked at the chicken tenders on the platter of fried stuff Dixon had ordered for us. And then-

"Body shots!" That was our server, who was now standing on the bar because the second quarter of the game was over. All the servers stood on the bar. There was a song playing with a thumping bass that practically made the tables rattle. All the guys hooted when the servers did shots out of each other's bras. Then they let customers do them if they'd paid extra.

I was almost impressed by how terrible this date was going. I wanted to crawl into a hole. The entire thing was giving me a headache. And worst of all, if I implied I wasn't into the scene, I was going to look like some kind of ice queen. Which didn't seem fair.

"Can we go somewhere?" I all but yelled it. I hadn't planned on saying anything. Dixon's friends rolled their eyes at each other. Not that I much cared about Dixon's friends.

"Somewhere else?" He said. He had to yell above the noise. "All my friends are here."

Weird argument, I thought. Since he was supposed to be on a date with me.

"Mind if we stay a bit longer?" Dixon smiled in a way that was just charming enough that I started to wonder if I was being unreasonable.

So it wasn't my scene. He didn't know that. Maybe I *was* being way too uptight.

I smiled, vowing to loosen up a little. "Sure," I said. "Yeah, of course. But I'm definitely going to need another drink."

Dixon winked at me and said, "That I can definitely do."

On my third vodka tonic, I was feeling more relaxed and trying to go with the flow. I really didn't care at all about the game, but I gave it my best shot. Dixon engaged me in conversation and we chatted a bit, the best we could with how loud the place was anyway. He told me about the construction business, how he liked to go hiking and camping. We talked about politics a little bit but nothing very in-depth or controversial.

"How's that drink treatin' ya?" Dixon had the bedroom eyes on now and suddenly there was a hand on my leg under the table.

I laughed and wagged my finger at him. "It's not treating me *that* well," I said, moving his hand from my thigh. He'd moved from about zero to a hundred and I hoped I could laugh it off.

Dixon laughed and said, "Well played."

I was about to respond when I thought I heard someone calling my name, yet it was more like an echo that had come from my own mind. I looked around the room, suddenly feeling a great sense of urgency. I looked to the front doors and breathed in. There was my lifesaver; the hot action hero guy who'd saved my life a couple of days ago. He was here with three other guys all as beautiful as him in their own unique ways.

Immediately, everything within me wanted to go to them.

I put it down to being frustrated with a less than stellar date and shifted my gaze back to Dixon. But not before Mateo saw me. I didn't miss the way his mouth dropped open when we made eye contact. He looked like he was staring into the sun and I smiled to myself.

I looked at Dixon and tried to think of something to say but I was distracted and when I glanced back at Mateo, he was still looking at me. Except now, all four of them were staring. I felt heated and swallowed.

"Who the hell are those guys?" Dixon said. He followed my gaze and glared at them. "Jesus, they're straight up gawking at you. I'm gonna go take care of this-"

"*Hey,*" I said, resting my hand on his arm. "C'mon. You don't have to do that. I'm here with you, not them. Ignore them."

Dixon turned his attention back to me and I sighed with relief. The last thing I wanted was a bar fight just when the date had been starting to turn around.

"You're right," Dixon said, with a wave of his hand. "Besides, what do I want with them when I got you?" He leaned in, diving right toward my mouth for a kiss. Everything about it seemed off and I reared back. "Whoa."

"Sorry," I said, laughing nervously. "Just um..." I gestured around us and rolled my eyes. "This place. Not a great setting for a first kiss."

"No," Dixon said, laughing. He looked around at his hooting friends and the loud crowd and the giant television screens as if seeing it all for the first time. "No, it's not. I apologize. Can I make it up to you with a beer?"

I shrugged and trying to be good natured, I said, "Sure." Dixon got up to get us drinks from the bar and I couldn't help but let my eyes stray to Mateo and his companions, whose dark eyes had turned from me. An image flashed in my head of myself, naked and sweaty, riding Mateo, leaning down for a heated kiss as his palms clutched my ass.

"Shit," I muttered, chuckling to myself. I should've been thinking of Dixon that way. I pounded the rest of my drink, determined to focus on my actual soulmate.

The rest of the date went reasonably well, especially once Dixon's annoying friends left and the game ended. We managed to have an actual conversation anyway. It wasn't mind-blowing but it was alright. I was starting to wonder if I'd had a mistaken idea of soulmates. Maybe...this was it. Maybe I'd had an overdeveloped sense of love and romance propagated by society and culture and all that stuff. Maybe I was thinking too much of it. And if I was, I certainly couldn't blame Dixon for it.

"I had a nice time," Dixon said, as we pulled up in front of my building. "But I think I screwed up."

"Yeah?" I raised an eyebrow, curious where he was going with this.

"Yeah...I probably shouldn't have taken you to Double's," he said, rubbing his face as if embarrassed. "I was excited when I met you, I thought it might be fun. You weren't having a good time…"

"It was fine," I said, too obviously lying through my teeth.

Dixon laughed out loud at that. "Alright," he said. "Clearly, you're a terrible liar. Another thing I've learned about you despite the shitty date venue."

I chuckled along with him and pursed my lips. Finally, I said, "Yeah okay, it sucked if I'm being honest."

"Ha!" Dixon clapped his hands. "I knew it. But hey, at least I'm realizing that now."

"Yes, you are," I said, nodding. "Good job."

"I'm also realizing that I wasn't reading your signals very well," he said, looking sheepish. "Sorry, if I was...I don't know, too fast, too weird-"

"It's okay," I said, waving my hand. "Dates are so tricky. People make mistakes. I hope I wasn't too uptight."

"You weren't!" Dixon said. "Listen...I just hope you're willing to give me another shot. Because the truth is, I feel really strongly about you. I can't really explain it. Maybe that's also why I brought you here actually. I was nervous at how intensely I felt? Afraid it might come off weird."

I sighed in relief. Everything he was saying seemed to agree with my anxieties as well as my reassurance that he was my soulmate. I felt as if we were making each other honest. And isn't that what soulmates are supposed to do? Bring out the best in each person?

"Of course, I'll give you another chance," I said softly. I looked at him and maybe I batted my eyes just a little bit, hoping he'd read this signal correctly.

Dixon's gaze drifted to my lips. "In that case, can I try for a kiss goodnight, Ellie?"

"Yes, you can," I whispered. Dixon met my lips and the kiss was nice if not electric.

Nice is underrated, I thought. There was just a hint of

tongue, but he didn't push it, which I appreciated. I smiled warmly at him and said my goodbyes.

Yeah, I thought, as I made my way inside. *He's definitely the one.*

And yet, after I brushed my teeth, washed off my make-up, walked Indiana, changed into my pyjamas, and climbed into bed, it wasn't Dixon who gave me some dirty thoughts in the dark.

It was Mateo and the three men with him.

ELLIE

In the morning, there was a text message from Dixon waiting for me.

Had a great time. Wondering if you'd like to come to my place for dinner. I promise- no basketball.

I did a little happy dance in my pyjamas, which I was grateful nobody could see. But it was early to be texting so I didn't respond yet. The giddiness followed me as I showered and got ready for work. I thought about that kiss again. Maybe it had only seemed underwhelming because of what a let down most of the date had been. Dixon wasn't a *bad* kisser, he was pretty decent. His lips were warm and soft. I figured any doubts I had about the guy were probably the fault of my subconscious. It's easy to self-sabotage when you're right on the verge of something good in life. And those four gorgeous men who'd been on my mind, they were probably just a distraction I'd latched onto because I was nervous about finding my true soulmate.

Yeah, I thought. That's it. Silly Ellie being afraid of a bright future and real love. At least I knew what the problem was. I'd go into this dinner date with Dixon with the best of expectations.

I had a few showings at one particularly hot house that day, so I dressed up a little in my best skirt suit. My ponytail remained sleek and low as usual. But I put on a bit of a smokey eye with the makeup. After the first two showings, I texted Dixon back. He responded quickly, seeming enthusiastic about me replying, and we made plans for me to come over that night.

The anticipation made me excited and I had to calm myself down so as not to be hyper around my clients. In my experience, people didn't want a hyper person selling their house.

We'd planned for me to come over right after work. That meant I couldn't change into date clothes. But at least I was wearing my best suit. When I clocked out for the day, I went to the restroom and took my hair down, fluffing it up for the date. I put on a darker lipstick I kept in my purse just in case and redid my eye makeup.

This date, I decided, was going to be fantastic. Dixon was hot and likable and the fates had destined us to be together. My doubts were just me being ridiculous and the assumptions that come with first impressions.

Dixon lived on the fringes of Boulder in a nice building with a flower garden in front. I took five minutes needlessly primping in the car and then took a breath and made my way in. I was barely done tapping on his door when he answered, a mischievous smile on his face.

"Do you like ratatouille?" Dixon said, slowly opening the door wider.

"You can make ratatouille?" The subject of cooking skills had never come up. But if he could cook things like ratatouille, I was impressed.

"I can *attempt* to make ratatouille," Dixon said, chuckling.

"No, I've made it before actually. I guarantee nothing. But I think it's good."

"I'm sure it's great," I said, as he took my coat. The thought that he could make something like ratatouille eased my mind. It was an interesting juxtaposition with the guy who'd taken me to a loud sports bar and it certainly got my hopes up. I ran a hand through my hair, feeling somehow both over *and* underdressed in my skirt suit. "Sorry about the formality here. I came straight from work and I had two showings today. I don't always wear a suit, but when I have a high end showing, I really go for it-"

"Hey, hey, hey," Dixon said softly, stepping into my space and giving me the bedroom eyes. He pressed a finger to my lips. "No apologies necessary. You look fantastic."

"Thank you," I said. I saw him bite his lip and his gaze roved up and down my figure. I supposed my skirt was a little short and my legs were bare, ending in heels that made me nearly Dixon's height. He nodded to himself and hang up my coat and I took a breath, feeling just a little self-conscious.

I took a look around while following Dixon into his kitchen. His place seemed pretty typical for a bachelor pad. My realtor's eye couldn't help but take stock of the place. He had nice hardwood floors and a few area rugs. It was minimalist with store-bought looking artwork hanging on the neutrally painted walls. The lights were turned down low and there were a couple of candles lit on the dining table. The style was a little generic, but very nice and another little surprise for me. It wasn't what I'd picture immediately for a construction worker who frequents sports bars. But there again were my silly assumptions.

Dixon's kitchen was as immaculate as the rest of his place, all whites and neutrals and steel accents. I leaned against the counter and watched him chop vegetables. He seemed to know his way around a stove.

My stupid brain immediately wondered if Mateo the Life Saver knew how to cook. I shook my head and stole a piece of bell pepper. "You cook a lot?"

"When I can and I'm not too tired from work." He held up a bottle of wine. "Vino?"

With that, the conversation flowed pretty easily. We sat down to dinner an hour later and the ratatouille was better than he'd given himself credit for, not that I was an expert on French cuisine.

I felt as if Dixon had paid close attention to everything I'd hated about our first date and done his best to go for the opposite. When dinner was over we sat for a while, sipping wine and talking. I felt a little stiff from work and rubbed my neck and Dixon perked up, watching me.

"You alright?"

"Oh, yeah," I said. "Just a little knotted up. Nothing serious."

"I can take care of that," he said, rising. He came around behind me and started rubbing my shoulders. The gesture made me smile and I relaxed into his touch. He was pretty good with his hands and I let my eyes close, enjoying his talented fingers working out the kinks in my neck and back. After a couple of minutes, I felt his fingers gently trace the line of my neck and I stiffened a little. I couldn't say why. There was nothing wrong with his touch. We'd kissed the night before and things seemed to be going well now.

It just felt...off.

I heard him rustling behind me and then lips were kissing my neck. I stiffened even more. I felt as if a stranger were touching me, but I felt bad saying anything. That was stupid too. Of course, I should say no when I'm uncomfortable. But I didn't understand what the problem was and didn't know how to explain it. He was gently licking my neck but it felt weirdly gross as if a snake was slithering over my body. His hand abruptly grabbed my breast and I pushed him away, getting to my feet.

"Hey," Dixon said, frowning at me. I backed up against the wall, feeling a little bit shaky, partly because I couldn't understand myself why I was so uncomfortable. "You alright?"

"Yeah," I murmured. "I dunno. Felt a little fast, I guess? I don't know. Maybe just..." I swallowed and shook my hands out. "Slow things down a little."

Dixon raised his hands and walked towards me, slowly, like he was approaching a frightened deer. "I can slow things down."

I chuckled, feeling foolish. "Good. Okay."

He stepped into my space so we were toe to toe and tipped my chin up so I was looking at him. "It's just me," Dixon said. He pecked me on the lips. "I like you."

"I like you too," I said reflexively. He kissed me, deeper this time and I rested my hands on his waist. I've always sort of enjoyed making out and this wasn't bad.

But that snakey feeling came over me again. I was just about to push him away and claim headache for lack of any better ideas when he shoved his hand up skirt. His palm sliding up my thigh sent blaring sirens off in my mind and I shoved him away hard.

"Hey! I said I wanted slow, and that's your move?" I moved away from the wall, thinking fast. This was *all* wrong, I thought with sudden clarity. This had *always* been wrong and I'd been trying to desperately justify it the entire time.

"What the hell is your problem?!" Dixon shouted. His entire face changed. He looked truly angry. "What did you think was going to happen tonight?"

I grimaced at his implication and said, "Whatever I agree

to is what happens," I said, sneering. "Ever heard of consent? Jesus."

"Oh my God," Dixon said, rolling his eyes. "Why is it always sluts who won't shut up about that shit?"

"You're disgusting," I said, practically hissed at him, already making my way to the door. "And I'm out of here."

I dashed out of his apartment without looking back, half afraid he was going to drag me back kicking and screaming. He was a terrible date and a shitty guy, that was for sure. But it was more than that. Something about him made my skin crawl and I'd been too blinded by belief in the spell to see it. I peeled out of my parking spot in front of his building and drove too fast, still feeling shaky. At a stop light, I realized that I'd left my coat at his place and also that he'd texted me several times.

I'm sorry. Please come back.

That was rude of me.

Come back, Ellie.

Maybe it was my abruptly soured opinion of him but the texts read as sort of menacing to me and I threw my phone in my purse, shuddering. I was all the way home before I realized that I'd based all my assumptions on him saying *he* thought we were destined to be together. It had probably just been a line and here I'd thought it was the spell working on him.

I was still shaky and I felt I needed to calm down and think somewhere quiet. Instead of going up to my apartment, I pulled out of my spot again and headed to Settler's Park. The spot where I'd conjured that spell was also nice for meditation. I'd done a lot of good contemplating there. It would be chilly there at night without my coat, but I felt I needed some time with my own thoughts and the sounds of the forests to comfort me.

I meditated for about an hour and slowly came to the

determined conclusion that Dixon had been a huge mistake and I should never see him again. But I'd also come to the conclusion that Mateo and his three companions meant something. The way we'd looked at each other at the bar, the world blurring around us, made me wonder if it hadn't been those men I was feeling pulled towards. I couldn't say for sure but the closest thing I'd felt to a magical compulsion had been when those men were around. And Mateo had saved my life, which made me think he was safe.

I resolved to find them again and see if my instincts were right this time. I just needed magic to guide me.

ELLIE

I waited until I got home to text Dixon one last time and tell him in no uncertain terms that I didn't want to see or speak to him again. I told him not to text me back or call me. I was probably overly polite about it too. Of course, he texted back immediately. Then he texted me back multiple times. The texts started out conciliatory and apologetic and eventually turned menacing again.

I think you'll come to regret this, he wrote.

It seemed to be worded very carefully, like a softened threat, and it sent a chill up my spine. At home, I got ready for bed and tried to ignore my phone. He was making me nervous and I hated that. I also hated the thought that I might see him outside work on Pearl Street. I assumed he was working close by since we'd run into each other at the deli. Maybe I could order delivery at lunch for a while just to play it safe. At least I could go to the office through the parking garage if I wanted to. Though it didn't seem at all fair that I had to go to such lengths to avoid a spurned guy who was freaking me out.

I crawled into bed that night and called Indiana up,

letting him sleep next to me just for the comfort. I put my phone on silent and watched some late night TV. But I was restless in bed. I was full of worry about what Dixon might do and I was also fearful that somehow I'd missed my chance to find out if Mateo or any of his three friends was the one.

I didn't sleep for hours.

The next morning, I woke up worried again. When I looked at my phone and saw that he'd called five times, a chill ran down my spine. He'd left voicemails and I deleted them without listening. I blocked his number, which I should've done in the first place. But I was still spooked. Aggressive guys like him could get really scary when they felt wronged. I knew I didn't have any showings scheduled so I called in for a mental health day. I figured I'd been working hard for so long, I deserved it anyway. Even my boss seemed to agree when he texted back. I just didn't want to risk running into Dixon somehow and I was also interested in maybe finding a spell I could use to protect myself from him just in case.

But first, a little self-care. I took a bubble bath and listened to some soft music. Indiana seemed very interested in what I was doing. He was probably confused that I wasn't going to work. In the bath, I let my fantasies about Mateo and his friends fly. I'd only seen the four of them together the one time but if I hadn't been with Dixon at the time, I wondered what might have happened. I certainly would've talked to Mateo and it would've made sense. The man was both ruggedly handsome and had saved my life. But I'd felt just as pulled to be near *all* of them if I was honest with myself, and I didn't know what that meant.

I let myself imagine Mateo suddenly showing up and me inviting him into my bath. I thought of him stripping off his clothes and slipping into the bubbles with me, his hot hands all over my body. I imagined his hands on my bare breasts, his thumbs flicking my nipples; teasing before he followed those touches with his tongue. The fantasy got me hot and bothered enough that I slipped a finger inside myself, thinking of him being sweet but seductive and caring the way Dixon hadn't been. I imagined riding him in the bath as I brought myself to the brink, furiously rubbing my clit by the time my fantasy became Mateo thrusting into me and heatedly kissing me, the stubble on his chin chafing my soft skin in the best way. When I came, I cried out, and hoped the neighbors couldn't hear me.

"Oh, wow," I muttered to myself, catching my breath.

It was hard not to wonder if the reality could live up to the fantasy.

After my bath, I treated myself to some French toast, but while it was cooking, I consulted some of my spellbooks. I figured if there was a spell out there that could keep away dangerous men, I could probably handle it unless it was too advanced. I fed Indiana and ate my breakfast while pouring over my books. Somehow I'd imagined it would be easy to find something I could cast on the fly.

A couple of hours later, I'd looked through every single spellbook page by page. The best I could do was a spell of protection against unwanted attention, but I'd need the feather of an entire peacock to pull it off. I didn't exactly have that handy and I already knew I wouldn't be able to get my hands on something like that in less than two days. I needed protection *now*. I considered inventing my own spell, but I'd never done that before. I'd only tweaked existing spells. Maybe I could find a base to start with...

It would be a lot of work and I hadn't devised many complicated spells in a while. That sort of stuff took thought and with how stressed I was over the Dixon thing, I really needed to clear my head. In my younger days, whenever I needed to have a good think, I went hiking. One of the reasons I loved Boulder so much was the access to nature. It had been too long. It was always something I thought of and never ended up doing. Occasionally, I would make a little time for some meditation up in the woods, but I hadn't been hiking in ages.

I decided to take myself for a little walk.

Since I had not been hiking in a while, I decided not to push myself too hard with anything arduous. The McClintock trail up in Chautauqua would do just fine. In the middle of a weekday, I figured there would hardly be anyone around. But the scenery around that area was always peaceful and pretty. It was the perfect place to spend some time with myself and get my scrambled head together.

I had to dig in my closet to find my good hiking gear. It had been *way* too long. I wore jeans and a sweatshirt and my favorite denim jacket that I'd had since college. My hiking boots were in the very back of the closet and it took a little while to beat the dust off the things. It had been deceptively overcast lately so I found a little bottle of sunscreen and slipped that in my pocket with a bit of insect repellent I'd dug up in my bathroom cabinet. I hooked a water bottle to my belt loop and wore an old ballcap of my mom's that I only wore when I went hiking.

I felt like Indiana was looking at me skeptically as I got ready and I raised my eyebrows at him. "You think I can't hike?" I said to my dog. "I can hike. It's just been a while. ...Don't look at me like that."

The weather was crisp and cool outside, but the clouds were moving quickly, the sun poking in and out as they moved across the sky and came back again like they couldn't quite make up their minds. I drove up into the mountains and it had been so long that I nearly got lost, not paying much mind to the GPS because the drive was so pleasant. When I found the parking for the McClintock trail, I thought at first I wasn't in the right place, it was so deserted. I'd been bracing myself for kids on field trips but the place appeared very empty.

At the start of the trail, I sighed and took a sip of water. I had friends in Boulder, mostly from work. Lately, we'd all been busy, but we still went out to happy hours or had game nights. None of them were very outdoorsy types though, which I'd always teased them about since they lived in Boulder. I think that made them even more resistant to things like hiking and camping. I couldn't get them out on a trail for anything. So, I had always been alone when I went out to commune with nature. Maybe that was for the best. As a witch, I had a relationship with nature that most humans didn't quite understand. Yet it had always felt a bit lonely, even when I was contented enough to find my peace in the murmuring trees and the whisper of the grass. I wished I had somebody to share it with, preferably somebody who could begin to understand it.

I wondered if Mateo and his friends were outdoorsy types?

I took a deep breath, reflecting on that, and set off on the trail. I felt so foolish for having ever imagined that Dixon was the person I'd be sharing things like this with. Perhaps I should have enhanced the spell for finding my soulmate. It had been far too easy to fall into thinking that that jerk was the one for me. Too bad the spell couldn't just put a mark on the forehead of my soulmate so I could pick them out in a crowd. Relying on a vague feeling of connection was a little bit tricky. If I felt that for anyone, it was for Mateo and his merry band of hotties. Which threw things a bit out of whack. How could I feel that same supernatural sensation of connection with four men?

My thoughts were busy, humming in my mind. I set them aside and focused on my senses. I breathed in and out, the air just cool enough to sting slightly in my nose. I smelled the trees. I smelled jasmine somewhere. I smelled wet earth. At a fork, I went left and up the steeper incline of a hill, and relished the good stretch in my legs as I made the climb. The crunch of my boots in the dirt and leaves and rocks was satisfying and rhythmic. My steps were regular and I found a kind of pattern with them and my breathing, the percussion under the song of leaves and wind. Poppies were in bloom in reds and yellows and I reached out to brush their petals with my fingertips. The effect was meditative. I felt like I was being recharged a bit. I walked for a good hour, almost entranced by the steadiness of my own steps and the buzz of the trees. I memorized each turn I took but I opted for the branches of forks that seemed like the least likely choices.

It occurred to me that taking the road less travelled might be a habit I should start getting into. I'd been in a strange position my entire life. I was a witch, which would be thought of as a strange and unconventional and even unbelievable thing by so many conventional people. Yet I didn't really think of myself that way. I'd taken a conventional job and I lived a very conventional life. But I suppose I'd always felt as if I were caught between the two worlds a bit. Perhaps more so than if I were a witch and making my living in the magical underbelly of the world, or if I at least knew more magical people and creatures. I'd never really sought them out. The only witches I'd ever known were in my own family.

I felt now as if things might be changing. Maybe I had to

fully embrace the unmistakably unconventional side of my life that I'd always ignored.

At the crest of a hill, I felt just a little bit lightheaded. I hadn't eaten in a bit and I took a seat on a nice, low, flat rock to enjoy the view and have some trail mix and water. The green hills rolled before me, fringed by lush trees and the occasional burst of bright poppies. The place was so deserted, it gave me the feeling of having the world to myself. I felt a keen sense of loneliness at that yet I had a feeling of peace as if everything was going to work out in the end. I sat there, breathing and drinking water, and listening to the earth. I closed my eyes and tried to access my instincts as a witch; everything I had been taught by my mother. I felt like I was being told to stretch myself, to look for that which wasn't the obvious choice. Dixon had been an obvious choice and he had been so wrong.

There was something terribly *not* conventional about the idea of Mateo and those three men. I kept thinking of them again and again.

Yes, the trees seemed to say. *Find them.*

"Well, okay trees," I muttered to myself, stretching as I sat there on the little boulder. I felt mildly silly about it. "If you say so."

I was about to get up again and make my way back down the hill when a rustling nearby took my attention. I had a *feeling* suddenly, an important feeling. The trees seemed to say I should wait, so I waited. The hairs on the back of my neck were standing up, but I stayed right where I was purely on faith, hoping that whatever this inexplicable feeling was that something important was about to happen, would not kill me at least.

I heard a low kind of breathing behind a bush. There was something close by and it was big. I waited patiently. My water and food were put away. I was suddenly rather glad I hadn't brought anything like beef jerky with me just in case. I sat silently, not moving a muscle.

It was the paws I saw first, peeking out from beneath a shrub. They were huge; cat paws in the unmistakable yellow-brown of a mountain lion. The cat was trying to hide, or it had been. Now it began to ever so slowly creep out from behind the bush. I saw its eyes next as the leaves and branches were gently shoved aside. It was moving so slowly, it took me a full minute to realize it was really moving at all. Yet eventually, the entire lion appeared, creeping out of the bushes. Its head was lowered, its great shoulders hunched up around its ears. I saw it sniff the air, its mouth slightly parted and its eyes wide and fixed on me. My heart pounded and my chest heaved as I breathed slowly. I couldn't remember ever coming so close to such a large predator. Deer had come right up to me plenty. I'd spotted bears before but always let them be. Yet I was absolutely certain I was supposed to remain where I was, and allow this encounter to happen. I was somehow sure I would not be hurt.

"Hello," I whispered.

The lion was not three feet away from me. It stood in the clearing, frozen in mid-stride, just *looking* at me. I felt as if it was trying to tell me it was safe. Usually with animals, it seems to be the reverse as you attempt to gain their trust. But the lion was now trying to gain my trust as it waited there, calmly looking at me.

I didn't know what I should do. I felt as if I were possibly meeting an important person and did not speak their language.

"I'd pet you," I said very softly, "if I was sure you wouldn't kill me. Oh my God, this is the stupidest thing I've ever..."

I could swear the lion smiled. He (pretty sure it was a he from what I'd seen of lions on TV) ducked his head and approached slowly. I couldn't imagine that he wanted me to pet him. People don't pet lions in the wild. People also don't sit on rocks and talk to lions. I'm pretty sure. This entire encounter was completely insane.

"You are so beautiful," I whispered. The depth of color in his fur and the amber tint of his eyes struck me as so handsome. Or at least, as handsome as an animal could be. I tried not to tense up. He wasn't showing any aggressive or predatory behavior. As far as I knew, lions didn't generally attract prey by lulling them into a false sense of security. "You're the most beautiful thing I've ever seen."

The lion had been moving so slowly, but suddenly I realized he was just inches away. I was sitting down and he was nearly at eye level. If he'd wanted to, he could have pounced and I would have been dead; mauled painfully and probably slowly and left to die bloody and maybe half-eaten on the McClintock trail for some wayward Boy Scouts to find. But every instinct within me said that this lion had only peaceful intentions.

The lion nuzzled my knee. I don't know what else to call it. He pushed his broad head against my leg as if cuddling up to me or leaving his scent. Strictly speaking, I wasn't sure if it was possessiveness or affection. But it was as sweet as if it had been a housecat doing it, even though it was impossible to forget the power and grace of that animal even as he rubbed his head against me. When I giggled he looked up and I swear he was laughing with me. Not literally perhaps, but his eyes were dancing. In that moment, I knew beyond a shadow of a doubt...

"You're a shifter," I whispered.

I knew about shifters but to my knowledge, I'd never met one. Not that I would know. When they're in human form, shifters are impossible to tell from regular humans unless you're also a shifter and can sniff them out. But there was something about this lion's eyes. He just looked too human.

Not that animals can't experience some deep emotions and have motivations of their own. But this lion was practically having a silent conversation with me and I could see a kind of deep sentience in his eyes that I'd never seen in an animal before.

Now I saw him register surprise. It had definitely understood me.

"You are," I said, smiling slowly. "You're a shifter, aren't you?"

The lion nodded and I nearly fell over. That meant he could also shift into human form whenever he wanted to though I sort of hoped he wouldn't. There was something sort of sacred about this semi-conversation, this intimate exchange between us. There was a magic to knowing that this lion could be anyone I met on the street. He could be the barista at Starbucks or one of my clients or anyone at all.

The lion nuzzled my hand that rested atop my knee and I got the feeling I was supposed to pet him. That did sort of surprise me. I'd always sort of assumed that humans petting shifters like house cats would be considered patronizing or something. But since this lion was making the first move, I went along with it. I felt like I was having some precious honor bestowed upon me.

"Your fur is so sleek," I said. "You really are gorgeous. I've never met a shifter before either. This is a first for me. I came out here just to think. I've been kind of… I trusted a man and he tried to hurt me. It...messed me up a little bit and I had to clear my head."

The lion looked very concerned by this. He turned his head and glanced over his shoulder as if trying to figure out what it might to do help. But it made me feel better just to pet his head, and he leaned into the touch. I had the strangest feeling as we quietly communed that we'd met before. He suddenly seemed familiar. For a moment the feeling was so strong that I was embarrassed at failing to recognize some old friend.

"Do I know you?" I said. The lion looked up at me, slightly wary. "I feel like I know you?"

He seemed to smile slyly then as if teasing and pushed at my knee with his nose.

"You're teasing me now," I said. "I'm sure I do know you. You could shift back now, couldn't you? And show me exactly who you are? But you're not going to."

The lion shook his head.

I laughed at that and he seemed pleased by it. "That's okay then," I said. "I don't want you to."

We sat like that for a while, content in each other's company. Eventually I felt as if I was probably holding the lion up. He doubtless had a human life to get back to, and things to do. It felt odd to make pleasantries and say goodbye but the lion was pretty good humored about the whole thing. He left me with one final sweet rub of his head to my leg when I stood up and I scratched him between the ears before making my way back down the trail.

As I headed back to my car, I felt better about things and more content than I had in a long while.

Oddly, when I got home, all I could think about was Mateo and those three men. I had perhaps erred in taking an entire day off. I felt better about things but also like I needed something to do. I had the strangest, most surreal feeling about my life, as if having made the decision to perhaps embrace the unconventional, something was already changing for me. I felt as if I needed to go out and find the thing, the soulmate, the change I was supposed to be getting or making. Maybe before it found me.

Having just had an encounter with a real-life lion shifter, I felt just a little bit restless to go find some other adventure too. At home, I showered, feeling sweaty and grungy from the long hike. I stood around my apartment, wrapped in a towel, trying to decide what to do next. Spellbooks were scattered across my dining room table but all that just reminded me of Dixon and my flawed attempts to interpret my soulmate spell.

What if he came back for me?

What if he tried to hurt me?

All those worries and fears threatened to harsh the strange but satisfying buzz I'd gained on the hike. I needed to get out and try to see the world with my new slightly unconventional eyes. I bit my lip and messed around on my phone, trying to think of what to do with the rest of my day. It wasn't even early evening yet but it was late afternoon. That made it a not inappropriate time for an early drink.

I never went to bars myself. I'd thought about it from time to time. It seemed like something a really confident person could do, to sit at a bar just to have a drink in your own company without any intention of picking someone up. I'd watch movies where a character struck up a conversation with somebody in a bar and feel jealous of that easy social interaction. Not that I have trouble with being social. But making conversation with a stranger in a bar always seemed like a particularly advanced level of sociability to me.

"I'm gonna do it," I muttered to myself, now changing into a skirt and a simple sleeveless top. "I'm going to go have a drink in a bar with myself...because it's something I would not normally do."

It seemed like a good way to take the edge off and enjoy my free day anyhow.

The question remained, which bar to frequent. I only knew the ones near work and that wouldn't be any fun.

There was a dark, quiet little place a few streets down from the office, just far enough away from work not to run into any of my colleagues and off the beaten path enough to retain some mystique. I decided to skip driving and took a Lyft over after looking up the place on my phone.

Leonardo's was even smaller and darker on the inside than it had looked from the outside, but it was long and narrow with plenty of little nooks and crannies to hide in. I ordered myself a Dirty Martini and forced myself to sit at the bar and not hide away. There were only three other people in the place and only one of them sat at a bar; he was hunched over on the end and I couldn't get a good look at him. My gaze kept straying in his direction though, as if magnetically attracted, as I sipped my martini. Jazz was playing softly. Billie Holiday was singing. It gave the place a noir kind of feel.

I had felt all day as I'd been trying on different parts of my life and I smiled to myself, thinking that I'd just entered the Noir Section.

"It's you." The voice was low and husky and it came from the end of the bar.

I turned my head and gasped slightly. The man at the end of the bar was Mateo Marquez and he looked at me now, blinking in astonishment. Somehow, each time I saw him, he seemed better looking. He had thick, black hair in a tight buzz cut but it only framed his handsome, lantern-jawed face, a bit of stubble decorating his jaw. His intense, dark eyes focused on me and I found myself smiling, tipping my glass in his direction.

"It's me," I said simply.

Mateo opened and closed his mouth and finally said, "Do you mind if I come over there-"

"Not at all," I said. I felt that sense again that I think was the sense I'd been waiting to feel with Dixon. I felt immediately as if I'd been meant to come to this bar and run into him here. I would have thought he'd been following me after running into him at Double's, only he was already here when I walked in. I wondered if he thought I'd followed him. "I promise I'm not stalking you," I said lightly.

"I didn't think so." He smiled warmly. He was drinking something clear and brown from a highball glass and we tipped our glasses together before each taking a sip. "So what brings you here at…" He checked his watch. "Four o'clock?"

I bit lip and shrugged. "It's happy hour, right?"

Mateo raised his eyebrows and look around him. "Not terribly happy looking here. But I guess so, yes."

"I took the day off today," I said. "I needed a little mental health day."

"Me time."

"I guess so," I said, chuckling. "And I assume you're here because at some point I may need you to save my life?"

"I mean, that's not why I *thought* I was coming here," Mateo said, grinning. He had a lovely smile; straight white teeth all in a line, and a deep dimple in his right cheek. "But if you do need some lifesaving, I will definitely keep an eye out."

"Thank you," I said. "That's good to know."

"You know, um…" Mateo cleared his throat. "I was just wondering, that *was* you I saw at Double's last night?"

"You know it was," I said, raising an eyebrow. "You looked right at me. You and um... your friends?"

"Roommates," Mateo said. "I mean, technically cousins but I don't really know how we're related, it's so distant."

"Oh."

How strange, I thought. But sort of interesting.

"Yeah," Mateo said, nodding. "Yeah, I know it was you, I just… You looked so…"

"Out of place?" I said wryly, taking another sip of my drink. "I was. Not exactly my scene."

"That guy didn't seem like your scene either," Mateo said. "If I'm being honest."

"I thought he would be," I said quietly. "But...no. Anyway, you know what, I'm not going to talk about that guy or that night or that bar. Tonight I'm..."

"Someone else?" Mateo said, tipping his head.

"Someone else who is also me," I said firmly. "If that makes any sense."

"I think it might," Mateo said. "I guess that's for you to say."

"Good. Then I say it's true." I leaned on my hand and fidgeted with the plastic toothpick bearing a giant olive that I was planning on saving for the end of my drink. "And what about you?"

"Me?"

"You seem like somebody who would be busy in the middle of the day," I said.

"I am," Mateo said darkly. "I haven't had a day off in a while. But I had a few hours to myself today so..." He held up his glass. "Drink"

"Needed to take the edge off too, huh?"

"You know, I really like my life," Mateo said, frowning into his glass. "It's just a lot sometimes. I feel like eh... Sometimes I think it's missing that final thing that could tie it all together. You know?"

"Yeah," I said, surprised at how much he was reminding me of me. "I definitely know. Is it a love you're looking for?"

"Yeah..." Mateo said. He eyed me like he wanted to say something and was holding himself back. "It's more like, I *have* a lot of love...my roommates and I, my friends, I should say. I'm very close to them. We have... a lot of love to give? It's like we need to put it somewhere. And we just need..."

"The right person," I said.

"Exactly."

What a lucky person that would be, I thought. I didn't completely understand what he was describing but it did sound like a sweet idea in general.

"But you can't force that kind of thing," Mateo said, frowning. "If somebody's not ready for it."

"No," I said, nodding. "Of course, not."

"Hey, so if you're not quite yourself right now... Then who are you?" He grinned at me again, raising his eyebrows.

Maybe I'm the woman who fools around with a stranger in a bar, I thought.

That was a pleasant if unbidden thought. Though not completely unbidden, I suppose, since I had been imagining Mateo surprising me in my bath just that morning. I'd thought about riding him and how he'd be so hot and firm beneath me. I started to feel warm just thinking about it again and I knew I was blushing. The bar was a little dimly lit. I hoped that would give me some cover.

"I am..." I drained the last of my drink and said, "I am a witch." I smiled, sticking my tongue between my teeth. For all he knew, I was just being fanciful. I could go with that. That could work for Afternoon Martini Ellie.

"A witch!" Mateo laughed at that and leaned on his hand. "I like that."

"Mmm." I sucked on my giant olive and took a bite and saw his gaze go to my mouth, watching me suck on the remainder of the olive for a moment before I ate that too. I watched him swallow, his expression only briefly flickering.

"Alright then, I'm a soldier," he said.

"Interesting," I said. "A soldier."

"A soldier who's come back from war," Mateo said. "Where I fought many battles."

"Oh yeah, well I've cast many spells. I've bent men to my will."

"I bet you have," Mateo said, sounding serious. He motioned for the bartender to bring me another. "I've got this round."

"Oh, that doesn't seem fair. You did save my life already."

"Then get the next one," he said.

The bartender brought me another dirty martini and I nodded my thanks before taking a sip. This one was stronger in the best way and it felt good going down. I peered at Mateo over the rim of my glass and frowned. "Have you really been to war?"

"No, not like..." He sighed. "I've been in a few...fights. A few big ones. I haven't been in the military. It's more like...I'm in charge. You know? I have to look after my people and sometimes the stakes are very high. I worry too much."

I frowned at Mateo, feeling a swell of that connection again, like I shouldn't let him out of my sight if I could help it. "Have you ever killed anyone?"

Mateo inhaled and stared straight ahead. I watched him throw back the rest of the liquor in his glass and I didn't really need more of an answer than that but he said, "Yep. I have."

I let out a breath and took a long sip of my martini. I hadn't intended things to get so heavy. But now I felt invested in Mateo and more than that, I felt as if I was *supposed* to be invested in Mateo. I had a hard time putting too much faith in those kinds of feelings though, especially after Dixon. But I found myself wanting to *know* him, or at least the version of him that hung out in bars alone in the afternoon.

"Who did you kill?" I found myself asking.

"When I was first living with my friends," Mateo said slowly, staring down into his empty glass. "We were living in

Italy at the time actually. We didn't live there long. It was just a whim really. There was a gang of… Well, there were some people who didn't like my kind… I mean people like me? Just wanted to start trouble, I guess. Very territorial types even though we were really just visiting. We were out one night. We were living in the countryside. My cousin, Javier, he wanted to go in this kind of pub? It was just a hole in the wall, didn't even have a name, but they were supposed to have really good wine. Javier loves his wine. But it was that gang's turf. People like us weren't allowed there, I guess. He walked in and before I knew what was happening, they had him up against the wall...jagged piece of glass to his throat…" Mateo frowned at his own hand, holding it up. "I remember the guy was holding this piece of glass in his hand, and he didn't even care that he was cutting the hell out of his own hand. That's how much he hated us. When I saw that I just… It's difficult explain. It's sort of like there's an animal inside me, and he comes out of me sometimes. When I saw somebody I loved in danger. I um…" Mateo rubbed his chin. I could tell he was about to lie a little bit and it made me curious about him, but it didn't bother me either. "I stabbed him. Then we had to run. We fled the country that night."

He took a deep breath and his gaze met mine. I felt like I'd just seen some secret part of him that maybe other people didn't get to see.

"He'll have another," I said to the bartender when he came by.

"I don't know why I told you that," he said, rubbing his eyes. "You must think I'm a complete psycho." He took his drink in his hand as it slid down the bar and gave me a nod of thanks before taking a sip.

"I think you protect the people you love," I said. "That's not a bad thing."

"It's the most important thing I do," Mateo said. "When

somebody I care about at all is in danger or somebody's threatening them I just…" He shook his head. "I get so angry, I can't see straight."

I dimly imagined Mateo punching Dixon's lights out. Wouldn't that be nice?

He was rubbing the sides of his sweaty glass with his thick fingers and I imagined sucking on one of them and gasped a little. I was getting pleasantly buzzed. Not drunk, but warm and loosened enough. I was also getting more than a little interested in the man in front of me who seemed mysterious and kind and strong.

I wanted something to *happen*, but I was nervous to make the first move.

"Sounds like you love the people you love a lot," I said. "No wonder you have so much to give, huh?" I smiled at that a little sadly. I couldn't help but wonder again what it would be like to be given that kind of love everyday. I'd been chasing my own dreams, focusing on my work and living a straight-laced, serious kind of life for so long. I had friends but not the kind of closeness Mateo seemed to have with his friends.

"I do," he said. "I just um…"

"Hmm?" I said, meeting his eyes again.

"You have a striking eyes," he said softly. "Sorry, I just… Having trouble thinking about anything else suddenly."

That didn't mean a whole lot to me. Dixon had told me I had beautiful eyes after all. It was hard not thinking it was just a line. "Sure," I said, shrugging. "What woman doesn't have pretty eyes."

"No, it's not that," He stroked his chin and squinted at me and then gestured with his hand. He looked like he was trying to figure out how to describe a painting. "I mean they're pretty, yes, but they're a little sad and smart and… They're kind, I guess. I like kind eyes."

I blushed at being read like that. I wasn't used to being under such close scrutiny. "You have…" I leaned toward him, too close maybe. "Intense eyes. Fierce eyes. Also pretty."

"I'm not usually called pretty," he said chuckling into drink.

"You are though," I muttered, feeling bashful. I was, I realized, trying to make a move now. My inhibitions were lowered just enough for me to be bolder than I usually was without doing anything I'd actually regret. I didn't know if it would work. Dixon had sort of made me feel as if I could only attract his kind of asshole. "You're very handsome."

"And you're gorgeous," he whispered. He turned toward me and I couldn't look away. Suddenly the two of us were locked into something. He raised his hand and I leaned forward just a little bit; wanting, hoping. He pressed his thumb to my bottom lip, parting his own mouth as he watched. "It's...hard not to stare at your mouth. It's so…"

"What?" I said, barely uttering the word.

"Sensual," he breathed.

The bar seemed to disappear around us and I reached up to hold his wrist in my hand, keeping it there and ducking my head a little, teasing his thumb with my lips. I watched him breathe in and thinking that this could be me being the version of myself I hadn't let out except in dreams, my tongue snuck out to taste his skin. I kept my eyes on his and kissed his thumb, ever so slowly and gently, parting my lips. He watched me with heavy-lidded eyes, his thumb cushioned between my lips. He tasted warm, salty, and a little earthy. He tasted like the outdoors in the best way.

I had no plan. I had not set out this morning to end up sucking the thumb of the guy who had saved my life a few days ago, but he was just so handsome and I felt we'd made a strange connection in the time we'd been sitting there at the bar. There was something between us. The spell, I hoped. It explained why I felt so close to him and his friends whenever I saw them.

I hope he's my soulmate, I thought dimly.

I found myself intensely hoping for that as I closed my eyes and forgetting that we were in a public place, I let his thumb slip into my mouth and sucked and licked it like it was my favorite candy. I heard him sigh and felt his other hand cradle the back of my head. I hadn't even kissed him, but I was getting wet at the strange intimacy of what we were doing there at the bar. I let his thumb slip out of my mouth and turned my head, sucking at the juncture of his thumb and finger and licking at his palm. I felt him leaning in very close and trembled with the hope that he would take it a little further and not leave me feeling like the biggest fool in the world.

When his lips met my neck, I sighed both in arousal and relief. It felt so good and I leaned closer into him as he gently tipped my head to give himself better access. His lips were hot and insistent, the stubble on his chin pleasantly tickling the sensitive skin of my throat, and he murmured my name. I kissed the inside of his wrist and he pulled back, breathless, staring at me with those intense eyes.

"Let's go in back," he said, his voice promisingly rough.

Me, the serious realtor, who performed magical spells for the practical reason of avoiding an uncomfortable date and who always did her taxes in February and who had never turned in a library book late, let the dangerously sexy man who'd yanked me back from the street, take my hand and lead me to a dark and deserted corner in the back of the bar. We were well hidden in one of those little nooks. There was a cushioned bench in the wall and he pushed me down, his eyes never leaving mine.

"Tell me to stop," Mateo said in my ear. "If you want-"

"*Don't* stop," I said. It felt like everything was the reverse of what it had been with Dixon, as I pulled Mateo to me. He sat next to me on the bench and pulled me half into his lap, giving me a long look that made my head spin before his lips met mine. He kissed me deeply and I wrapped an arm around him, my heart pounding in my chest as I slid my hand up his back, feeling the quiver of the strong muscles in his back as he wrapped his arms around me too. He tasted like whiskey and a little bit like lemon and like *him*, whatever that wonderful and mysterious flavor was.

"I really never do this," I whispered against his mouth.

He smiled against me and licked inside my mouth, making me moan before he said, "I do... But...this feels different."

I believed him somehow. I figured if it was just a line, he would have said he never did this either. And honestly, I loved the way he took control while asking for permission at the same time. He licked a stripe up my neck and impulsively I threw my leg over his lap, wrapping my arms around his neck. I looked down at him and kissed his bottom lip, lost in the taste and the heat of him. I took his hand and placed it on my thigh and he squeezed, leaning back to look at me hard as he slowly slid his way up my skirt. I nodded, breathless with anticipation and wet for him. Two thick, rough fingers pressed at me through my panties and I whimpered. He bit my bottom lip and pressed, teasing and rubbing through the cotton of my underwear.

"Ellie?" he whispered.

"Yes..."

Suddenly he was fevered and quick and I ducked my head, shutting my eyes, and praying we wouldn't be caught as his fingers yanked my panties aside. One finger slipped inside me and I moaned into his neck, pulling him close. His other hand held me firm and now it slipped down to squeeze my bottom and I ground into him, riding his finger as he plundered me with slow but firm strokes.

"Look at me now," he breathed.

I leaned back to look in his eyes and gripped his shoulders and I shook as he added a second finger. His fingertips were calloused and I bit my lip hard as they now pressed at my clit, rubbing in sure circles as I quivered, ever closer to the edge.

"You feel so good," I said in his ear.

"How good?" He whispered. "Are you going to come for me in the middle of this bar, witch?"

Something about that sent me over the edge and I bit his shoulder for something to do that wasn't screaming as an electric pleasure engulfed me, his fingers expertly working my clit as I gripped him, riding his hand. I could feel his hardness pressing against me.

"Like that," he whispered, his other hand coming up to lazily squeeze my breast. "Just like that."

He kept rubbing me there even as I was coming down, sending little shock waves of pleasure through me as I kissed his neck and the corner of his jaw and then his mouth, rocking against him. I felt *so* dirty and yet also so like *myself*; the other self that I'd been hiding for so long under that serious realtor Ellie. I had a feeling this adventurous Ellie wasn't going anywhere.

"I want to see you again," Mateo said, when I'd slid off his lap. I straightened my skirt, blushing terribly, but somehow we'd been discreet enough not to attract attention.

"You will," I said, knowing without a doubt that it was true.

He combed his fingers through my hair as I tucked my dishevelled shirt back in. He sat back in his seat on the bench, looking sick with desire and it made me smile to myself that I had caused it.

"When?" He said.

I thought to myself: *What would Adventurous Ellie the Witch do?*

"You'll find me," I said, and stood, hoping that my wobbly legs wouldn't give out underneath me. I requested a Lyft even as Mateo got up and slid an arm around me from behind, kissing my neck.

"I *will* find you, witch lady," he said softly.

I squeezed his hand and flashed him a smile of goodbye before making my way out.

ELLIE

"Oh my *God*," I said to myself, but I couldn't help but smile as I bit my lip and shut my front door behind me, sliding to the floor.

Now that I was home and back on the familiar turf of my own place, I couldn't quite believe what I had just done and I giggled into my hands, feeling sort of delicious and naughty and sexy after that impromptu rendezvous with Mateo.

I was absolutely certain that I would be seeing Mateo again. I hoped I'd be seeing his friends too. Indiana ran up to me and I swear the dog looked at me funny, like he knew I'd been up to no good. I hugged him and got up to feed him, kicking my shoes off, as I made my way to the kitchen. I plugged my phone in and didn't even look at what he'd sent. I wasn't planning on seeing him ever again.

I spent the next couple of hours just puttering around, listening to podcasts and cleaning, tidying up my spell books and doing some housework I'd been putting off. When there was a knock at the door while I was doing the dishes, I jerked, startled. My building has a buzzer and I tensed up.

How had whoever it was gotten in without buzzing? I didn't like that at all.

"It's not Dixon, scaredy cat," I muttered. But at the door, I checked the peephole. I didn't see anyone.

I thought they'd gone when there was another pounding on the door that made me jump.

"Delivery!" The voice through the door didn't sound at all like Dixon and I relaxed. I'd ordered some special eye cream from Amazon and it wasn't scheduled to arrive for another couple of days, but I figured that's what it was. "I just need a signature, please."

I opened the door just a crack, inwardly lamenting my lack of door chain. I opened it just wide enough and peaked out to see that, sure enough, Dixon was standing there, an angry glare on his face.

"Shit!" I started to shut the door but he was faster and stronger, shoving it inward and knocking me back.

I couldn't get my bearings before Dixon was grabbing me. I tried to hit him and he took both of my wrists in his meaty hand, rendering me powerless with an iron grip. We didn't speak. There were only grunts until I thought to scream and he mumbled for me to shut up, shoving me against the wall. I twisted and with one burst of strength, I managed to break away and make a run for it. I made it out the door and I yelled for help as I dashed to the staircase and raced down to the street.

"Help help help!" I was frantic and half hysterical. My building was quiet and there was no one about as I ran for the front door, but when I tripped on the wrinkle of an area rug in the lobby it slowed me down just enough for Dixon to grab me again. "GET OFF ME!"

I didn't even see them coming but all at once, Mateo and his three friends arrived, bursting through the doors of the lobby. They wasted no time in attacking Dixon and quickly getting him off of me. The fight was quick but brutal and I scrambled back to the wall as one of Mateo's friends got Dixon in a lock from behind and Mateo threw one single punch that seemed to nearly knock him right out. That wasn't quite enough though and another one of the men threw a punch, a third kicking Dixon in the stomach. Dixon stirred and Mateo grabbed him by the collar, his friend releasing his grip. Mateo shoved Dixon up against the wall and I took another step back. It was all happening so fast, I hardly knew what to think.

"You stay away from Ellie," Mateo said, locking eyes with Dixon. He hissed his words, looking ready to murder. "If you ever contact her or come anywhere near her again, we will end you. Are you hearing me?"

Dixon mumbled something inaudible and Mateo shoved him again. "Sorry!" Mateo shouted, and his hand came up to grip Dixon around the throat, choking him. "Speak a little louder?"

"Yeah," Dixon whispered. "I get it."

"That's what I like to hear, asshole." Mateo looked half crazed. He shoved him toward the doors and one of the other guys gave him a kick in the butt that sent him stumbling. After the rush of violence and terror, it was sort of funny, and I stifled a laugh. I think it was a little bit of hysteria giving me the giggles and I had to bite my lip to keep it all in. But then Dixon was gone and I took a deep breath and then another.

The five of us stood there for a moment, getting our bearings.

Mateo met my eyes and I said, "You saved my life again." The anger had gone from his eyes and when he looked at me, he softened just a little bit. "This is getting to be a habit for you."

"Yeah, I'm starting to get used to it," he said lightly, and the rest of us tittered. He winced, rubbing his hand, and I saw his bruising knuckles.

"Um, I don't know how you happened to be here," I said. They all looked at each other a bit apprehensively. It was probably *weird* and it was probably not a coincidence but I didn't know how to explain my comfort with them to myself except to say that I felt safe with them and more than that, I felt the intense pull towards them I'd been waiting for. I felt all the things I'd only been pretending to feel with Dixon. "I don't know and I don't really care. Not that I wouldn't like to know." I spoke slowly, meeting all their eyes. One looked serious with a long face, one was shorter with rounder cheeks and he was smirking a little. The third had such a beautiful face, I wondered if he modelled. They all looked at me with a similarly intense expression, except Mateo, whose expression was somehow more focused as if he were poised to protect me on a hair trigger. "But if you all have some time right now, I'd like to invite you in." I nodded at Mateo's hand. "I have some ice for that hand. Maybe we could catch our breath. If nothing else, I think we have something to talk about. Don't we?"

"Oh, I like her," the most serious looking one said softly.

I smiled at him and said, "I think I like you guys too."

"We do have some time," Mateo said. "We'd love to come up."

JAVIER

I'll tell you a secret. When Emi read aloud that bit from the clan lore about a mate who would be shared among us, I got a chill up my spine. I've *never* gotten a chill like that in my life...except once. That was the day my father introduced me to Mateo, Al, and Emi, my future pack mates. I was living with my family in a modest little house in the Basque Country. It was idyllic but I was used to it and I was eager for something new. I was especially excited to be in my own pack within the clan. Right away, I knew these men would mean everything to me. I even knew it at sixteen, flexing to try to impress them. But I'd gotten that tingle up my spine. And from the moment Mateo had said, "I'm Mateo, I'm the alpha," we were a single unit. All for one and one for all, like the three musketeers say.

Now I was feeling that tingle up my spine again so even though the four of us were paying a little lip service to the question of whether or not this Ellie woman could be our shared fated mate, I wasn't uncertain at all. I knew beyond a shadow of a doubt. She would be ours, and we would be hers.

Still though...following her into her apartment felt weird. At least Mateo had met her before. The rest of us had only seen her in that douchebagey sports bar. We'd ended up there because we felt the pull again. We were down the block, having a drink at a much different kind of place, one without servers in tube tubs. It was one of Emi's favorite spots although maybe a little *too* quiet for me. I was explaining the Marie Kondo method of tidying to Alejandro, sipping on my Jack and Coke, and then I'd felt it. We *had* to go to Double's. There was no way around it. We'd all experienced the pull at the same time. Even taking the time to close out our tabs had made us feel itchy and restless. We only felt better when we walked in the door and saw her.

God, she was beautiful. She looked miserable though, like somebody was subtly holding her hostage. She'd been sitting with that asshole who clearly wasn't appreciating her at all. I could tell, because he didn't look completely awestruck like I did just laying eyes on her in that little black dress as she sat at the table, one leg crossed over the other, her shiny, dark hair softly blowing because the AC in the place was blasting. Then she'd looked up at us and I'd thought: *I'm home.*

We couldn't stop talking about it for the rest of the night and nothing else had even happened.

Ellie let us into her place and we all kind of stood around awkwardly.

I liked Ellie's place. It made me smile. I didn't know her yet but I could tell a lot from looking around her apartment, especially when her little Welsh Corgi ran up to us. Dogs can be tricky with us. They sense that we're actually cats and that can go either way.

"That's Indiana," Ellie said, laughing as her dog ran up to us and stopped short. Her laugh was funny. It was a shrill little yelp that levelled out into something throatier. The moment I heard it, I wanted to hear it again. "Don't mind her."

Indiana froze and stared at us. Ellie's dog despising us would be easy to explain away, I figured, but it would be easier if he liked us.

We all looked at each other and Mateo crouched down and lowered his head. I snorted a laugh into my hand and glanced at Ellie, who seemed amused. If she knew Mateo was imitating a play bow and showing submission for the sake of her dog, she was dismissing it as a joke. Indiana bowed, lowering his head to his front paws. Then they were playing and Ellie laughed again, delighted.

"He likes you!" She said.

"He's cute," Mateo said, scratching Indiana behind the ears.

We all took a few minutes to adore Indiana but I hung back, taking the opportunity to get to know Ellie via her living space.

She loved elephants. I smiled to myself, spying both a small modern sculpture of an elephant that had been turned into a lamp and an area rug with an elephant border. She also had a couple of elephant figurines on a shelf. Her walls were painted peach and she had teal rugs. There was plenty of personality in the place. I liked that about it.

"Can I get you guys something to drink?" Ellie said, backing toward the kitchen. "Or eat? I've got hummus and..."

"I'd love some coffee," Alejandro said quickly.

"Sure thing!" Ellie said.

"Make yourself at home, why don't you?" I said, nudging him.

She disappeared into the kitchen and Mateo followed her. Emi was busy examining her bookshelf. Knowing him, that would take all day.

Alejandro leaned into me and quietly said, "When people

offer you something in their home, they're trying to feel more comfortable themselves. It's always better to accept."

"Huh. Interesting." I shoved my hands in my pockets and went to the kitchen. "I'll have some coffee too, if that's cool?"

"Sure!" Ellie smiled at me and I think I probably looked like a complete dope. It hit me like a mallet to the head. I felt dizzy for a second. "So…how did you guys happen to be here? To fend off Dixon?" She sounded like she was frowning as she poured water into her coffee maker. I was really worried she'd decide we were weird stalky creeps even if we had been in time to save her from a bigger creep.

"Dixon," Emi muttered, following Alejandro into the crowded kitchen. "Figures. Stupid name."

We all looked at each other again. I think we were collectively trying to figure out how to answer the question, because the truth was we'd been scattered across town as usual. Alejandro and I had been at the office, though that wasn't far from Ellie's place at least. Mateo had been in town 'running errands' (which often meant he needed a couple of hours to himself), and Emi had been at home. We'd all felt the pull at the same time, and more than that, we'd sensed that Ellie was in terrible danger. We hadn't even texted each other first, we all just started running, following our noses and the strong pull that urged us on until we heard Ellie's screams and saw her fighting that asshole off through the glass doors of the lobby.

Mateo cleared his throat and said, "We were in the neighborhood."

Ellie's eyebrows shot up, but she was smiling wryly. "You were in the neighborhood," she repeated. "Just happened to be here when he attacked me…"

"Yep." Mateo nodded.

"That's not entirely true," Emi said. "We were…not too far. And we just got this feeling. So we ran over here."

Now she looked serious, as if she absolutely believed him. But she didn't look frightened like I felt a normal person would. Because Emi's explanation made absolutely no sense if you didn't believe in things like magic or fated mates.

Ellie said, "Did you? That's interesting."

"Yeah," Emi said. He looked like he was about to say something else and stopped, blushing.

"I'm sorry I didn't say hello at Double's," Ellie said to Mateo. "God. I'm sure I would've had a much better time with you guys that night. I was just...I had a mistaken idea about him. I had reason to think he was...special? Turned out to be a complete asshole, of course. So much for my genius instincts." She shook her head and glanced down at the coffee maker, as if for something to do.

Mateo nodded at that and looked briefly a little surprised. I saw them exchange looks I couldn't read.

Mateo always thought he was so slick, but I was sure he'd met Ellie again by himself. He'd run into her or something. They were just being secretive about it. Which wasn't very surprising. And yet I didn't even feel jealous. This fated mates thing was strange in that way.

I thought of what Ellie had said about this Dixon guy. Special? That was interesting. I did sense magic about her. She wasn't a shifter, that was for sure. But I wondered if she was maybe a witch or something. But regular humans can have magic about them and not even know it, so asking could be dicey.

"Don't worry about it," Mateo said. "Didn't look like you were having a good time though."

"I wasn't," Ellie said darkly.

"You don't look like somebody who would have a good time at Double's," I piped up. It was true but I also had an urge to make her notice me. I felt as if I wanted to make some kind of impression so I would stand out a little bit, even if I wasn't jealous exactly. We'd discussed that too. We'd had some long conversation about fated mates. We were all just sort of fine with the idea of sharing a woman between us who we would all adore while drinking up whatever love she gave us back. We couldn't explain it. "You're sophisticated," I said. She met my eyes and I sighed a little. "Refined but kinda quirky. In a quiet way. And...beautiful."

The others all snickered and my cheeks burned. I felt like a stupid teenager. "Well, she is!" I blurted out.

Ellie looked a little taken aback but not unpleasantly. She stared at me and just whispered, "Thank you."

Success! We'd made a connection, I felt. Even if it was small. For a moment I felt as if all five of us were connected somehow and it was about the most satisfying sensation I could imagine.

Ellie licked her lips and looked away from me at Emi, Alejandro, and Mateo. "I feel like we're all talking around something," she said slowly. "We're pretending whatever it is that's going on here is normal. But it's not. Is it?"

The rest of glanced at each other nervously. She didn't know we were shifters and she certainly didn't know about fated mates. It was too strange seeming. She was going to push us away-

"Listen, I don't care that it's not normal," Ellie said. "I know I might seem like a pretty conventional person. I'm a realtor and I have a nice apartment... I do the crossword every day." She laughed lightly at herself. "But I'm not quite as conventional as I seem. So if this isn't quite normal... maybe that's okay? Because I know there's something between us." She gestured to all of us. "And I can't explain it, but I really want to get to know you better, all of you, I mean. Would that be okay?"

"We're all super into you!" Alejandro blurted. He clapped a hand to his face. "Oh god."

I slapped him on the back. "Smooth," I said. "Real smooth, buddy."

Ellie laughed at that and this time it was more of a giggle and she covered her mouth. I was enchanted. "That's sweet but it's not as if I can date all of you. I mean...that would be crazy. Right?"

That alarmed me for a second but I met Mateo's eyes. I've known our alpha for almost twenty years. He can say a lot with his expressions. Of course, being an alpha, a lot of the expressions are 'shut up' or 'just do what I'm telling you, Javier, holy shit' but this time I read his face as saying, 'give her time'.

That I could do. I had a feeling I would be willing to give Ellie all the time in the world if she wanted it.

"I don't see why not," Mateo said. "But let's put it this way. Why don't you get to know us. All of us. And then..." He shrugged. "We'll see what happens."

"See what happens?" Ellie poured coffee into a mug and smiled at us. "I can try that."

ELLIE

We stood around chatting and talking for so long, it was getting dark before we noticed how much time had passed. The conversation ran the gamut. I told them all about Dixon and I could sense their rising anger at how he had treated me but I also saw them trying to contain it. But we also talked about our work. They were just as interested in me being a realtor as I was in their investigative work. It all sounded pretty exciting to me. Mateo tried to play it off. He insisted that most of their job consisted of surveilling potentially cheating spouses and doing background checks for suspicious people. Still, it was more exciting than talking about the attractive backsplash in a kitchen or extolling the benefits of a hardwood floor.

There was a growing kind of tension in the room, but it wasn't a bad thing. It was more like anticipation. I wanted so badly to keep spending time with all of them and they all seemed just as interested in me.

Finally, I had to bid them goodbye. It had been a strange day. I made myself some dinner and kicked back on the couch with Indiana. I turned on the TV but I didn't really watch it. All I could think about were those Marquez boys. Although I did sleep much better that night.

In the morning, I woke up giddy. I had three showings that day, and the guys and I had agreed that they would come and hang out with me while I worked. That wasn't anything I'd done before with a guy, yet this had been my idea. I had to work, but I simply had to see them also. They needed to work too, so they decided they would switch off.

That morning at the office, I was practically on the edge of my seat with excitement. I was walking on air thinking about seeing Javier in a little bit, and then Alejandro, and then Emiliano… I kept muttering their beautiful names under my breath, picturing what Alejandro's silky, dark hair would feel like between my fingers or how Emi's elegant hands could make me feel…

"Ellie." That was my boss, Myra. She was waving a hand in front of my face.

I sat up and smiled tightly. "Hey."

"Hey," she said, chuckling. "I've been saying your name…"

"Oh, sorry."

"That's alright. You just seem like you're in a great mood today actually. I was curious."

"Oh." I ducked my head, a little bashful. "I just met some… somebody. A guy. One single guy." I shrugged. "I like him."

"That's good," she said, leaning in the doorway. "You seeing him later?"

I felt like some scandalous woman, quasi-dating four men at once. The possibilities made my cheeks burn. "Yeah," I said. "Just casual. See what happens."

"Well, that's great," Myra said nodding, peering at me over her wire-rim glasses. "Be casual. Explore your options. Good luck with your new guy."

"Thanks." I watched Myra go and muttered to myself: "Explore your options…"

The only thing that threatened to wreck my giddy mood was trying to figure out how the spell factored into the Marquezes. I'm a pretty good witch. I'm not a genius but I know what I'm doing. There was no way I'd accidentally called the fates to show me four soulmates. How would four soulmates even work? I'd called for one. All I could figure was, one of them was meant for me and maybe the feelings were so strong, I was projecting them onto all four.

I suppose what I needed to do was focus on that connection I felt with them. Surely, I would discover that it was only really pointed at one man. At first, I assumed it would be Mateo. But having spent a few hours talking with them over coffee, I felt the same about all of them.

I just needed to figure out what the fates were really telling me.

At eleven, I hopped up from my desk to go to a showing at a remodelled three-bedroom across town. I made it in record time and let myself in with a little time to spare to ready the place. I opened a couple of windows and sprayed just a little bit of Febreeze around some furniture. The owners had already moved out and left to itself, the place could get a little bit musty.

The doorbell rang and my heart leapt. When I saw Javier waiting on the other side of the screen, I beamed.

"Hi!" I said, a little bit breathless. "Glad you came."

"Me too," he said and produced two cardboard takeout containers. "I brought lunch. Hope that's okay?"

"Yes!" I said, and checked the time on my phone."Please. I've still got some time before the prospective buyers show up."

Javier was the most compact of the four Marquezes. He was just a few inches shorter but he was muscular. He had sort of a thick, solid build but was somehow still cute though, his face was nearly always smiling or smirking or cracking a grin. He was clearly the most generally cheerful of them all, and he had long, wavy black hair that nearly touched his shoulders. He was wearing a nice button-up and black pants. The day before, he'd been wearing a t-shirt and jeans. I wondered if he'd dressed up especially to visit me. I liked the thought.

Javier handed me a take-out box. He'd bought me a big Caesar salad from my favorite place. We sat on the front porch to eat since I was always very careful about crumbs during a showing. Javier didn't seem to mind at all.

"You know we had to draw straws to pick who'd visit you when?" Javier said, sipping his soda.

"What do you mean? Why?"

"Alejandro and Emi both wanted to go first," he said. "I didn't really care when I went, as long as I got to see you. But they were very nervous, I guess. About wanting to be first, maybe? So we drew straws to make it fair."

"And you ended up being first," I said, laughing. "That's hilarious. And maybe a little sad."

"Maybe so," Javier agreed, but he was laughing too. When we were done eating, Javier got to his feet and said, "So give me the hard sell."

"What do you mean?" I said as he followed me inside to throw out our take-out containers.

"For the house!" He spun around on his heel, gesturing around. "I want to see you in action!"

I rolled my eyes but Javier would not be dissuaded, so for the next ten minutes, I gave Javier my spiel; large bedrooms, dual vanity sinks, new plumbing, updated central air…

Javier abruptly cleared his throat as we loitered in the master bedroom and said in a terrible, posh British accent, "Now my wife and I, you see, we're looking for something with a, eh…a moat."

"A moat," I said, blurting a laugh.

"Yes, of course, my dear, a moat. Also, gun turrets would be preferable. Keep out the neighbors and such forth-"

I burst out laughing and Javier stared at me, his lips parted, his dark eyes wide. "You are so goddamn beautiful when you laugh," he said softly.

Javier was about exactly my height and we stared at each other as I realized how close we were standing.

"I wanted to make you laugh," he whispered. "Just to see it again."

"I'm…I'm sure you'll be seeing a lot of it," I said, feeling dizzy as he stepped a little closer.

Javier was looking at my mouth but he said, "I'm not expecting anything of you, Ellie. I'm not expecting you to-"

I cut him off with a kiss. It was impulsive, as I leaned forward and my lips met his. His mouth was soft and wanting and there was a kind of buzz inside me as his hands came up to rest on my arms and tug me a little closer. I wrapped my arms around his neck and he pulled back slightly so that I chased his mouth until he let me catch it again. I liked that. I liked that he was letting me be the pursuer. After Dixon, that made me feel like I had a little more control.

I pulled away just a little and nuzzled his nose, feeling him chuckle against me, his fingers lightly tracing my arms. He was gentle and sweet. I wondered if they were all like that.

"You are so lovely, Ellie," Javier whispered in my ear.

I was about to respond when the doorbell rang and I jerked away, though I hardly wanted to. "Shoot." I nodded behind us. "Um. The um, buyers."

"Oh yeah," he said, blinking. "I should go."

"Oh, do you have to," I said.

He smiled and pulled me forward to kiss me softly on the lips one more time. "Don't worry. I'll see you soon."

I almost got so wrapped up in another kiss, I forgot about the buyers, until the doorbell rang again. I winced, stepping away from him toward the door. It felt almost physically painful. "I'll definitely see you soon," I said.

"I'll let myself out the back," he said. And with a wink, he was gone.

~

The showing went well, except that I had to pinch my arm not to laugh, remembering Javier's little British characters every time one of the buyers asked about something. But his visit had made me cheerful and confident and it went well.

The next appointment was closer into town, a little bungalow in the middle of a line of bungalows. It was small but it would sell easily, I suspected.

When I got there, I found Alejandro waiting for me. He was parked on the street to leave the driveway for me and the clients. He leaned on his car, wearing aviator sunglasses, and grinning from ear to ear. He took off his sunglasses and bit his lip, briefly looking me up and down so subtly I almost missed it.

"Hey there, beautiful!" he chirped.

I blushed reflexively and led him inside. All the Marquez men are attractive but Alejandro is absolutely gorgeous. His features are almost delicate but I also haven't seen him without a little beard growth which only makes him more scrumptious. He'd joked to Mateo the day before that he liked to grow stubble because he was tired of being called 'pretty boy'.

I didn't tell him that he only looked prettier with the stubble.

"Hi," I said, taking him into the kitchen to talk. Somehow my ponytail had come loose, and a lock of hair fell in front of my eyes. That's not exactly a big deal, but for me, it was odd. I am immaculate the majority of the time. "Good to see you," I said.

"Good to see you too," he said. He was wearing a big, beige coat with a sheepskin lining. It looked like a designer piece which only made him look more like a model. He sidled up to me and smiled a crooked little smile as he reached up to tuck the loose lock of hair behind my ear.

"There ya go," he said, his voice low. His eyes were lighter than the other Marquezes I noticed, now that he was standing so close.

"Thank you," I murmured. I blinked at him. All my coherent thoughts seemed to have run off. It was some combination of the intense pull I felt to be close to him and his heart-stopping beauty. It was making me feel like I was in junior high all over again. "You um…you look nice," I said. I couldn't remember the last time I'd ever been so tongue-tied. I was so used to being confident and well spoken.

"God, you are so adorable right now," Alejandro whispered.

"Um…"

This is absurd, I thought. Or at least somewhere in the back of my mind, I might have been thinking. Right now the bulk of my brain power was focused on Alejandro's pink lips and heavy-lidded eyes.

"Oh gosh," I breathed, before grabbing his coat collar and yanking him forward into a kiss.

Alejandro's lips slotted with mine and I felt his tongue touch my own as our mouths parted. Javier had kissed so sweetly and I thought I'd love that best, but I loved this too as Alejandro kissed me dirty, opening his mouth wider and licking my tongue. His hands went to my hips and squeezed and I pulled him closer. I was up against the dishwasher and he pressed against me, our tongues curling around each other's before he laughed lightly and smiled against my slick lips.

"You're adorable *and* sexy as hell," he said huskily. "Now, that's not fair."

"Ah...back at you," I breathed.

Alejandro ducked his head and laughed into my neck and on impulse, I hopped up on top of the counter. I pulled him closer and parted my legs so he could step between them and he growled low in my ear before nibbling at my neck. The prospective buyers would be here any minute and this was so unlike me but I couldn't keep my hands off him. He rested his palms on my knees and I covered them with my own before slowly sliding them up my legs, underneath my skirt.

He nibbled on my earlobe. "Ellie," he whispered, pleading. He squeezed my thighs and I gasped, wrapping my legs tight around him.

Things were on the verge of getting quite *involved* when the doorbell rang.

I was really starting to hate doorbells.

"I kissed Javier!" I said when I pulled away.

"Aw, that's okay," Alejandro said, smoothing my hair back for me. "We knew what we were getting into. It's fine."

That seemed much too good to be true. "Really?" I said, disbelieving.

"You're getting to know all of us," Alejandro said, shrugging. He kissed me once more and I nearly melted into his arms again but managed to control myself and hopped down off the counter. "Now go answer the door. Just tell them I'm another buyer who's bothering you."

"Good idea," I murmured. I started to turn away and then turned back to kiss him one last time before going into realtor mode.

~

The second showing went well and I headed off to the third, feeling cheerful and confident. As far as I knew, I had no other Marquezes coming to hang out with me, but I was anticipating the next time I would see one. The thought of Alejandro and Javier's kisses made me smile to myself. And yet I was starting to hate the thought that I would eventually have to choose between them. They might be fine with me 'getting to know' all of them, but that surely wasn't going to last long. Nobody was *that* cool with sharing.

I chewed on my lip and tapped my fingers on the steering wheel. I wasn't going to think about having to choose *now.* I would let myself enjoy this. I would just focus on the moment, on those kisses, and the sensation of Javier's tongue touching mine and Alejandro's hands sliding up my legs.

I was getting myself all riled up again and at a stoplight, I took a deep breath. My phone buzzed and I glanced at it, careful to watch the light. The prospective buyer had cancelled the showing at the next house. Well, that was weird. They didn't give a reason either. As soon as I got a chance, I turned back around and headed for the office. I didn't get many short notice cancellations and it was annoying when they did happen. Making appointments around everyone's schedules was always such a pain. This particular buyer had seemed so excited about seeing the house too.

As it turned out, the fun was just beginning. I returned to the office, intent on eyeballing some potential properties online, only to find that a few possible sellers had cancelled their appointments with me over the coming week. I rarely got cancellations to begin with, much less so many at once. It just didn't happen. It was a little bit apocalyptic and it all sent a chill up my spine.

I had to wonder if somebody had cast a spell on me. A hex for financial trouble or bad business dealings. The only person who had it out for me would be Dixon. I hadn't smelled magic on him, but then that was its own sort of talent that I'd never been particularly strong at.

I tried not to panic. It was probably just a fluke. But as soon as I got home that night I cast a spell to detect any nefarious forces that might be working on me. It took an hour to brew and when it was done, I peered into the smoke of my cauldron. I didn't see anything in the marbling, oily surface. That was sort of disappointing. If I could just find out what it was then I could fight it. When I was done with the spell, I poured out the brew, spent a half hour scouring out the pot, and brewed up another spell for protection. I already had the Marquez men 'looking out' for me. I wasn't sure what that entailed but they'd been worried on my behalf, in case Dixon came back. That made me feel better, especially when I remembered the way they'd kicked his ass and sent him running.

The protection spell made me feel better too. There was no guaranteeing it would change anything. There was every chance I was just having a bad week. For a moment I wondered if the housing market had suddenly gone belly up and somehow no one had mentioned it, but that was impossible. I concentrated on the spell, carefully measuring every ingredient and repeating the words as I stirred clockwise then counter clockwise and then focused my power. The smoke turned from green to white signalling that the spell had worked and I poured out the brew and scoured my cauldron again.

I fed Indiana and ate dinner, all the while answering texts from the Marquez men. I had individual texts going with each of them as well as a group thread. They kept me *very* entertained.

That night I went to bed, sure that the next day would be

better. Either I'd had a little run of bad luck for a day or else there was certainly a good explanation for all this.

But in the morning, when I checked my email at work, I had a flood of cancellations even worse than the day before. It was as if I'd been put on a blacklist and every prospective buyer or seller in Boulder had been warned not to work with me. It made my blood run cold. I had some query emails from people who hadn't even set appointments yet and when I replied to them over the course of the morning, they either didn't answer back or changed their minds about working with me without explanation.

I was starting to legitimately panic. I also had nothing left to do all day which made panicking a lot easier.

To make matters worse, my boss popped in the door, looking dour. That didn't help my state of mind either.

"Are you alright?" she asked. She had doubtless gotten wind of my downward spiral.

"I... I guess it's just a bad week?" I said shrugging.

She shrugged. She had always been an understanding kind of person. "It happens, you know. Maybe not this extreme though.Try not to freak out. Let me know if I can help, okay?"

I nodded and smiled tightly, but inside, I was definitely freaking out. My calendar was empty and the promise of some future commission had just completely disappeared.

I had no idea what to do.

ELLIE

For a few minutes, I just sat frozen at my desk, as if waiting for an epiphany. When none came, I resolved to just keep plugging along, assuming that things would improve. I worked hard, tracking down some new leads and putting the hard sell on people who hadn't answered me or who had cancelled. Nothing seemed to be working. I spun around in my desk chair, taking deep breaths. Outside my window, there was a nice view of the mountains. I looked out and wished I could be up there somewhere, not worrying about work. I wondered again if the Marquezes liked to go hiking? How nice it would be to go up there where it was peaceful and listen to the trees with four handsome men who looked at me the way they always seemed to be looking at me.

My stomach rumbled and I winced. I'd only eaten a small container of Greek yogurt for breakfast and it was about lunchtime. I'd totally spaced on making a plan for lunch. Originally I'd planned to bring my own, just to avoid potentially running into Dixon for a while. But now I didn't want to buy take-out for lunch anyway if I had no new money coming in. The Marquezes had texted me here and there but I didn't tell any of them what was happening at work. I felt a little embarrassed about it.

I was sitting at my desk, feeling pathetic and hungry when reception called to say somebody was waiting to see me in the lobby. At first, I assumed it was a client and hoped my bad luck spurt was turning but I admit, my heart leapt when I saw Mateo waiting for me by the front desk. When he saw me, he looked up and smiled warmly.

"Hey," I said. I wished I'd thought to freshen up in the restroom for a minute.

Mateo gave me a smile that reached his eyes. "Hey there, beautiful," he said. Just that gave me butterflies. I ushered him into my office. He was carrying a bag and he set it on the desk. "I thought I'd come by and bring lunch? I hope that's okay with you."

"Oh, you godsend." I kissed him on each cheek. "I'm starving and I didn't want to go out."

"Perfect," he said.

I cleared my desk and helped him set out the food. He'd brought sandwiches from Lovebird's, chips, cookies, and drinks. My mouth watered at the sight of all the food spread out on my desk.

"Would you like chicken salad or roast beef?" Mateo said.

I jumped at the chicken salad and Mateo laughed, claiming he'd wanted the roast beef, to begin with. We sat in chairs facing each other as we ate and I couldn't believe how much my mood improved just seeing him.

"So, how's your work?" Mateo said, between bites.

I sighed around my chicken salad, noticeably deflating. I took a sip of iced tea and shrugged. "Not good. Not good at all. All these clients cancelled out of nowhere. Like just as of yesterday? I've been doing really well and suddenly I'm persona non grata. It's the weirdest thing."

"Oh, no," Mateo said, looking deeply concerned. "That's not good at all. You have any idea what's causing it?"

"Nothing concrete," I said. "Although..."

"What?"

"It occurred to me that maybe Dixon's involved," I said. It *had* occurred to me but I also wasn't letting myself think about that idea too much. The thought of Dixon affecting my career was too frightening for me to actually consider it. But I did feel a bit easier with Mateo right in front of me.

It had also occurred to me that even if I hadn't smelled magic on Dixon, maybe he knew somebody with the gift, like a wizard who didn't mind hexing some woman he didn't know for the right amount of cash. But I couldn't tell Mateo that. He'd think I was insane.

"That was actually my first thought too," Mateo said darkly. "Guys like him, sometimes they don't give up so easily. I've seen a lot of cases like that. But I'm guessing you know that already."

"I can guess," I muttered. I tried to think of something I could say instead of 'evil wizard'. It would be good to have them on the alert for Dixon, even if they didn't quite know what they were looking for. "I don't know. Maybe...maybe he's threatening my clients. Or something. Maybe he put a scathing review of me on some realtor website. I haven't looked at them. People really stick by those reviews when they're looking to work with somebody."

"It's very possible," Mateo said. "I'd really like to look into it for you if that's okay?"

"Please," I said, feeling a little safer already. "I can use all the help I can get."

"You should know," Mateo said, "any of the four of us...we'd do anything we could to help you."

I smiled softly, genuinely moved. "That's sweet of you," I said, feeling a bit tongue-tied. I ate my sandwich and Mateo smiled at me, changing the subject to more cheerful things. He told me about a weird case he was working on. An old lady had hired him to find out if somebody was secretly feeding her cat because she thought it was getting mysteriously fat.

"Why doesn't she just keep the cat inside?' I said, laughing.

"I have no idea," Mateo said. "She lets it wander off and now she wants to know where it's going and who's secretly feeding it. It's really the cat we're investigating. I've been surveilling a cat for three days."

The thought was so ridiculous that I couldn't stop laughing. When I finally caught my breath I said, "Well, how hard can that possibly be?"

"Harder than you think!" Mateo said, his thick eyebrows shooting up. "Cats are very stealthy!"

When we were done eating, Mateo helped me clean up, but I convinced him to stick around a little while since I still had some time left on lunch. I asked him if he and the guys liked hiking and he lit up. Apparently, the Marquez boys were huge on outdoorsy activities. He promised we'd all go hiking as soon as we had a chance. Then somehow we started talking about books. The guys were all big readers but all in very different genres. Mateo's thing was history and lots of books about war and battles. Javier read a lot of sci-fi and fantasy. Alejandro liked biographies and literary fiction, and Emi read a lot of hard science and politics.

Apparently, all four of them were huge on *Harry Potter* and the very thought of that amused me to no end.

"This is easy," I said, draining the last of my iced tea. "You're Gryffindor, Javier is Hufflepuff, Alejandro is Ravenclaw, and Emi is Slytherin."

"I'd take issue with a couple of those," Mateo said, laughing. "Especially since Ali insists he's Gryffindor. You're going to have to fight him on that one."

The time got away from me and I went way over on lunch. It took Mateo noticing the time and he winced, hopping up from his seat and apologizing for keeping me.

"Don't apologize," I said firmly. "I've been in a terrible mood all day." I stepped in close to him. It was hard not to want to get close to any of the Marquez men when I saw them. I felt so drawn to all of them, like a moth to a flame. "It was wonderful to see you. Thank you for lunch."

My words said "thank you for lunch" but I was pretty sure my eyes were saying "please bang me on this desk." Mateo seemed to read me correctly because he stepped into my space so that I could see the golden flecks hidden in the dark of his brown eyes when he spoke. I could see exactly how thick his eyelashes were.

"I meant what I said before," he said softly. "We'd do anything for you, Ellie. All of us. We care about you. Deeply. Might be hard to explain because we haven't known you long, but-"

"I believe you," I whispered, my eyes straying to his mouth. I swallowed, wanting more. Wanting him not to leave. "Mateo..."

Mateo began to lean in and I took that as a green light and kissed him, tugging him forward by his collar. My heart was pounding, anticipating the kiss of the man who'd made me come in the middle of a bar in the afternoon. His kiss was powerful, almost ferocious, his mouth covering mine as if he would make me his own. Yet I didn't mind it at all. I felt like I wanted him to claim me. I wanted all four of them to claim me. I wanted to belong to all of them, and I wanted them to belong to me. But I knew it was impossible.

Mateo acted like he'd been dying to kiss me since I'd left him at the bar, and now he was going to make it worth his while as if this might be the only opportunity he got. He plundered my mouth and I surrendered happily, clutching at his shoulders as he pressed me against my desk. He sucked on my tongue and I moaned as his hand reached up to take down my ponytail. He tangled his fingers in my hair and heatedly moved to kiss my neck and nibble on my ear.

These Marquezes would be the death of me.

"God, I want you," I breathed, and my cheeks burned. I hadn't intended to say it out loud.

"Ellie, I would take you right here if I could," Mateo said, gently biting my shoulder.

I was wet, practically aching for him, and I pressed my knees together. I might have moaned just a little bit.

"I wish," I muttered.

"Soon enough," he whispered in my ear. The promise of him in my bed only made it worse and I kissed him again before forcing myself to gently push him away.

"I hope you mean that," I said.

He reached up to press his thumb to my bottom lip and I sighed as he pulled it down and then leaned forward to kiss the spot.

"Of course, I do."

With much regret and longing, I bid Mateo goodbye. My head was swimming. I had to go to the restroom and splash some water on my face just to get a proper hold on myself.

Mateo had me feeling...well, not just turned on, but also confident. This work situation was not the end of the world. Things would turn out alright. I decided to try to look into this problem with work myself too, as much as I could. So I called up one of my most loyal clients. I'd helped Dorine flip several houses. She'd started with some money, and now she has much more because of me. She's worked with only me for the past five years.

The phone rang four times before she answered, which was unusual for Dorine.

"Hey..." She didn't sound too happy to hear from me either.

"Dorine!" I said, stubbornly cheerful. "Hi, it's Ellie. I just wanted to give you a call and check in..."

"Right," she said, sounding very uncertain. "Okay."

I cleared my throat. Dorine sounded weird as hell. "I've just been having some weird responses from my clients lately? And since we've known each other so long now, I just wanted to check in and ask you if you've heard anything? Has anyone maybe told you not to work with me for some reason or... Honestly, you can tell me, Dorine. I'd just like to know."

"I can't answer your calls anymore. I'm sorry." She sounded spacey when she said it. As if she were hypnotized.

"Oh, no," I said lightly as if this all wasn't very disturbing. "Well, that's not great to hear. Can you tell me why? Give me any reason? Has there been some bad buzz?"

"I can't...I can't take your calls anymore. I'm sorry."

I pursed my lips. I knew a spell when I heard one. This was all I would likely get from Dorine. She was on autopilot. Something had clearly messed with her head.

"Okay," I said, sighing. "Well, I'm going to let you go then, Dorine."

"I can't take your calls anymore-"

"And you're sorry," I said, nodding. "Got it. Bye now."

I hung up and rubbed my eyes.

This was definitely down to Dixon.

My next call was to Mateo who was back in his office by now.

"Hey, Mateo," I said, tapping my desk with my fingernail. "I'm gonna need you guys to do me a favor. If that's okay."

"Anything for you, sweetheart," Mateo said. "Like I said."

"I know you said you'd keep a lookout, but I think Dixon's seriously fucking with me," I said, to put it in the clearest terms. "I'd like you to investigate him. I'm willing to pay-"

"You're not paying a cent," Mateo said. "We were going to anyway. I hope that doesn't freak you out."

"No," I said, chuckling. My heart swelled with affection for him and the others. "No, it makes me feel like I'm not alone."

"You're not," Mateo said quietly. "If you want, you never have to be again."

I spent the next few days pretending I didn't know that Dixon was definitely using magical means to ruin my life. I suspect he was either powerful and I just wasn't sensing it, or somebody was helping him. I guessed my spell of protection wasn't working because the hex against it had already been cast or else my magic was too weak. But without knowing for sure, there wasn't much else I could do. I was hoping the Marquezes would solve this little mystery and scare Dixon away for good.

In the meantime, I chased new leads and tried to repair the old ones. I finally landed a new appointment and I thought maybe things were looking up. I guess I've always been an optimist by nature. I let it slip to Alejandro in a text, and he made way too big a deal out of it, though it did amuse me. He kept sending me emojis and gifs to celebrate.

It's just a meeting to look at his house, I texted. *Nothing is settled.*

I believe in you! Alejandro replied. He made me giggle at least.

That evening I went to dinner with him and Emi. It was just casual and they still had to work that night on some stake-out, investigating a potentially cheating wife, so they didn't have all the time in the world.

The two of them drove me crazy. Emiliano was serious

but he had a broody way about him that I found sexy. I also hadn't kissed him yet and I kept fixating on his lips as he spoke even as Alejandro's foot found my leg under the table and slowly slid its way up my calf. I nearly spit out my wine when I felt it and met his eyes across the table.

There had not been a good time to be alone somewhere private with any of them for too long. But I'd certainly imagined it plenty, alone in bed at night, with only my hand for company. I was scrambling at work and their cases kept them busy. I felt like if I didn't get naked with a Marquez soon, I might actually explode.

ELLIE

On a Friday afternoon, I had my appointment with the new client scheduled. The circumstances were slightly unusual. I only knew his first name and the house was way out on a mountain road by the park. As far as I knew there weren't many properties ready to sell up there yet, but I wasn't going to argue with a new client.

I wore black slacks and a simple button up for the meeting. With new clients, I don't like to look as if I'm trying too hard. I like to be a little casual yet project confidence. It usually works for me.

I was looking forward to the meeting especially, because Emiliano was taking me. I'd taken the bus to work that morning after some resistance from the Marquez boys, who were happy to cart me around. Javier had brought me lunch and his Greek chicken wraps had been delicious. Now, my office day was over. It had not been very fruitful though as far as I could tell. But it was four o'clock and Emi would be on his way soon.

At four-fifteen, he hadn't shown and he wasn't answering his texts. The others didn't know where he was either and apologized for his lateness. They offered rides, but I knew they were busy and told them I'd take a Lyft.

My ride came quickly. I'd been doing this long enough that I'd factored in the possibility of running late and allowed for some extra time. I absolutely cannot *stand* being late for a client ever, much less for a first meeting. It's a difficult first impression to get over.

On impulse, I took my ride to my place and picked up my car rather than going straight to the client's house. I don't know why. I just had a feeling like I might need my car. A little voice in my head was screaming at me not go without it.

My meeting was scheduled for five and I got there in plenty of time. I pulled up on the winding road and squinted at the property. It was an old, decrepit looking house. This was going to be a fixer-upper for sure. I hadn't had one of those in a while. The front yard was all overgrown and even this far from sunset, I got an eerie feeling about the place. I made my way down the crooked, dirty path toward the half-collapsed porch and saw a dark figure standing there. My client, I assumed.

"Hi there!" I waved in a friendly matter. "I'm Ellie!"

The figure didn't move or speak and I started to get a creepy crawly feeling in my stomach.

"Have you been waiting long?" I said, though I started walking more slowly. I had an urge to stop. I also had urge to turn around and run the other way. "Hello?"

The figure stepped into the light and it was Dixon.

I should have known. I felt like a complete fool for not knowing.

"Ellie," he said, "I just want to talk."

"I don't want to talk to you," I said, slowly backing up down the path.

I was wishing I'd thought to bring an amulet or something simple for protection. I wished Mateo was there with me. "I told you I never wanted to see you again."

"That's a mistake," he said.

"Are you the reason I've lost all my clients?" I said, anger replacing fear within me. "I can't even get arrested in this town. Is that you?"

"It's not my fault," he said, fixing his eyes on me. He curled his lip, his fists clenched at his sides. "You upset the fates! It's the fates working against you! We're meant to be together."

"The fates would never pair me with you," I said, practically hissing. Magic, I well knew, would never be so cruel. "You don't know shit about fate."

"Just stop for a minute," he said, trying to sound so calm and reasonable. "You're upset-"

"Oh, fuck you," I snapped. It took a lot for me to get angry at a person. Dixon, I would have liked to see dead. "You attacked me." I was still backing up. I had my keys in my hand.

This was why I needed my car. Though I wished instinct had told me not to come at all.

"I'm sorry I did that," Dixon said, in that creepy voice of his. "But I want to apologize properly. If you just come with me, Ellie. Everything will go back the way it was."

I counted in my head.

One...

I held my keys tight in my fingers.

Two...

He was walking towards me and I backed up a few steps.

"Ellie, it's not too late-"

THREE.

I turned and ran like my life depended on it, picking up brambles and thorns from the overgrown weeds in place as I stomped through the grass. In the car, I locked the doors and fumbled with the keys for a second as Dixon thundered outside, pounding on the windows. I peeled away and sped down the road and he ran after me and as I watched in the rear view, I could swear I saw a wolf suddenly appear on the road.

I sped back into town and waited til I was just a little calmer before calling Mateo. I wasn't as calm as I thought though and my voice shook as I spoke. I told him everything that had just happened and I could hear him fighting to stay calm himself though I suspected he wanted to tear Dixon limb from limb. He told me to go home and if I liked, they'd come over.

"Yes!" I said, tears in my eyes. "Yes, please come over!"

When I was finally safe inside my own apartment, I dead-bolted the door. I hugged Indiana to my chest for comfort and I managed a giggle when he licked my nose even as I wiped away a stray tear. I was filled with anticipation to see my boys now and I drank some wine to calm my anxieties.

Just after five, the buzz from downstairs sounded from my intercom and when I pressed the button to see who it was, Mateo's voice said, "Sweetheart? It's us!"

I buzzed them in but Dixon had me so turned around, I was slightly suspicious even though I recognized Mateo's voice, and I checked the peephole when they came up. Javier seemed to sense me watching and waved at me, though he looked just as concerned as Mateo.

I threw open the door and Alejandro, Javier, and Mateo wrapped me in a hug. I'd never felt so safe and comforted in my life as their arms embraced me. Though I was starting to get worried about Emi. They peppered me with questions. Was I okay? Did he hurt me? I should carry mace, they said.

They made me sit down. Javier wanted to make me some kind of special tea until told him I was happy with my wine, thank you. I told them everything I remembered and I could see them all trying to contain their anger at Dixon, though Mateo most intently.

"I don't know," I said, staring down at my hands. "The more I see him, the more I think he doesn't just want to have me, I think he wants to...hurt me. It's almost like he needs me for something. Or he needs to hurt me. It's not just regular scary ex stuff."

"I'm sorry we weren't there," Mateo said, frowning down at the floor. He sat on the arm of the couch, his arms crossed.

"It wasn't your fault," I insisted. "You can't be with me every second. And I don't need a babysitter."

"We should keep watch on your place though," Alejandro said. "I hope that not too much? It's just that we have training, you know? Can you let us do that? Please?"

"Yeah," I said, sighing in relief. "That would make me feel a lot better actually."

"Good." He reached over and patted my knee. "But listen, you guys, do you know where Emi is? Have you accounted for him?"

"No," Mateo said darkly. "I was about to leave and go look for him actually. I'm getting worried."

"Good," I said. "Yeah, please go find him."

"But we'll stay with you," Javier said. "If you'd like?"

"Yes, please," I said. I felt a little silly but I saw both Javier and Alejandro visibly relax when I agreed.

Mateo got up to leave and I followed him to the door. I did worry that he might go too far with Dixon if he happened to see him. And I was doubly worried for Emi.

"Be careful," I said softly.

"I will be, sweetheart," he said, and stroked my cheek.

I leaned forward and pecked him on the lips and he leaned into the kiss. I knew it would be easy to get carried away with Mateo and I made myself pull away, squeezing his had once before he went.

When I spun around I saw beautiful Alejandro and adorable Javier on my sofa, looking up at me with big eyes.

"Well…" I ran a hand through my hair. "What should we do?"

Alejandro swallowed and said, "Um…"

I felt like there was only one thing on all of our minds and it wasn't about my safety or about Emiliano. It was odd but things were so charged between all three of us.

"You guys like wine?" I said, heading to the kitchen.

"Yeah!" Alejandro said, getting up to come with me. "Please, please. I could use something to take the edge off."

"Me too!" Javier chirped. I trotted to the kitchen and came back with another full bottle and the corkscrew. I popped the cork and Alejandro followed with wine glasses. I poured them two drinks and we clinked our glasses together.

I downed the rest of my glass and poured just a little bit more for myself, wanting to feel more relaxed.

"So, other than Mr. Asshole," Javier said, after taking a long drink, "how was your day?"

"Oh, work is awful right now," I said, shrugging. "I'm sure Mateo told you about it."

"Yeah," Alejandro said. He looked apologetic and leaned toward me to push a lock of hair behind my ear. "I'm sorry you're having a rough time."

"I've always been pretty optimistic," I said. "I'm guessing things will turn around eventually."

"That's what I like about you," Javier said, his eyes lighting up. "One of the many things."

I ducked my head, feeling just a little bit pleasantly shy. "Anyway, I'll do my best. Power through. I think it's just a rough patch. And I have you guys." Even saying it, I blushed.

I wanted all of them.

I wanted all of them at once.

"You do have us," Alejandro said, his eyes locking with

mine as he sipped his wine. I took another long swallow of my wine and sat back, relaxing into the couch. I was so turned on over almost nothing. I pressed my hands to my thighs. The tension in the room felt so thick I thought it might crack the walls.

I'd drunk a *little* sloppily and I felt a drop of wine spilling from my lips and down my chin, sliding down my throat. I felt Alejandro and Javier's eyes on me and the anticipation made my breath short. I wondered if they could see down my shirt. If they noticed how flushed I was, how my breasts swelled as I breathed.

"You got something..." Javier turned sideways, his eyes screwed on that drop of wine. "The wine..."

Feeling bold, I whispered, "Drink it up then."

Javier's eyes flashed and hesitantly he leaned forward. When I made no move to stop him, he bowed his head and I felt his tongue touch where the drop of wine had slid to my collarbone. he pulled the open collar of my shirt away and licked the line of wine up my throat, all the way to my chin, before kissing my mouth.

I looked to Alejandro, half expecting him to look annoyed or jealous or something. Instead, his mouth was parted, his eyelids heavy as he watched. "That's really hot," he whispered, sounding a little stupid.

I smiled at that and tugged gently on his shirt. "C'mere, Ali."

Alejandro looked like he was being given some great gift and lurched forward to kiss me as Javier mouthed at my neck.

I hadn't planned on a threesome tonight. I hadn't planned on a threesome ever - until a couple of weeks ago.

Life was funny that way.

"Ellie," Javier whispered, his hand at my throat as he nibbled at my ear. "Are you sure this is-"

"Yes!" I said, between Ali's kisses. "Please. I've thought about all of you so much, I'm...I'm...Please..."

Alejandro pulled away, his lips swollen and pink. I felt dizzy just looking at them. His eyes wandered to the buttons of my shirt and I nodded permission. He went to work unbuttoning and I turned my head to give Javier my attention again, kicking off my shoes as he kissed me deeply, his hands tangling in my hair.

I scrambled to help Ali get rid of my shirt and then, blessedly, there were hands all over me. I writhed under the attention and threw my head back and Ali palmed my breast through my bra, kissing me there. Javier was leaning forward, an arm around my waist until his hand found my ass.

"God, Elli," Javier murmured and pulled aside a bra strap to kiss my shoulder. "So beautiful..."

It was dizzying and a little manic and then their shirts were gone and without any plan of exactly what we were doing, they were pressing up against me and then getting rid of my bra.

"I want to eat you out," Javier whispered in my ear. His hand hovered at my zipper and I gasped and blinked up at him.

"You really know what to say to a girl, huh?" I said, breathless. "Yes..."

Javier tittered and kissed me again and he slid off my pants. He pushed me sideways so I was lying on the couch and the both of them kissed me all over it seemed.

I never would have dreamed that they would be okay with this but now Alejandro had one of my nipples in his mouth and when I gasped he squeezed my breast as Javier tongued his way down to my entrance, his hands grasping my thighs.

He whispered, "You smell good," and it made me blush.

His tongue licked at me, teasing and tentative. I knew he wasn't shy, he was making me beg for it and I reached down to tug at his hair, urging him on.

"I like that," he said and grinned up at me. "Pull my hair."

I was trembling already, not just from the sensation of everything but because I could feel a kind of closeness to both of them like I'd never felt with anyone before. I tugged harder at Javier's hair and he moaned, the slight vibration of it making me cry out. He shifted around and then two fingers were spreading me open. Sometimes I could be a little self-conscious with someone for the first time in bed, but the two of them were making me feel so sexy and wanted. I felt wanton. I felt like the sexiest girl in the world as Javier murmured sweet nothings before his tongue flicked out at my clit.

"Does it feel good?" Alejandro asked. He was kneeling on the floor beside me and he turned my head to look at him.

"Oh God, it feels so good," I babbled. He kissed me and his tongue plundered my mouth just as Javier's tongue entered me below. Alejandro massaged my breast and I thought I was levitating, I was in such a state of bliss, my clit swollen and pushing me to the edge already as Javier worked at it, my thighs spread open before him.

Alejandro pulled away just to look at me, his pupils blown out and I was at eye level with his crotch. He was obviously fully erect in his jeans and he bit his lip, palming himself.

I was dizzy and I felt so wonderfully dirty as I said, "Take it out. Take it out, I want it."

Ali scrambled to unzip his fly and his cock sprang out, erect and leaking.

"A-are you sure, Ellie, are you- oh!"

I guided it into my mouth and it was satisfying; firm and salty as I sucked at it. Ali met my eyes and he looked helpless as I curled my tongue around. He was being so careful with me, trying not to push into my mouth and it made me want him more.

I looked down at Javier and saw his little smirk as he watched us. I pulled his hair hard and he groaned and his tongue plunged inside me, making me buck, and I sucked my cheeks in. Ali cried out and began to pull away. He was coming in my mouth but trying to be polite about it, pulling out quickly. I swallowed a little of his come and some of it fell on my lips as he reached to finish himself off. The sight of him helpless, shaking with pleasure because of me set me off just as Javier's fingers began massaging my clit, fast and furious and making me scream so loud, I thought I would wake up the neighbors. Ali laughed at that and covered my mouth with a kiss.

I moaned and cried into him as Javier sent me soaring until he sensed I couldn't quite take it anymore and he finished me with a tender kiss to my swollen clit before sitting up, gazing at me adoringly as he stroked my thighs.

The three of us were breathless and silent for a couple of minutes. Ali pet my hair and lazily drew circles on my breasts as I came back down to earth.

"So," Javier said, "have you chosen one of us yet?"

For a moment I thought he was serious and looked over at him in surprise, only to see him smirking. I burst out laughing instead and that set him and Alejandro off and we all sat there, sated and giggling helplessly at the strangeness of our situation.

MATEO

I didn't like to leave Ellie but concern for Emi pulled at me, and I trusted Javier and Alejandro to keep her safe. I also had a rage in me toward Dixon that was making me want to tear through the city, sniff the bastard out, and tear him limb from limb. I figured I would distract myself by doing something more useful, namely finding out what Emi had gotten himself into.

It was probably nothing, I told myself. Sometimes while on a case, one of us got into a bit of a scrape. He was probably just stuck somewhere with a dead phone battery.

I knew his schedule for the day. He should have been in town somewhere unless a target had flown the coop and he'd had to pursue somebody, but it would have to be pretty serious for him to take off with a dead phone without leaving a message for somebody on a payphone.

I do tend to be a worrier and to cover for myself, I get angry. The guys like to tease me about it. Now I drove, clutching the wheel with white knuckles.

If anyone had hurt Emi, I'd murder them.

If anyone hurt Ellie, I'd murder them too.

Javier teases me the most about being the alpha of our pride. He always says he wouldn't want the responsibility. But to me, it makes everything very simple.

You fuck with the people I love, I end you.

It's pretty cut and dry.

I could smell faint whiffs of Emi's scent on the air if I really concentrated. That was a good sign. I drove back to our office and started there, intending to track him. From the office, his scent took me in the direction of the mountain, not far from our house. It looked like he had been on his way to go meet Ellie, but something had stopped him.

On a side road, I found his car. It was totalled.

My heart leapt into my throat. I felt as if all my blood was rushing down to my feet. I pulled over and ran to the car, but I already knew he wasn't there. I would have smelled him.

The front end of the car was smashed where he'd run straight into a cluster of tall tree stumps. But something had also hit him from the side.

Someone had run my pride mate off the goddamn road and since Dixon had been waiting for Ellie at that house up the mountain, I was sure I knew just who that asshole was.

I forced myself to take a couple of deep breaths and then I followed the scent. The driver's side was caved in a little but I only saw a little bit of blood. I suspected he wasn't too badly hurt, especially if he had escaped on foot. If I knew Emi, he might have even been trying to find Ellie.

I shifted and it felt good to wear those lion's muscles again as I trotted along, sniffing the ground. My senses were always much stronger when I shifted. I followed my nose through the brush, deeper into the woods. Even as a human, I can smell strong fear. But now I sensed that Emi was not just scared but lonely. That meant he was probably shifted too. We miss our pack mates much more keenly when we're in lion form.

I finally got a perfect lock on Emiliano's scent and went running through the woods to a cave where I found his lion huddling inside. His shoulder was bleeding and he was crouched. He looked like he'd been a little beaten up, though he mostly appeared shaken. He recognized me and laid down on his stomach, resting his head on his front paws. I licked his face in greeting and knelt beside him, licking at his shoulder and nuzzling him. He closed his eyes, signalling I was comforting him. That was good. He'd be alright. He was still trembling though. I wondered if he was stuck.

When I shifted back, Emi looked up at me with scared, lion eyes.

"Can you not shift back?" I said.

Emi shook his head. I sighed and chewed on my lip. I suspected something had locked him in but maybe if I calmed him down enough he could break whatever the spell was.

It took me the better part of an hour of stroking Emi's head and whispering that he was safe before he finally stopped trembling and eventually shifted back into himself. That did make sense though. If anyone was susceptible to get locked into a form, it was Emi, who was more prone to anxiety than any of the rest of us.

"What happened, man?" I said, wrapping an arm around his shoulder, careful of his injuries.

"I was on my way to pick up Ellie," Emi said, shrugging. "Some asshole came out of nowhere, ran me right off the road. I got knocked out. When I came to, I was shifted and I couldn't shift back. I wanted to find Ellie." He looked sheepish then, and he ducked his head. "But I was too shaken up and I was afraid she'd flip seeing a lion coming right at her even if I did find her. I'm so sorry, Mateo."

"Hey, don't apologize." I reached around to squeeze the

back of his neck. "You're fine, man. You didn't do anything wrong."

"I didn't get a good look at the guy," Emi said, sighing. "But I'm guessing it was Dixon. I'd bet on it."

"It was definitely Dixon," I said darkly. "He tried to go after Ellie again at that house. He was clearly pretending to be a client. He lured her there."

"Shit! Is she okay?"

"Yeah yeah," I said. "She's with Javi and Ali at her apartment. Let's get over there, okay? Unless you need to go to the hospital for your shoulder-"

"It's just a scrape," Emi said, rolling his eyes. "I was more panicked than anything else."

"Alright, well let's get you to Ellie," I said, helping him to his feet. "She was really worried about you, ya know?"

"Was she?" Emi stood up straight and looked at me with hopeful eyes and it made me chuckle.

"Of course she was, numbskull. Come on."

When Emi and I walked in the door at Ellie's, everyone was dressed and composed, but the smell of sex was strong in the air and I didn't miss the way Ellie's face turned red when she saw me or the way Javier was smirking. The thought of what had likely happened while I was gone didn't make me *jealous* per se, not of them being together. I was only jealous that I hadn't had a chance to be with Ellie again myself. But I couldn't ignore the chemistry between her and, well, all of us.

When Ellie saw Emi walk in, she turned to goo.

"Emiliano!" She hugged him gently, careful of his injury, and led him off to the bathroom. There was a lot of fluttering and offering of tea.

The rest of us watched from the hallway, hovering in the

background, as Ellie looked after Emi in the restroom. He seemed to be drinking the attention up like water in a desert and the three of us smiled knowingly at each other.

"I'm alright, Ellie," Emi said quietly as she bandaged up his shoulder.

"I'm just glad he didn't hurt you worse," she said, wiping a tear from her eye.

"Hey, hey, it's okay." He patted her shoulder. It was rare to see Emi open up to somebody. It might have warmed my heart just a little bit. "I'm fine. Really."

Ellie abruptly kissed him and Javi whispered, "Way to go, Emi." I saw him press a quiet high five to Alejandro's palm and rolled my eyes but I couldn't help smiling.

ELLIE

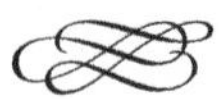

The Marquezes started keeping watch outside my place. It was strange, maybe, to have my boyfriends patrolling my apartment just in case my attacker felt like messing with me again. But then, it was strange to have boyfriends at all. I was starting to wonder if fate was just being generous. Could I really be blessed with all four of them as my soulmates for life? It just seemed too good to be true yet they always seemed to be nudging me toward each other and not in a way that was crass or disrespectful.

For the rest of Friday night, we hung around at my place until late when everyone started yawning. Alejandro wanted to stay behind on guard and the others agreed.

On impulse, I held Emiliano back.

"Can he stay over?" I said. I was starting to feel increasingly possessive over my Marquezes. I hadn't had much time with Emi to begin with and now, after what he'd been through, I really didn't want to let him out of my sight. I felt like we could sort of comfort each other. I looked at Emiliano, pleading. "Can you stay over? With me? You don't have to-"

"I could," Emi said quickly. "I'm feeling much better though. And I can take care of myself, Ellie." He grinned then, and I saw the strength in him and the light of his confidence. "Took Dixon running me off the road in a truck to knock me out."

"I know," I said, squeezing his hand. "But will you? For me?"

"Of course," he said, squeezing back.

With that, we let Mateo and Javier leave. I'd heard them muttering together while we were hanging out. I got the sense they were eager to go hunting for Dixon. A part of me worried that they would get themselves in real trouble, even if I wasn't so much worried about their physical safety. On the other hand...I was a witch, even if they didn't know that about me yet. Operating outside of the law really wasn't so crazy an idea to me.

When the others were gone and Alejandro was posted outside, I took Emi's hand and led him to my bedroom. I knew we were both very tired after all the excitement, and nothing much was probably going to happen tonight, but it was still exciting to me to have him in my bed. I also couldn't help but admire his body as he stripped down to his boxers.

Emiliano was the brainy Marquez, the one who always had his nose in a book and was seemingly more reserved. But he was still built. Somehow he found the time to get nearly as buff as Mateo, even if he was a little longer and leaner. I suspected that was down to Mateo keeping them trained and in shape for their P.I. jobs.

I bit my lip, trying to contain myself, and climbed into bed, pulling back the covers for him.

Emi smiled at me and climbed into bed beside me and I scooted up close to him and softly kissed his lips. "I know you can take care of yourself," I said. "Mateo said you tried to find me after you were hurt."

"I would have," he said, frowning, looking almost ashamed. "But I… There are things you don't know yet about us, Ellie. I can't explain right now, but I was afraid I would scare you more if I found you. That you wouldn't understand. But it killed me to think you were hurt." He spoke quietly and reached up to stroke my hair. I was wearing a little camisole and shorts and he leaned over and kissed my shoulder. "If I'd found him, I think I would've killed him."

"I don't know if that's a good thing," I said, smiling slightly. "But it does make me feel safe with you. That's why I wanted you to stay over. I mean...I wanted to get you alone too if I'm being honest."

Emi smiled at that and kissed me and I felt myself responding hungrily, even though I'd sworn to myself that we would just sleep. Under the covers, his palm covered my thigh and pulled at my leg until I threw it over him. The feel of his body pressed up against mine spurred me on as his tongue curled with mine.

"Emi…" I whispered.

He pulled back to look at me and his hand found my breast, massaging me through the camisole and I pressed into the touch.

We kissed lazily, writhing together until his hand slid down my body and pressed at me through my shorts. I whined for more and his fingers slipped under the waistband of my panties as I held him tighter. When his long and talented finger entered me I moaned and kissed him harder. A second finger entered quickly and I was gasping as he plunged two fingers in and out of me, burying his nose in my neck as I hugged him to me. His fingertips found my clit and I cried out, tangling my hands in his hair and on the very edge of coming, I stopped him. He looked up, his wide mouth parted, confused and worried.

I mumbled, "No, I mean I just….

I rid myself of my shorts and panties under the covers and yanked his boxers down, climbing on top of him. Emi gasped and rolled us over and the power of him, the way he manhandled me only brought me closer to coming.

"Emi, yes," I breathed.

He pushed the covers aside and pushed my legs apart, looking down at me. Somehow I felt more naked like that than I ever had and the anticipation made me moan. I threw my head back, begging for him.

I looked at his cock, long and engorged, and trembled as he guided himself inside me.

"Fuck, Ellie..."

He clasped my hands and I wrapped my legs around him, urging him deeper, feeling him fully within me. He rocked into me and when I cried out it seemed to unleash something and he began to thrust in earnest, pounding into me. I kissed him sloppily, barely able to manage it as I cried out, riding the bliss of him plunging in and out of me, teasing my swollen clit just enough to make me see stars as I came for what seemed like ages, shaking as he kissed me and fucked me like it was the end of the world.

He seemed to have total control and I was happy to let him have his way, even as tears leaked from my eyes and I became too sensitive to bear much more.

"Are you going to come for me, baby?" I whispered. "Will you come kissing me?"

Emi gasped at that and yanked my head up to kiss me, deep and bruising, my body wrapped around his as he came inside me so hard I could feel it everywhere, our heartbeats throbbing in time with each other.

When he collapsed on top of me I couldn't help but chuckle breathily and I stroked his back, slick with sweat. I felt his cum leaking out of me and I smiled slyly to myself, feeling so pleasantly wanton.

"I didn't expect that to happen tonight," Emi said, still panting. He kissed my breast and rested there.

"Me either," I said, and kissed his hair. "But I'm so glad it did."

~

"He has been making threats." Mateo was looking at me sternly as I sat in Javier's lap in a big, leather chair in the Marquezes living room.

It was Sunday and they'd decided to have me over to see their place, make me lunch, and show me what they had on Dixon. Javier had his arms around my waist and I covered his hands with mine, seeking a little strength. He kissed my neck absently. We'd mostly been talking about the Dixon situation. I'd hardly had a chance to appreciate their lovely house.

"It'll be alright," he whispered.

I smiled at that and took a breath. We were all sitting around in the living room, sipping wine. But now Mateo had his laptop out. He had some surveillance, he had phone records, he had all kinds of things.

"We think he has blackmail on a couple of people," Mateo said. "But mainly it's just straight up, vague threats. Work with another realtor or else. And um…"

He exchanged a look with Emi who shook his head. I wondered if they'd found out Dixon was using dark magic and didn't know how I'd take it. I was going to have to tell him I was a witch soon. But this relationship was already so unconventional, I wasn't looking forward to yet another complication.

"This guy needs to be taken out," Mateo said fiercely.

I tensed up and Javier squeezed me a little tighter. "You can't just murder him," I said slowly. If he was a wizard, well, there were different rules in the magical world. But the

Marquezes weren't magical even if I did sense something different about them. I couldn't condone humans just up and killing humans. Those rules were pretty clear, no matter what he'd done to me. Most importantly because I didn't want any of my boyfriends going to prison.

Emi said, "Well..."

I watched Mateo's jaw clench and unclench. "I understand why you're saying that," he said. "But..."

"I know you *want* to kill him," I said, rolling my eyes. "And I certainly wouldn't mind him dead. But there are laws, Mateo."

All the guys seemed to be exchanging looks with each other and having some kind of silent conversation with their eyebrows. I didn't know how to read their eyebrows so I was lost. I made a note inwardly to learn how to read the Marquez's eyebrows.

It had occurred to me more than once that the Marquezes might be magical in some way. I felt that vibe from them even if I didn't know for sure. I didn't think they were wizards. It was something else. But on the other hand, it was only a hunch, and I wasn't quite ready to tell them I was really a witch. I had to assume they would think I was nuts if I told them that. So far as they knew, I was an innocent human.

"If we have so much evidence," I said, "we should go to the police."

"If we go to the police," Mateo said, "and then...something should happen to him, just hypothetically speaking, we'll be the first suspects."

"That's true," I said. I started to wish they were wizards or something. I found the magical non-human way of dealing with threats like Dixon a lot more effective than human laws. "What if we warn him?" I said hopefully. "Let him know we've got the goods on him. Maybe then he'll back off."

The guys all looked doubtful and I didn't blame them. I'm sure they thought it was a weak move. The truth was, I agreed with Mateo. If I went to the police and then things got real with Dixon after that, they'd come to us first. I thought it would be fair to give him one last chance to stay away. After that...I think I'd be ready to sic the Marquez men on him for good, although it would be safer for me to just hex him to death or poison him with some strong potion.

"I'm going to call him," I said firmly, getting to my feet. I stretched, feeling a little regretful at leaving the comfiness of Javier's lap, but I figured I might as well get it over with. Mateo had paper copies of the phone records showing that Dixon called every one of my clients and I grabbed one, heading off to the privacy of the kitchen to make the call. Every Marquez looked at me with grave concern and I rolled my eyes. "It's a phone call, guys. He's not going to kill me through a phone call."

I said that, and yet it took me a few minutes of psyching myself up before I had the nerve to make the call.

When the call went to voicemail I was only relieved and I put on my sternest voice when I spoke, even though my hands were shaking.

"Dixon, this is Ellie. I want to let you know that I've compiled a lot of evidence concerning your attempts to ruin me. I know you've been threatening my clients and I know you ran my friend off the road. If you don't want me to go to the police, you'll back off. I don't want any more contact with you, I want you to stay away for good. Or else. I'm sending you a photo of phone records I've obtained that prove you've threatened my clients. Do not contact me again."

I hung up and it took me a few tries to send the photo after which I took a lot of deep breaths and pocketed my phone before shaking my hands out and walking around in circles. When I was a little more composed I went back out to the living room and pretended I was calm.

"Done and done," I said, shrugging as if it were nothing. "Let's just see how that goes, okay?"

They all looked very doubtful and I didn't really blame them.

"We'll try it your way," Mateo said gravely. "Temporarily."

I raised an eyebrow. "Oh, thanks for your permission."

Mateo narrowed his eyes and I watched that jaw clench and unclench as he chewed his lip. I kept waiting for him to respond, say something. I think it was taking all of his self-control not to just tell me exactly what to do. I got the strong impression that he was using to calling all the shots all the time.

Finally, Mateo breathed out very slowly and it sounded something like a big cat growling.

"Fine," he said.

I smiled at that and stood on my toes to kiss the tip of his angry nose. "Thank you."

I changed the subject quickly enough and Mateo settled a little. Javier had made us dinner. It was his apparently famous seafood linguine dish that was so good, he teased me that I liked the pasta better than I liked the four of them. After dinner, we just sat around talking and drinking wine. I'd sort of assumed something would *happen* that night but instead, I fell asleep on their couch in Emi's lap, my head on Alejandro's shoulder. I woke up in their guestroom, snuggled under a duvet.

It felt good to wake up in their big house in the woods. It felt right. I could easily picture waking up here all the time with the four of them and spending the rest of my life with these Marquezes. Maybe it was a pipe dream - but I thought it was a beautiful one.

In the kitchen, I found the four of them, already up and drinking coffee in the kitchen in their boxers and t-shirts, laughing and lighting up when I walked in the room. I couldn't help but grin, feeling a kind of warmth in my heart and realizing it was something that felt like home.

ELLIE

Mateo was apparently set on me staying at their house for a while, at least until things with Dixon were resolved. I admit it was sorely tempting. But if I was honest with myself, my reasons for wanting to stay there would have nothing to do with my safety, and that would just be moving whatever this five-way relationship was much too fast. It was already oddball enough.

On Sunday, I went home, though Alejandro came to stand watch. I was grateful for him playing guard...although it didn't stop me from inviting him in before I went to bed which ended up with me riding him until he made me scream into his hand.

I did find that sleeping after sex with any Marquez gave me the best night's rest.

On Monday, I went to work feeling good about things. We hadn't heard anything further from Dixon yet. I was hoping maybe things had resolved themselves, but maybe that's because I'm an optimistic person.

He did seem to have stopped whatever mayhem he was causing with prospective clients, as I managed to score some appointments and house showings, much to my great relief.

At lunch, Javier brought me a salad he'd made himself, and we ended up making out like teenagers on top of my desk, I had to regretfully stop things before I wanted to so that I could end lunch on time for once.

Javier left me with a, "Bye, beautiful," and lipstick on his cheek.

I did notice a couple of co-workers looking at me slyly after that when I went to the breakroom for coffee and it occurred to me that they'd also seen Mateo bring me lunch.

Well, if they asked, I would just tell them that I had, in fact, four boyfriends.

It wasn't like it was illegal.

On Monday night, I found Javier and Alejandro ready to guard my place for the night. Two guards felt like overkill but it was hard not to feel comforted by their concern. I invited them to have dinner with me and then, as all three of us probably expected, we ended up fooling around again. At ten, they dressed in a hurry and left me with heated kisses before going outside to keep watch.

Sated and sleepy, I curled up in bed, feeling safe and adored.

I was hardly asleep before a sound like the howling of a dozen wolves woke me up. It was so loud, I shouted as I jerked awake, breathless and suddenly alert. Out my window, I saw Javier and Alejandro looking alert but in no danger.

I wondered if I'd imagined it. I'd probably dreamed it and the imagined sound had snapped me out of the dream.

I curled up back to sleep and everything felt fine if a little eerie.

When the sound of howling wolves woke me up a second time, I reached for my phone, even though everyone looked fine outside.

I called Mateo, just to hear the sound of his voice really. I felt a little guilty waking him up, but he assured me he was safe, Emi was safe, Javier and Alejandro were obviously safe as they'd just checked in with Mateo and said they were taking a look at the road that led up into the woods from my place. I was probably being ridiculous.

I bid Mateo goodnight and tried once again to get back to sleep. It had made me feel better to hear him tell me I was safe.

Hours later, I woke up again. This time I didn't hear the sound of wolves. I didn't hear anything, not even the hum of the street outside or the breeze or anything at all. It was also so dark, that I couldn't tell when I had opened my eyes. There was usually some light through the blinds even when they were closed, and the blinking light of my router in the corner. Now there was nothing. Just pitch black.

I had a bad feeling all the sudden; so bad that I felt I couldn't breathe.

Outside, I heard it pouring rain suddenly and thunder rumbled. Somehow the sound was comforting to me but I was still breathless with fear.

I had a strong feeling that somebody was in the room and I couldn't see them.

"Is someone there? Javier? Ali?"

I heard a sharp intake of breath and almost screamed. If it had been a Marquez, they would have said something.

I tried to think of something I could grab for a weapon. The only thing nearby was my phone. I'd have to make a run for it, except that I couldn't see a goddamn thing.

"Dixon," I whispered.

Lightning cracked outside and lit up the figure of Dixon, looming over me, a huge knife in his hand.

I screamed bloody murder.

JAVIER

We were on alert as we guarded Ellie's place, yet we were spending most of the time talking. It was cold out and I'd worn my favorite leather jacket. I shoved my hands in my pockets and walked beside Alejandro as we paced Ellie's block. We'd been lucky so far that no neighbors had thought we were suspicious.

"I have to be honest with you," Alejandro said, smirking over at me as his breath puffed in the cold air. "When we became pack mates, I really didn't think we'd end up in threesomes together."

That made me burst out laughing and Alejandro patted my back as he joined in. The two of us had, perhaps inevitably, grown just a little closer lately.

My cheeks flushed and I shrugged, feeling sheepish. "I think it's really hot, to be honest with you."

Ali cleared his throat and said, "Yeah." He scratched his neck and seemed a bit embarrassed. "I agree."

"I wonder how Mateo would feel about it," I said, cackling.

"Oh boy," Ali said. He trilled his lips and we both laughed, hearing the echo of it in the empty street.

It was drizzling out and my hair was getting damp. I sighed, pushing it back, squinting up at the sky. I hadn't counted on the weather when I'd agreed to stand guard with Ali that night. I wished one of us had thought to bring an umbrella.

"I think it's gonna start pouring," I muttered.

"I think you're right."

Abruptly the howling of wolves startled us and we whipped around, sniffing the air for danger. They weren't nearby wherever they were. They sounded like they were coming from the woods.

"That's close to town for wolves," Ali said.

"Yeah…" I wished I had a cigarette suddenly but I'd quit on Mateo's insistence a few years ago. "Should we check it out?"

"Let's hang back a minute," Ali said. "Don't want to get far from Ellie if we don't have to."

When it started to rain in earnest, we found a bus shelter to stand under that still had a decent view of our surroundings.

When we heard wolves again and a little bit closer, we started to worry.

"Can I tell you something?" Ali said quietly. "I've wondered if Dixon is a shifter."

"Me too!" I said, widening my eyes. "I could swear I smelled shifter on him when we fought? But it wasn't like us…"

"Yeah," Ali said sighing. "I don't know my shifter scents. I couldn't really tell. Maybe he's just…"

"An animal?" I said wryly.

"I mean in a bad way," Ali said. "I don't know. Maybe we should check."

"I say we stick close," I said.

When nothing happened immediately, we started to relax. It was raining and a little eerie out. It felt like a ghost story kind of night. When the thunder and lightning began, I had to laugh. If nothing else, I supposed it would keep us awake.

I was freezing cold and soaking wet. I was tempted to say we should just go to Ellie's apartment and stay in there with her. We could keep her nearly as safe and get warm. But then we couldn't stop a danger at the door. So I nixed that. Besides which, I knew Mateo would read us the riot act if we pulled that without telling him first at least.

When we both smelled a pack of wolves far too close we looked at each other and shifted. We both took off in the direction of the wolves. Even if they really were just animals who'd found their way into town, it was too much of a threat. God knew what Dixon was capable of. For all we knew he could control wolves or something.

As lions, we could cover a lot of ground quickly, but soon we'd gotten pretty far from Ellie and I could tell that Alejandro wanted to hang back. He tipped his muzzle back in Ellie's direction and I gave him a nod. Ali went running back to Ellie and I continued on to investigate the wolves.

I figured it was better if just one of us went to investigate anyway. Mountain lions aren't always the stealthiest and one is easier to hide than two.

I was as careful as I knew how to be, keeping a long distance from what smelled like multiple animals. I tracked the scent deep into the woods and crouched behind a boulder to see a full pack of wolves clustering in a clearing.

I was sure they smelled me somewhere yet they didn't seem alarmed. I think the thunderstorm might have been throwing off their senses, or at least I hoped so. But when my stupid, big lion paw stepped on a twig it cracked as loudly as the thunder in my ears. I saw them all look in my direction and they didn't hesitate. They were off, coming around the boulder to discover me. I took off running and it was slow going through the mud. I tried to calculate my odds. One puma against a pack of wolves? I definitely had a shot but I would've felt better with my brothers.

Sometimes when one of us in danger, another one of us can feel it far away. I concentrated every bit of brain power I possessed in Mateo's direction and then fixated on Alejandro in case Mateo or Emi was too dead asleep. Although I didn't really want Ellie any less safe.

Hear me, I prayed as I ran for my life in the forest. Somebody help me…

I was trying to at least lead them away from town but found that the road and the woods was forcing me to come back around in the direction of Ellie's place.

Oh God, somebody hear me…

ALEJANDRO

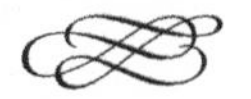

I don't know how I knew, but I knew.

I'd reached Ellie's place and just as quickly as I got there, I felt guilty for not staying with Javier. I felt like I was losing either way. Boulder is completely dead in the middle of the night and it was also the middle of the week. Nobody was around to see a puma prowling a quiet residential street so I prowled the block freely, licking my chops, almost wishing for something to happen.

None of us had forgotten our intense bloodlust for Dixon.

I think all four of us were itching for a fight, maybe especially Emiliano who I highly doubted was actually asleep back at home.

I felt a lurch in my heart as if it were trying to jump out of my chest.

At first, I thought of Ellie and I was about to run up to her apartment and check on her but then somehow I knew it was Javier. It was just one of those pack mate things, I guess.

I was a split second from running for Javier but Ellie...

Instead, I shifted back into human form and reached for

my phone, hurrying to text Mateo and alert him to what was going on. He texted back immediately that he and Emi were on their way and I should stick by Ellie unless I was about to be ambushed.

I practically growled at the text.

How could I protect Ellie if he wanted me to run when trouble actually arrived?

Alphas. I swear to God. It's like they think they're the only ones who can fight. But that was Mateo for you.

I could hear them coming and I shifted, ready to pounce.

All at once I knew instinctively that we'd been right about Dixon: he was a shifter.

I was sure somehow that the wolves after Javier were shifters.

Except that now they weren't after Javier, they were after me.

The ambush came just as I'd feared and with Mateo's orders fresh in my head, I felt forced to run from Ellie's place and I kind of wanted to kill him.

Five wolves all coming straight for me.

If nothing else, I figured I could lead them away from Ellie, which I suspected Javier had also been trying to do. Although this was on the assumption that one of the wolves was Dixon. I hoped so. Otherwise, we were falling right into a trap.

I suspected the wolves had been chasing Javier and he'd probably tried to lead them away and then they'd turned around and come after me.

I tried to throw them off, run one way and double-back in a different direction. Then I smelled Javier nearby. I didn't particularly want him in danger, but right now it was five against one. I followed his scent, the wolves hot on my tail. I was nearly all the way to the woods again when Javier came bounding out behind a stone wall.

Now it was two against five.

Javier ran up next to me and even in puma form I could read his eyes saying: *I'm with you.*

The wolves made a big show, growling and snapping without attacking.

The two of us, being feline about it, slowly paced, only flicking our tails in warning. I glanced over at Javier and tried to give him a look with my puma face that said: *Shifters?*

It was a little bit more specific than our conversations via facial expressions generally went. But somehow Javier understood me and he nodded.

We agreed then.

Javier abruptly reared around and roared at the wolves like I'd never heard him roar.

They growled back yet nobody made a move.

That was fine with me. Two pumas against five wolves? I think we were going to kick their asses. But I don't love fighting if I'm being honest. I was happy to wait and see if Mateo and Emi showed up.

Just then, as if on cue, the cavalry came running up the road.

Mateo, being your typical alpha, absolutely loves a fight. He did not hesitate and leapt right at the alpha wolf who was standing in front of the others. Then it was a battle; the four of us going to town on the five wolves, all teeth and claws and fur flying. A wolf snapped, nearly taking a bite of my haunches and I got his neck in my jaws before one of his mates nearly disembowelled me just as Emi came in for the rescue.

Mateo just about ripped a wolf's throat out and we were clearly winning.

Then suddenly...it was all over.

The fight couldn't have lasted more than three minutes

when all the wolves abruptly stopped as if commanded by some unseen force, turned around, and ran off.

We all stood there, feeling as if we had won, if only for a moment.

And all at once we knew without speaking to each other.

Ellie.

It had been a trap. We'd been pulled off our guard to leave Ellie unprotected.

Abruptly, we all began to run full speed back to Ellie's apartment.

ELLIE

Dixon was holding a knife to my throat. I couldn't move, I couldn't think.

I didn't understand where he'd come from. How had he gotten past Javier and Alejandro?

"You should have just come peacefully, Ellie," Dixon said. "I didn't want to have to do it this way."

He spoke so matter-of-factly as if he wasn't about to kill me.

"There are different ways to do this," he said, calmly thoughtful. "I was trying to go the non-violent route. I take away everything from you...the power is last. You would have been left with nothing but your life. But hey, life is something, right?"

I didn't understand what he was talking about but I was now positive he wasn't just some regular human. I squirmed, trying to get out from under his hold, and the knife dug in a little more as he tightened his grip.

I screamed as it broke the skin on my neck, a couple drops of blood oozing down my throat. Dixon climbed up on top of me over the covers and leered down at me.

"I was supposed to take you that night, you know," Dixon said. "When those assholes fought me off. That's part of it. Alright, well, I guess that bit would be violent, wouldn't it? Still. I would have left you alive. I wouldn't have really hurt you… "He leaned down and whispered, "Much."

"They're gonna kill you," I said, forcing myself to smile. I hated him knowing how afraid I was, though I couldn't control the way I shook as the full weight of him settled on top of me. He could crush me if he wanted to. For sure he could just slit my throat and then it would be over.

I suddenly felt a loss for all the years I was going to miss with the Marquez men. I was sure now; if I had ever really doubted it since I'd met all of them. They were *all* meant for me. I was supposed to love them and they were all supposed to love me. My spell had worked. They were fated to be with me forever.

But if they didn't find me in a few seconds, forever wasn't going to last long.

Tears slid from my eyes as I thought of all the things I'd lose. No morning breakfast with Mateo grumbling about whatever the agenda was supposed to be the for the day. No Emiliano talking about the latest book he'd read. He was always reading some new science book that ended up playing into their private investigations. Alejandro teased him about it, but Mateo had told me that if it wasn't for Emi, they wouldn't have nearly as high of a success rate in their cases. There would be no cooking lessons with Javier, who had promised to teach me how to make a proper roux. He'd become interested in Cajun cooking as of late. There'd be no late night watching of terrible movies with Alejandro. He got a real kick out of that. It seemed to drive Emi crazy and the two of us would make fun of the way his nose scrunched up when somebody in a terrible movie was particularly stupid.

There'd be no self-defense classes with Mateo. He was set on at least teaching me how to throw a proper punch. I think he wanted me to take up regular boxing classes if I liked the idea. He kept hinting about it. He hated the thought of me unable to fight back.

Like right now for instance.

I was supposed to be with them. I'd already fantasized about it to no end in my head. They'd said I could have that guest room whenever I wanted it and I took them at their word. I wanted to live in the mountains with my guys, to go on hikes and explore the wilderness. I'd imagined how I'd tell them I was a witch a million times. I trusted them to accept me for that, especially since I was sure they were keeping a secret about themselves too. I knew it to be true now from the way Emi had spoken to me the first time we made love. I wanted to show them the spells I could do and learn all about them.

There was so much I still didn't know about the Marquezes. They weren't closely related at all, according to Mateo, though they shared the same last name. They'd come together through friends and family and ended up as a sort of unit of friendship, never to be parted it seemed. The P.I. business had been Alejandro's idea initially because he'd always been interested in it and thought Mateo had a good head for detective work.

But I wanted to know so much more. What had they been like as children? I wanted to see pictures of them as little kids in Spain. I wanted to know every stupid story about them and their favorite parts of their favorite movies and what they were like when they were grumpy or had a cold.

I wanted them in my bed. I wanted to memorize every inch of every one of their bodies and know from a touch who was with me in the dark. I wanted to wake up with a different Marquez every morning and sometimes two at once and maybe three and why not four?

I was overcome with such love for my four men that I found myself smiling up at Dixon even as he held a knife to my throat.

"I'm going to steal your power," Dixon was telling me. "That little stone my aunt gave me is really handy." He dug a little glowing, green crystal out of his pocket and showed it to me. "Lights up when you get near some power, particularly witches. I researched for years how to steal a witch's power. The best way is to seduce her." He leaned down and licked my cheek and I squeezed my eyes shut as I turned my face away, repulsed. "Seduce her, take away everything, then you drain her. But if that doesn't work..." The knife dug in a little deeper and I shrieked, less from pain than fear. "You kill the bitch. I should know..." He chuckled and shrugged as if it was all nothing. "You're not my first witch. A few more and I'll be the most powerful wizard this side of the country."

He'd killed other witches before and taken their power. The thought of it made my heart ache and I clenched my teeth, hoping that even if I didn't survive this, that he would end up dead.

I kept my eyes closed and decided to just ignore Dixon. I couldn't stop him from killing me. Maybe Javier and Alejandro were dead already though the thought was shattering. But maybe Mateo and Emiliano could still be saved if the damn fates could just help me out for a minute.

I was a good witch, a skilled witch, if not super advanced. But I had magic in me that I knew was untapped. Now, I focused hard on Mateo and Emi and thought as strongly as I could: *Run, my loves. Run away.*

I knew if they heard me, they would likely try to come find me. But I just wanted them to be safe. I didn't know what else I could do for them, but the overpowering sense of love for all four of them wanted me to sacrifice myself even if it meant I died and never saw them again.

I focused on my sense of connection to them as hard as I could, trying to send out that warning when all at once I somehow felt the presence of all four of them inside me. It was like I could hear echoes of them in my head in my heart somehow, even if I couldn't quite make out their thoughts; a faint psychic connection. It at least let me know that all of them were alive.

Run run run…

They wouldn't get here in time, I was sure. Dixon could kill me in a second and then he would take my power. If he wasn't lying it would make him a powerful wizard. Certainly, he'd already used powers on those clients just like I'd initially thought. He'd done more than threaten. It explained why that one loyal client had sounded so strange on the phone, as if she'd been hypnotized. God knows what else he'd done.

"You think those four little lion cubs are going to come save you?" Dixon said, practically spitting in my face. "They're so stupid, I headed them off without even trying."

Lion cubs? Shifters!, I thought. That was it. The four Marquez men were a pack of lion shifters. And the memory of the shifter that day on the mountain came rushing back and I understood why he wouldn't shift that day.

My beautiful lions.

I giggled in Dixon's face and he sneered. I was just thinking of how much sense it made that Mateo was obviously the alpha. He sure acted like one.

"Stop laughing," Dixon hissed. He slapped me across the face. "Slut!'

"They're gonna kill you," I said, and somehow I couldn't stop giggling. "They're going to KILL you!" I was helpless with laughter and Dixon almost looked afraid.

Then he drew back the knife and I shut my eyes again, readying myself for death.

Mateo, Emiliano, Alejandro, Javier, I love you-

The crash, when it came, was simultaneous with a crack of thunder. I had no idea what had happened until I was on the floor. I was expecting my throat to be slashed, sharp, stinging pain and the rush of life with my blood spilling from me. I was fully expecting that - instead, thunder crashed and what sounded like a truck had ploughed through my bedroom window. Glass and plaster went flying and then something horribly heavy and warm was half on top of me for a split second and I was on the floor, the knife gone from my neck.

It was chaos.

I was buried under the covers. I'd been ploughed against the opposite wall and a terrible weight had slammed into me before disappearing again, while around me it sounded as if giant monsters were destroying my apartment. The sounds were wild and riotous.

I was terrified but I figured I wasn't dead so whatever was happening was...good?

I crawled out from under the covers. I was turned around, but I thought I was heading in the direction of my bedroom door although I was pretty sure I'd just heard the wall between my bedroom and the kitchen come down.

When I crawled out from under the sheets I saw what I'd sort of suspected.

Four mountain lions had attacked Dixon. The Marquez shifters had jumped right through the window which...was impressive since I was on the second story, but I suspected they'd jumped from the stone wall just opposite. I really didn't know the climbing abilities of mountain lions.

I wanted to shut my eyes again. I wanted Dixon dead,

sure, but I didn't know that I wanted to watch my four lion boyfriends rip his guts out.

Then I saw Dixon turn into a wolf.

He was backed into a corner, blood dripping down his face, and he turned abruptly. He was a gray wolf and he bared his teeth as the Marquezes reared up at him. I backed up into the living room.

My apartment was completely demolished. Somebody had broken right through the kitchen cabinets. Two lions stood where before there had been stacks of pots and pans now somehow thrown through the shattered living room window.

I watched Dixon the wolf bolt for the window, attempting to escape and all four lions pounced at once.

Now I did close my eyes, yelping as I heard jaws snap and huge cats growling as they attacked him all at once.

It didn't take long.

The cats all went quiet suddenly.

I heard a whimpering behind me and turned my head to see poor Indiana shaking by the sofa.

In retrospect, it seemed silly but I found myself crawling over to him, muttering, "Oh, poor baby."

I hugged Indiana to me and sat on the floor by the sofa. Through the wreckage, I saw the bloody remains of Dixon the wolf as the lions parted before shifting back into the Marquezes. Mateo spun around, looking around for me wildly.

"Mateo," I said softly.

He saw me and closed his eyes for a second before pinching the bridge of his nose. "Jesus, I really thought we were too late."

"Almost," I said, smiling faintly. Alejandro rushed over to me and plopped on the floor before wrapping both me and Indiana in his arms. "Somebody pushed me off the bed."

"That was me," Ali said sheepishly. "Sorry if I was rough. Hard to pull that off and be gentle after crashing through a window... as a puma."

"Don't be sorry," I said. "You saved me. You all did."

Alejandro kissed my cheek and rested his head there the others knelt by me until we were all wrapped around each other in a five-way embrace with a very confused Welsh Corgi in the middle.

"I'm sorry about your apartment," Javier mumbled into my shoulder just as a pendant lamp hanging by a thread in the ceiling crashed to the floor.

That made all five of us laugh and I said, "Yeah, I might need that guest room."

When I heard the police sirens, doubtless alerted by concerned neighbors, I groaned.

An hour later I was standing outside answering questions to the best of my ability while lying through my teeth.

"You're saying that wolf crashed through your bedroom window," the cop said, frowning at me. "And did all that damage?"

"That's right," I said, nodding. "I'm pretty sure it was rabid. But who knows."

I watched animal control dragging Dixon outside half covered in plastic. For all they knew, it really was just a wolf.

"And who...did that to him?" The cop said, vaguely motioning to Dixon.

I chewed on my lip and said, "My boyfriends. But I mean, the wolf pretty much destroyed himself tearing up the place. He was just...crazy, I guess."

"Mmm-kay," the cop said, frowning. I felt like he knew I was telling an insane lie but he couldn't figure what crime had been committed other than disturbing the peace. "And which one's your boyfriend?"

The cop pointed to the four Marquez men who stood on

the sidewalk with their four pairs of eyes trained on me as they drank coffee.

"Boyfriend*s* - plural," I said in the same tone I used to sell a three bedroom with a great backsplash. "They're all my boyfriends."

EMILIANO

I've always been a lore nut, so when I discovered the bit in the lore about us having a shared fated mate, I started digging a little deeper. The guys tended to tease me when I get deep into lore and because I enjoy being right about things and knowing things before the rest of them, I didn't really talk about it too much.

Basically, I knew that Ellie was a witch. I didn't mention it to the guys and I hadn't told Ellie I knew. I figured she would tell us in her own time. And it wasn't particularly fair, I thought, to spring that I knew her secret when she didn't know ours. I'd already alluded to it. I'd been hoping I could make her feel a little more comfortable about things if I hinted. But she probably already knew something was up. Witches can usually at least smell the whiff of magic around people who aren't quite human.

Shared mates, from what I'd read, were commonly witches. Once in a while, they were regular humans but if you dug into their ancestry, there was usually a witch in there somewhere, some magic that was calling out to the shifter blood.

I almost let her know that I knew the first time we made love. But afterward I'd been so dizzy and incoherent with my affection for her, not to mention high on the bliss I'd shared with her, I hadn't been able to form much of a thought once it was over.

Now the five of us were back at our house where, I thought, Ellie truly belonged. I felt bad for her apartment and everything. The building was insured at least and even if the damage hadn't exactly been an act of God, I don't think any of us minded letting the bill fall on the insurance company.

But Ellie couldn't stay there. We all knew that. The place was a wreck.

She didn't seem too torn up about it either which amused me a little bit.

Most of her actual stuff was in okay shape, it was mainly the furniture that was in pieces and some of her breakables.

For the night, since we were all exhausted, we packed up a couple night's worth of Ellie's stuff and lifted back to our house.

We were all exhausted yet we were too wired up from everything to actually sleep yet. And besides that, I knew we needed to clear the air on at least a couple of things.

"So, you're shifters," Ellie said later, cradling a cup of coffee in her hand. She was curled up next to Mateo on the couch, Ali on her other side. We were all huddled up in the living room. Poor Indiana was doing his best to acclimate to the new environment, but he smelled a powerful cat somewhere and I tittered to myself, watching him jump around trying to figure out what kind of cats smelled like that.

"Yeah," Mateo said, nodding, and then did a little doubletake and gaped at her. "Wait, how do you know what a shifter is?"

"Because she's a witch!" I said as if it should be obvious. Though to be honest, I say at a lot of things to my brothers as if they should be obvious. I looked at Ellie and raised an eyebrow. "Aren't you?"

"Yes," Ellie said. "How'd you-"

"Shared fated mates are often witches," I said proudly, as the other gaped at me, seeming slightly annoyed. "I read it."

"Nerd," Javier said.

"The nerd who's always right," I cracked.

"Still a nerd," he said, but he was smiling fondly.

"Shared fated mates?" I heard Ellie mumble. I saw her frowning over it. Oh, right. I needed to explain that to Ellie. In fact, none of us were completely sure that was what she was signing up for.

"Wait, what?" Alejandro said. I snorted at that, enjoying their surprise.

Even Mateo was thrown for a loop. "Wait, you're really a witch?" He said. "I thought that was just something you said at the bar?"

"When were you guys in a bar together?" Javier said, and I saw both Ellie and Mateo turn red. Aha. I'd thought they'd met up together at some point. Mateo never keeps his secrets well.

"I did a spell," Ellie said. She smiled at me and I liked to think she was proud of me for knowing first. "Weeks ago, I did a spell to find my true love, my soulmate. When I met Dixon, I thought it was him. Just because of the way he talked about meeting me. Ridiculous, right? But then every time I saw any of you..." She slumped against Mateo and he wrapped an arm around her. "I should've known from the start."

"I love that you're a witch," Ali said softly.

"I suspected that you were magical in some way too," Ellie said. "I just didn't know how." She blushed a little and laughed into Mateo's shoulder. "I would not have guessed puma shifters."

"Reowr!" Javier pretended to hiss and waved his hand around like a paw and Ellie giggled.

She gasped suddenly, her eyes wide. "Wait a minute, I met one of you up in the woods," she said. "It must have been one of you. C'mon, fess up! Who was it? You know exactly what I'm talking about!"

It had not been me and I looked around in surprise to see if I could guess who had been loitering in the woods and lucky enough to bump into Ellie. It had not been Mateo, who could not hide anything he was feeling and looked surprised. That left Javier and Alejandro. Javier was looking around with surprise but he was sometimes a decent actor.

Finally, Alejandro, blushing, raised his hand. "That was me," he said sheepishly. "I was just out having a run and then I felt that pull we keep talking about... Saw you walking up the trail. And I recognized you from Double's. I'm glad I didn't scare you."

Ellie beamed at him and said, "You didn't scare me at all. That meant a lot to me, you know."

"Yeah, that meant a lot to me too," Ali said.

And alright, maybe I was just the littlest bit jealous. But then I thought of the night Ellie and I had shared together. It seemed that each of us had made our connection with this woman and when I thought of it that way, I didn't begrudge my pack mates anything.

"Yep," Mateo said. "So, that's the Marquez clan. All puma shifters. We're all over Spain. The four of us came together when we were teenagers. Sort of like an arranged marriage between our parents. We came out to the states not long after that."

"Was that after Italy?" Ellie said.

Javier blurted out, "Wow, you told her about Italy?"

Mateo coughed and said, "Yeah, that was after Italy."

"Do you guys still visit Spain?" Ellie said.

"We haven't visited in a while," I said, trying to think back. It had been at least five years since we'd been home. But we tried to keep in contact with our families generally. Javier had always been the closest to his parents. He was often telling us what new crazy thing they'd just posted on Facebook. I'd never been very close to my own parents. My mom had died when I was little and my father was pretty cold. I'd always considered the other guys my real family. I think they mostly felt the same.

Yet it has never been quite complete before.

Until now. Until Ellie.

"Yeah," Javier said wonderingly, "we haven't been back in forever."

"We should go soon," Mateo said. "It's important to stay in contact with our home packs, even if there aren't really battles anymore." He shrugged and said, "At least not big ones," clearly thinking of Dixon.

"I've never been to Spain," Ellie muttered. "I've barely been anywhere. I was always just so driven with my career and one thing and another. Never took the time to travel."

"Do you want to go to Spain, sweetheart?" Mateo said, kissing her temple. "We can take you to Spain."

"I'll take you to all the best vineyards," Javier said, throwing her a wink.

"Oooh," I said, stroking my chin as I started to get excited at the idea. "There are so many museums I would love to take you to. And the architecture, oh God, Ellie, you'll really appreciate the architecture. I could take you on a real tour. You'd actually enjoy it unlike the rest of these slugs."

"I'd love to," Ellie whispered.

"Will you really go with us?" Alejandro said hopefully. "Because we'd seriously take you in a second."

"Yes, we would," Mateo murmured, stroking her hair.

"Of course, I would," Ellie said. "Who's turning down Spain with four hot men? But..there's something I have to tell you because I feel like we haven't properly discussed it..."

She looked genuinely worried then and I felt all of us tense up a little bit at once. I wondered now if she was going to say this shared mate thing just wasn't for her. I would understand if she did. Only the fates seemed to have designed it and the fates didn't usually pair people up who would be unhappy. Though I supposed it wasn't impossible.

Ellie wrung her hands and I saw that whatever it was, truly upset her a bit. Her eyes were glassy and she swallowed before she spoke. "I know a couple of you have said you don't get jealous. That it's fine if I get to know you all." She glanced over at Ali and Javier and blushed especially deep. "I know we've...done some things. Together. Um, well, all of us."

I didn't miss the way Javier smirked at that before his expression switched back to concern.

"But I can't assume..." She cleared her throat. She seemed to be having a hard time getting it out and Mateo encouraged her, whispering in her ear, though I didn't hear what he said. "I can't assume you're all just..." She started to cry and I leaned forward as if to catch someone falling.

My mate is upset, I thought helplessly.

Mateo held her close as she spoke, choking on her own words. "I can't assume you're all j-just okay with...with all being with me but..." She shook her head, tears sliding down her pretty face. "I can't choose just one of you. And I've made peace with that. I'm in love with all of you. I don't know how else to p-put it. And I've been thinking of you all as my boyfriends. B-but is that okay?" She clapped a hand to her mouth, her eyes wide with panic. "Can I really have all of you?"

I felt all of us simultaneously relax. Of course, it wasn't good that Ellie was needlessly upset but I think we were all quite relieved that she didn't mean to be and that we were all on the same page here.

"Baby," Javier said lightly. "We don't want you to choose."

"Yeah," Ali said, nodding. "It's like I said the first time I really met you. We are all *super* into you. Like, all of us. And this shared fated mate thing means...you're with us. *All* of us. As long as it's good with you, it's good with us."

Mateo reached up to wipe her tears away and kiss her softly sand said, "I'm so glad you *want* to be with all of us."

"Oh God, so much," she said, smiling sweetly before breaking into a yawn.

"Oh man, you must be so tired," Mateo said. "After all this excitement."

"I was thinking of going to bed soon," Ellie said, rubbing her eyes. "I'm so happy though, you guys. I can't really explain how happy I am."

"We're happy too, my love," Mateo whispered.

I couldn't help but smirk at how sweet Mateo was with Ellie. It was such a different side than I usually saw of him.

"Can I show you to your room?" Ali said, extending his hand to her when he got up.

She nodded and we all stood up and stretched. I winced, feeling the ache of sore muscles. Mateo generally liked to keep us in shape, since with our jobs and being shifters, there was no telling what kind of action you'd suddenly need to swing into. But it had been a while since there'd been quite so much excitement and jumping through a window and throwing down like we'd just done had put me to the test. When I stood up, I realized I was about to pass right out. I thought I'd go straight to bed, but as I passed everyone else,

Ellie tugged me over by my sleeve and kissed me. Not just a peck either, but a real kiss that would have had me changing my mind about sleep if I hadn't been so exhausted.

"Goodnight, Emi," she whispered.

I kissed her one last time and said, "Goodnight."

My dreams were sweeter and more restful that night then they'd ever been before.

ELLIE

Alejandro took my hand and let me through the Marquez's impressive home. I *loved* their house. I'd never really had a dream house in mind for myself. I'd always sort of imagined living in the woods, but being a realtor who saw so many different types of houses and design styles and architecture so often, I'd never really been able to decide on one thing. Yet I felt like the Marquez's home with its dark wood siding and big windows and gorgeous cliffside view of Boulder, was exactly the kind of house I would choose if I could choose any house in the world.

The rest of the guys were still talking in the living room and it was nice to have a minute alone with Alejandro. He clasped his hand in mine and we ambled through the living room and the dining room and I eyed the pretty stained glass windows here and there and the nice refinished hardwood floors. It was hard not to also look at it through a realtor's eye.

Ali led me up the stairs and said, "Are you really tired? Or are you mostly overwhelmed?" He smiled slyly and I nudged him.

"I was overwhelmed," I said. "How could you tell?"

"I'm good with people," he said, wrapping an arm around me. We climbed the stairs and he kept smiling at me. "We're all pretty excited you're here now. Can't lie."

"Me too," I said. A lock of hair fell in front of my eyes and at the top of the stairs and he stared at me, looking a little lovesick and making my heart thump in my chest. He tucked my hair behind my ear and swallowed.

"You don't have to be shy," I said softly. "About touching me. Or anything like that." I stepped into his arms and kissed his cheek and his chin and his bottom lip. "I'm yours. I'm all of yours."

"God, Ellie," Ali murmured. "You're amazing."

We ended up just making out at the top of the stairs for a while until we heard somebody coming up the stairs behind us and clearing his throat.

"Oh, *I* see why you guys wanted to be alone," Javier said, grinning cheekily.

I felt as if I'd been a given a kind of permission now to embrace what I'd been (only a little bit) shy about before and now I pulled away from Alejandro and turned around to tug Javier closer by the sleeve of his shirt.

"Um, do you two guys feel like, um...tucking me in?" I said, turning a little red.

Alejandro wrapped an arm around me from behind and kissed my neck. "Anytime."

Javier's smile turned sly and he stepped in close to kiss me slowly. "Baby, we'd love to."

There was an attempt at giving me a tour of my bedroom, though it was a little weak in execution as all three of us were pretty distracted. The room was nice and big though, with a huge, comfy bed all freshly made in white sheets and a crisp, white duvet and big windows that looked out on the forest below.

Javier led me inside, laying little kisses along the inside of my wrist, and Alejandro shuffled along behind me, moving my hair aside to kiss my neck, his palm firm against my stomach. At the side of my bed, I tugged Javier close again and he kissed me, heatedly. The press of him from the front as Alejandro embraced me from behind made my breath short just from the implications. I pulled away to catch my breath for a second and Javier looked at me, slightly worried, until I took off my shirt and let it fall to the floor. Behind me, I heard Alejandro doing the same and I giggled, giddy, as I helped Javier get rid of his.

Javier had the longest hair of all the brothers and I reached up to tangle my fingers in it as I kissed him and Alejandro pressed me closer to Javier and the bed. When I felt Alejandro's palms kneading my breasts through my bra, I sighed into Javier's mouth. Alejandro murmured behind me and I didn't even realize I was taking off my own pants before they'd joined my shirt and my shoes on the floor.

"Lay back on the bed," I said to Javier, and he nodded and kicked his shoes off, his eyes big, as he sat on the edge of the bed and scooted up. Where Ali and Emi were muscular but lean and Mateo was huge, Javier was thick and it made my mouth water as I climbed up on the bed. There was something impressively solid and sexy about his body. He had abs like the rest of them but they were nestled in a little bit more belly and there was so much to hold onto. I crawled up to straddle him and leaned forward, kissing him deeply, sliding my hands down the warm, brown skin of his chest to his stomach and pressing my fingers there. Alejandro climbed up and knelt behind me and it was already overwhelming in the best way as he unzipped his jeans and pressed himself, hard and firm against my bottom clad only in a thin layer of lace.

Experimentally, I rocked into Javier and Ali rocked with

me. I could feel Javier erect under me and Ali behind me as his hands came around to massage my breasts again, Javier's hands sliding up my thighs to press at my stomach. I threw my head back and Ali licked at my throat as we all rocked into each other again and again. Just that would have gotten me off and I thought it might but I couldn't help *wanting*, wanting so badly to feel what it would be like to have both of them inside me at once.

"J-Javier..." I said shakily.

He knew what I meant immediately and he scrambled out of his jeans and his briefs, his erection thick as it sprang free. I heard Ali rustling behind me and then he helped me off with my panties and we were all naked together, the connection between all three of us humming and buzzing like a live wire that made us even more aroused. I inched up a bit more and smiled softly at Javier when I saw that both our hands were shaking as I helped guide his cock inside me. Behind me, Ali seemed to read our bit of nervousness and murmured sweet things and softly kissed my shoulder and my back, but when I felt Javier fully inside me I gasped and lurched forward a little, bracing myself on his chest. Ali pressed himself against my ass and the promise of that was enough to make me whimper as I slowly began to ride Javier.

"Is this good?" Ali whispered in my ear. "Is this okay, sweetheart?"

"Yes," I breathed. "Do it, do it, please..."

Ali pressed himself inside me slowly, slowly. I started to get impatient. But when he pushed himself inside fully and I felt the two of them in me at once, I shook and he held me, his arms around me as he whispered in my ear how much he and the others loved me and how they belonged to me and me only. I bit my lip, becoming used to the sensation of both of them in me and slowly I began to move. I felt like I was right on the precipice of bliss and it was taking every bit of effort not to fall off of it as Javier gripped my hips and moaned, thrusting up into me just as Alejandro began to push in and out from behind. I could feel them both holding back a little, scared to hurt or overwhelm me and I leaned on my hands, staring down at Javier. I smiled and he pushed my hair behind my ear, staring adoringly.

"Let go," I whispered. "Both of you. You can let go. Do it."

I saw a tear slide down Javier's cheek and I pressed my thumb to his mouth and he bit it just as he thrust up inside me, Ali pounding me at the same time. I cried out so loud I must have awakened the dead but pleasure was coursing through me, the bond between all of us vibrating like a plucked bass string and I rode Javier, bouncing and rocking with no particular rhythm as Alejandro whined and moaned against my back pressing ever deeper inside me until all once he gasped and I felt him come, the pulse of him thrumming through my body. That set off Javier and I felt him spill inside me as he arched up, clutching my hips so hard it would likely bruise.

We were all together in our pleasure, wrapped around each other as the bliss rushed through us in waves and finally I keened and slumped over on top of Javier, breathless. Alejandro pulled out of me and fell beside us and threw an arm over Javier and I, grinning and catching his breath.

"Oh my God," he said, panting. "I've never felt like that before."

Javier just stared at me and whispered, "I can't believe you're ours."

"I am," I said, and kissed him and then Javier before moaning a little as I let him pull out of me. I slid across Javier so I was resting between the two of them, the three of us slick with sweat and cum but I didn't feel weird or gross about any of it. I only felt sated and happy as I spooned

Alejandro and Javier spooned me. "Are you sleeping here with me then?" I said giggling.

"I really don't think I can't move," Javier murmured into my neck.

I squeezed Ali's hand and felt his soft laughter and the three of fell asleep like that, naked atop the covers.

~

"Well, what do we have here?" The voice was Mateo's and he sounded pretty amused.

I smiled when I heard him but I didn't open my eyes. I was much too comfortable and I attempted to burrow into Javier's back. My arm was wrapped around him, a warm and thick body and I squeezed him and hummed, refusing to be moved. Alejandro kissed my neck and I heard Mateo laugh to himself.

"Looks like you guys had some fun."

I cracked an eye open and looked up at Mateo who stood by my head, grinning like the cat who ate the canary. "Um… I thought I'd break in the bed?" I said.

"We sure did break it in," Ali said, gently biting my shoulder.

"If you're willing to actually get out of bed," Mateo said, "Emi's making French toast."

"Hmm." Javier hummed. "He does make good French toast."

"I need a shower," I mumbled. I rolled over on my back and stretched, unashamedly bearing my breasts. When I opened my eyes again all three of them were gaping at me. "Don't make me feel bashful," I said, smiling shyly now.

"You're our first shared mate," Javier said, his voice hoarse from sleep. "Takes getting used to."

I kissed his nose. "First and *only*, I think you mean."

"Obviously," Ali said, rubbing my shoulder.

Mateo backed toward the door and said, "I was just about to shower but if you want to go first-"

"*Or* I could join you," I said, sitting up and kicking at the sheets.

Mateo grinned at that and leaned in the doorway. "Well, I'm not saying no to that."

Our shower ended up going a *little* long once I ended up with my legs wrapped around Mateo who was strong enough to hold me up against the shower wall as he pounded into me. I'd never had successful shower sex before but trust the Marquez alpha to make it an award-winning experience. I braced myself on the shower bars attached to the wall and my legs gripped him around his back as he thrust inside me. I was still a little sensitive from the night before and now I threw my head back and whined and moaned as he leaned forward to bite and lick at my breasts.

The French toast was cold by the time we came down to breakfast.

I shuffled into the kitchen in a bathrobe, feeling just a little bit shy, as happy as I was. I'd texted work to let them know I had a serious home emergency and was staying elsewhere. Myra had told me to take a couple of days off to deal with it when I'd explained that *actually* my apartment had pretty much been destroyed. I was a little worried about what that meant with how my clients had been going lately and feeling like I needed to be honest, I'd told her so. She'd texted back that my phone was ringing off the hook. I supposed Dixon's death had broken whatever kind of spell he'd had them all under.

"Hey," I said, greeting Emiliano at the stove. He smiled a good morning to me and I wrapped him in a hug, forcing him to turn around and embrace me back. I got the feeling that Emi wasn't a natural hugger and I chuckled to myself as he sighed and then relaxed into it and kissed my neck before turning back to the stove.

"Are you grumpy in the morning?" I said, nudging him.

"I'm only grumpy because I have to remake your French toast," he said loftily. "Because you took so long it got cold."

"I don't mind if it's cold," I said.

"*I* do," he said. "Sit down and have some coffee."

"Yes, sir." I pecked a kiss to his nose then and sat at the table. Immediately, Indiana came tapping into the kitchen as the boys stepped around him, getting their own coffees and plates and utensils. Indiana looked sort of befuddled but contented. I think he was still getting used to the scent of big cat that must have been everywhere around him and the half-cat people who were now his new family. He jumped at me and I scratched between his ears as Javier set a cup of coffee in front of me and kissed me on the head.

"So...I don't have to work today," I said with some sense of triumph. "But my clients are coming back so I might send some emails and make a few calls from here. I don't want to take anything for granted. I assume you guys are all working today?"

Javier, Mateo, and Alejandro all nodded, looking a little annoyed that their jobs had not disappeared the moment their mate had arrived but Emi cleared his throat.

"I don't have anything for today actually," he said quietly. "If you'd like to spend the day with me…"

"I'd love to," I said brightly. I would have been fine on my own but I was so excited about this big, new, crazy relationship. I was relieved I'd get to spend some time with one of my guys. "Hey, could you show me some of that lore stuff you were talking about? I'd like to learn more about shifters."

The other three smiled knowingly and Emi spun around with his spatula in hand, his eyes big. "You actually *want* to learn about lore?"

"Oh my God," Mateo said, chuckling. "You're his dream woman."

I blushed at that but only looked at Emi. "Yes, of course. I'd love to."

Emi nodded at that, looking pretty happy about it. "Well, I'm not grumpy now." He flipped a slice of French toast so that it flipped in the air.

"You're all my dream men too, you know,' I said, looking at each of them. "Each of you. That's why it would have been impossible to pick."

"Soulmates," Mateo whispered in my ear.

"Soulmates," I said, and leaned back into his arms as he sat behind me, the two of us waiting for Emi to finish making me a nice hot batch of French toast.

EPILOGUE

S*ix months later...*

"I don't like flying," Javier said queasily. "I don't get sick or anything but I don't...I don't like flying."

He may have been a cat, but Javier was giving me puppy eyes. I stuck out my bottom lip, pouting in sympathy. We were all buckled into our business class seat on a plane bound for Atlanta and then Barcelona. I sat back in my seat between Javier and Mateo and reached up to rub the back of Javier's neck because I'd discovered that could calm him when he was a little freaked out about something. He sighed and leaned into it and Mateo nudged me on the other side.

"He'll be alright," Mateo said. "It's just take off and landing that's rough on him. Once we're up, he orders a gin and tonic and he's right as rain."

"Good," I said, chuckling with relief. I leaned my head on Mateo's shoulder and sighed happily.

The first decision to visit Spain had been made just days after I'd officially moved into the house. But then it was one thing after another keeping us from taking the trip. I was too busy with clients. I'd sort of overcompensated after the scare with Dixon had nearly ruined my career and worked so hard with such determination that my career had sort of exploded. A small explosion maybe, but I'd had a big spike in sales and that had attracted new business. The commissions had been amazing and it had been fun to take my guys out on the town and treat them. We'd taken some day trips out to Denver and eventually when I'd had a real weekend free, they'd taken me camping...although most of the camping trip had been spent on a pile of sleeping bags in the tent and then cuddled around the fire.

I'd also learned a lot about the Marquez's investigation business which I found endlessly entertaining. They were always telling me about interesting new cases and I pestered them even for information about mundane cases. It was all new to me after all. Even the tenth unfaithful husband they were surveilling was fascinating to me. And after enough begging, Mateo had let me go out on a stakeout with him. That had been a lot of fun. Everyone had claimed it would be a lot more boring than I expected. But they were all wrong, of course. Even when nothing exciting had happened, I'd been stuck in a car with Mateo. When the others got wind of it, suddenly I was invited on a bunch of stakeouts - to my delight.

Time had been passing by so quickly as everything seemed to fall into place. There was always something (and someone) to do around the Marquez place. Emi had been delighted to teach me all about shifter lore and then he'd wanted to learn about my spells and potions. Between the two of us, we kept pushing each other to learn more about our respective magical worlds.

Then there was Javier - who had discovered that I had a good palate for wine and his favorite game became testing it. He was more into wine than I'd realized...which is how he'd figured out he wanted to be a sommelier. He'd been shy about admitting it. He felt a loyalty to his job with the P.I. firm but after I'd pushed him a little he'd confessed to Mateo he would study it if it was his passion. Now he was studying to be a wine steward and everyone was proud of him.

Alejandro and I also shared a special kind of bond. It wasn't really based on anything like a skill or a passion for some kind of work. It was people we both seemed to understand. I'd realized after spending enough time with Alejandro that he was a very empathetic person. It was how he'd known just what I'd needed when he'd run into me in the woods while he was shifted. He seemed to have a talent not just for talking to people but making them feel a little bit better about things. Whenever the two of us were alone and talking, we were discussing people and their behavior. A lot of my most meaningful conversation with the Marquezes were with Alejandro.

Meanwhile, Mateo and I had a sort of soulful connection. Sometimes I could look at Mateo and just know he needed me to take his hand, as much as he pretended to be eternally strong. The more I got to know him, the more I saw how seriously he took his duties as alpha and as my mate and as the head of his investigation firm. He was the most focused and intense person I'd ever known and every single day I woke up in bed, snuggled up between a couple of my Marquezes, I thanked the fates that I grew sick of dating and did that spell in the woods that day and that Mateo's reflexes were quick enough to yank me back from getting run over in the street.

"What are you thinking about?" Mateo said now. I glanced over Javier, who looked a little sweaty and took his hand in mine, giving it a squeeze.

"How happy I am I guess," I said quietly. "And excited! I can't wait to see where you grew up."

Mateo leaned over to peck me on the lips. "I'm glad we

could make the time for the trip. We should try to make it a regular thing. Or maybe in another six months, we could go somewhere else too? Paris or London..."

I smiled a secret little smile to myself and took a deep breath. I'd been meaning to the tell the guys something. I'd thought I might wait until we were in Spain, maybe make an event out of it when I got to see the countryside where they'd grew up, but I didn't think I could contain it any longer.

"Six months from now might be tricky." I said, biting my lip.

"Oh yeah?" Mateo raised an eyebrow. "Why's that? What have you got lined up in six months?"

I took yet another deep breath and met Mateo's eyes, squeezing Javier's hand next to me so that he looked up in interest, forgetting for a moment that the plane was about to take off.

With my free hand, I patted my stomach and cast Mateo a meaningful look. "I might not be in the greatest condition to travel that far six months from now."

Javier squeezed my hand hard and I heard his intake of breath and he made a funny little sound like a meow. It made me laugh. Behind us, Ali and Emi immediately popped up between our seats, gaping up at me.

"You're *pregnant*?" Emiliano said. He never sounded so animated and I nodded, beaming. "Oh my *God*. That's fantastic! I mean, isn't it?"

"I'm happy about it," I said, shrugging. It hadn't really occurred to me not to be. There hadn't been a very formal conversation about it but there had been vague references to 'cubs' here and there. And there was no reason to wait that I could see.

Alejandro was crying. I'd guessed he would be the most emotional about it and I leaned over and kissed his lips. "You're a sweetheart," I said.

He sniffed and ducked his head. "Sorry. I'm just surprised is all."

Mateo was just staring at me. I thought he looked happy. But for the first time, he was a little bit hard to read. He rubbed his face and I did see his eyes glisten a little bit. I couldn't remember ever seeing him close to crying before.

"My mate having cubs," he whispered. "*Our* mate."

"Our mate," the other three said, firmly in unison.

"I don't think I could possibly be any happier," he said as if he were genuinely trying to think of a way for that to happen. "Little lion cubs?"

"Little lion cubs," I said. I took his hand and rested it on my stomach and kissed his cheek. "Congratulations. You'll have a new Marquez puma pretty soon."

The hug was a little awkward, as Emi and Ali tried to hug us around our seat. And Javier had completely forgotten to be nervous as the plane began to taxi. The four Marquez men squeezed me and I wiped my eyes. I could sense the curious looks from passengers around us. It would have been difficult *not* to eavesdrop and I could only guess what they were theorizing about our unconventional little family.

But none of that bothered me as I sat back in my seat and nuzzled Mateo's shoulder. What did I need of convention? I had love.

AFTERWORD

A Final Note from Jade:

I hope you enjoyed this story. Well, the good news is that there's more to come. If you want to be the first to hear about my new releases, promotions and giveaways, I urge you to join my Exclusive Reader's Club:

[Yes. Sign me up, please!]

I love supporting my readers and I want to be able to provide more to you, you can also join me on Facebook **here**.

ALSO BY JADE ALTERS

Magic & Mates

The Sharing Spell

Fated Shifter Mates

Mated to Team Shadow

Mated to the Clan

Mated to the Pack

Mated to the Pride

In the Heat of the Pack

Protected by the Pack

Claimed by the Pack

FATE OF THREE

Acknowledgment

Without you I have no motivation to move forward. For that I thank you with all my heart.

Love,
Jade

❀ Created with Vellum

KATE

"Ma'am? Did you want that iced or hot?" The barista is looking at me like there might be something wrong with me. I don't blame her. I've been staring blankly at her for a few seconds too long.

I shake my head and manage a tight smile. "Hot, please." I pay for my latte and nod just as my phone buzzes again. I get that familiar tense feeling in my shoulders again. Funny, but when I was an executive assistant at an auction house, I never used to get that tense feeling in my shoulders. But that was before I made the mistake of being flattered by the attention of a man representing a very secretive, very rich, very underground collector whose representative was 'impressed' by my conduct and work at an auction one evening. I still remember it like it was yesterday. He never told me his name. He was just a well-spoken balding man in a very nicely tailored suit who said his client was looking for a new assistant who could conduct herself with the utmost professionalism and discretion and had some solid experience with collectors and tracking down objects of great worth. I remember the knowing smirk on his lips as he handed me the bright red business card that had an address but no name on it. I remember being flattered and only later did I realize that the criteria the man didn't mention was that he needed somebody just young enough and just naive enough to be easily manipulated and cowed.

Three days later I met Mr. January for the first time and my life was never the same.

I work at Mr. January's warehouse where he keeps many of his 'treasures'. Some of them he has flown out to his estate in Mill Neck on Long Island. But underground down on the Lower East Side, there is a hidden place full of incredibly valuable as well as incredibly dangerous things he's picked up over his long life. That's his dragon's horde. That's his great treasure. That's where I go to work every day.

I wish I didn't.

The entrance to the warehouse doesn't look like anything because it's not supposed to. I sip my latte and make my way down a bustling street headed toward Chinatown. Just like I do every morning, I nod hello at Mr. Zhao who runs the grocery next to the rusted metal door that leads to an elevator. On the other side of the door is a shoe store that never sells shoes. I'm pretty sure the shoe store is some front that January's also running, but that's none of my business. The less I know about Mr. January's business outside of my job, the better as far as I'm concerned.

"Morning," Zhao says, squinting because it's bright and crisp out on this cool day.

I adjust my scarf over my shoulder. "Good morning, Mr. Zhao."

I take out my key and unlock the door and head down a dark and narrow hallway to a dodgy looking freight elevator that will take me to the warehouse. Nobody's supposed to know I'm going through that door every morning. January likes to stay on the down low, to put it mildly. Mr. Zhao gets paid a couple of thousand dollars a month to make sure nobody's noticing, and anyway, he knows if he said a word about who goes in and out of that door, he wouldn't be waking up the next day.

Mr. January is pretty good at keeping his bases covered.

There's only one button in the elevator and it only goes to one floor. The elevator ride is always a little terrifying. The thing rumbles and shakes and goes down down down deep under Manhattan and half the time the subway is thundering by and it feels so close I think it'll bust through the walls. I step out and clutch my latte and my purse, taking another sip to buck myself up for the day.

I've been working for Mr. January for two years now and I haven't gotten used to it. Sometimes I'm afraid of what I'd be like if I did get used to it.

My heels clack on the stone floor of the long corridor and I slide my keycard through a scanner and pull the heavy door into the warehouse. You'd think working for somebody with the wealth of a person like Mr. January, a man who has his fingers in who knows how many unsavory business pies, the environment would be a little bit more luxurious. Not that it's my biggest problem with this job by any means. I've had to go down to the estate at Mill Neck a few times, one of those gigantic, luxurious mansions that somehow seems hidden in the middle of Long Island's fanciest neighborhood. But, most of the time, I work at a big, boring desk in a big, boring warehouse full of very unboring *stuff* as men walk around and occasionally talk about doing frightening things. When I'm working on my own at my desk, I'm okay. But I have to deal with January a lot and I have to go handle transactions a lot. I hate those parts of the job.

"Kate Bloom!" Mr. January says. I hear his voice seemingly all around me as I make my way through the warehouse, passing the men January hires to do 'special projects' for him. Right now three of them are sitting at tables cleaning guns so that's a clue as to the special projects. January sounds happy. I guess that's a good sign. I spin on my heel and see him heading towards me.

January is somewhere close to seventy. You can tell he used to be really handsome. I guess he still is. I'm not sure if I don't think of him that way because he's so much older or because he scares me half to death. His age makes him no less intimidating. He's got several inches on me too. His gray-blonde hair is receding but he makes up for it with a beard and a gravelly voice. He has blue eyes that pierce you like a laser target. When they're fixed on me, I feel like I can't even move.

"You're just the girl I want to see," January says, grinning at me. He's doing his folksy thing like I'm his daughter or something. He strides up to me in one of his good suits and grips my shoulders in his hands. I breathe in and smile.

Ready to serve, sir. Whatever you need. Please don't murder me.

"I have a little transaction for you to handle," he says. "Over on the west side. Very important item. You'll be carrying the money."

When I buy things for Mr. January I have to verify the authenticity of the object. If I'm wrong, he'll be very upset. So far, I've never been wrong. But I really hope it's an item I already know about.

"Anything familiar?" I say. I like to keep my tone light.

"The Kanyite necklace," January says, rubbing his hands together.

I'm probably visibly relieved. The Kanyite necklace is just a stupid magical crystal that improves health and vitality. The last recorded possessor of the thing was an empress who lived to be one hundred and thirty years old. Since then it's been bounced around and rumored about, like just about everything January ends up buying that shouldn't be in his hands in the first place. But at least this thing sounds pretty harmless. Worst case scenario, he'll end up living a long life.

Now, I'm pretty jazzed. A transaction will take up most of the day, even if it's just uptown. I could stop for lunch at the Russian Tea Room maybe…

I mean, I hate this job and I'm not allowed to resign. I might as well enjoy the perks.

"There's a second object of great importance," January says more quietly, stepping in close to me. I don't like the way he says it. It worries me. "But don't worry about the authenticity. George will authenticate it."

George is one of January's suits who's really a henchman. If January ever does decide to kill me for some reason, I'm pretty sure George will be the one to do it and then somebody right under him will do away with the body. The guy barely ever changes his expression. His face looks like it's made of plastic. He scares me more than Mr. January does.

"Okay," I say, putting on my most agreeable voice. "Of course, sir. What time will I be-"

"They'll be expecting you at eleven…" He glances at his watch. "And I need you to take a look at some listings."

"Yes, sir."

The listings will be for auctions happening right now on the dark web where anything January is likely to be in the market for would be sold. A lot of my job involves combing through the absolute cesspool that is the dark web. Typically, January gives me a list of items he'd like to find and I start looking. Sometimes this means searching the dark web and sometimes this means meeting really weird people in really weird places. I've gotten to go to some exotic locales. But today I don't mind sticking to my desk, especially since I get to go back out later.

Three hours later I have a headache because January's

apparently looking for the skeleton of one *specific* dodo bird that supposedly once belonged to some king from...somewhere. I really shouldn't complain. He once had me handle the buying of an amulet that captures souls. As far as I know, he hasn't used it. But he is keeping that one up at Mill Neck. He probably shows it to prostitutes when he brings them over.

At ten-thirty, George waves me over. Time to go uptown. I ride in the back of one of January's limos. I'm not sure he doesn't have some other magical amulet or something that makes traffic disappear. Streets always seem to clear for his cars. Even in the middle of the day. In *Manhattan.*

I catch up with the seller and read the dossier on the way over. Next to me on the seat is a metal suitcase containing a million dollars. That's just the security deposit; the little tip that means January is for real. The buying price is fifty, which seems high for an amulet with unproven magic powers. I'm guessing it's the second object that's the real prize. That worries me. He's bought weapons before. He's bought powerful dark objects that he's sold to others or just talked about using someday. For the most part, January is a thug and a mercenary. He doesn't want to take over the world or anything because he's not interested. So, the real damaging stuff he passes onto somebody else. Which is just as dangerous as if he used it himself. It's probably more dangerous a lot of times. At his worst, January is a gangster. But there are people out there who want real power and some of these artifacts would be deadly in their hands, for the entire world.

"Mrs. Oleskaya," I say. The heiress is from Ukraine. Her penthouse is lavish. She's wearing a mink and drinking vodka from a crystal glass. Some tiny dog barks from another room. My back-up stands behind me in their black suits. George has the briefcase full of cash. "I'll be handling Mr. January's transaction today. It's a pleasure to meet you."

People always seem sort of relieved when they're buying from or selling to me - as if they didn't expect somebody who wouldn't be threatening for no reason. I'm the kind face that gets some of January's dirty work done. It's all a lie. If January wanted somebody dead or if a deal went south, George would tell me to duck and somebody would have a bullet in their head. And I'd duck. Because I'm interested in staying alive.

If I could leave, I would. But he'd find me and kill me. He's told me so multiple times. You can't just leave Mr. January. I didn't know that when he hired me, of course.

Mrs. Oleskaya offers me a drink and I take one because why not. I'm worried about whatever this second mysterious object is. I could use something to take the edge off.

I'm sitting on a white velvet chaise. The entire place is white and gold. It's just bordering on horribly gaudy.

"I have something I know you're quite interested in," Oleskaya says, winking at me like this is a cute little game. She nods at a pearl inlaid mahogany box on a gold side table. "It's right there. Go ahead and authenticate it."

I nod at George who motions to one of his guys and they bring me my case of tools; a light and various magnifiers among other things. This part I'm comfortable with anyway. I take a sip of vodka and go to work, carefully opening the box to reveal the necklace sitting on a pile of black velvet. I've been studying the thing. I've even studied 3D models of it. I can't test its magical veracity although I have learned how to do that with other magical objects. I'm about half witch at this point, though never formally trained. But all I need to do with this thing is to make sure the crystal is real.

"It's perfect," I finally declare smiling at Oleskaya. I nod at George again and he brings Oleskaya the briefcase. "And I understand there's a second piece you're selling to us?" I doubt I can keep the tension out of my voice. I just have the worst kind of feeling.

"Yes, of course." Oleskaya gestures for the men to come help in another room and when they walk out I stand there, feeling awkward and uncomfortable in this palace of a living room at the top of a tower in Manhattan. But I guess I don't feel totally out of place. Not completely. I've sold my soul to the devil. And the devil pays me very well. My own place might as well be just as gilded.

I hear something that sounds like whimpering and that's enough to make my heart pound. I turn and see the guys rolling out a young woman who is tied to a dolly like Hannibal Lecter, except they've put a kind of silver helmet over her head. She's also wearing silver bracelets on her wrists that look chafed and raw. The silver must be spelled to deflect her magic, though presumably she's gagged. Not many witches can do magic without verbalizing the spells. If this one can though, she might be worth all that money.

A person. January's buying a person.

I feel sick. I clench my fists and fight not to give anything away. I've seen other terrible things on this job. I've seen both bad and innocent people get very hurt and I've seen a lot of objects that shouldn't even exist get bought and sold from one villain to another. But they're usually *objects*. This is a human being.

"Oh," I say simply.

"They call her the Sewer Witch," Oleskaya says, looking far too excited. "She's from Austria. One of the twenty most powerful witches in the world. Or so they say. They say a lot of things, don't they? She lived under the city in Vienna. Tell January, I said 'You're welcome.'"

The witch is a skinny little thing. Judging by her shaking, clenched fists, she's terrified. But there's nothing I can do for this woman. Not that it excuses anything, but it's very likely that January won't even know what to do with her. He may just have her do some parlor tricks at Mill Creek and then sell her to somebody else...which might be worse. Maybe she's as powerful as Oleskaya says and she'll be able to escape. I hope she does. I'm not involved in security. It wouldn't come back on me.

Or the witch will be able to escape and take some great revenge and kill me. I wouldn't blame her for it.

Or maybe I'm just telling myself all this to make myself feel better.

George is apparently involved in authenticating because he walks up to the Sewer Witch, grabs the helmet off her head just long enough to get a look at her face, and slams it back on. But in just that brief second, the witch's eyes flash and all the mirrors in the room shatter.

Oleskaya jerks and yelps out loud. "Oh, dear."

George heaves a sigh and pulls out his wallet, taking out a couple grand and handing it over to Oleskaya. "Apologies for the mess."

"I don't blame you," she says darkly, eyeing the witch. "I blame this awful creature. She nearly killed my Coco." She pouts at the football-sized dog in her arms who doesn't look any happier to be here than I am.

"It was a pleasure doing business with you, Mrs. Oleskaya," I say firmly. I feel nauseated and my head hurts. "Please let us know if you have any more items of interest in the future. Mr. January is always buying."

"Of course, dear," she says, all sweetness and light. "Good luck with the Sewer Witch. I would not remove that helmet unless you've got a solid ward up."

"Thank you for the advice, ma'am," I say.

He'll probably have me put up the wards. But I might try to convince him to hire his own in-house witch. I've long thought he should. My magic is okay, but it's not strong enough to hold back one of the twenty most powerful witches in the world.

The guys load the witch into the back of the SUV like she's a suitcase.

I'm riding shotgun and George is driving. He seems far too amused when he says, "Did you say you wanted us to drop you off for lunch at the Russian Tea Room and get your own way back or-"

"No," I say quietly. "It's fine. Let's just go back."

Mr. January is happy about his necklace but he's even happier about the witch. He's rubbing his hands together in excitement as the guys roll her through the warehouse. They have cells back there. I don't know if they've ever been used before. I don't think I want to know.

"The Sewer Witch!" January says. "An incredible find."

"What are you going to do with her?" I say. I try to sound indifferent but I'm sure I'm failing.

"I don't know yet," January says thoughtfully, stroking his chin. He regards me warily. "Do you have a problem with this, Kate?" He tips my chin up.

I hate it when he touches me.

"Of course not, sir," I say, not meeting his eyes. "You're right. It's an incredible find."

"Good," he says, nodding. "That's good. Because I have a lot of nice, empty cells back there. If you ever said a word to anyone-"

"I keep all your business in the strictest confidence," I say firmly.

It's true. I don't even know who I'd talk to if I were to say anything. If I go to the cops and say my boss is a dangerous gangster, they might listen to me. If I tell them the weapons are *magical*, I'll be laughed right out on to the street.

"That's what I like to hear." He gives me a joking little

punch to the chin. "You do a wonderful job here, you know." He smiles, almost friendly. He can go from threatening to jovial in less than a second.

"Thank you, sir," I say, before clasping my hands behind my back and going to my desk.

SCOTT

Wizards sure run slowly, I think to myself, scaling a second chain link fence. The climb is a little awkward with a clay vessel under my arm, but I'm still quick enough to outrun the spells being cast at me by the sluggish wizards. I dash down the alley, grimacing at the thick traffic of cars and people on the other side. Suddenly, I see people scatter as a black van skids to a stop and the side door slides open.

The guys have never quite gotten used to driving in Bangkok.

Dennis's head pops out and he waves his arm. "Scott!"

I feel the sting of a spell hitting my hip and grimace as I run to the van and hop inside and Dennis shuts the door as Miguel peels out. The van would not have been my first choice for a chase generally but so far the wizards are on foot and we'll lose them quickly enough.

I hand the clay vessel, aka The Vessel of Toontoon, over to Dennis. It supposedly holds the ashes of a powerful dark wizard from centuries ago. A mercenary gang in Thailand was planning on reviving him in order to bring some despot to power in Laos. Some chain of requests via under the radar diplomats then became a mission directive to us. The people who send us on our missions are a small group, some from the US and a few outside of it. They are the only ones who officially know we exist. Even the people that provide our resources and manpower from time to time have no idea who we are. They certainly don't know *what* we are.

We are Jaguar Force.

I hiss and clap my hand to my hip. "I need a healing tonic."

"Gotcha," Dennis mutters. He taps his lips and throws open the metal door of a cabinet on a wall in the van as it screeches down the street. Usually, Dennis drives and Miguel is the one with the tonics. I don't know why they switched it up and I clench my jaw, resisting a lecture. "This should ease any nasty hexes." He pours a bit of potion onto a cloth and presses it to my hip as I hold up my shirt. "If it were *me,* I would've shifted-"

"I don't know, Dennis, I thought a jaguar running through the city *might* have attracted some unwanted attention."

"I'm just saying," Dennis grumbles, "what is the point of being shifter spies when we never, ya know, *shift.*"

"We shift sometimes!" Miguel says from the driver's seat.

"For ourselves!" Dennis says, his voice going up a little high and hysterical like it does when he's making a point. I snort a laugh because Dennis is funny when he's like this. Sometimes that's annoying but since we've just accomplished our mission and have now lost the wizards, I guess I don't mind being a little amused.

The pain in my hip is easing up and I lean against the wall of the van and sigh as the vehicle swerves around another corner and jostles as it hits bumps in the road. We'll be making our way to our safehouse now. With any luck, we'll get some days off to relax. I wouldn't mind trying out an actual hotel room with a hot tub for a while before we jet off again to God knows where. Dennis has also been threatening to take us on a 'real' night out on the town in Bangkok which, knowing Dennis, is probably a terrible idea.

"I'll try to work a nice shifter moment into the next mission," I say wryly, grinning at Dennis. "Maybe we can play with a giant ball of yarn to take down the bad guys or something."

"Ha ha. Hilarious."

Now he's fooling with his laptop. He's the tech guy. Dennis sometimes acts like I'm the badass of the group because I'm the alpha and the toughest fighter, but the truth is, Miguel and I would be completely lost without him.

"Just saying...we should be called Jaguar Force for a reason," Dennis says, smirking. He's grown out his goatee and with his black-rimmed glasses, he looks like a fashionable nerd. Although calling Dennis a nerd is a little bit deceptive. We're all jaguar shifters and we're all well trained. Dennis might look like the computer guy but I'm the only person I know who could take him down.

The drive seems to take forever as Miguel takes us on a circuitous route to make absolutely sure we aren't being followed. Miguel is, generally speaking, our magic guy, though he's generally more about having the knowledge of magical objects and spells and beings than doing magic himself, although he can do some spells here and there. He's pretty good at brewing potions though. I'm guessing a hex would have taken me down by now if it weren't for Miguel.

Finally, we pull up in front of the safehouse and I get out to raise the shutters so Miguel can park inside. The sun is just setting. Nobody on the street seems particularly interested in us. The safehouse is just an abandoned warehouse.

We've been here about a week, tracking down the vessel. Pretty straight forward mission. They never saw us coming.

I watch Dennis carry the vessel and he tosses it in the air before catching it again. "Jesus, be careful with that thing. I don't know how dark wizard ashes work. The last thing we need is Voldemort suddenly appearing."

"Relax," Dennis mutters, striding up to the warded safe constructed just for this particular object. He punches in a long string of numbers and letters into the keypad before the little door opens and he sets the vessel inside before shutting it again. "We're all good. Anybody smart will try to forget the combination. And off this goes back to Peru, where it came from in the first place."

We need to pack everything up and head to the JF jet and get out of here.

But God, I am tired.

We've had four missions in a row with no real break. That's a lot for us, considering how much each mission takes out of us. I stand in the middle of the warehouse and rub my eyes, sighing. I want to be lying on a deck chair on a beach with a Tequila Sunrise in my hand and a scantily clad woman sitting on top of me. I don't know what the woman looks like yet. I'm sure I can think of something though.

I feel a nudge and open my eyes to see Miguel handing me a cold bottle of beer from the mini fridge. "Take a load off, boss. We'll handle packing up."

"Oh, you don't have to-"

"Don't worry about it," Dennis says, already packing up his computers as Miguel starts stowing our weapons into their cases. "You did all the heavy legwork on this one. Who knows? Maybe they'll even give us a break this time."

"Somehow I doubt that," I say darkly.

There's been a lot of work lately. Too many dark, magical objects floating around out there and too many people who know what to do with them. I've felt more and more lately like we're playing Whack-a-Mole.

I'd love to take a whack at a *big* mole. I know there must be one out there.

I take a sip of the beer and head to my bunk and my laptop to report our mission accomplished. Or at least, accomplished as soon as we hand off the artifact to our man in London who will take the thing to Peru.

All in a day's work.

We're just starting to relax on the JF jet, finishing up writing up our debriefing reports, when our new mission comes in. We all cast each other knowing looks. I figure if we get two more missions with no break, then I'll have to talk to Colonel Sachar. He sort of handles our HR issues and acts as a go-between for us and the commission who oversees us, while also doing the research to recommend missions for us that are usually then approved by the higher-ups. Ten years ago, Colonel Sachar started training us for Jaguar Force, which was his idea. Jaguar Force was intended to be one extremely elite team that would handle the sorts of intelligence problems that no one in intelligence even knows exist: the supernatural ones.

Before Jaguar Force, the three of us were babes in the woods of the CIA, intent on hiding our shifter identities while we handled regular old missions and legwork in the field. We were still within a pretty elite circle of intelligence operatives, but nothing very special. But Sachar knew what to look for when he started recruiting. He is a shifter himself. The advantages of utilizing shifters as spies were obvious. We have somewhat enhanced strength and senses. And sometimes actually shifting during a mission really does come in handy. It can certainly help out in a fight, although we try our best to limit visibility.

Now I'm getting a notification on my laptop; a new message coming in from Sachar.

"Let's get this over with," Miguel mutters.

We're whining, but the truth is...we totally love this job.

"Hello, team," Sachar says. He's mainly speaking to me from the laptop on the fold-out table in front of my seat. But Miguel and Dennis lean on the chair to watch. Sachar has a mop of white hair and a bushy beard. When he first told me he was a shifter and I guessed that he was a bear, I guessed correctly. He looks kind of like a bear. "Good job in Bangkok. Good job as always. I know you guys have been hard at it. I'm giving you three days of R and R on your way to your next mission. Let's get that out of the way..."

All of us collectively sigh in relief at that. Three days isn't much for how hard we've been working lately, but it's more than I thought we'd get.

"And what *is* our next mission?" I ask.

"We have a lead on a target who could bring down a big chunk of the black market in magical goods," Sachar says.

A big chunk?

Sounds like a big mole. He's got my attention alright.

Sachar says, "Have you ever heard the name 'Mr. January?'"

"I think Sachar's trying to take this guy down too soon," Miguel says. He's fidgeting with his lip. That's what he does when he's worried.

The hotel in New York is a five star. We never get accommodations this swanky. It's certainly a far cry from the stripped down safehouse we were just bunking at in Thailand. It makes me think Sachar is trying to butter us up for this mission. Because I think Miguel is right. We are going in too soon.

Our materials are spread out on the coffee table since Dennis has already swept the room for potential bugs. Twice. We don't like to take chances and we're right out in the open staying in a popular hotel right on Fifth Avenue. Of course, we have a cover and fake names for our hotel stay. We have a lot of those.

I squish down into the couch and take another sip of sparkling water. My stomach rumbles and I reach across Dennis for the room service menu. He's looking at the blow-up photograph of our 'in' to get at January on his iPad. This is our potential informant.

"Kate Bloom," Dennis mutters. "Former assistant at Christie's. She was recruited about two years ago."

"Did she know what she was getting into?" Miguel says. "Also, are we ordering room service? I need like, three steaks, at least."

"Yeah, sure," I say. "And it's unclear what she knew. All we really have to go by is some surveillance of her around Chinatown. Sachar thinks that's where January keeps his treasure trove."

"It's too soon," Miguel mutters again.

Dennis says, "It's not if he really does have the Ares stone."

According to the dossier Sachar gave us, January is right on the verge of selling an item called the Ares Stone. In terms of hot items, it's about the hottest there is if you're interested in utilizing dark magic to gain an insane amount of power. If you're in a fight and you've got the Ares stone, you're going to win. If you're in a *world war* and you've got the Ares Stone, you're going to win. Sachar has reason to suspect that somebody of ill repute out there is trying to get his hands on the

Ares Stone via January. He just doesn't know who it is yet and if January even really has the thing. there are a lot of question marks on this mission but even if we don't get to the Ares stone, January still sounds like a big fish worth taking down.

The only part of the mission I don't really like is the idea of handing the Ares stone back to my own government if we do find it. *Nobody* should have the Ares Stone. The thing should be destroyed. We're lucky if it's only been in the hands of a regular gangster and not the kind that runs a country.

"Sachar isn't sure that he does," Miguel says. "It's all rumors on the dark web."

"Still worth taking down, " I point out. "But I mean, I'm not sure whether this is the type of woman who would flip." I take the iPad from Dennis and take a long look at the girl. She's young. I already know she's twenty-seven but she looks slightly younger. She's come up fast to go from executive assistant at Christie's to a buyer for a guy like January. Which makes me think she *didn't* know what she was getting into. Maybe he deliberately recruited somebody young who he could scare more easily. Would someone like that really be willing to go up against a guy like January? It's a massive risk to take.

I hand the iPad back and pick up my phone to order room service on the hotel app. We know the basic facts of Kate Bloom's life. She's a nice suburban girl from Connecticut who majored in Art History at NYU before getting in at Christie's. Her parents are alive. She's had two long term relationships but nobody serious since starting at January's. But we don't know anything about *her*. Not really. Presumably, she's familiar with magic and the supernatural in general just by virtue of working for January. We're not sure if she was before but there's no evidence of it. I order us all a bunch of steaks and potatoes and some shrimp scampi and wedge salads on the side while I think.

She looks scared in the pictures to me, but maybe I'm reading too much into it. If she's scared, she'll resist helping us. We have to put our best foot forward.

"Miguel," I say, looking up at him. "You should initiate communication with her."

"Sure," Miguel says shrugging. Miguel is the prettiest of us. He was born in Costa Rica before coming to America as a teenager and joining the Marines, eventually getting recruited into intelligence. He has refined features and startling light brown eyes. Women love Miguel. "But why me?"

"Because you're hot but non-threatening," I mutter.

Dennis snickers at that and Miguel flips him off. "Whatever, nerd. The ladies love me."

"Exactly," I say, sending our order in. "Do that puppy eyes thing you always do.

"I don't do puppy eyes," Miguel says, sounding faintly sulky.

"It's a compliment!"

Dennis is laughing at us and I roll my eyes. "You'll pose as a seller. Dennis, you'll have to pull a name from one of his recent buyers or sellers. That's your connection." Dennis is humming in that way he does when he doesn't like what I'm saying and I shoot him a dirty look. "What?"

"It'll be better if I make some noise on the dark web. As an invented seller. We can't just go in cold. She'll freak out. We should dangle some bait and let her come to us."

"That might take a while for her to take the bait," I point out.

Dennis raises his eyebrows and says, "Then we'll have to make it some very good bait."

KATE

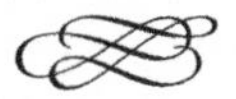

The postings on forums I keep tabs on are talking up a statue of a tiger. It's not just any statue of a tiger, of course. It's called the Blue Tiger and anyone who's really in the know is aware of its history. It was used to imbue the possessor with magical talents beyond their inherent means. Anyone really in the know also knows it was destroyed by monks in 1983.

Not many people *are* really in the know, of course. But I am. And I can't imagine why somebody would pretend to have it. If the seller is targeting rubes who don't know any better, it would make sense. But that shouldn't be happening on this kind of forum where only the elite buyers like January (or rather their representatives like me) hang out. Not many people even know about it. I think it's a test. I'm guessing they're really in possession of something else. Maybe something much bigger. I'd be stupid not to at least follow the lead. January's got a long list of items he's on the look out for. He gets impatient when I can't track down a certain number of them. So far, I've managed to stay in his good graces. But I once saw him direct George to break a guy's knee because he brought him the wrong kind of latté, so I'd rather not test his patience, thank you very much.

I send the seller a message. I don't tell them I work for Mr. January, of course. I wouldn't reveal that kind of information right off the bat. I tell them I work for a 'reputable client' and I'm curious as to their possession of the Blue Tiger. If they're going to play a game, I can play one too. At least for a while. People in this industry can be weird as hell. We go back and forth a little bit, both of us a little bit vague as we get a feel for each other. They don't admit that the Blue Tiger no longer exists but going by their tone, I'm ninety percent sure I was right.

I would like to speak to you about this in person, the seller says.

That's not unusual. People tend to hammer out the details of a deal in person. Even on the dark web, there's plenty of reason to be paranoid.

I say, *Where and when?*

The seller wants to meet me at The Blue Bar at the Algonquin Hotel when I get off work. Seems a little touristy but I guess there's some romance about the place. They haven't even given a name yet. Their handle is GrayGuard89 and I go by The LadyEve1777.

I agree to the terms of the meeting. This is good, I guess. Maybe they'll have something January really wants. Most of the time that's bad. At least for the world. But it's good for me. I get commissions along with the insane salary Mr. January pays me. Sometimes I try to stave off the guilt by throwing money at charities, but it doesn't help much.

I describe to the seller what I look like and what I'll be wearing. I'm petite and dark-haired and I have green eyes. Today I'm wearing a black Armani jumpsuit. The seller describes himself as early 30's, Hispanic, and 'devastatingly handsome' in a charcoal suit.

Modest too, I think to myself.

The rest of the day, despite my general unhappiness and anxiety working for January, I find myself getting kind of excited to meet the seller. There was something sort of charming about him online. Not that I'd ever actually get involved with one of these people.

Since I started practicing magic, I do feel as if I've become more in tune with my instincts. I'm not saying I'm psychic or anything like that but there are times I get particularly strong feelings about things and then it will turn out I'm right. I've known a couple of deals were about to go south, just in time to tell George we needed to get to the car just before shots were fired.

Right now, I have a feeling that this meeting is important. But I don't feel any kind of dread about it like I so often do. I can't really explain it. I buy and sell for January. It doesn't really have anything to do with me. Maybe, I think to myself, something important is going to happen on the way to the meeting or coming back. That would explain it.

At five, I shut down my computer and make my way out. More and more often, January handles *all* of his business from this warehouse. Sometimes that could be every day or it could be a couple of days a week and, some blessed weeks, I never see him at all. The rest of the time he's up at Mill Creek or jet setting around.

Today he's here, and I think he's unhappy with somebody because I hear the echoes of screams coming from the back of the place. It sounds like a guy at least. So it must not be the witch. Still, it makes my stomach lurch and I hurry to the elevator.

The Blue Bar is nicer than I remember. I met a buyer here once but I was probably in a bad mood that day and didn't remember the pleasant ambiance. I find a seat at a table near the middle of the place. I make sure my panic button is easy to find in my pocket. If I press the button, George comes running. I always bring it when I meet a new buyer or seller, but I leave it at work at the end of the day because it creeps me the hell out too.

Mr. January doesn't want anything happening to his property (unless he's doing it himself) and that includes me.

I order myself a dirty martini and keep my eyes peeled for devastatingly handsome men in charcoal suits. I wonder if he's a flirtatious type? He did seem a little flirtatious online but I only gave him enough to keep him talking. The very last thing I need is to get involved with either a seller or a buyer. They'd probably only be interested in getting closer to January anyway. That doesn't sound very confident, but my confidence has been in the toilet since I started working for this man.

My dirty martini is perfect; stronger than I thought it would be and not *too* dirty. Just how I like them. The seller promised to arrive sometime before six and it's exactly 5:45 when a man who is apparently honest and not egotistical at all sits down at my table, wearing a flawlessly tailored charcoal suit and an easy smile. He has high cheekbones and thick, dark eyelashes framing sparkling light brown eyes. I have to tell myself to hold it together. God knows what kind of snake is hiding behind that gorgeous facade...except that my decent instincts aren't registering any danger from this guy. I'm getting a good vibe from him. But that doesn't mean I'm not going to be on my guard.

"Hi there." The guy sits down at my table and gives me a smile that looks designed to be charming. He's carrying a laptop bag that he rests under the table when he sits down. "Have you been waiting long?"

"No, not at all."

"Good good." He motions a server over and orders a scotch and soda. It's not until he has his drink in front of him and has taken a sip that he says, "So, how long have you been working for Mr. January?"

That he knows I work for January isn't too surprising if he's inside this industry enough to have been on that forum. It also means he must know the truth about the Blue Tiger.

I fold my hands on the table and smile slyly. It's not too hard to play this cool, collected version of myself who knows the ins and outs of dealing with these people even though they're scary. I've gotten good at it. "I'll tell you that when you tell me how long you've been pretending the Blue Tiger still exists?"

He laughs at that. It's not a cackle either. It's kind of a warm laugh. His eyes are sparkling too. Who is this guy? "I was pretending for your benefit," he says. "I was hoping to pique your interest."

"Well, consider me piqued," I say wryly. "What is it you're *actually* selling?"

"Answer my question first," he says. "How long have you worked for Mr. January?"

I squint at him. His eyes are sparkling but they're also knowing. I feel like I don't need to answer this question at all. "You already know," I say slowly. "Don't you?"

"Two years," he says. "Did you know who was hiring you when you took the job? Or what kind of business it was?"

"No..." I'm starting to panic a little. I have a stinging, itchy feeling in my hands. I force myself to stay. I'm so tired of giving in to fear these days.

"I didn't think so," he says, smiling sadly. "Kate..."

That makes me gasp a little. It's one thing to know I work for Mr. January. It's another to actually know my real name right off the bat. "How do you know my name?"

"I have nothing to sell you," he says quietly, his gaze flickering around the room. "What I have is a proposal. It's a proposal that could free you from this job that I don't think you like very much."

"What, you want me to work for you?" I say frowning. "Sounds like it's a lateral move."

"I told you," he says. "I'm not a seller. I'm not a buyer either."

"Then who are you?" I say, clenching my teeth a little.

"I'm under the auspices of American intelligence," he says much too calmly.

"Under the auspices of... " I can't breathe. All the blood is rushing to my feet. "The FBI?" I whisper. "Are you fucking kidding me? You're going to get me killed-"

"It's not the FBI," he says. Now we're leaning forward over the table, close enough to kiss. There's a chance this guy is full of shit. But I don't think so. Not with what he already knows. "Not the CIA either but you might as well think of it that way. We want to take down your boss. And we want you to help us."

My panic button is in my pocket. I could just slip my hand in my pocket and press it. Probably what would happen is George would come and this guy would see him coming and scram. Then all this would be all over. Even better, I would be considered a stellar employee for calling the heavies in when presented with the authorities. It's exactly what I'm supposed to do. January would probably move his entire warehouse or go dark for a while to put them off the scent.

"I-I can't," I stutter. "He'll kill me. I can't...I can't even be *talking* to you. You don't understand what...what he traffics in. You wouldn't even believe me if I told you." I'm already committing a cardinal sin. I'm telling this guy about January. I must be crazy and yet some part of me that's been scared for so long is starting to crack. I never get to talk to *anybody* about this job or how stressful and terrifying it is. My family thinks I work for an elite auction house with quiet but legit customers. But I can't help but think that even if this guy is CIA or whatever, he can't have any idea what January is really into since probably ninety-eight percent of the human population doesn't.

"I think I would actually," he says. He mutters something under his breath and leans on one hand, twirling his finger in the direction of the rose in a vase on the table. The flower rises out of the vase, hovering in mid-air for a moment before it drops again.

I narrow my eyes. "You're a wizard? You're a...CIA wizard?"

"Sort of," he says, shrugging. "Listen, I know this is a scary thought for you. But if you did help us, you'd have our full support and protection. We would do everything necessary to keep you safe."

"You'd do the best you can, you mean," I say darkly. I notice he's not guaranteeing my safety. He knows better than that.

"Yes," he says, nodding. "And you'd be helping us destroy a monster."

It's strange but hearing someone else say that makes me feel better. I've never heard anyone refer to January as a monster because everybody I speak to about Mr. January is trying to stay on his good side. But still…

"I can't," I say, shaking my head. "I shouldn't even be talking to you at all."

"But you are," he says thoughtfully. "Listen, I'm going to take two books out of my bag. And that's all I'm doing."

"Okay…"

He slowly reaches into his bag and places two books on the table in front of me. One is *The Catcher in the Rye* in the familiar bright red cover I remember from school. The other is *The Great Gatsby* with a bright blue cover.

"My name is Miguel," he says softly. "That's my real name. I'm going to give you these two books and then I want to let you think about this for a day. If you decide to help us, I want you to go to Kat's Coffee in the Village. Do you know it?"

"Yes," I murmur.

I can't believe this is happening. I don't even want to make this decision. I feel like my panic button is burning a hole in my pocket. I don't understand why I'm not pressing it.

"You go to Kat's Coffee after work and sit by the window," Miguel says, his pretty eyes intensely focused on me. "If your answer is yes, you put Gatsby on the table. Gatsby is yes. If your answer is no, you put *The Catcher in the Rye* on the table. You leave the other one in your bag. Do you understand?"

"Yes."

"Who'd you tell about this meeting?"

I sigh and rub my temple. "No one. I didn't even say anything about the messages. I wasn't sure it would come to anything. I don't tell January anything if I don't have to."

"Okay. Good." Miguel taps his ear. "Doesn't sound like anybody followed you tonight. That's good. He trusts you right now. But we'll be careful. Anybody asks you what you did tonight, you were on a date. If he read your messages, I'm still a date. I met you on the forums. You thought you'd get a good deal out of me because I like you. Hopefully, none of this comes up though. We'll be watching outside the coffee shop tomorrow. If you put a red book down, we disappear. You'll never see me again."

I nod and then realize the real rub. "What if you have another way of getting inside January's operation?" I say. "Say somebody else does help you take them down; I'll be screwed then, right? Pretty good incentive."

I don't have a choice, I suddenly realize. This is going to

happen. My best option is to help them even if it gets me killed. I feel so sick.

But Miguel says, "Yeah well, I wouldn't worry about that."

"Why not?"

"Because we don't have any other options, Kate," Miguel says, sighing. "You're it."

"Shit," I mutter. "I think I liked it better when I didn't have a choice."

"I think you're gonna say yes, if that helps," Miguel says as casually as if we were talking about the weather.

"Is that so?" I ask. I think I'm getting a headache.

"The two guys I work with, who you'll meet if you say yes, they think you'll say no. I thought so too, at first. But now that I've met you...I've got a good feeling about you, Kate Bloom."

"That's great," I mutter under my breath. "I'm not sure I do."

MIGUEL

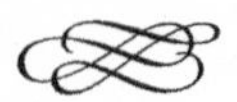

I like Kate and I wasn't just bullshitting. I think she's going to say yes. I'm not just saying that because she's cute either. But damn, the photographs of her we found do not do her justice at all. She looks like a million bucks in that Armani suit too.

But the poor thing is obviously scared out of her wits. It's hard sometimes to have sympathy for people who work for thugs like Mr. January, and I'm sure Kate is very well paid for her trouble. But I'm also sure she had no idea what she was getting into when she walked into January's office at twenty-five. I'm also sure she doesn't sleep well at night, even if you wouldn't know it to look at her.

When she leaves, I watch her walk away, the two books poking out of her purse. For how petrified I'm sure she is, she carries herself very well. I wonder if she's always been like that or if it's a skill she's picked up on the job.

Dennis speaks through the earpiece I've been wearing the whole time. "She still there?"

"She just left," I say under my breath.

"You were awfully soft on her."

I put three times what our drinks cost on the table. I'd already told Kate I would cover her. Which was probably unnecessary. I'm sure she makes about ten times what I do.

I grab my laptop bag and take a casual look around the bar as I make my way out. Nope. Nobody looks anything like somebody who would be following Kate for January. That's good.

"What did you want me to do?" I mutter. "Read her the riot act?"

"It doesn't hurt if they think they're gonna be in trouble if they don't go along is all I'm saying," Dennis says in my ear.

Out on the street, I straighten my jacket and head east three blocks toward the waiting car. "She's already scared out of her mind, Dennis. I could tell. If I'd scared her anymore, she'd rat us out to January."

"I guess. I think you like her though."

"I just met her!" I yell this out loud right there on West 44th Street which these days really doesn't look too weird because everybody else is also talking on a Bluetooth.

Dennis is laughing at me. I hear his husky chuckle and I roll my eyes. "You didn't say no."

"She is cute," I say begrudgingly.

"Eh."

"No, man," I say, hustling my way down the street. "You didn't see her. She's really very cute."

About a half a block earlier than I expected, the door of a shiny black Lexus opens and Dennis leans out. "Just get in the car, pretty boy," Dennis cracks.

I hop in the car and sit back in the seat. All I did was have a conversation but it took a little bit out of me, trying to figure out what Kate would want to hear from somebody like me in this situation. But I didn't want to lie either. I don't think I did.

"She's going to say yes," I say under my breath. Somehow

I'm absolutely sure of it. That part wasn't bullshit. But it doesn't make me happy either. It's going to be scary and dangerous for her and she does seem like a nice person who just got wrapped up in something bad.

"I doubt it," Scott cracks from the driver's seat. "I think she'll go running straight to January."

I squint at Scott. I can see his eyes in the rearview. He's frowning. "No, you don't. You think she'll say yes too."

Scott is quiet. Dennis and I exchange a glance. Finally, Scott sighs and says, "I have a weird feeling. I don't know if it's good or bad."

"So do I," I say slowly. "But it's definitely good."

"I feel *weird* too," Dennis says.

"It's probably nothing," Scott mutters.

"Hey, don't dismiss instinct," I say. "You never know what the fates have in store."

"Aaaah, wizard Miguel is on the case," Dennis says laughing.

"Ha ha ha," I say rolling my eyes. I sit back as Scott drives us back to the hotel through crawling traffic. "We'll see who's laughing soon," I mutter the rest absently and stare out the window. My muscles feel kind of tight and I realize the reason I'm just a little bit more drained than I should be is that we haven't shifted together in so long.

Shifting into your jaguar form to stretch your muscles is just a little bit more difficult in a metropolis like Manhattan. But we are spies. We can be incredibly stealthy when we need to be.

"Let's go on a run tonight," I say. Just saying it out loud makes me feel a little better.

"Um..." Dennis gestures vaguely around him. "Where are we supposed to a run?"

"There's a giant park in the middle of the city," I say, grinning.

"Miguel..." That's Scott, raising an eyebrow suspiciously.

"Oh, c'mon," I say. "We've shifted in cities plenty of times. We'll wait until it's late, like two, before we head out. No one's going to see us and anybody who does see us in the park in the middle of the night isn't up to any good anyway. What are they gonna say? C'mon. My big cat needs to *run*. I know yours do too."

I peak over the seat and see Scott tapping his fingers on the steering wheel as he sighs. That means he's going to say yes. It'll be nice. I'm already looking forward to it. Being the most experienced of the three of us with all things supernatural, I know that us shifting together is important for our relationship as a pack and as a team. I always feel closer to the guys when I shift. I know they feel it too.

Dennis isn't saying anything. I know he's waiting for Scott. Unless he feels strongly about something, he usually follows Scott's lead.

"Yeah alright," Scott says. "But we gotta be *careful*."

"Well, we are one of the three most elite and highly trained intelligence operations teams on the planet," I say. "So, I think we're good."

Scott snorts a laugh at that and makes eye contact with me in the rearview mirror. "Okay."

We spend the rest of the evening doing basic mission prep stuff. We research January and the known items he's bought or sold that we've uncovered. Dennis finds Kate's Facebook page which she deleted when she started working for January. I was dumb enough to think that recovering a deleted Facebook page was impossible but then, I'm just the magic guy.

"I feel a little weird about this now that I've met her," I say, reading over Dennis's shoulder.

Scott frowns at me from the other end of the couch. "I don't remember you ever saying that about an informant before."

"She's different," I murmur. They both groan and I can't help but flush a little. "It doesn't *mean* anything. She's just not the type of amoral asshole trying to save their own skin that we've become accustomed to."

"Get your head on straight, Santos," Scott says gruffly. I know he means business when he's using surnames like when we first knew each other. "She's a mark just like any other mark. We protect her, be courteous, utilize her as intelligently as we can. But do *not* get attached."

I think about those big, scared green eyes staring at me, trying to figure me out. There was no chance she didn't want to bolt. But she kept talking to me...

"I know, " I say, a little stiffly. "I'm not an amateur, you know."

I see Scott and Dennis exchange a look like they don't quite believe me and it rankles. I'm the one that's supposed to be exchanging a look with Dennis about Scott. I'll have to be on my best behavior and stop talking about the cute informant.

Though I would put down money that once Scott and Dennis deal with her, they won't be any less fascinated than I am. Maybe more so. Not that Scott will give himself away. He never does.

We eat a late dinner with plenty of protein so we're not too hungry when we go on our run. It would be nice if we were somewhere we could eat. But I don't think New York will look very kindly on a couple dozen squirrel carcasses littering their favorite public park.

At two, we head out in human form. It's New York after

all, so there are still people around at two, even on a weekday. But we find a deserted spot where we can shift before running into the safe darkness of Central Park.

Of the three of us, I'm the only one that can trace my shifter line directly through my family, back several generations. My people have been jaguars in Costa Rica for a long time, whereas Dennis and Scott were born in America and their shifter line is more muddled up with humans. Some people in their families are shifters and some aren't. It depends on how the genetics work out. Scott's great grandfather came from Panama and he was a jaguar shifter. Dennis doesn't even know where his shifter line originates from other than that his uncle is one.

Like me, they both managed to find a pride in their teen years but once we all ended up in Jaguar Force together we re-formed our own pride with Scott as alpha.

It's weird when you find that pride formation that suddenly makes sense. As if all along there was this family out there just waiting for you. That's how I feel about Scott and Dennis. Sometimes they drive me crazy, but in the end, we would all give our lives for each other without question.

All we're really missing are mates...or *a* mate. I once explained the concept of a shared fated mate to Scott one night after a few drinks. He turned red and cleared his throat and got up to make himself another drink so I never mentioned it again. But it made me chuckle at him for the next few days. I'd never seen Scott blush before.

We have fun in the park that night. I don't remember the last time we all three of us ran around in the middle of a city and there's a fun sense of mischief about it as we race each other and climb trees and climb around on the Alice in Wonderland statue. We drink at the big Bethseda fountain and even splash around in the water before giving chase again. We do see a few people who look mildly alarmed but also not like anybody who is going to report jaguars in Central Park to the authorities. They look like people who avoid authority.

At four in the morning, we head back. We'll get a few hours of sleep. It wouldn't be nearly enough for a normal person but we're able to function really well on very little sleep. At this point, I'm not even sure if it's because we're spies or jaguar shifters. But either way, it works for us.

I pass out on top of the covers of the queen bed in the suite I'm sharing with Dennis (who totally snores). I feel satisfied and tired in the best way. It was nice to get out on a run with my guys and let our cats run free for a while.

That night I dream of Kate Bloom. I dream that she's our shared fated mate and that we make love to her and she makes to love us. I dream that she's a part of our team. I also have vague but arousing dreams of all four of us together in bed, naked and writhing together. When I wake up, I'm hard as a rock.

But that's just a stupid dream, I tell myself in the morning.

The next day in the late afternoon, the three of us are camped out in the Lexus near Kat's Coffee in the village. It's not our van. We have one waiting at a garage in Queens that we can use later. I feel like we're too out in the open just sitting here in a car with untinted windows but then, nobody was following Kate that I could see. If she is saying no, however, there's a very good chance somebody *will* be following her today. And that's if she even shows up. Scott's got a scope that can zoom in on all the tables in the window.

I check my phone for the hundredth time. It's still a little early.

"We do have other options if she doesn't show," Dennis says.

I snort at that. It's only the truth in the sense that there's always *some* kind of other option. But we don't have any other leads. All we could do is try to bait January again and get him out in the open. We don't even know where he's based. We do know about his mansion in Long Island. There's always undercover gigs. We could get Dennis in there as his butler or something. Going in that way always takes *forever.* We really need somebody who's already on the inside.

"Hey," Dennis mutters, tilting his head as he squints down the tree-lined street. "Is that her in the red dress?"

I see her coming a block down and smile to myself. She's wearing a deep red dress that hugs her curves and her hair is pinned up. She looks like some 1940's bombshell as she strides down the sidewalk in her heels and glances around before going into Kat's.

"Yeah. That's her." I look at Scott who's watching her through the scope. He and Dennis were listening in when I met Kate at The Algonquin, but they never even got a good look at her.

"She's a dish," Scott says.

"I *told* you," I say.

Dennis punches my shoulder. "Yeah yeah. Whatever. It's a nice dress."

"It's a nice woman," I mutter under my breath. From my seat in the back, I can't see what's happening well enough in the shop. "She get a table?"

"She's getting a coffee," Scott says like it's the craziest thing he's ever seen.

"Well, that makes sense," I say. "If she's supposed to be a customer."

"But most marks wouldn't bother to get a coffee," Scott

mutters. "They'd be too nervous. they'd just sit down and tap their feet. She's sitting down...stirring her coffee..."

"No book?" I say.

"Wouldn't I have mentioned whether she took out a book?" Scott huffs.

"Okay okay."

"She's just sitting there..." Scott heaves a sigh. He always gets impatient when people aren't quite cooperating. He's long ago forgotten what it's like to be a civilian. He hasn't been one since he was about eighteen. "She's reaching into her bag... And she's stopping again. C'moooon."

I take a deep breath, drumming my hands on my knees.

"She looks like she's thinking really deeply," Scott says. "Which I guess is... Wait, which is yes and which is no?"

I sit up with a jerk. "*Gatsby* is a yes, *Catcher* is a no."

"Well, well, well," Scott says. "Fitzgerald is on the table. She's just sitting there sipping her coffee and staring at it."

"I knew it," I say, biting back a smile.

"Go make contact then," Scotts says. His voice sounds strange. I think he's either genuinely surprised or surprised that he's not too surprised.

I hop out of the car. This time I'm not wearing the charcoal suit. Kate's 'yes' means that I'll be posing as her boyfriend, which hopefully won't *really* come up. At least not for a while. So, I'm casual today in dark jeans and a sweater. I go inside and see Kate look over at me as the bell jingles over the door. I nod hello and grin and I'm a little surprised when she smiles softly and then looks down at her book, sipping her coffee. I order myself a chai latte and sit across from her. The guys will be driving back to the hotel now and we'll be meeting up with them.

"Good book?" I say.

"Yeah, well... I never could say no to Fitzgerald." She has a look of resolution on her face. Relief too, I think. "Wow. I actually feel better. I mean I'm terrified but I also feel better. Is that weird?"

"No," I say, shaking my head. "I think that makes perfect sense."

"What happens now?" she says. She's fidgeting with a napkin, shredding it up. I suddenly smell magic on her. I didn't get it from her before, though that doesn't mean it wasn't there.

"Now, I'm your boyfriend," I say, smiling slyly.

"Oh, really?" She says, seeming a little wary.

"Yeah," I say, nodding. I take a quick survey of the place again and look outside. Nobody of note. But we'll still be careful. "Especially if we run into anyone from work. Though it's not in our plans so far."

"What *is* in the plan so far?"

"You come down to our hotel," I say slowly. "Hang out with me and my friends and we talk about things. You didn't tell anyone about our date yesterday or today?"

"Of course not," she says firmly. "So should we go?"

"Let's finish our coffee first, huh?" I smile, casual and easy. She seems to relax a little bit. This certainly isn't how Scott plays it. He's always emphasizing how *important* everything is and how matter of life and death every mission is when he talks to informants. I happen to think that kind of pressure only makes them stiffen up and get more freaked out. I much prefer to put them at ease if at all possible. "So, Hitchcock, huh?"

Kate blinks at me, looking confused. "Sorry?"

"Oh, you like Hitchcock a lot." I blush just a little bit. I'm sure she would no longer be surprised by the idea that I know a creepy amount about her, especially after Dennis got a hold of her Facebook page but still. "According to our research. Although *The Lady Eve* is your favorite movie. Strange choice."

Kate makes a startled little chirp of a noise and says, "It's a great movie! Have you seen it?"

"No. It's like an old screwball comedy, right?"

"Barbara Stanwyck and Henry Fonda," Kate says. "It's great. It's a classic. You should see it. What's your favorite movie?"

I shrug at that. I don't think I've thought about a question like that in fifteen years and I sit back, stroking my chin. I've even come up with favorite books or movies for people I was pretending to be on missions, but never for myself. There's no reason to really get to know Kate and it might be better if I didn't.

But on the other hand, Scott and Dennis drove away. For the few minutes we have while we finish our coffee before we head off to the hotel, we can at least talk like normal people

"I mostly just watch movies on planes," I say, frowning. I don't remember the last time I went to a theater except for once when we had to chase a vampire through a theater, but that wasn't really 'going to the movies'. "Or in hotel rooms. I guess maybe *The Dark Knight*? That's one of my favorites. I liked all those, even the last one that everyone hated."

"You walked around doing Bane all the time, didn't you?" she says wryly.

"Of course, I did."

She takes a long swig of her coffee and says, "So, do it now."

"Absolutely not. I need you to respect me."

She laughs at that. It's a genuine laugh. She even throws back her head a little and her mouth is open just enough that I notice her cute overbite. I love an overbite on a woman. I don't know why.

"I have another question," Kate says seriously.

Without moving a muscle, I take another quick look

around the place in case she's about to ask something sensitive. I'd rather things like that come up in the hotel room though. Plus, Dennis hasn't swept *her* for bugs and as good a time as we're having together and as much as I'd like to keep her relaxed after making such an important and dangerous decision, there is a protocol to follow.

"Have you read *The Great Gatsby*?"

"Oh." I chuckle at that, dropping my shoulders a little. "I think in high school? I do read though." I feel just a little defensive about it. This work keeps us busy but there is a lot of sitting around waiting too. I usually have a book in my hand once I've gone over the dossier for the third time. "Mostly non-fiction. I like true crime a lot..."

"I *love* true crime!" Kate says, her eyes lighting up. Her hand covers mine on the table and she seems to think better of it and pulls away, her cheeks a little pink.

Suddenly this really does feel like a date.

I think of Scott telling me to get my shit together. I don't think it's going to be easy around her.

SCOTT

I was starting to wonder if there was something seriously wrong with Miguel. Of the three of us, I guess he is the most touchy-feely. But he's always been as professional as I am and able to look out for an informant without getting attacked, and we've dealt with attractive women as informants a couple of times before. I couldn't imagine what was different this time.

Then I saw Kate.

I'm not saying it was love at first sight or anything ridiculous like that. I wouldn't put any kind of weight on it at all even. But I did have that zing moment as if somebody hit me over the head with a block of wood. I got a *weird* feeling again too as if she must be important to us. On the upside, I'm pretty good at compartmentalizing. I put that feeling right away. I put it in a box and I taped the box shut and I put the box on a shelf at the back of my mind.

I'm blaming that damn red dress if anything.

Dennis and I head back to the hotel to wait for Miguel and Kate. They should be here shortly. My suite adjoins

Dennis and Miguel's suite and we usually hang out in their room.

We're not always very neat about things either.

"This place is a pigsty," I shout as if yelling at the mess itself.

Dennis plops down on the couch and puts his booted feet up on the coffee table, his laptop in his lap, a can of Pringles leaning against his leg and a can of Monster at the ready. That's pretty much default Dennis but now he watches, seemingly baffled, as I throw out empty take-out boxes, soda cans, and beer bottles. I put away anything that doesn't need to be out. At least there's not much paperwork anymore. Everything is digitized.

"You're cleaning up for her," Dennis points out, smirking.

"I'm being polite," I say, growling just a little bit.

"Okay."

"I'm being *polite*."

"Where are they?" Dennis checks his phone. "They should have been coming right behind us in a cab."

"I'm sure they're on their way," I mutter, making my way to the bathroom.

I am *not* checking my hair for the girl. I'm just looking at the beard scruff I've managed to grow out so far. It's for my role as a thug working for January. He's hopefully going to hire me. At least, that's the plan.

But we'll get to that.

I'm feeling kind of restless. Although that run in the park last night did do us a lot of good. I guess I'm always a little edgy at the beginning of a mission before the action really kicks in.

It's kind of like foreplay.

Dennis has a hole in his sock and I tell him to change them. He freezes, one hand holding a Pringle halfway to his mouth, and looks up at me.

Finally, he says, "What exactly does me having a hole in my sock have to do with this chick being a good informant or us doing our jobs competently?"

"Making a good impression isn't actually against protocol, Dennis," I grumble. "Throw those out and put on a decent pair of socks, wouldja?"

Dennis makes an inordinate fuss as he gets up and follows my orders. We should probably order lunch while she's here. She wouldn't have eaten and we haven't eaten properly yet either. I wonder if this woman will be a tightass. To a certain extent, a tightass is good for a mission. They follow the rules. On the other hand, a tightass can be terrible too. They can't improvise. They're also not much fun to hang out with, not that it's relevant per se. But being able to talk to your informant casually is good for morale if nothing else. I can't tell yet with Kate. Her opening conversation with Miguel wasn't enough to go on.

That dress though...

Miguel and Kate finally arrive and I guess they didn't take too long, assume they stuck around to finish their coffee and there was probably some traffic. When they walk in, I'm at the suite's wet bar, drinking water. I don't much react. But that's only because I'm trained not to react if I don't particularly feel like it.

Her pictures didn't do her justice and neither did my view of her walking down the street from too far away. She's gorgeous. She's maybe not like a supermodel or anything. She reminds me more of some old movie type, especially that dark red dress that swings when she walks and has a heart neckline and little black heart buttons. She has one dark curl that keeps falling over her eye.

But I don't react to any of that. I just say, "I'm Scott Morales. I'm the mission leader for Jaguar Force."

We're all sort of standing around somewhat awkwardly. *I*

don't react but Dennis sure does. It's kind of hilarious considering how he's been talking but now his mouth is hanging open as he stares at her, obviously fighting the urge to look her up and down in too lewd a manner.

"Jaguar Force," Kate says, shaking her head. "Jesus Christ. What a name."

"We have identification, of course," I say firmly, going right into alpha-on-a-mission mode. I head back to the coffee table and sit down, bringing up the dossier on my laptop and Kate comes over but does not sit. "And we need to show you our materials on January. We think he's about to sell a very dangerous item he's had for years. That's the chatter. We're pretty sure we know what it is but we don't have hard confirmation. It's this item that's the real target or equal to January in importance anyway. That will be the focus of the operation-"

"Whoa, boy," Kate says, interrupting him. "Buy a girl dinner first."

Dennis blurts a laugh at that and I look up in surprise. "Ah. Actually yes, I did mean to get us some dinner if you haven't eaten, we haven't eaten-"

"Well, I didn't mean literally, I just meant-"

"I know..." I look up at her and we kind of size each other up inside a second. I feel like she can tell I'm a little off my game and she doesn't know why. That's good anyway. She doesn't need to know why. I definitely need to just go get laid and clear my head. But I'll think about that later. "Let's order some food though. What do you like?"

"Oh! Chinese?" She looks around at each of us and we shrug and nod.

"Oh good," Kate says. She whips out her phone. "I know just the place and the order. Any allergies for you guys?"

We all mutter in the negative and she taps out an order on whatever deliver app she's using and is about to slip it in her purse before she holds it up and says, "Oh, sorry. Do you need to scan my phone or check that I'm not-"

"We have," Dennis says, shrugging. Kate looks mildly alarmed at that but she just nods and puts it away.

"Can I have some water?" Kate says, sounding nervous. Something about it makes things feel a little more normal again and Miguel goes to pour her a glass. She finally sits down on the couch and crosses her legs neatly like a lady, folding her hands on her knee. She takes a long drink of water and sets the glass on the table and says, "Okay. I'm sorry, I'm very nervous actually, don't let the witty repartee fool you. I have no idea how this works."

"Yeah, we understand," Miguel says, raising his eyebrow at me and sitting on Kate's other side. "Scott just comes on a little strong. He forgets not everyone is a super spy. We'll ease you in."

Dennis says, "First off, we should reiterate what I think Miguel already told you. We're an elite team of intelligence operatives. We work for the U.S. government but very few people know we exist. And we work slowly on operations that involve...eh...."

"Magic shit," Kate cracks.

We all snicker at that and Dennis nods, grinning. "Exactly. I'm pretty sure 'magic shit' is in our official protocol description."

Miguel digs our government IDs out of the same case that holds some weapons since we use them as little as possible. Kate nods, frowning at them. They show us as working for the CIA which is not even accurate anymore technically.

I shrug and admit what often comes up. "It can be difficult to prove our positions when we're this deep. The budget for our team is listed under the Army Corps of Engineers for God's sakes."

Kate says, "But you're out to get January, right? Take him down?"

"Yes."

"Then I'm in," Kate says firmly. She's looking at me hard like she's afraid I won't believe her and I smile at Dennis and Miguel.

She's going to be good at this, I think to myself. I'm sure of it.

"I like her," Dennis declares.

"Oh, gee thanks," Kate says, but she smiles at him.

I get the sense that she's going to fit in with us quite well.

"There's something else we should tell you," Miguel says slowly, eyeing Dennis and I. "It's a lot easier since you're already aware of the supernatural realm. Are you familiar with shifters? As in animal shifters?"

"Oh, sure," she says easily. "January talks about them. I've met a couple. He bought some urn that's supposed to grant good health from a wolf shifter once. He's always wanted to hire one too. Why?"

"We're shifters," I say. "Jaguars. Hence the name of our team. Jaguar Force."

"*Jaguars?*" Kate says, her eyes lighting up. "That's so cool! Can I see!"

I'd sort of expected hesitation but not excitement and we look at each other in surprise. I guess it's good she's not afraid of us though. Sometimes even people who have heard of shifters fear them. Abruptly, I let my jaguar out and there I am; a full-grown jaguar sitting on the couch. I have the most intense urge to shred the couch but we try to avoid crazy hotel bills if at all possible. Kate is right next to me and she jumps when I turn, giggling a little hysterically as she clutches her chest. I look up at her, patient. The shifting might never come up but there is literally no telling. It's always good to be prepared. So, we might as well get her used to seeing us suddenly turn into big cats.

"You can pet him," Dennis says.

Nobody's petted me in ages. And it's not usually something I would even allow but when Kate slowly reaches out, I raise my head to bump into her palm, encouraging the pet just like a house cat would. Kate giggles again and pets me in earnest, stroking me between the ears and scratching me under the chin.

I don't mean to start purring, it just happens. But Dennis and Miguel snort laughs at that, and I shift back abruptly, a little bit mortified. "Alright, alright. Anyway, yeah we're shifters," I mutter.

Kate grins at me. "Good kitty."

"Ha!" Dennis barks.

"Back to work," I say firmly. But I can't help but be just a little bit amused.

I bring up the dossier again and let her browse a bit so she can see what we know and show her that we're legit. She mutters about how some of our information is incorrect and Miguel grabs a pen and scribbles down what she's saying before I tell him that we'll go over that piece by piece. Maybe after dinner, if there's time.

"The gist," I say, slowly this time, "is that we know some things about Mr. January but we don't know a lot. We don't know details. We don't even know where he works from exactly. Just that he has a place in Long Island."

"The Mill Creek mansion," Kate says, rolling her eyes. "Yeah. Lives there all by himself with a rotating cast of hired staff. Just him and his toys. The warehouse is on the Lower East Side. Chinatown really. That's where I work. Here, I'll write down the address." She grabs that hotel pen from Miguel and writes it down on a pad of hotel stationery. "It's a totally nondescript door next to a Chinese grocery and it leads to a freight elevator that goes way down to a warehouse. It's practically in the subway."

I'm about to explain some more when the food comes and I realize Kate paid for it. I find some cash and hand it over and we dig into the feast. I would've taken a break from the operation talk, being very aware of 'foreplay' and 'easing in' but Kate is eating out of a container of chow mein as she hunches over my laptop and clicks on the list of items we know January to possess. She scrolls through it, chewing, and her eyebrows arch.

"Short list," she says.

"Yeah, we don't have much," Dennis admits. "If you can help with that list, it would be great-"

"I don't know everything, but I could write a pretty good inventory to start with anyway," Kate says. "At least of the important stuff. He has about twenty times as much as is listed here and a lot of it is wrong."

"Maybe she could upload a list from the warehouse," Dennis starts to say. "I could fix up a phantom dropbox for my forum avatar?" He looks at Kate, "Ya know, the same one I was using to talk to you on the forum?"

Kate does a little doubletake, looking from Dennis to Miguel who is a little sheepish. "Wait, I was talking to you on the forum? Like when we first met?"

"Right," Miguel says. "I forgot to mention that."

"Yeah," Dennis says, scratching his goatee. "That was me, Lady Eve."

"I should've known," Kate says, smiling a little mischievously. "You're more of a geek than Miguel. The tone was a little different. I thought it was just a difference between talking online and in person."

"I don't know about *geek*," Dennis says, his voice going up a little.

"No no!" Kate says, waving her chopsticks around. "Not

in a bad way. It's a compliment. I mean you seemed so knowledgeable but like you were playing me a little bit? It was good, it got me to meet you. Plus you dropped that reference to *Battlestar Galactica* out of nowhere."

"You got that?!" Dennis says. Miguel and I shoot him a look and he frowns. "Sorry."

"Not that you're not knowledgeable!" She says to Miguel, resting her hand on his knee. "I didn't mean it like that-"

"No, no," Miguel says, waving a hand. "Dennis is all brain. I get you."

"You're very charming," she says quickly, sounding a little conciliatory. "You're probably the one that charms people right out of their secrets, huh?"

Dennis says, "One hundred per-"

"I mean *I* kind of do that," I say at the same time.

Dennis raises an eyebrow and I shrug. "Okay, maybe that is more Miguel."

"And you're the action hero," she says to me just before taking a bite of orange chicken.

"Yes," Miguel and Dennis say together.

I shrug and smile, just a bit smug. "I'm not denying it."

"Okay," Kate says, after swallowing. "So, hit me. What is the big plan then?" Her gaze flits away. We're all trained pretty well at reading body language and behaviors, and at being able to have at least an educated guess as to what somebody's thinking whether they're a target or an informant or just a chump in the wrong place at the wrong time. Kate has been pretty charming herself since she walked in. Easy and cooperative, like one of the team. But I can see the undercurrent of fear. I read her as the kind of person to throw herself into something wholeheartedly once she agrees to do it. That's good for us but it's going to be very difficult for her and I can see the fragility under the exterior.

"So," I say, taking a deep breath. "As I said before, we

think January is right on the verge of selling a very significant item in his possession. That's the chatter. Have you heard anything about that?"

"Selling? No. But he just bought a witch."

"A witch?" Miguel says. "As in a person?"

"Yep."

"We'd have him on human trafficking," Miguel says.

"I'm guessing he's into plenty of that normally," she says. "I know he's into other business outside of his collecting, I've always suspected human trafficking might be happening on the side. But if you can ever manage to rescue this woman..." She looks to me, her eyes pleading.

I wish I could promise it but I can't. "We'll try," I say shortly. If I go into it any more than that right now, it would just be a lie. "The item we're talking about might be a stone. Anything on the docket to sell?"

"I haven't heard anything about a stone," Kate admits. "Nothing huge. A lot of times with sales, he finds those buyers himself. I'm often looking for items on his wishlist and buyers will find me in the forum or elsewhere. But something big? It's probably a private connection I don't know about."

"That's okay," I say, putting up a hand. "We're gonna keep our ears open. We're also going to get somebody else on the inside with you."

"Who?"

"Me," I say, spreading my hands. "The plan is to stage an attack on you. You report to January that you feel unsafe and *hopefully* he decides to hire you protection. A bodyguard doubling as a driver would be ideal. Then I put myself in his line of sight for the hire."

"Is that why you've got the sexy scruff going on?" She says, rubbing her own chin.

"Ah..."

Miguel and Dennis look a little taken aback and Kate blushes (which certainly isn't cute except that it absolutely is). "I'm being objective," she says. "If it is, it's a mistake. January likes his henchmen looking like businessmen. Clean shaven, shirt and tie."

I can't help but grin and I sit back on the couch, rubbing my chin. "That's very helpful."

"Well, that's what I'm here for, I guess. It's a good plan though. January is protective of his people in his own fucked up way. He always says if somebody is going to fuck you ever, it better be him."

"And I'll be posing as your boyfriend," Miguel says it in a rush like it's all one word, but Kate looks pleased, if a little amused, by that.

"Ah, right," she says. "I guess it's a good thing we've already been on two dates then."

"Heh," Miguel ducks his head and rubs the back of his neck. This doesn't bode well for staying detached.

"What about Dennis?" Kate says. She gestures towards him with a chopstick full of broccoli. "Or are you just doing tech stuff behind the scenes and thinking about Cylons?"

"Ha *ha*," Dennis says, smirking.

"We're going to try setting Dennis up as a potential buyer," I tell her. "See what we can see from there. Get him to bite on something big enough, it might be all we need. Even better if we can get him in as a buyer for whatever this big ticket item is."

"You'd *really* need to clean up," she says to Dennis but he only nods, smiling as if he expected that. To be fair, he is wearing a pretty ratty Superman t-shirt and torn jeans and his faded old jacket from the Marines.

"Tomorrow, we'd like to stage the mugging," I say, wiping my hands on a napkin. "That address for the warehouse would be good. We'd like to actually pull it off close to your work just in case we can get some eyes on it, put on the hard sell. Do you think you could pull off some tears or something? It would be good if you could freak out."

"Mmmm," Kate heaves a sigh and leans on her hand, regarding me wryly. "Oh, I think I can manage freaking out right now."

"Alright," I say nodding, feeling like the real work is about to begin. "Let's get into it then."

KATE

I quickly learn that every step of this spy thing is completely different and there's no telling how I'm going to feel about it. I felt comfortable with Miguel so quickly and then when we left the coffee house to go meet the guys at the hotel, I was incredibly nervous. I was so nervous about seeming inept and not meeting expectations for these government spy boys, it nearly overrode my fear of going against January in the most dangerous way possible.

But then I met Scott and Dennis.

I can't quite explain what happened, only that I walked in the door and I immediately felt as if I'd met them before. I felt in a few minutes as if I'd been hanging out with them, eating Chinese food and talking about how to take down January for years.

Which is *weird*.

They seemed impressed by me too, which gave me a nice confidence boost. I even asked Miguel afterward if they'd only seemed that way for my benefit and he'd assured me that Scott didn't bother to fake good opinions of anyone unless it was to get something out of them. And Scott wouldn't imagine that faking anything with me would be helpful. If he was impressed, he was impressed. That made me feel pretty good, a little less scared anyway.

The next day we fake the mugging right there in Chinatown, just a couple blocks from Mr. Zhao's grocery. We don't want January to get too spooked and think somebody has found out his warehouse. Dennis disguises himself and pulls off the attack. He tells me to wear a sweater and a thick coat that day as we're wrapping up that night at the hotel.

"Why?" I say, stretching and slipping my heels back on.

"I might have to slam you against a wall or something," he says. "Don't want you to get hurt."

"Thanks."

They're weirdly sweet, these guys.

I actually think he doesn't go as far as he should have. I mean that would be my review if I was his 'mission leader'. When it goes down, I throw myself into the role. I just think about how scared January makes me, and that makes it pretty easy to scream as Dennis shoves me in the street after work when it's dark. He looks briefly alarmed like he's worried for me, but he shoves me again as he grabs my purse. He has a gun and a few people are watching as he digs the barrel into my throat and demands my phone and my necklace. I hand it over and he takes off. That's it. If January asks around, there are witnesses.

The tears are easy to whip up and I still have my keys so I can run back to work, mascara impressively running, and take the elevator down to the warehouse to announce that I've just been attacked and mugged and it was terrifying. We figure it makes sense that I'd run to work since it's so close and there are still people there, instead of going all the way home.

January is still there, which is good. He sees my fresh terror.

I hate Mr. January so much that I think sometimes I could live on that hate if I ever was stuck somewhere without food or water.

Now, he's all concerned. He has these watery blue eyes and his brow furrows as George leans on a desk nearby and I sip from a bottle of water, relating my story.

"My poor girl," January says. "Accosted right in the street? You know, you think this city is getting safer and then this kind of shit happens."

The irony of him saying that is not lost on me but I just keep crying, dabbing my eyes with a Kleenex. I honestly did not wear waterproof mascara on purpose today. I thought some scary looking mascara streaks would be more effective.

"I'm just glad I didn't have any confidential information on me," I say, sniffing and shaking my head. "I wouldn't want anything about your business to slip into the wrong hands."

There's an extremely tiny microphone pinned to the front of my bra. It's so small it looks at first glance like a tiny embroidered flower decoration. It's supposed to pick up our conversation. It's kind of nerve-wracking to not know for sure whether it's doing its job but Dennis told me he tested it several times at various equivocal distances.

"You're very thoughtful, dear," January says gravely.

"You're such an important man," I say seriously. "I try to be as discreet as possible but I've handled so many transactions it's possible people know I work for you, right? I know this is a lot to ask, but if I could just... " I swallow. My hands are shaking. Which makes my act look good but I'm not actually trying to make them shake. "Maybe if George could drive me around or escort me like a bodyguard, I don't know-"

George coughs. It's an insult. His job is much higher level than that. "Not George, of course." I pretend to be apologetic, sniffing again. "I'm sorry, I'm upset."

"Sure," George says, shrugging. "Whatever."

"A bodyguard," January says, shrugging. "I think you've needed one for a long time now. We should not take any chances. It's a good idea. Somebody to keep a close eye on you, huh?" He rubs his beard. I'm sure the idea is appealing on multiple levels. He'd have somebody making sure one of his possessions, me, is kept safe. They'd also be keeping an eye on me for the sake of making sure I don't step out of line. Which, of course, only works for us if it's one of *my* guys. I told them in detail about January's henchmen and what their responsibilities are. For the most part, they go out on other jobs not related to his collecting and then they provide back up during a transaction. Of course, I don't know how busy they are. I've been worried that January would say one of them could double as a guard for me.

But Scott explained that they had eyes on one guy who they'd already targeted. Scott had approached him and made contact, making it known he was an experienced heavy and he was looking for work with the right person. The hope is that it's enough to put him in January's sights as the hire.

"My boys are pretty busy," January says, sighing. I try not to look happy about that. I just whimper and dab my eyes. "But I may be able to scrounge somebody up in the next day. For now, why don't you take a Lyft home tonight? George will wait with you."

"Oh, thank you, sir," I say, and I sum up a watery smile. "I really appreciate it, Mr. January."

"There's just one more thing," January says, his voice is a little cooler now. I think he looks at me like a daughter in a totally fucked up way but now he has his scary boss voice on.

I raise my eyes. "Yes, sir?"

"I know you got that new boyfriend," January says, narrowing his eyes. "Met him on the collector's forum?"

That's the story we're going with. We figure if it does look bad that I'd date someone from that forum, that's *good.* January will assume that's all I'm hiding; a fairly innocuous secret about a clandestine lover I met through the dark web while doing business as usual and nothing more than that.

"I was going to ask you about it," I say, wringing my hands. I drop my gaze to the floor in shame. I'm so impatient to get out of here, I could bust. I'm going home afterward, straight to my apartment where Miguel is supposed to be waiting to debrief. If I can just get through this and go to Miguel… "I didn't know what the rules were." I sniff, looking pained. This part is not much of an act. "He's just so handsome and charming," I say, tittering a little. "I think he does want to buy from you, but I doubt he's thinking big enough, you know what I mean?'

January smiles warmly now, or warmly for him. "Eyes too big for his stomach, huh?"

"Yeah. Well, he's young."

"I'll have to meet him sometime," he says. "Make sure he's good enough for our girl."

Gross.

I don't pretend not to be a little scared by that. I know he wants me to be. "I...That would be nice. I guess. Sure." It would come off fake if I weren't uncertain about that.

"I'll keep it in mind. The point is, Kate…" He whispers and tips my chin up so I'm looking at him. "Don't. Ever. Hide. Things. From *me*."

I look appropriately cowed, shaking in my boots. "Yes, sir," I say, nodding rapidly. "I really didn't mean to- I mean. Yes, sir."

"Good girl," he says, patting me on the shoulder. He nods at George then. "Let's get her home, huh?"

I'm about to walk away when he grabs me by the arm hard and I freeze up. "You ever keep anything like that from me again, I'll have that witch flay you alive," January whispers in my ear.

The microphone will hear that. They'll hear the little gasp I let out when he says it, his breath still puffing against my ear. I'm suddenly so scared, I'd like to pass out.

Get home, get home, get home.

"Go," January says simply.

I can't think of any moment in my life as awkward as standing outside Mr. Zhao's grocery with George, waiting for the Lyft to come. Somewhere close by, Dennis and Scott are watching as they listen in. I think Miguel can listen in from my place. Those guys and their devices. I don't like them knowing how scared I am, but I guess that's obvious.

George doesn't speak as we wait. That's not surprising. In two years, I've never once heard George speak when it wasn't about work. I don't know anything about the guy, but he seriously freaks me out. The dude is like a robot. I can't ever picture him so much as having a friend or going on a date. He's just a henchman, like an automaton. I saw him smile exactly once and it was one time when January ordered him to go torture somebody. That makes him impossible to reason with and probably willing to do just about anything - like make sure a witch successfully flays me alive. I breathe slowly as we wait, in and out, sniffling into my Kleenex.

When the Lyft finally comes, I almost cry. I cast George a tight smile. "Thank you, George."

George only nods and in the car, I let out a long breath. I stare down at my hands and squeeze my fingers. The driver glances at me in the rear view mirror. I must look like a disaster with my running mascara and my red face.

"You okay, ma'am?" The driver says.

"Yeah, I'm fine. Thanks."

When we're well away from Chinatown, I finally reach into my bra and detach the tiny microphone flower. Dennis stuck it there for me himself. He was kind of adorably awkward and flustered about it, but I was too nervous to feel modest. I stick the mic in my purse. They said they would turn it off once they knew I was safe, but I just want to be sure. I trust the guys but they don't need to hear me blubbering in the car.

I'm not fine. I'm not fine at all. Now I can't stop thinking about getting flayed alive. I don't know what the deal is with that witch. Maybe she'd have no problem flaying a person alive, but I doubt it. I know enough about the magical world to know that plenty of witches are just regular people and not any more evil than anyone else. Every second that woman wastes away in that cell, I feel bad. I feel like it's my fault for handling the transaction. It must be. Maybe I deserve to be flayed alive.

By the time I get home, to my walk-up in Brooklyn, I'm shaking. I bid the driver goodbye and step out, looking around me. It's dark but the streetlights are on. There are plenty of people around and somebody is playing a steel drum on the corner of the tree-lined street. I feel like I'm being watched. I can still feel January's breath on my neck. He's threatened me before like that and it has always been terrifying, but I wasn't actually working to actively betray him before. I wasn't wearing a goddamn wire.

When I walk in the door, Miguel is waiting. He looks worried, his hands shoved in his pockets as he stands in the living room in the dim light. He looks at me with hopeful eyes. If I didn't know better, I'd think these guys care about me. Maybe they do. Maybe they felt the same way I felt meeting them; like we were already friends. Maybe they also feel almost like we've met in another life; that powerful sense of connection making me think and try to remember if I've ever run into them before and forgotten. The point, of course, being that if I'd run into them before, I could never have forgotten it.

"You did great," Miguel says firmly, as I hang up my coat. "I'm serious, Kate. Not just saying it. We couldn't have asked for better." I approach him, swaying on my feet. Nothing even *happened* but this whole situation is so terrifying… "You were amazing," he says softly. "I know you're scared-"

"He's gonna kill me," I whisper as if it's already written in stone.

"No," Miguel says, shaking his head. "That's not going to happen."

"He said he would have me *flayed*," I say, and Miguel steps closer. I can hear him breathe and I shut my eyes. I'm glad he's here. I'm getting used to Miguel. He's kind. If it's all just to make me an amenable informant, that's fine. It's working. He's good at his job. I swallow hard. I don't want to cry again. This time it would be for real. "He said he would…" But I can't stop the tears. I *did* do a good job. I don't know where it came from. I just listened to what they told me to do and did my best, thinking on my feet. I've had two years to learn what January likes to hear. I guess that's a good skill for spy craft. "And the witch," I say, shaking my head. "They've got that poor woman locked up, Miguel, we have to help her, we have to…" I'm babbling now, a little hysterical.

But it's still a surprise when Miguel wraps his arms around me. "Hey, whoa. Okay. Okay. It's okay."

He's holding me in his arms and it's been I don't know how long since somebody held me. I wrap my arms around his waist and shut my eyes, resting my head on his chest.

"Tighter," I murmur.

"Okay," Miguel says, chuckling. "You are so brave. I'm not just bullshitting you, honestly. You pulled that off like you'd been doing this for years. I swear, Kate. We were really impressed." He squeezes me and I hang onto him, soaking up his words. "Just breathe, okay. Breathe in...breathe out..."

I breathe with him and then we're just sort of swaying slowly together, locked in each other's arms. He hums and rests his chin on my head.

"Do you always hold informants like this?" I ask him.

"Um...not exactly."

"Because they don't fall apart at the first sign of danger?"

"No, I just..." Miguel heaves a sigh and pulls away and suddenly I can see the vulnerability in his face, even in the dim light. "I like you, Kate. What's not to like? You're charming and intelligent and real and... It's possible I care about you more than I have other informants. And I'm not supposed to say that." He smiles weakly. When he reaches up to stroke my hair, he stops, thinking better of it, but I lean into the touch.

"I'm not gonna stop you," I murmur. "Better for me if you do care."

"Might not be better for the mission."

I sigh and lean back again, looking up at him. I fix him with a firm stare, although I don't know how effective it is with the streaks of mascara on my face. "I won't let you compromise the mission for me," I say firmly. "I'm scared, yeah. But I said I was gonna take January down with you and I *will*. So if that means telling you to shut up when you're too worried about me, then that's that. Alright? Deal?"

Miguel looks quietly astonished at that. He opens his mouth and closes it again and finally says, "Oh shit, I really do like you. Goddammit."

"I like you too," I say. I don't tell him that based on that hours-long meeting in the hotel room, I like Scott and Dennis too. But Scott and Dennis aren't here right now. It's just Miguel and I in this moment. And I feel a sense of connection with him as he rests his forehead against mine. That familiarity I've had with all of them seems significant now. It's like something out of a dream I've had a hundred times. Right on the tip of my mind.

"We shouldn't..." Miguel is looking at me and I feel too warm. His mouth is right there; I can see the little dip of his top lip and the shadow there. I can see the tiny shaved hairs in the stubble above his mouth. I can smell his faint cologne and something else that's just him. His nose brushes mine. He strokes my cheek. I feel like I might pass out if he doesn't kiss me. "Fuck this," Miguel growls, and he covers his mouth with mine.

I moan into Miguel's mouth as his arms wrap all the way around me. He lifts me off the ground a little bit and our tongues meet. The kiss is deep, our tongues curling around each other. My bottom lip keeps chafing against the stubble on his chin and making me shiver and he squeezes me a little tighter. I wrap my arms around his neck. I don't care about protocol. I don't care about anything but Miguel's mouth on mine and how he is licking my tongue and now slowly sucking on my top lip and biting me there until I press closer against him and his hands slide down and rest, uncertain around my hips. He pulls away and we glance at each other until he lurches forward again to kiss my neck. I grab his hand and place it on my thigh, looking him right in the eye. I push my dress up with his hand, guiding it, feeling his breathing get heavier. I don't know if I'm stepping backward or he's pushing me but suddenly I'm up against the wall and Miguel is mouthing at my neck as his hand slides up inside my dress to clutch at my ass through my panties. I hold him tighter against me and feel him getting hard, pressing against my belly.

"Please, Miguel," I whisper, and all at once he's yanking my underwear down and I'm furiously unzipping his fly. He picks me up off the floor and I wrap my legs around him. It's not romantic and there's no foreplay here, just a passionate distraction from the danger and the fear and when he slides inside me I gasp and my head bumps against the wall behind me. He's strong enough to hold me up and fuck me and I moan as he thrusts in and out of me, our breath hot and even between us before he kisses me again, swallowing my moans. Miguel isn't small but I want to be full of him and I flex my legs around him; closer, closer, tighter, deeper inside...

An orgasm I didn't even feel coming sweeps over me like an electric shock and I scream out, shutting my eyes and Miguel bites my neck. It sets him off and he comes inside me, pulsing and filling me. It's not safe and that's really stupid but I'm at least on the pill but there's still no real excuse for this impulsivity. Not that I care at the moment as we quiver and come down from our bliss and he lets me down so I can lean against the wall, my legs feeling like jelly now as I catch my breath.

Miguel is still breathless when he says, "I didn't *intend* for that-"

"I know." I smile weakly at him and he looks a little uncertain so I stand on my toes and kiss him again. "But I needed it. And I wanted it."

"Well, it wasn't a chore," he says, rubbing a thumb along my bottom lip. I titter at that and he says, "I'm supposed to stay here tonight. Just in case."

"Sleep with me," I whisper against his mouth. "Hold me."

"I can do that," Miguel says, stroking my cheek. "I can definitely do that."

KATE

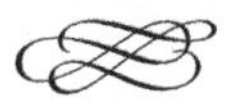

Miguel is sweet and polite about things, but if I had to guess, I think he's feeling pretty conflicted about us having sex. I'm not. I have too much to worry about to think about the proper protocol of spies and informants. Besides, I *like* Miguel. So far, I like all three of these guys. If something good can come out of this outside of whatever happens with January, I won't let go of it if I don't have to.

In the morning, I wake up in Miguel's arms. He doesn't bolt or act weird. He kisses me; just a little peck in consideration of morning breath, and gets up to put on coffee.

At this point, I'm not completely sure if he's just pretending to be my boyfriend or how deep these feelings go or what. But I don't feel inclined to ask either.

Today, two things may or may not happen depending on how things are going. January will hopefully hire Scott to be my bodyguard and driver. If the day is going well, then just before lunch I will tell Mr. January that he has a new potential high-end buyer who would like to meet him which will be Dennis. To help direct me, I'm wearing not just the microphone on my bra this time but also an earpiece so small I keep asking Dennis if it could potentially fall out. He claims it won't.

I drink coffee and eat jam toast with Miguel and he helps me fix the mic to my bra and put in the earpiece.

At eight o'clock I say, "Dennis? Scott? You guys hear me?"

"Coming in loud and clear, Kate," Dennis reports. "Over?"

"Yeah," I say, sighing. "Over. Or...whatever."

Miguel can't hear Dennis but he stands near me and says, "Hey, guys. I'm on my way back. See you soon."

"You guys okay last night?" Dennis says. "Nothing suspicious?"

I choke a little bit and say, "We were alright last night." Miguel and I share a sheepish look.

"I kept watch most of the time," Miguel reports. "I think she had eyes on her from the street. Far as they know, I'm just the boyfriend. Did another sweep of the house for bugs and it was clean."

I gape at Miguel. "When did all that happen?" I say, my voice going up a little. "Somebody was watching me from the street?"

"I didn't want to worry you," Miguel says, scratching his head. "I only slept for about an hour. I'm stealthy."

"Jesus."

"Okay, guys," Scott says, a little snappish. "Let's argue about this later? Kate should be getting to work."

"Right," I mutter. "Yeah, okay."

I shoot Miguel a dirty look as I take one more gulp of coffee and he shrugs. "You wanted me to put the mission first - if I'm doing that, I'm not going to worry the informant unnecessarily."

"I *guess*," I say, a little waspish.

I feel okay about things all the way to work but when I get there, I have to immediately lock myself in the restroom to calm myself down. I really hope January ends up hiring Scott today. I'll feel a lot better when Mr. Muscle Bound Action Hero who has a look that says 'no mission is impossible' is here with me all day.

I don't cry or anything, which is good. I was upset yesterday but I feel like if I were too upset today, it would just come off more suspicious. I sit at my desk and work steadily. Messages come in from Dennis's new fake buyer character and I feel better when I engage with him, just in case somebody hacks in to look at my work at some point or somebody asks, they can see this backlog of establishing contact with this buyer. We chat in the deceptively casual tone I'm used to using with buyers. It's like I'm establishing a rapport while luring them in. At the same time, it's all business. I notice Dennis speaks differently, even though I'm sure it's him. He's not giving himself away; if anyone ever compared these messages to the ones he wrote as Miguel there would be no link. He's careful. He's good at this. I smile softly to myself thinking of him cutely furrowing his brow as he fumbled with the tiny microphone he had to attach to my bra. Dennis has medium brown hair that's a dark gold when the light hits it. He has hazel eyes and a goatee that should probably be more carefully manicured, but the scruffiness of him is kind of adorable. I told him I needed to talk to him before he introduced himself as the buyer in person. He needs to be *very* cleaned up. I wanted to be able to approve his look in person. He seemed amused by that but I think he was a little bit impressed too.

"Kate," January says just moments later as I'm walking back to my desk. "I have someone for you to meet."

I raise my eyebrows and straighten my jacket. Every single time January speaks to me now I'm on the edge of panic but I think I'm covering it okay so far.

"I think I've found a very talented bodyguard for you,

Kate," January says. He looks too happy and suddenly I remember that January always wanted to hire a shifter. I even mentioned that to the guys. That must have been their angle for Scott getting hired. He takes me by the arm in that way that's deliberately too firm, as if he always wants to remind me that I belong to him. He's left bruises before because he's grabbed my arm so hard, even when he was smiling in my face. "Come meet Joe."

A figure in black slacks and a blue button-up turns around and I think I should win an Oscar for not sighing in relief when I see that it's Scott. He cleaned up like I told him too. I smile politely and he reaches out to shake my hand, looking casually indifferent as he looks me up and down. He looks good, like mouthwateringly good. His sky blue shirt is tight on his chest. I hadn't quite realized just how big and built he is and his sleeves are rolled up, revealing all kinds of muscles. His shaggy, sandy blonde hair is the same, just brushed back, but he's clean shaven.

"Joe Cisco," Scott says, giving my hand two solid pumps. January won't let go of my arm and his grip is a little painful. But I keep smiling. He clearly wants even the bodyguard to know very well whose property I am. I see Scott's gaze shift to where January's fingers dig into my skin. But he doesn't show the slightest reaction. "Nice to meet you."

"Nice to meet you too," I say. January's grip tightens and I let go of Scott's hand quickly like a trained dog. "Thank you, Mr. January. I really appreciate this."

"And I haven't shown you the best part," he says. He makes a little waving gesture with his hand. "Joe, show them?"

Scott gives him a curt nod and abruptly shifts into the big, beautiful spotted jaguar I met just the other day. George and the few henchmen nearby gasp and titter and a couple of them clap. I hear someone mutter 'freak' too.

"Whoa!" I say, clutching my chest. I very nearly forgot to be surprised but everybody was watching Scott so I don't think it was noticed. "A *jaguar* shifter? That's incredible."

"Isn't it?" January says, beaming proudly. "Always wanted a shifter working for me. And a jaguar to boot. Might need to borrow him for client meetings once in a while. Everyone would admire him so. Okay, Joe. Turn back."

Scott turns back and clasps his hands in front of him. He doesn't say a word, which is about right for the kinds of guys January hires for these positions. They're always strong and silent types. They usually seem dumb as rocks to me too, except for George. Though Scott is coming off more quietly professional than stupid.

January lets Scott go. Presumably, he has some other duties to attend to when he's not driving me around. He might even end up scrubbing a floor. Mr. January finally lets go of my arm. It's definitely going to bruise but I resist the urge to rub it, I hate him knowing he hurt me.

"Mr. January," I say, now following him to his office, "I have a buyer who's very eager to meet you. He's based in London, has a small collection going. Just goes by Daltry. Interested in very big-ticket items. I've been speaking to him..."

"Big ticket items?" January says, taking a clove cigarette from his pocket. He seems faintly amused. "How big?"

"He says his pocket book is bottomless," I say. I roll my eyes a little as if even I'm wary. "I told him you only do business with connections but I know he's done some business recently in Prague. That's how he's found his way onto the collector's forum on the dark web. He suggested I set up a meeting if you're amenable?"

"Sounds like somebody who doesn't quite know what they're doing," January says darkly, lighting his clove. "Fresh-faced? Bright-eyed and bushy-tailed. Kinda like you were when I found you!"

He swats my ass which he has done a few times before and I swallow the yelp of indignation. Out of the corner of my eye, I see Scott look over from where he's sitting across the warehouse with two other guys.

"Yes," I say quietly. "Like that, I imagine."

"Fine fine," Mr. January says, shrugging. "Set something up next week."

"Next week?" I say, choking on it a little. We'd been hoping to have them meet potentially the next day.

"Next week," January says shortly. "Thank you, Kate."

He only ever says 'thank you' like that when he's making it clear that he's done speaking to me, so I just nod and return to my desk. It takes a lot to resist the urge to look at Scott across the room, but I manage it. I do already feel a little calmer knowing he's nearby.

That evening, Scott is driving me home for the first time, in a car that January is letting me use. It feels strange to act so cold and let him open the door for me and pretend I'm just a stranger he happens to be guarding. In the car, I know we can't speak, but our eyes meet in the rearview mirror and I feel like he's trying to tell me he's there for me so I smile back. The plan is for him to drive me straight home and then we'll leave from there to meet the others at the hotel, together as long as nobody is tailing us. But Scott *is* supposed to be my tail. If someone's following me now, they're also following him and our cover is blown.

"Are you alright, ma'am?" Scott finally says.

I lean forward from the back and peak over the seat. He's gripping the wheel with white knuckles.

"Yeah," I say softly. We have to assume the car *might* be bugged. He hasn't had an opportunity to check, I don't think. "Had a fight with my boyfriend."

"Yeah?" Scott says, the corner of his mouth turning up. "I bet it was his fault."

"He's doing his best," I say shrugging, smiling as we play this little game. "I really like him."

"Hmm." Scott frowns at the window, tapping the wheel now as we're stuck in traffic.

"I really like his friends though too," I say then, softly, meeting his eyes again in the rearview. "I like his friends a lot."

He smiles at that and nods and I sit back in my seat. Even if I could speak freely, I'm not sure what I would tell Scott that could explain it better than that. It's not as if I've known these men long, it hasn't even been a week. But they give me the strangest feeling of connection and deep trust and maybe even something more than that. But with all of them. It's a crazy kind of dream to imagine being with three men in a relationship. But...it's a lovely fantasy anyway.

Scott still doesn't say anything once we've arrived at my place and he's parked the car. He gets out and scopes the area and gives me a curt nod as we get out and walk around the corner to where Dennis is waiting in a different car to pick us up. I glance at him as we walk down the sidewalk to the Lexus waiting for us and, his eyes straight ahead, he reaches down to squeeze my hand.

Once safe inside the Lexus, Dennis says, "We good?"

"Yeah," Scott says, as we drive off.

"Except January doesn't want to meet your buyer until next week," I say to Dennis.

They both groan at that. It's just a little more of a wait than we wanted. Although I guess moving too fast can also be dangerous. In the passenger seat, I sit back and sigh, rubbing my eyes. Just existing in January's orbit takes energy. Being a spy who's working against him takes double the energy. Even if nothing is actually happening.

"Well," Dennis says, shrugging. "That'll give you more time to get my look right."

He smiles over at me and I have to chuckle. "That's right."

At the guys' hotel room, I feel much more at ease. I kick my shoes off and I wish I could change into jeans and a t-shirt. I actually wish I could take a hot bath to decontaminate. I'm wearing a skirt suit and I drop the jacket on the couch and plop down on the couch next to Dennis, who automatically hands me a bottle of beer.

"You're doing good," Dennis says, tipping his bottle toward mine.

"She's doing *great*!" Miguel says, appearing from out of the bathroom.

"Hi, boyfriend," I say wryly.

Scott's standing in the middle of the suite with his hands on his hips, staring at me, his mouth a tight line. He looks pissed, but definitely not at *me*.

"What's your problem?" Miguel says.

Scott looks at me again and turns, stomping off to his room and slamming the door.

"Oh shit," Dennis mutters. "He's in a mood. I thought today went well? I mean, didn't it? I was listening."

They were both listening, I assume. But they didn't have eyes on us. They didn't see January grab my arm or *spank* me. I'm pretty sure that's what Scott's upset about. It wasn't horribly traumatizing or anything but I find myself not wanting to get into it right now with Miguel and Dennis, if only because I don't feel like having another couple of angry jaguars on my hands when I was the one getting manhandled.

"I'll talk to him," I say, getting up. I take a long drink of beer and set it down on the table.

Scott's room is mercifully unlocked, so I just walk in, where I find him pacing around as a jaguar. I snort at that. I guess it relaxes him or something but the sight of this large jungle creature casually pacing a hotel suite bedroom is making me laugh.

"Scott," I say dryly.

Scott shakes his head and growls, continuing to pace.

"It wasn't that bad," I say, shrugging. He huffs through his nose. "I'm used to it."

Scott abruptly shifts and his face is pink with anger but he holds back when he turns to face me. "You should *not* be used to that!" He snaps. "No woman should be used to some asshole putting his hands on you like that and especially not you!"

"Why...*especially* not me?"

Scott's jaw clenches and he spins around. "Forget it. I can't... This is so stupid."

"I slept with Miguel," I blurt out. "Um..."

Scott looks at me blankly. "I know."

"You know? How do you... You weren't listening, were you?"

"No," Scott says, shrugging. "Your mic was in the purse, wasn't it? But it was kind of obvious?"

"It's not weird?" I say. "I mean, call me crazy, I feel like you're interested?" I wince. I couldn't possibly be more awkward about this.

Scott laughs at that. He's not even sardonic. He laughs genuinely, throwing his head back and comes to me, taking my hands in his. "I'm pretty sure it would be useless to pretend that I don't have an interest in you at this point, Kate. So does Dennis, but..." He sighs heavily and runs a hand through his hair. "We're not... It's not like... We're not fighting over you. We're not jealous. There's kind of this thing with shifters? It's called the shared fated mate? Sometimes somebody comes along who's the mate of a pack of shifters and...she's *with* all of them. And they're with her."

I blush at the very suggestion but the thought also makes me weak in the knees. "As in, if it were us...all three of you would be my boyfriends?"

"Yeah exactly," Scott says. He's being sweet and even a little nervous, but now he locks eyes with me. "I'm not saying that's what's happening here at all. But I am saying *if* it was, even in this situation where it definitely should not be happening because you're our informant and it would be totally against protocol, as far as I know, we wouldn't have a problem with it. With...sharing. I mean. Though God knows you probably wouldn't-"

"I would," I say quickly, and my cheeks burn.

I might as well have said, *Yes, please let me fuck all three of you.*

Way to be thirsty, Kate.

"For the record," I say, shifting from foot to foot. Without my heels, I'm quite a bit shorter than Scott who looks dumb with surprise as he slowly walks over and stands toe to toe with me. "Well...that's good to know."

He looks at me and my breath is short, we're standing so close. He tips his head toward me as if falling into a kiss and leans back again, perhaps thinking better of it. "I just hated seeing him putting his hands on you like that. I wanted to kill him, Kate."

"I'm glad you're there," I whisper. "It makes me feel like I'm safe."

"We *will* keep you safe," Scott says quietly.

"So how much *do* you care about protocol anyway?" I ask him, looking up into his eyes.

Scott purses his lips and when he steps away, I feel like I

have my answer. "Enough that it's getting to be really annoying," he mutters and stomps back into the main room.

I take a deep breath and clear my throat. Well, now I know that the three of them are down to take part in some kind of three-way polyamorous romantic relationship...theoretically. Too bad this goddamn mission is in the way.

I spend the evening listing every item in January's possession that I can think of and every item he wants to buy. We order dinner. Italian this time. There's something so comfortable about hanging out with the three of them. Scott even ends up rubbing my feet as Dennis models various suits they've picked out for his prospective buyer.

"That double-breasted is ridiculous," I declare. "Do the black suit. Gray tie. And you need a haircut and get that goatee cleaned up."

Dennis tosses me a nod and says, "I think she should be the mission leader now."

"I think I agree," Scott says, grinning at me.

I toss them a little salute. This is not so bad at all. I wish I could have a free day with them. I know they're just working this job. More than likely, they'll just move on and forget about me when it's over. But I wish I could have one day; just the four of us together just for fun and not thinking about Mr. January at all.

The next week goes by quickly and slowly at the same time. Nothing important happens. I'm sort of shocked by how mundane a spying job can be as I fall into a routine. Scott picks me up in the morning and the ride with him is fine. He was able to sweep the car and it turned out there were no bugs in it. That's good. We can talk freely in there. There's not too much to talk freely about though in terms of the job.

I spend most days talking in the forums and trading emails and searching the dark web for the items on January's wish list like usual. The most exciting thing that happens is that January sends me out to wine and dine a few potential buyers with him at an exclusive nightclub downtown. I've done it before and I hate it. I feel like I'm on display. I see Scott hating it as much as I do as he stands by, just one of the guards, and I watch his fists clench every time January puts his hand on my knee while he laughs at something somebody said and drinks his champagne.

He makes such a big deal about it later, but I keep telling him, I feel safe when he's around even when Mr. January is trying to frighten me. I feel safe with all of them.

Finally, it's time for Mr. January to meet Dennis.

DENNIS

I'm usually just fine with being the behind-the-scenes guy. I'm the tech guy, the 'geek' as Kate aptly described me. I'm the one that sets up the wires and the bugs and hacks into mainframes and Scott is the one who takes action and so does Miguel. But this mission feels different. Every mission is the most important mission ever, but this one is about Kate. I know all three of us feel it and I think all three of us have felt it since we met her. I know Miguel has. We want to take January down for Kate's sake as much as we want to because he shouldn't have his hands on dangerous artifacts that can cause damage to the world.

That's why the whole week of waiting to jump in as a prospective buyer for Mr. January feels like agony. I'm waiting in the wings while everyone else is onstage and I feel like I'm going a little crazy. But I'm a professional after all, so I try not to let it show.

The plan for me as a buyer is to cozy up to January, and if given the chance, worm my way into his office with a bug I'll stick to his desk that will allow me to hack his laptop from the outside. If I can get anything else done in this role, that's gravy, but this is the real mission. One proposed idea was to let Kate deliver the device but we all decided it was too dangerous. It's small, but not small enough and after she'd described her job in detail to us, it didn't sound like she was often invited into his office. We want to play it safe with Kate if we can, not just because she's our greatest asset on the inside but because we've all come to care about her...possibly too much. We were worried at first that buyers wouldn't be invited into the warehouse but Kate has assured us that if we could get January to want a buyer's business and he signaled he wanted to see the treasure trove, he'd get an invite.

On a Tuesday afternoon, I'm finally making my way to the Russian Tea Room to meet the famous Mr. January. Kate will be there and Scott will be waiting in the car. That leaves Miguel in a van parked two blocks away.

I'm helpless when it comes to things like 'style' and 'fashion'. Miguel is as smart about it as Kate is, however. He takes me to a salon that gives me a nice cut and tames my goatee. It's shocking to me what a difference it makes. I haven't had to play a role undercover in a while.

The only problem I'm having with playing this role is that Kate insisted that January likes to be told no and wants what he can't have. So I'm supposed to act like I'm not interested. Which can be a smart play and something Scott or Miguel have much more experience pulling off.

It makes *me* nervous as hell.

"Mr. Daltry," Kate is finally saying that afternoon as she greets me with a smile and a handshake. "It's wonderful to finally meet you in person. I'd like to introduce you to Mr. January."

"Excellent!" I say, letting go of Kate and letting January squeeze my hand like he might be about to rip it off my arm. "Good to meet you. I haven't heard a lot about you."

January guffaws at that. "Well, that's how I like it."

"Makes you all the more enticing, doesn't it?"

We all sit down and order drinks and a weird appetizer with a name I can't pronounce that Mr. January points out. There's a lot of vague chit chat and I think I'm doing alright, at least Miguel isn't yelling at me in my earpiece and Kate hasn't shot me any dirty looks. She'd told me to act like somebody with new money who expects to get whatever they want whenever they want it.

Douchebag, I thought immediately. *I'll do my best.*

We ease into talking about specific artifacts. I can feel that January is sizing me up, and figuring out how much I know. I try to speak knowledgeably. I want to be a rich douchebag who doesn't understand the business quite yet but does pretty much know what he's talking about in terms of the items January would be willing to sell. January does seem impressed and I count that as a win. But Kate told me to make him want what he can't have. I have an idea for that and I have no idea if it's going to work.

"As it happens," January is saying, "I have a significant item I'm putting on the market soon."

That piques my interest. This might be what the entire case is built around in the first place.

"Do tell," I say, taking another sip of my martini.

"Let's just say there might be quite a bidding *war* over such an item," January says. He's been drinking a little. Kate has been keeping him plied with vodka. His eyes are practically glittering. He's not going to say what it is, but he's dancing around it. "A buyer approached me a few months ago with the right offer. If somebody made a better one... Well, I'm not married to him."

I feel like this is my chance to make him chase me and my snippy tone isn't a mistake when I say, "Well, how am I going to make an offer if I don't know what the item is? What is it?"

"Little soon for that," January says, enjoying the mystery. "We've only just met after all."

"You know, I heard a little rumor that you bought the Sewer Witch," I say, staring at my martini glass tracing my finger along the rim. "I've been looking for that witch for ages. I'd be willing to part with…" I shrug. "Twenty million for her."

I see Kate tense up but she doesn't say anything. She watches me steadily. Miguel mutters in my earpiece. He seems wary but he's not yelling at least.

"Sewer Witch isn't for sale," January says easily. "Only just bought her and I want to see what she can do. New toy and all."

I resist the urge to look at Kate then. I can feel how upset she is when it comes to the witch and I don't blame her. I huff and loosen my tie. I act up the aggravation, shrugging my shoulders. "Alright fine. If you change your mind, the offer stands. I'm willing to entertain a higher price. So what have you got that's so special then?"

"I've got a lot of special things," January says. "I have a crystal cat that can make people disappear. I have other items that are merely of interest. I have an urn full of the blood of a wolf shifter who fought Vlad the Impaler. I have all sorts of things."

"I'd like to see the toy box," I say wryly.

"We can arrange that."

"Excellent," I say. Maybe we have him already. All I need is to get inside the warehouse. "I'd love to see it as soon as possible."

"We can arrange that *someday*. Perhaps." January laughs at me. "So eager."

Not what I wanted, but it does lead to my original strategy.

"I don't appreciate these *games*, January," I snap. "Do you want my business or not? There are other collectors who I'm sure have items of even greater interest. I'm happy to give them my business and I have plenty of money to spare on them."

I stand, feigning outrage, and throw down my napkin. January looks sort of annoyed, yet amused. His eyebrows are raised. He's not offended. That's good. This is probably all just entertainment for him anyway.

"I am sorry, Daltry," Kate says quickly. "Perhaps we could work something out if-"

"Kate," January says, "please. Daltry, why don't you sit down and we'll talk about this-"

"We have nothing to talk about if you're just going to jerk me and my money around. My time is worth much more than this. You can call me when you've decided you're actually serious."

Miguel whispers in my ear: "I hope you know what you're doing."

So do I, I think.

With that, I leave the table and stalk out of the Russian Tea Room, leaving January sputtering behind me and stopping Kate from following. Feigning offense is the kind of move Miguel is great at and I hope I did it passably. Miguel is a better poker player than me though. He always beats me. I just hope I've learned from watching him bluff.

I think I might have screwed up. Scott is with Kate. Miguel is parked not too far from the warehouse, still working surveillance. I didn't hear a thing from Miguel after I stormed out. He just kept telling me to 'sit tight' and he thought I did okay. But 'okay' doesn't sound great. I finally took out my earpiece, figuring that on the off chance I hadn't screwed up an important part of the operation, it would be a miracle. I'm usually happy for the brief time I can get a place to myself when we're out on a mission, but right now I just wish I had a distraction.

When there's a knock at the door that evening, I figure it's housekeeping. Miguel and Scott never forget their keycards. Of course, just to be on the safe side, I grab my gun.

"It's Kate." Her voice is light, sounding faintly amused.

I crack the door and see her smiling wryly. She's still in her work clothes I saw her in at lunch; another one of those cute old fashioned pin-up dresses and her coat. This one is in a royal blue. A dark curl falls over one eye as she smiles at me with her glossy, red lips.

"It worked," she says, as I let her in. "He sent me over to win you back. In fact, my instructions were to seduce you."

The thought of that pisses me off and I clench my jaw. "Seduce me? He really just pimped you out like that? That's fucking-"

"Okay okay," Kate says, rolling her eyes. "Trust me, I was offended too. Point is, you played him well. So, good job. Scott said so too, he just went to meet Miguel. He says I wasn't followed."

"I guess that's good," I grumble. It *is*. I just feel like beating January senseless. I think we all do.

"You looked the part too," Kate says, taking off her coat. I guess she's sticking around a while and we should. There's always a debrief, although we should wait for Miguel and Scott. Miguel wanted to stake out January and catch him coming out of the warehouse if possible, maybe follow him. They could be a while. Kate walks up to me and runs her hand through my hair. I put some product in it and it's just a little bit crunchy, but that doesn't seem to bother her. Miguel had to help me 'master the coiffure' as he put it, but I think I got it down. "I like this haircut."

"Thanks," I murmur. This close to her it's hard not to breathe her in; her perfume, her shampoo, the subtle but primal scent of her humanness that is specific to Kate. My gaze drops to her lips and her cheeks go a little pink as she drops her hand.

"I didn't mean you weren't handsome before," she says.

"I didn't think so," I say, a little amused.

"The scruffy geek thing is kind of cute."

"You don't have to pander." I grin now. I haven't seen a girl flustered in front of me in… I don't know how long. I've always been a handsome enough guy but I never felt like The Handsome Guy like Miguel and Scott clearly do. I usually feel like the scruffy geek. I'm comfortable with being the scruffy geek. I guess I usually tend to put out scruffy geek energy.

"I'm not pandering!" Kate looks good-naturedly offended and shoves me slightly, but she laughs. "I'm serious. If I did have to seduce you… It wouldn't exactly be a chore."

"Aww. You mean I'm not getting seduced?" I say, stepping just a little closer.

I know she slept with Miguel and I know she's into Scott. I also know she told Scott she wouldn't at all mind it if she had the opportunity to be with all three of us, or even be in a relationship with all three of us. I haven't put much thought into that since Scott told me. I think if I do, I won't be able to think about anything else.

Kate looks at me and her lips part. She looks like she doesn't quite know what to say. She chuckles in a throaty way and just her laugh makes my cock twitch. She doesn't have to do hardly anything to be sexy, this woman. "Would it need to be a seduction?" Kate says. "Is that really necessary?"

"God, no," I whisper. It's the flutter of her eyelashes that does it. I lean forward, slowly, showing my intent. Kate gives a little nod and I kiss her, slotting my lips with hers. She half falls against me and grips my shoulders and I feel her desire. It spurs me on but when I lean back, I find myself wanting to please only her. "Tell me what you want, Kate. Anything you want."

"Um..." Kate gives me a long, deep kiss and whispers, "Take me to bed and taste me."

That makes me growl and I pull Kate closer, backing up in the direction of the bedroom. Kate is petite and her curves are subtle. That means it's not hard for me to pick her up off the ground even though I'm not a hulk like Scott is. She wraps her arms around my neck and I carry her, kissing her all the time, as I haul her off to the bedroom.

I've fantasized about a couple of informants before. But it was more of a fleeting thought; a distraction from the danger and the tension of the job. But this is different. I know there's something between Kate and all of us that's so real and so hot at the same time. It's like we're almost afraid to touch it and yet we're physically unable to resist and Kate is too, I guess.

We reach the foot of the bed and Kate leans back to give me a long look. I feel like she's looking right into my soul, touching a part of me that's never even been seen as she softly kisses one cheek and then the other. She kisses the tip of my nose and my forehead. She kisses my chin and then tips her head up, her tongue flicking out to touch the little bit of stubble that remains under my lip.

I take my time, feeling every inch of her. I feel as if I have to memorize her body with my hands. I don't know if I'll get this chance again for sure. So I slide my hands slowly along the plains of her body, paying attention not just to the obvious delights like the curve of her breasts but the softness of her stomach, the place where her lower back meets her ass. I palm her bottom and bring her closer to me and she hums into my mouth, biting down on my lip. I reach around to unhook the top of her dress and slowly unzip her and help her step out of her clothes. My cock is hardening quickly in my pants and as I spin her around she willingly falls back onto the bed.

For a moment I only look at her as she kicks off her shoes; the way her breasts heave just a little bit beneath her black bra and the black lace triangle that makes me narrow my eyes. I kick off my own shoes and crawl up on the bed to kiss her just once before moving to make my journey down her body with my mouth.

Kate's body quivers and writhes, responding so well to every bit of attention I give to her. I mouth at her breasts through the lace of her bra and she arches, encouraging her. I love the friction of lace against skin on a woman and I torment her for a little while, raking my teeth along those gentle swells. I taste the roughness of that lace with my tongue and gently sink my teeth into her breasts, my hand reaching down to palm her over her panties just once, like a promise. She tangles her fingers in my hair and I take the hint, chuckling against her skin, slowly laying kisses down the middle of her chest and her stomach and pushing her thighs apart. I move to suck a hickey on the inside of her thigh and she sighs, pressing up against me, tugging on my hair.

"Dennis, *please...*" She moans my name and I press my cock up against the bed, a little desperate for release. But this moment is about her pleasure.

I pull her panties down slowly and then I can't bear to take my time anymore and she doesn't seem to want me to either. I plunge my tongue inside her with abandon before licking at her clit as she writhes and gasps on the bed. I raise my eyes to look at her and see only her throat as she tips her head back and the sight of her massaging her own breasts as I taste her makes me groan into her. I wrap my arms around her thighs and taste and lick to my delight until she's thrashing on the bed and I feel such a joy in making her feel this way. I don't let up until she's whimpering, melting into the mattress, and then I crawl my way up to her, absently leaving kisses along her body.

"You...you like to do that don't you," Kate says shakily, looking at me with hooded eyes.

"Yeah, uh...it's my favorite," I say.

"Oh," Kate says, giggling. "Bless you, Dennis. May you live a thousand years."

I laugh at that and pull her into my arms.

SCOTT

The idea of the shared fated mate was something even my grandmother told me about. Except when she explained it, it sounded more like a nice family unit. The sexual implications didn't occur to me until I was grown up and then it was something I really didn't think about too much. I thought about having a mate sure, and I thought about the strong bond within my pride. Regular old jaguars who aren't shifters are more individualistic creatures, but shifter jaguars need to be with each other just as all shifters do. We bond into small groups and then we never let go of each other. I'd die for Miguel or Dennis in a second and I know they'd do the same for me. While I've always wanted a mate of my own, the thought of distance between us also makes me sad. Those bonds are strong. The shared fated mate is a solution to that, which I suppose was always the intention. Our bond would only be stronger if we shared a love for our mate and I don't feel any sense of jealousy about it.

How Kate would ever fit into our life as intelligence operatives, on the other hand, much less having been an informant, I have no idea. But it's difficult to deny what I think all of us are feeling so strongly and so quickly. I'm starting to think that only the fates could be the cause of it. She might just be the one for us. On the other hand, the idea of that is so exactly what I've always wanted in my life that it's hard to accept it could actually happen.

I'm not always the most optimistic person.

When Miguel and I get back to the hotel the day of Dennis's meeting with January, Kate has already gone but Dennis is acting a little weird, a little off. I know she came here because I dropped her off. Judging by the way Dennis keeps looking away, I suspect something happened.

"I think she's our mate," Dennis says that evening.

Dennis and Miguel are sprawled on the couch with their laptops. I'm cleaning a gun at the dining table. I stop abruptly and glance up at Miguel who's looking at me in question as if I can decide whether this is true or not.

"It's not impossible," I say, frowning down at the handgun. I sit back and sigh. I imagine it going different ways. I imagine us coming home to her. When we're home from operations, we share a big condo in D.C. Though who knows if Kate would want to live there, although she'll obviously need a new job if this mission goes well. There are auction houses in D.C. Or maybe she'd like a new line of work.

I've been thinking about this too much already. Sometimes I even think she'd be good as a permanent fixture to our team with the right training. She certainly has a great background on supernatural artifacts.

"Not impossible from him means he's half in love with her already," Miguel says knowingly.

I flip him off and he smirks. "There's no way to prove that stuff," I say shrugging. "From what I know. It's just something we'd all feel strongly, including her. And if it's true and we denied it, we would be pretty miserable for the rest of our lives. From what I know of the lore."

Miguel and Dennis glance at each other, looking hopeful. "We feel strongly," they say simultaneously.

"What about you?" Miguel says. He's smiling like he already knows the answer.

"I care very much about her," I mutter. Even on a good day, I'm not the best at discussing my feelings. "She makes me… I care a lot about her." My face goes red, I'm sure.

Goddammit.

"You liiiiike her!" Miguel croons.

"Shut up," I say. I point my gun at him. It's not loaded of course. Dennis snorts at that. I roll my eyes and go back to cleaning it. "What's not to like? She's very...charming."

"Think she's charming now, just you wait," Dennis says, smirking.

"You *did* sleep with her!" Miguel says.

"Well…" Dennis has the good sense to blush. "Apparently she has a thing for scruffy geeks. Or formerly scruffy geeks."

Miguel sighs and sits back. There are practically stars in his eyes. "I can't stop thinking about it. It was fast but it was passionate. I just want her in my arms again."

I want her in my *arms too,* my brain shouts. The thought is so loud, it's a clap of thunder. I mercifully have a bedroom to myself, so Dennis and Miguel are ignorant of the number of times I've furiously jerked off thinking of Kate.

There has been opportunity, and plenty of it. But Kate isn't just any woman. I feel increasingly raw around her. She looks at me like she understands me, as if even when I don't want to admit what I'm feeling she's going to know it anyway. If I'm honest, that's scary. Not that I'd ever admit that either.

"Scott," Dennis says from the crouch. "You're doing that thing where you growl."

I *was* growling. I do that sometimes when I'm annoyed. I clear my throat. "Frog in my throat."

"He's emotionally repressed," Miguel says in an exaggerated stage whisper.

"How about I repress your face?" I say loudly.

"That doesn't even make sense."

"I can make it make sense."

Dennis says, "You notice how he can make literally anything sound like a threat?"

"That's why I'm mission leader," I say, packing my clean gun away. "I'm going to bed."

"He's going to jerk off," Dennis says, and Miguel cackles.

Goddammit.

"You better sleep with one eye open," I grumble.

When I'm back in my own room, I lock the door and fall on my bed, sighing. When I close my eyes, I see her; her full red lips and the curve of her breasts under one of those cute dresses she wears. I imagine her beneath me, letting me make her mine. My cock swells and my hand slips under my waistband.

I don't get to sleep for a long time.

Since I've started my role as Kate's driver and bodyguard, the mornings are my favorite time. I still sweep the car for bugs very carefully, but we don't even talk about the job in there. We talk about other things; anything. Kate finds out about my love of John Le Carre novels. Apparently, she's read a couple herself. We both have always wanted to visit Peru. My work has taken me all around the world, but I haven't made it to Peru somehow. Kate wants to hike Machu Picchu. I want to hike Machu Picchu with Kate. There's enough traffic on the ride from Brooklyn to the warehouse that the ride can be slow and it's always a nice conversation. She always brings me coffee from her place in an extra thermos and takes it back from me when I drive her home. She asks me if I eat enough because she said she thinks spies would probably be very busy and distracted and 'forget to eat'. She said Pringles don't count.

Alright yes, I'm falling for Kate. It's not my fault my heart swells up like a goddamn spider bite whenever she gets in the car and smiles at me and says, "Good morning, sweetie," like we're used to each other, the affection just rolling right off her tongue.

This morning is no exception. I stop in front of her apartment and honk before getting out and going around to stand and wait for her so I can hold her door open, like a real chauffeur. Kate teases me about it, but it's all an excuse at this point. Now she comes outside, locking her door behind her, and makes her way down the front steps. She's wearing a red blouse with a sailor collar and a black and white polka-dot skirt. Her hair is in pin-curls and she smiles at me with bright lips. When she walks up to me, she hands me my thermos of coffee.

"Good morning, sweetie," Kate says. I can smell her coconut scented shampoo and her perfume which I think is Obsession and which Miguel says Eternity, but we haven't asked yet.

"'Morning, Kate," I say, opening her door for her. I smile softly, and I know I give myself away a little.

The part of me that is all alpha and all mission leader is pissed off for getting complacent. We've fallen into a kind of routine as we watch January's movements, waiting for a kind of shoe to drop. It's a stasis but it's a pleasant one. As long as we're waiting, Kate is ours and I can show up every morning and watch her walk down the front steps and smile at me, the scent of her coconut shampoo carried by the breeze as her skirt swings around her knees.

On the ride this morning, we somehow end up talking about our childhoods. I end up telling Kate about the first time I remember shifting and how I walked around feeling like I had the coolest secret in the world. Kate says she used to dress up as a witch every single Halloween with no exception.

"I sort of forgot about that," she says, her head tilted and one little curl falling over her eye like it often does. "I wanted to be a witch so badly when I was little."

"Can you do any magic?" I ask her.

"I can do a little," she says, winking. "Be good and I'll show you someday."

She's killing me.

At work that Friday, our complacency all comes crashing down.

When I'm not carting Kate around and looking after her, I'm paying attention to January and his men but *officially* I'm doing whatever he tells me to do. That turns out to be a lot of manual labor; reorganizing the incredible number of boxes and crates that line his warehouse. Other times, I'm sent to pick up a package from one place and cart it off to another. I note everything; locations, names, anything I can find. I stop short of opening packages because it would be noticeable. I don't want to blow my cover only to have discovered some useless trinket that January is palming off on an heiress in Connecticut for fifty grand. I bide my time.

Today, January has me unpacking crates from the back of some old shelves for inventory. Nothing looks especially significant although that doesn't mean much when it comes to magical artifacts. I try to memorize as much as I can. Dennis suggested a hidden camera but useful photos would need to be taken carefully and there are always a few other guys working closely with me. I look for distinctive markings and anything else I can think of to ask Kate or Miguel about.

Late in the afternoon, January is speaking to Kate when he calls me in. At this point, whenever I'm near Kate, I have a physical reaction and it takes a lot of effort not to even acknowledge her because I think the person I'm pretending to be wouldn't. Kate is frowning at her phone, probably in the middle of a conversation with January but I sense her attention on me.

"Joe, I need you to move a body," January says.

Kate's head jerks as she looks up at him with big eyes. Of course, we know shit happens with January, it's part of the reason we're after him. He's had me put the hurt on a couple of people already and I've lost sleep over it. But I haven't been asked to move a body or kill anyone.

I don't react at all. I just say, "Where?"

"Sewer Witch," January says, his eyes on his own phone while he speaks as if it's an everyday occurrence. "Back in her cell. We tested her power. It was not what was rumored. Complete waste of money. There oughta be a crate big enough around to throw her in. George'll tell you where the body dump is."

I can't help but glance at Kate then. The mouth is a straight line and her eyes are watering. I only nod at Mr. January. "Sure thing, sir."

I hear Dennis in my ear say, "Did he just say they killed the witch?"

"Yes, sir," I say again, really speaking for Dennis's benefit. "Will do."

"Shit," Dennis says.

The body dump isn't pretty. Especially when I have to wheel the crate right past Kate's desk and I see her heart-broken face. She told me she kept meaning to speak to the witch but she didn't know what she could possibly say and felt she was as much at fault as January for her situation. There's been nothing any of us can say to console her. I'm just sorry we couldn't free the witch before it was too late.

The ride home that evening is not as cheerful as the morning was.

Kate is a gladiator for the couple hours left of work but once she's in the car and the door is shut, she bursts into tears. I grip the wheel hard and make for Kate's place. I'm not good at this kind of thing. I've seen upset informants before, sure. But Miguel was always the one to comfort them. I'm gutted about the witch too and I didn't even get to know her.

"It wasn't your fault," I say quietly, as we make the drive to Brooklyn.

"Yes, it was!" Kate says, through her tears. "I could have...I should've stopped it. I should've stopped the sale. She was a *person*, she was..."

"He would've killed you, Kate," I say calmly. "At best, he would have fired you. But January doesn't fire people. He would have killed you or tortured you. Chopped off a finger or God knows what."

Kate is inconsolable and it's difficult to comfort a person when they're in the backseat and you're driving. When we reach her place, I don't just hold the door open for her this time. I wrap an arm around her and help her inside. I feel like I can't leave. I'm not good at this but I have to try, even as Miguel is talking in my ear and asking if Kate is okay.

"No, she's not," I say, knowing Kate's mic will pick it up. Kate sniffs and I help her off with her coat and she detaches the little mic on the front of her bra.

"I need to..." Kate shakes her head and rubs her eyes. "I-I need you to..."

"Go lie down," I say, in a voice that won't be having an argument. "Change into your pajamas and lie down. Are you hungry."

"No."

"Lie down then."

"Scott," she says softly. "Will you stay?"

That's the question, isn't it?

I nod and that's all she needs as she toes her shoes off and pads into her room. I feel like I'm supposed to bring her tea or something. I don't know who decided tea is eternally comforting. I don't find it particularly comforting myself. I find a shot of vodka and the chance to punch somebody who deserves it pretty comforting. I wish I could punch January right now. Though honestly, I have been wishing that since this started. For lack of a better idea, I pour Kate a glass of water and bring it to her. She's sitting on the edge of the bed in a t-shirt and cute little pajama pants with kittens on them. I hand her the glass and she takes a long drink, smiling up at me.

"I wish I could have saved her for you," I whisper. "I didn't see this coming. I'm sorry, Kate."

"If it's not my fault, it's certainly not your fault."

"Maybe it's our fault," she says, leaning on my shoulder.

"Maybe," I say, unable to disagree.

"Scott," Kate murmurs.

"C'mere." I prod Kate to lay down on her side and I lay down behind her, spooning her. When I wrap my arm around her, she holds my hand and clutches it to her chest. I close my eyes and revel in the feeling of her against me, in the smell of her soft hair, and the sound of her heart beating and each breath I feel as my own chest swells against her back. "Kate...I've never felt this way about anyone before."

"Good," she says, and I hold her a little tighter. We fall asleep just like that.

MIGUEL

On Friday night, Scott ended up staying over at Kate's. We figured on that when we heard what happened. I knew the loss of the witch would hit Kate hard. I was glad at least that Scott could be there for her. Dennis and I spent Friday evening researching the known items of January's that Kate had listed for us so far and stuff that Scott had described for us since being on the job. Sometime around two, we were both still awake and feeling restless, so we went on a run in the park again.

There was something very liberating and probably kind of insane about shifting into jaguars in the middle of Central Park and going on a run. On our way back, we decided that Kate needed something special. The next day was Saturday and she wasn't going into work. Surely we could give her one day where she didn't need to think about goddamn Mr. January.

"So, take her for a date," Dennis said, as we walked back to the hotel from the park.

We were sweaty but invigorated from the run and the air was crisp and cool on our skin. I shoved my hands in my pockets and looked at Dennis askance. "A date? Like a *date* date?"

"Well, you are supposed to be her boyfriend," Dennis pointed out. "It wouldn't exactly be frowned upon."

I felt somehow like I was cheating Dennis and Scott if I got to go on a date with her and they didn't. "What about you guys?"

"We can't go," Dennis said, shrugging. "What if somebody saw us out with her? Very low chance of it, but still a chance. You're *supposed* to be her boyfriend."

"I wish you could come," I mutter.

"We can always hang out in the hotel," Dennis says, shrugging. "Don't sweat it. There'll be time for all of us."

"Will there?" I say, raising an eyebrow at Dennis.

He stops in the middle of the street and raises his eyebrows at me. "I mean don't you feel it?" he says. "She's our mate. We all three belong to her and she belongs to us. I'm sure of it. As sure as I've ever been about anything."

I feel a kind of electric excitement in my blood and I rub my hands together, nodding. "I do. Good to hear you say it out loud though."

"We may have to convince Scott it's real," Dennis says. "But his heart will win in the end. He's just stubborn."

"Yeah, no kidding," I say, chuckling. I bite my lip and smile, thinking about all the possibilities this portends. I don't know what that life would look like but it would have love in it; the kind of love that I know all three of us have been waiting for our whole lives.

"A mate," I say quietly, kicking a pebble down the sidewalk.

"A mate," Dennis says, and grins at me. I don't often see him looking so genuinely happy.

~

Early on Saturday afternoon, I wear something almost but not quite casual. It's generally agreed that I'm the best dresser of the three of us. Scott just wears stuff a size too small to show off his big muscles and Dennis dresses like he's making his weekly run to the comic book store most of the time, so I don't have much competition. Today I wear a good, dark jean that hugs my ass and a nice sweater with a jacket. I take longer than usual on my hair. We thought Scott would have some kind of problem with me taking Kate on a date since the role of me as her boyfriend is all but an excuse for me to show her a nice time and hopefully cheer her up. But Scott only frowns and says it's what Kate needs and I should spare no expense. He seems a little dazed when he gets back from Kate's place. I can guess what happened there but I'm not so sure it was sex actually. I think it was something deeper than that.

I call ahead, of course. I don't want to spring a date on anyone. She's had such a rough time of it. For all I know, she'd rather stay in and vedge out all day. But when I ask her if she wants to spend the day together she says she'd love to, so I take that as a good sign.

When I knock on the door, Kate answers as if she was standing right there waiting. She's wearing jeans and a cute sleeveless top with giraffes printed on it. Her hair is up in a messy bun. She really doesn't have to do much to look adorable.

"Hi there," I say, smiling genuinely.

"Hey, boyfriend," she says, grinning. She tugs me forward and kisses me and I lean into it. If I let myself go, there will be no real date and I pull away. Every time this woman touches me, I feel like she's holding onto another piece of my heart. I rub my lips together, feeling a bit dizzy. "Um...what would you like to do today? I had some ideas..."

"I bet I'll like your ideas," she says, shrugging. "I'm curious."

"I mean it's kind of cliche for you probably since you live here. But do you feel like going to The Met?" I ask her. "The art museum, I mean."

"Yes!" She says, lighting up. " I haven't been in ages."

"And we'll find some place fun for lunch," I say.

Kate takes my hand and it feels like it's real. It feels like this is our every day. It almost makes me think that's possible.

At The Met, Kate wants to show me the Impressionists. She even acts embarrassed about it, as if it's too obvious a choice. I tell her she's overestimating my knowledge of Art History. It's fun to be with her. She gets excited about the paintings and tells me everything she knows and I just watch, fascinated and enchanted by this beautiful woman with the lovely brain. It's when we're standing in the crowded galley displaying the giant wall of Monet's lily pads, that she brings up work. It doesn't spoil things and I can't exactly blame her for not being able to just drop her worries over January even for a few hours. But it brings me down to reality pretty quick.

"Do you guys have any new info about what January is trying to sell that's so dangerous?" She asks me. "Anything that you haven't told me yet?"

I heave a sigh. We do and we were planning on telling her on Monday, leaving her the weekend to try to process the murder of the Sewer Witch.

"We have a strong theory," I say, shrugging. "Nothing is totally confirmed. But some surveillance we've gotten from Sachar says January is looking to sell the Ares stone. Which, if it's true..."

Kate turns to me, her eyes wide. "He has the Ares stone?"

She says. "Are you sure? I didn't know about that one. Not for sure anyway."

"You know what it is?" I say. I'm sort of impressed. It's an obscure item. Obscure because it's so powerful that most doubt its existence. "That was what put us on the mission in the first place."

"The possessor will win any war," she says darkly, turning back to the pretty, purple lily pads. "Find victory in any fight and vanquish any enemy... Which isn't the end of the world if it's possessed by a two-bit gangster but in the wrong hands..."

"The potential buyer is in Monaco," I tell her, glancing around for nosy figures out of habit. "But the real buyer is likely a man named Andre Bouchard. He's a dark horse candidate for the president of France."

"Jesus."

"Yeah," I say, sighing. "I guess the real question is, is a political campaign considered a fight? Because if it is, he'll win it with that thing."

"He'd also win any war he decided to declare if he wanted to declare one," Kate says, and I see her shudder. "He'd win any fight he started."

"He'd start a lot," I crack. "He's a nut. Total fascist."

"Oh, great."

"Yeah so, pretty important we get our hands on that thing. Assuming we're correct. But don't worry, we're also devoted to taking down January. And the buyer for that matter."

"But we need confirmation," Kate says.

"Yeah."

She knows as well as I do that 'Mr. Daltry' has been invited to the warehouse, Kate having successfully won him over and back into January's good graces. That means he can stick the bug to his desk. Scott actually tried it but had no obvious occasion to get anywhere near January's desk without arousing suspicion and we voted he shouldn't try again. Kate wanted to try it but we all voted that down. The original plan is the best plan; Dennis.

"No more work talk," I whisper in Kate's ear.

"Sounds good to me," she says and leans her cheek against mine. I kiss her there in the gallery, in front of the lily pads and we decide to skip our late lunch and go back to her apartment.

We're stuck in traffic on our way back to Brooklyn and I raise my eyebrow at her. "Are you sure you want to go home? I could take you somewhere to eat? Or do whatever you like?"

She smiles and leans over to kiss my neck and I gasp and grip the wheel, my cock swelling a little. "I'm sure," she whispers.

At Kate's place, the door is barely shut before we're on each other. It's not like last time. There's no desperation or burning need to get out of ourselves. Instead, I take my time to learn Kate's mouth what makes her shiver and gasp.

Or, at least that's what I'm doing before Scott appears.

He clears his throat and walks into the living room from the kitchen, looking vaguely embarrassed.

"Hi," he says, throwing us a little wave. "Sorry. I'm just leaving."

"What's up?" I ask him. Scott knows the two of us were going out and I know him. He wouldn't barge in even if he were jealous, it's not his style. He also wouldn't stop by Kate's house for no good reason.

"I got jumpy about bugs," Scott says, shrugging. "I've been watching the place. Thought I saw something a little while ago but it was somebody putting out junk mail. Swept the house again for bugs just to check. I'm just gonna get out of your hair."

Kate is still half in my arms, my hands resting at her hips. It's not exactly awkward, this situation, as Scott stands there looking uncertain in his tight jeans and t-shirt. Then Kate squeezes my hand and says, "Don't leave?"

Scott looks mildly confused by that. His razor-sharp jawline twitches. I breathe in, getting the sense of what Kate is saying. Scott smells like the tiny bit of cologne he wears and a little bit like sweat and a little bit like the strong alpha scent of the jaguar he is. I imagine Kate sandwiched between us and it's suddenly what I want more than anything. I look at Scott while moving Kate's hair aside, laying soft little kisses along her neck and her shoulder.

"Yeah," I say, watching him. "Stay with us."

He steps closer and I let the hand resting against Kate's stomach slide up to massage her breast, feeling her sigh and lean into me. Scott watches the movement and I see his crotch swell under his unforgiving jeans.

"Is that what you want, Kate?" Scott says.

"Yes," Kate whispers and tugs him closer by the front of his shirt. "Very much."

I watch them kiss and somehow it sparks no possessiveness in me. Instead, I feel as if it's something I've been waiting for and the sight only excites me. I press up against Kate and mouth at her neck as Scott plunders her mouth. I knead her breast and she presses into the touch.

"Bedroom," she says when Scott pulls away again.

Scott looks at me over Kate's shoulder, the hint of a dazed smile on his face. "Miguel?"

I look at Scott like I've never looked at him before and nibble on Kate's ear before murmuring, "Bedroom."

In the bedroom, Kate climbs Scott like a tree and he chuckles, falling back on the bed and taking her with him. She pushes up his shirt, raking her nails through his chest hair and pressing her hands to his muscles and I interrupt just long enough to get Kate's top off, and she unzips her jeans and lays on top of Scott so I can pull them off her body. She sits up and straddles Scott, helping him get his shirt the rest of the way off and then we're all busy for a while. Kate makes out with Scott and I sit behind her, moving her hair to tongue at her neck and put my hands all over her as she grinds into Scott while he arches up into her. My cock is engorged and throbbing with want and I press up against Kate, watching Scott unzip his pants and shove them down with his briefs just low enough for his cock to spring out, thick and leaking.

Kate strokes Scott and I watch, enjoying how lost in pleasure he is as I massage Kate's breasts, hugging her too me.

Soon enough Kate is riding Scott and ever so slowly I slide into her from behind as she reaches back to grip my neck. I think it's going to be too much for her but she whispers for me to keep going, bracing herself on Scott's chest. Then none of us can speak, the three of us entwined and connected on a level that I've never felt before. Somehow we all come at the same time which is a thing I've never thought really happened but the three of us are shouting our ecstasy loud enough to disturb the neighbors as I feel Scott throbbing inside Kate while I thrust into her.

We're sticky and sweaty and sated when Kate and I finally collapse on top of Scott, catching our breath.

"Um..." Kate swallows and gazes at me with heavy-lidded eyes. "Good date."

"Yeah, good date," I mumble.

The rumble of Scott's laugh makes us bounce on top of him and he says, "Fucking awesome date, guys."

KATE

The good and bad part about waking up on Sunday sandwiched between two hot jaguar shifters in my bed is that I feel delicious for the rest of the day and into Monday morning. Which is *good* except that I should really be on my toes. I've never been in a more dangerous situation. Except now I feel as if my heart is as much as a risk as my life when Scott meets my eyes in the rearview on the way to Chinatown and my heart swells even as I blush terribly.

I'm still in a bit of a daze into the afternoon.

Then January invites me into his office and announces that he's inviting Mr. Daltry down to have a look at the warehouse. I smile genuinely when he tells me which only makes sense as he's cozying up to the 'buyer' I introduced him to. But it snaps me out of my daze quickly enough. This means Dennis will be coming and that he'll hopefully be attaching that bug to January's desk. The bug will allow him to hack January's laptop and see what we can't. I feel as if things are about to move much faster.

"He mentioned you, Kate," January says knowingly to me. He leans in a little, leering.

The creepiest thing about how January talks to me is that sometimes he looks at me like I'm his daughter and sometimes he looks at me entirely differently.

"Guess you did a good job winning him over." His tongue makes an appearance and he licks his bottom lip. My stomach recoils. "Maybe your talents are being wasted."

I don't even know how to respond to that but I certainly don't like the way it sounds and I just bat my eyes and say, "Happy to have helped, sir."

"There's something else," January says, sitting back in his chair. "I'm selling an item of great significance this weekend. I have a buyer down in Monte Carlo. I want you to come, of course. Make a trip out of it. I'll tell you about the item on the way there. When's the last time you took a vacation?"

"I-I don't know, sir," I say, blinking rapidly. "It's been a while."

I wonder if this is about the Ares stone. If he's not telling me what it is now, he's not going to.

We need that bug.

"You'll come," January says, waving a hand. "Wine and dine. Make me seem more sophisticated than I am. You can even bring that boyfriend of yours so I can get a look at him."

"Yes, sir."

January winks at me and says, "Buy yourself a bikini and a ball gown, Kate. You're going to Monte Carlo."

Dennis makes it sound so easy but the next day, I'm faking a smile as we all three stand in January's glassed-in office in the middle of the warehouse. I feel like I'm going to have a heart attack and I'm not even the one planting the bug. Dennis looks nervous too. It can be played as 'Mr. Daltry'

being nervous about this meeting but knowing him, I can tell he's not the one who does this sort of thing usually.

All he has to do is stick the thing under the rim of the desk. It's so tiny, January will never see it. But the movement would definitely be noticed. We just need January to look away for a minute. George isn't here. Nobody else is watching. Dennis is sitting in one of the two antique side chairs that January has there for guests.

They're talking about their supposed crystal collections now. Dennis is holding his own as he crosses one leg over the other, wearing a dark gray suit. He fiddles with his tie. Occasionally he casts me an interested little look since I'm supposed to have seduced him. It's a nice touch. I see January notice it.

After a half hour of chit chat, I'm starting to lose my mind a little. Dennis has already been given a tour of the place. This meeting isn't going to last much longer and he hasn't had a chance to plant the bug. Dennis is freaked out too, I can tell. I watch a drop of sweat slide down his cheek and he casually wipes it away as he sits up straighter in his chair.

"Are you thirsty, Den- Mr. Daltry?" I bite down hard on my tongue at the slip but it seems to come off as a random slip of the tongue as January's gaze turns to Dennis.

"I wouldn't mind a drink," Dennis says, pulling on his collar a little. "I won't lie."

It's a long shot but I'm hoping…

"I know just the thing," January says, rising from his chair. He has a few prized bottles of booze in the mahogany cabinet in the corner. My gaze flicks around the warehouse, searching out any prying eyes through the glass walls of the office out on the dimly lit floor beyond. Nobody is looking as January turns his back and Dennis looks to me. I give him a nod and see his mouth twitch and tighten as he sits up silently and takes the bug from his pocket. "Barrel aged from

Belgium…" He turns around again and I panic for a second but Dennis only looks as if he's sitting up in interest and January turns around again. "A wonderful bourbon…" Dennis reaches around the side of the desk and silently sticks the bug under the rim before sitting back.

I feel as if I haven't breathed in ten minutes and now I relax, feeling slightly dizzy as I cast Dennis a little smile while January pours the drink.

"Here," he says, handing Dennis a highball glass bearing a finger of his bourbon. "Have a taste."

Dennis takes a sip and nods approvingly. "It's delicious."

By now, when I go to the hotel where the guys are staying and kick off my shoes, I feel just as at home as I do when I'm actually at home. I toss my cardigan on a chair and plop down on the sofa between Dennis and Scott, who hands me a beer. Miguel is sitting on the arm of the sofa and everyone seems enthralled by Dennis's laptop.

"Are you in?" I ask him.

"Yep. Been in for a while."

"Yeah?" I perk up. "Anything good? Is he selling the Ares stone in Monte Carlo?"

"Yep."

"Well, this is great," I say. I look around and see three much too serious faces. Everyone looks like they're...plotting. "I mean...isn't it? Great?"

"Yes and no," Miguel mutters. "The Ares stone belongs to January but it's not at the warehouse… And we definitely need to get our hands on it and switch it for a fake before the sale. We can't risk anybody taking possession of that thing."

I rack my brain. I know the gist about the Ares stone but I don't know the finer points of its lore. It's something I wasn't even sure really existed until recently. "Hold on, if he's the possessor of the Ares stone and anyone who has it can win any fight, aren't we kinda doomed here?"

Miguel smiles at me and waves a hand. "I know, it's okay though. You can win any fight but not in relation to the stone itself. Right? Like someone can still take it from you. Or else we'd *really* be in trouble."

"You're sure about that?" I say.

"Trust me, I've read everything there is to read on the Ares stone in the last few days," Miguel says. I relax a little and take a long drink of beer. "So...it's not in the warehouse, it's probably at Mill Creek? You guys have to bust into his mansion and switch the stones before the trip."

"It's not in Mill Creek," Scott says darkly.

"Oh?"

"It's in Paris," Dennis says, sighing. "In a *very* secure vault."

"Oh," I say. "Shit."

"Yep."

"Makes sense," I mutter. "You can win any fight but somebody can still just swipe the stone from you and then they can win any fight…"

"So, you'd want the stone to be as secure as possible," Scott finished. "Exactly. And it's pretty goddamn secure. We're just gonna have to bust in."

"Into the vault? In Paris?" I squint at Scott, trying to imagine the logistics. "We'd have to do it before Monte Carlo which is in just a few days but it would have to be just Dennis and Miguel then, right? If Scott disappears for a day, January will definitely get suspicious."

"I'm not disappearing for a day," Scott says. "Too risky."

"Then it'll just be Dennis and Scott-"

"We can't do it," they both say, snorting a little. Scott puffs up just a bit at that.

"So…" I shake my head. "How are we…?"

"We'll have to do it on the way to Monte Carlo," Scott says, shrugging. "We're all flying there together and George is supposed to pick it up in Paris and follow. This is according to the messages flying between January and George that Dennis has hacked."

I snort a laugh at that myself. We're supposed to leave on Thursday in January's private jet. A straight shot to Monaco from New York. Scott's been invited along as security, which was a relief to me. And Miguel will be there since January wants to cozy up to my boyfriend. But...

"I'm confused," I say, laughing a little and looking back and forth between them. "What are we supposed to do? Politely ask January if we can stop in Paris on the way for pastries and then switch the stone without him knowing?"

"Close," Miguel says. "Except we don't say it's for pastries. And we don't ask."

"How...?"

"We drug January," Scott says, smirking. "And the pilot. I can fly a jet. We have Dennis go to Paris ahead of us so he can meet us on the runway. We drug January and the pilot for long enough that we can land, switch the stone, get back on the plane and in the air just as they're waking up. We'll leave the real stone with Dennis and he'll meet us in Monte Carlo. Meanwhile, George will arrive in Paris to pick up the fake stone."

Dennis and Miguel both look at me as if awaiting my response and I just blink at them all. "That's insane."

"That's Scott," Dennis says dryly.

"Look, that part is easy," Scott says. "The real trick is getting into the vault."

KATE

If I had the option to pull this caper off while on some heavy dose of barbiturates, I might consider it. Some Xanax at least would be nice, as I feel as if I'm about to pass out from the anxiety of this crazy mission. I guess I'm outwardly covering it well though because Miguel keeps asking me how I'm used to this already as we go late that night planning everything out. He seems surprised when I tell him I'm not even a little bit used to this.

Dennis leaves for Paris the next day but not before I pull him aside and give him a long, hot kiss just in case things go sideways. He looks a little googly eyed when I pull away but he pecks a kiss to my nose.

"Do good, geek," I tell him.

"I'll see you in Monte Carlo," he says with a wink.

On Thursday I wake up with my nerves frayed but I feel oddly excited too. Scott tells me the mission has gone well so far though perhaps it hasn't moved as quickly as they would like. He's grateful for that too though as he can't deny the feelings they all have for me. The question of what happens after this is still open.

But I know what I want.

I want my jaguar shifters. All of them.

I'm packed and my passport is up to date and I'm about to combust from both anticipation and anxiety. Yet I feel a lot better when I step outside and see Scott waiting for me by the car. We're picking up Miguel, my 'boyfriend' and then heading straight to the airport where we'll board the jet with January.

"Are you nervous?" Scott says, raising his eyebrow in rearview at me.

"I think I might pass out," I say, only half kidding.

"You're gonna do great," Scott says firmly. "Just like you have all through this mission so far."

I'm glad he has confidence in me anyway. The drugging at least is rather simple. I've taken flights with January before. Every single time I've gone, the pilot has had a Coke brought to him just before take off, and January has taken a whiskey sour. They both have their little routines. The jet isn't too big. As in, it's decent sized for a private jet but it's small compared to a big passenger airplane. But we all have a little room to maneuver. Scott will slip the drugs into the drinks. For extra security, Miguel will charm January's private flight attendant because, well, he's very good at that.

But first, he has to charm January.

We pick up Miguel and I feel better with my two guys by my side. It would be even better if Dennis was here too. But we already know he's on track to Paris. I lean against Miguel in the car and he strokes my hair. If nothing else, I'll at least get a free trip to Monte Carlo with some hotties out of this. Maybe I'll even get in a few hours by the pool at the luxury hotel we're staying at. That is, before the sale is supposed to go down, at which point they put the hammer down on January.

At the airport, I have an urge to straighten my skirt,

except I'm not wearing one. I don't like to fly in skirts. I'm wearing my 'jet capris' and a tunic blouse and boots. Still stylish and professional enough to pass for a high-powered executive assistant for a rich and powerful man, which will come up again at the vault. We park on the runway where the private jets are parked and the wind blows our hair around when we make our way to January's limo as he's getting out and greeting the pilot. He nods good morning to me, looking giddy. January loves going somewhere exotic to buy or sell something.

"Mr. January, I want you to meet someone," I say, grinning widely. I have to shout over the wind and the ruckus of the planes on the runway. I put on a show of being the jubilant daughter, introducing the boyfriend to dad. Which completely grosses me out. But January seems charmed. I tug Miguel forward by the arm. "Sir, this is Edward Calvarro," I say, using the name they picked for Miguel.

"Wonderful!" January says, shaking Miguel's hand. "Good to meet you, Edward!"

"Call me Eddie, sir!" Miguel says, yelling it as a plane takes off. "Kate's told me absolutely nothing about you!" He says cheerfully. "Except that she greatly admires her boss."

"She's a good girl!" January says, tossing me a wink. "C'mon! Let's go to Monte Carlo!"

January is in magnanimous rich guy mode. It's a good mode for him to be in if your intention is to dupe him. He does really get into a good mood when he travels. He didn't grow up with money from what I understand and he so loves private jets. Good for us.

Except that once on the jet, after he finds his seat and settles in while the pilot heads to the cockpit and Scott heads for the kitchenette, January starts making his way to the kitchenette.

"Oh, Mr. January?" I say, choking on the words a little bit

so he'll turn around. Scott is at the counter. He's got a vial in his pocket. He's chatting up the flight attendant who's giggling as Miguel stows our bags away. January turns to me, looking mildly annoyed. "Are you going to...gamble much this trip? I know you love your roulette."

"Ah yes, well I don't want to get in too much trouble," January says, glancing back at the kitchenette.

I watch Miguel head over to get the flight attendant to double down on the charm and soon she's actually blushing. I don't blame her. The vial makes an appearance and now Miguel is turning the attendant around to ask something stupid about airplane bathrooms.

"I've never played roulette!" I say, speaking a little loudly.

January squints at me. "Well...we'll have to remedy that."

"Maybe you could teach me!" I grin with all my pretty, little white teeth. January always seems to like it best when I'm sexy in a kind of innocent way, like a school girl or something. Even though I'm in my mid-twenties. Creepy. That slow lecherous smile comes over his face.

"Maybe I could at that," he says, chortling. "Excuse me, sweetheart."

I'm about to go too far and arouse his suspicion probably but then I turn my head just in time to see Scott covertly pouring the contents of the vial into a bottle and a cup and pocketing it again, turning casually, and grabbing a mini bottle of vodka. It all happens in about two seconds while the flight attendant is facing Miguel and January's head is still turned towards me.

"Of course, sir," I mutter. I feel like I've lost about ten pounds in the last minute. I've probably perspired through my shirt.

Scott casts me a grin and wink and passes me the vodka as he walks by. "Relax and have a drink, Ms. Bloom."

"Thanks, Joe." I go straight to my seat and plop down. I

can't quite see what's happening but the pilot has come out, presumably to get his Coke and January is now pouring from the drugged bottle. That leaves the flight attendant. I couldn't think of ever having seen the flight attendant pour herself a beverage or anything.

"Chloroform," Scott said, shrugging. "I'll have to sneak up on her and put her out. Can't be helped. Don't worry, we'll be careful."

Maybe I'm dismissive of innocent flight attendants, but I'm not thinking about that too much. I'm more worried about the pilot zonked out in the cockpit.

The guys had to talk to me for about half an hour to make me feel better about that little part of the plan. The drugs work pretty precisely, they insisted. They'll see when the pilot takes a drink and when January takes a drink and watch the time. Assuming they both take a drink around the same time, they should pass out around the same time. And when they wake up, they will have no idea that a bunch of time has passed. Or so Scott assures me. Anyway, when the pilot passes out, he says the plane's not going to immediately crash or anything. It won't even lose altitude. Autopilot yadda-yadda. He talked a lot about how airplanes work and my eyes glazed over.

"And if January is asking questions, I'll just scramble his thoughts a little," Miguel said, shrugging like it was nothing. "I'm not a hugely powerful wizard or anything, but that I can handle."

The plane takes off and most of the flight is leisurely. It's nice to be there with Miguel anyway, even if Scott has to keep to himself and pretend as if he's just my disinterested bodyguard and driver. Every once in a while, I meet his eyes and smile a little so he knows he's not left out. It's probably unnecessary, but I feel so connected to all of them. I find myself thinking of Dennis and wishing he was here too.

January mostly entertains himself online and watches a movie while getting toasted. Which is good for us. I cozy up to Miguel and chat about things like books and movies, nothing incriminating. For a while, I fall asleep on his shoulder and he wakes me up later to have some lunch.

I check my watch as I nibble on the chicken wrap, the flight attendant serves me. The drugs should be kicking in soon. I make myself eat more than I want. I'm not sure when I'll get the chance again.

It's about a half hour later when Miguel gives me a slightly worried look and then his eyes go to the cockpit. The kitchenette is just behind the cockpit. Scott looks over and they exchange a look that must be some kind of non-verbal shifter language of expressions because Scott hops to his feet and casually stretches before making his way to the kitchenette. The flight attendant is reading something on her phone. I get the impression that the pilot might be out but January isn't and they're worried. The plane won't immediately crash...but it won't fly itself forever. Scott digs around in the mini fridge, pretending to look for something. January doesn't seem to be paying attention. Scott knocks on the cockpit door and it doesn't seem to be answered. Which probably means the pilot is out. He looks back at Miguel who frowns at January, leaning on his hand and casually watching Netflix or something.

The plane feels like it dips slightly.

Oh shit.

Everyone stares at January who blinks up at us and says, "Something wrong?" Just as quickly his eyes glaze over and his head tips. He's out.

The plane dips again and the flight attendant sits up, looking alarmed. "Hey, what's happening?" She says. I grip the arm rests of my seat and try to breathe and watch Scott nod at Miguel who hops to his feet and approaches the flight attendant from behind her seat.

"Hey," Miguel says, catching her attention. "I think it's fine, we're just... " He leans over the seat and produces chloroform, clapping it over her mouth and I squeeze my eyes shut, taking deep breaths as she shrieks. I hear the slam of the cockpit door and some wrestling around and then the plane dips a little again before leveling out. The flight attendant's shriek finally turns to a whimper.

"Hey, Scott!" Miguel shouts to the cockpit. "We good?"

"We're good!" Scott shouts back.

The pilot is out, the flight attendant is out, and January is out. And now I feel the slight turn as Scott changes course toward Paris.

"I can't believe that worked," I say, as Miguel plops down next to me. "How the hell did that work?"

"It's not the first time we've done it," Miguel says with a wink. He leans over and kisses me and I shake my head.

"Buncha jaguars," I say, chuckling.

SCOTT

Now comes what I like to call 'the fun part' which is why Dennis likes to call me 'certifiable'. I haven't actually flown in a while (which I didn't mention to Kate) but I keep skills like that fresh enough anyway. You never know when you'll need them. Kate seems wired up, nervous that somebody will wake up during our mission and she pokes her head in to check on me a couple of times. But everything is going pretty well so far.

We land pretty smoothly outside of Paris (alright, maybe not as smoothly as I would have liked but it's not bad for a not-professional pilot). Kate seems happy to step off the plane. The mission is going to be nerve racking but I think she's relieved any time she can put some distance between herself and January.

"Hey, losers!" Dennis shouts, leaning out the window of an SUV.

Now is the time to rush. We all hustle down the stairs. Paris is cool and crisp today and it smells just a little bit like wet smoke, like something I can't place which is always the way with flying overseas in my experience. We landed outside Paris on a runway reserved for intelligence operations that does not appear on any map. Sachar gave the clearance. From the road, it just looks like a farm. Now we pile into the car and the door is barely closed before Dennis is taking off.

We're not on the road five minutes when Dennis says, "Hey, Scott. Are you sure you want to-"

"Yes," I say. I know what he's asking me already. He's probably asking the same question he's asked me twenty times.

The vault break-in is a little dicey.

The thing is, parts of it would be easier if I was shifted and parts of it would be easier if I was human. So I'm going to shift a couple of times depending. Except that I won't be able to hear Dennis when I'm shifted. The ear piece will have disappeared with my clothes and everything. It's the nature of shifter magic.

"Don't like you going in without ears," Dennis grumbles.

"If you get the doors open when you're supposed to, it won't matter," I say, clapping him on the shoulder from the passenger seat. He doesn't look very comforted.

Forty minutes later, I'm standing on the roof of a nondescript office building just across an alleyway from *La Banque Vierge*, an extremely exclusive place of banking and safekeeping for people like Mr. January. It's a bustling part of the city but at least it's dark now what with the time difference. Which also means I have jet lag working against me, but I'm more than used to that.

Below, I know that Miguel and Kate are going to play customers trying to open a safety deposit box while really carrying a device that will scramble the signals of the computers handling security, allowing Dennis to hack in and open doors for me - among other things. That includes the door on the roof.

All I have to do is get to the roof.

The neighboring roof is three stories higher, which means it's ziplining time.

I love ziplining. Although I suppose it's more fun when there aren't enormous stakes involved. I swing the grappling hook in a circle next to me a few times, feeling its weight, inwardly estimating the distance I need to throw. I toss it and watch it hook around a solid metal pole on the edge of the roof and affix the other end to a steel arch implanted in the cement of the roof nearby.

"Nobody looking up?" I say, knowing Dennis will hear me.

"Well, I can't account for everyone in Paris," he says in my ear. "So, try to be quick."

I hook my pulley to the cord, step off the roof and throw my feet out in front of me, the wind blowing in my hair as I rush downward, the adrenaline rushing through me like a rolling wave. My boots absorb the shock as I bounce against the bank and I pull myself up to the cord and with two quick tugs, climb up over the edge of the roof, landing neatly. I dislodge the grappling book and toss it back to the roof of the other building where it likely won't be noticed for, possibly, months.

Now, it's time to wait.

"How are Kate and Miguel doing?" I say. I crouch down by the roof's mechanical doors. They are locked and unlocked by computer. I'll have to wait until they can get in with the signal scrambler so Dennis can hack the system.

I check my watch. Everyone on the plane will wake up in about twenty-three minutes and the drive back to the runway at this time of night will take about nine.

"They're at the front desk schmoozing," Dennis reports. "I'm trying to get them closer... Guys?" I hear a click and then the audio from the mic Kate is wearing is in my ear.

Kate is speaking French but I can't make it out. She and Miguel laugh and I hear a door opening.

"Elevator," Dennis says.

"I got thirteen minutes now," I say. "At best."

"I'm aware."

"Can't Miguel like...do a spell or something?"

"I'm pretty sure he just hexed the guy at the front desk," Dennis say. "But he's not Harry Potter so..."

"Almost there..." Dennis says.

I take a deep breath. The point in catching January making the sale of an extraordinarily restricted weapon like the Ares stone is to get him on the greatest possible crime. The Ares stone is the kind of object that's so illegal the laws against possessing it are not even on the official books. He could be tried for treason just for owning it, but selling it to a political candidate outside of America is particularly juicy.

I've fantasized about January wasting away in a federal prison without his toys for days now.

Eleven minutes. Deep breath.

Dennis say, "Okay..."

"Now?"

"Just a sec..."

I sigh.

"Open the door," Dennis says.

A little light on the door handle has now turned green and I push it open, entering a narrow corridor. Dennis is directing me where to go after which I'll need to shift and I won't be able to hear him anymore.

"The duct above your head...right there," Dennis says. I stop and look up and sure enough, I see a vent just big enough to fit a big but stealthy jaguar. At the end of it will be catwalks to navigate. I figured it would be easier to manage them if I was actually a cat. I drop the small black bag I'm carrying, hop up, and detach the vent and set it next to me.

I shift and duck my head, grabbing the bag in my jaws, and rear back before jumping up and gripping the edge of the duct in my paws. It takes all my strength to pull myself up and into the duct.

Now I can't hear Dennis, but hopefully, I won't need to.

I've memorized the ducts at this point. Right, straight, straight, left...

I have about two minutes to accomplish this. When I find the right duct, I grip the vent in my claws and yank it back. It hurts like hell but I manage to pull it inside. Now to walk the catwalk down to the vault.

There are about six guards below me. I just have to cross over their heads, shift back, jump down, knock out the guard in front of the vault which has been opened by Dennis, and slip inside.

I cross one catwalk, my paw slips, and I fall.

I'm a cool, well trained, professional intelligence operative.

I almost lose my shit...but I *don't*. Instead, I manage to catch myself, hooking my paws over the beam, the little black bag carrying the fake stone gripped in my teeth. I'm sort of glad nobody is here to see this travesty of unstealthy shifter spycraft especially as it amounts to a big cat looking quite silly. But I do manage to climb back up on the beam and trot right over the guards on their walkways all the way to the open corridor where *two* guards are in front of the vault.

Oh, great.

Nobody's supposed to know we were in and out. Dennis is supposed to get them distracted away from the vault by pulling a false alarm down the corridor. The seconds feel like years. I'm used to keeping calm no matter what but I can't deny that the fate of a possible future with Kate feels like it's on the line as well as the mission itself.

Finally, the two guards move.

I have to shift before I jump down because I have no way of knocking two guys out as a jaguar. I could kill them but...that would be bad. This part I have been a little unsure about. I've shifted in precarious places before, but never while standing on a very narrow beam. I grip it with my paws, hope for the best and shift.

The shift throws me off and I lose my balance but I manage to somersault myself mid-air and stick the landing.

Now, to get in the vault.

"Dennis," I say.

"Hey!" Dennis says in my ear. "Kate and Miguel are in the car. Tell me you're at the vault."

"Affirmative."

"Okay, I'm scanning in your thumb print to the system…"

"That's not done yet?" I hiss. "How's our time?"

"Not good. Shut up. And…"

"Dennis, I swear to God."

"That's not gonna make it go faster… And go!"

I press the sensor on the front of the vault with my thumb and it turns green. I turn the giant wheel until the thing opens. Inside I find a small circular room. The entire place is full of private vaults and this one is Mr. January's. The stone is under glass in the center.

"No time for love, Dr. Jones," I mutter to myself before grabbing the stone from the bag, removing the glass dome, and making the switch.

Luckily, *I* am now holding onto the Ares stone.

Which means anyone can take it from me. But it also means if anyone fights me, I'll win. I'm back on the catwalk and shifted into a jaguar with the black bag in my mouth in seconds and I trot back, keeping calm as a rock, to the vent and back up into the tunnels.

I make it all the way to the roof and take a deep breath. On the other side of the bank, there's another smaller building across a different alley. This time, I'm jumping. As a human, I don't love huge jumps like this. I usually have to rely on an adrenaline rush to make myself do it.

Luckily, my jaguar doesn't mind so much.

With the bag in my mouth, I back way up and start running at full speed. The gap between the buildings didn't seem that wide but now I feel like I'm flying, my paws outstretched as I descend and land light and sure on the next roof, the Ares stone safe in my jaws. I drop the bag, shift back, and grab it again.

The building I jumped to is a regular old, fairly unsecured office building with an unlocked door on the roof and from there it's just a mad dash down several flights of stairs to the street where the SUV is waiting for me, two blocks down.

Dennis peels out before my door is closed.

Kate says, "I think I'm going to have a heart attack." I'm squished into the backseat next to her and she burrows into my shoulder. "Holy shit."

"We'll make it," I say, breathless. I kiss her hair and she laughs a little hysterically. "Time?"

"They should be waking up in eight minutes."

Dennis breaks probably several laws on the way to the airfield where Dennis takes the stone and the rest of us pound up the stairs to the jet with about ninety seconds to spare. I half collapse into the cockpit and we're just beginning our ascent when they all start to stir.

The pilot jerks and looks around, baffled. "I… Oh my God, what just happened?"

I haven't even caught my breath yet but I smile at him.

"What's that? Oh, nothing. I was telling you I've just gotten my pilot's license and…" I sit back, laughing slightly.

"Are we over...Paris," the pilot mutters, rubbing his eyes. "I could swear…"

"Are you okay?" I ask him, doubtful. "You said we had to deviate our flightpath slightly? Can't remember why."

"S'fine," the pilot says frowning. He looks panicked. He'll be alright. He'll just be doubting himself for the next several months probably but then he does fly a private jet for a murdering gangster so I'm not overly sympathetic. I watch him for a minute to make sure he's actually functioning. If he flips out or something, I can always take over.

In the kitchenette behind the cockpit, I find Miguel pouring himself a vodka and soda.

"We good?" Miguel says.

"Looks like. How's the asshole?"

"S'like nothing happened."

"Nice."

MIGUEL

The last time I was in Monte Carlo, Dennis and I ended up nearly getting eaten by an ancient troll summoned by some grumpy wizards. But that was a few a years ago and most of the fight took place in the sewers. We hardly even got to the beach and we certainly weren't staying in a fancy hotel. As much as I'd like to shove this big, fake Ares stone right down January's throat, I can't really quibble with the accommodations as the limo we're riding in pulls up to The Hermitage, the most luxurious hotel in Monte Carlo and probably all of Monaco. We've flown through the night and its early morning. I watched Kate make a show of being surprised by January's 'reveal' that it's the Ares stone he's selling on the trip. He seems impressed that she already knows all about its existence. She plays her part well.

The only thing that makes this whole mission a few degrees less glamourous is the feeling of having gone too long without a nice shower and a change of clothes after so long in the air but I'm hungry more than anything else.

I wrap an arm around Kate as bell boys take our bags. Everything smells like money and the ocean. January gives us a vague little wave before heading off to his penthouse. Later this evening we'll be needed for the buyer's party where the sale is supposed to go down. That gives us plenty of time to plan...and even some time to enjoy the amenities of The Hermitage, assuming I can actually get Scott to relax for five minutes. At least our rooms are a couple of floors beneath January's and Scott's adjoins ours since he's Kate's bodyguard.

The suite at The Hermitage makes our suite back in Manhattan look like a fleabag motel. When we step inside, I hold a finger to my lips. I've done it before. It doesn't really mean 'don't speak' as much as it means 'don't speak freely'. We have to sweep the room for bugs. It's extraordinarily unlikely that January would bug a hotel suite ahead of Kate arriving if he really found something amiss, but we like to be thorough as always.

Kate nods in understanding and says, "I'm just going to take a shower."

It takes a long time to check an entire hotel suite for bugs and by the time I'm through, I'm starving. Half the battle is just putting everything back the way it was. I hear Scott knock on the wall between us which means he's clean and I knock back.

A minute later he shows up and says, "Can we order like twelve lobsters or something, I'm starving."

"Twelve lobsters?" Kate says, walking in from the master bath in a truly gigantic white bathrobe. "That seems like it's pushing it just a tad."

"Hey," Scott says, smiling at her. He tugs her forward by the belt of her robe and I just stick my hands in my pockets and watch, smirking. "Come here."

They kiss and if I wasn't so hungry, I would jump in and join them. But my stomach is growling at this point. "I'll order up some food."

"Order for Dennis too," Scott says, in between laying kisses along Kate's neck. "He'll be here soon enough."

"All my boys here with me in Monte Carlo," Kate says, wrapping her arms around Scott's neck. "What a lucky girl I am."

"What would the lucky girl like to eat?" I ask as I pick up the phone.

"Something pasta," Kate says, sleepily leaning into Scott. "Something with lots of meat and cheese."

"I'll see what I can do," I tell her. I'm on hold on the phone for a minute and I watch Kate and Scott lazily make out. It makes me feel warm and sort of blissful. Ever since I spent that night with the two of them, I've felt much closer to Scott as well as Kate. I wouldn't have seen that coming. I feel as if the four of us are becoming something like a single unit. Which I suppose is how it goes with a pack and a shared mate.

I order a ridiculous amount of food and when I hang up the phone, Kate is in my lap and Scott's gone to change. "Oh, hello," I mutter.

"Hello there," she says and leans down to kiss me slow and sweet. She leans back but she's frowning. I press a finger between her brows. "What's the matter, dollface?"

"I feel like it's almost over," Kate says, resting her forehead against mine. "The closer I get to the end, the scarier it is. And I don't know what comes next."

"We're gonna take him down," I say firmly, meeting her eyes. I reach up to stroke her hair and cup her face, kissing the tip of her nose. "And after we do... No matter what happens, you're gonna be there. At least I hope so."

"Are you sure about that?" Kate whispers. "Don't lie to me. You wouldn't lie to me, would you?"

"Kate," I whisper. "You're the one. You're the one for all of us. We all feel it. I don't know what it will look like yet, but we want you in our lives."

She still looks uncertain and if I'm being honest, I can't promise more than that because nothing has been decided. All I know is that all three of us are certain by now that she's our mate, the one that brings us all together and completes us. It's as if we have always been missing her and never knew it. Kate smiles softly and kisses me and then she's straddling my lap and we're lazily making out again. When she grinds up against me, I start to get hard, but then there's a knock at the door.

"Housekeeping," the voice says. But it's obviously Dennis.

When I open the door, he's wearing a blonde wig and a hotel uniform, carrying a towel over his arm.

"This hotel will hire anyone," I quip.

"Oh, ha ha," Dennis says. He nods at Kate. "Hey, beautiful."

From the under the towel, he produces a black velvet bag and tosses it to me. "Don't leave home without it."

I glance inside. The Ares stone is blue and so bright it glitters and the light isn't even hitting it. I take it out and hold it in my hand. It feels oddly cold. It's also much smaller than I'd imagined. It's only about the size of a small rock. "We should put it in Scott's room."

"We should destroy it," Kate says.

"We can't," I say apologetically.

"Yeah, I know," she says, waiving a hand. "In a better world…"

Scott comes back and eventually, the food comes. We dig in and it feels almost like a regular day, albeit in a luxurious hotel suite overlooking the beaches of Monte Carlo. But we're so comfortable with Kate now. We eat oysters and drink champagne even though it's still early in the day. There's not a lot to be done today before the party tomorrow and I saw Kate get some napping in on the plane. The rest of us have pretty good stamina being shifters.

When we're done eating we laze around a little bit. Kate curls up on Dennis's lap on the couch and I rub her feet. She practically begs Scott to shift for her and then there's a jaguar stalking around and finally curling up next to her so she can scratch him between the ears. It takes every bit of self-control I can muster not to laugh when Scott starts purring.

"Is the French guy going to be there?" Kate says. She's resting her head on Dennis's chest and rubbing little circles under his shirt. Dennis is smiling softly and looking at Kate like she's the best thing he's ever seen. It's an expression I'm sure I've worn myself. "The presidential candidate?"

"He's the one throwing the party," Dennis says, massaging her knee. "Someone else will most likely be handling the sale but I imagine he'll make an appearance whenever it does go down."

"You'll all be careful, won't you?" Kate whispers. "I don't want to lose you. Any of you."

"You know we will, darling," I say. I slide my hand up her leg and she moans a little and kisses Dennis.

She says, "Keep doing that," in my direction and Dennis kisses her in earnest as I scoot up moving her legs into my lap. I massage her thigh, my hand sneaking up inch by inch as she parts her knees for me. Scott hops off the couch and shifts into human form and kneels by Kate's side. She turns her head and kisses him and Dennis massages her breast as she arches up into it. I let my hand wander up to her panties and press my fingers there, teasing her through the lace. I duck my head to kiss her knee and watch her tongue curl around Scott's. Dennis tugs the front of her dress down and leans to kiss her neck and her collarbone. I feel as if there's no particular goal, as if it's not assumed we're going to have sex. We're just sort of enjoying each other and I feel the electric tingle of our connection to each other shiver through me like it's a physical thing. I bite Kate's thigh and slowly pull her panties aside, slipping a finger in and she moans into Scott's mouth. It's making me painfully hard and her foot is pressing against my crotch. She toes at it, deliberate, and I get a bit of delicious revenge; fingering her clit so that she writhes, driving us wild. She turns her head and kisses Dennis again and Scott goes to kiss her neck. I slip a second finger inside her and she bucks, gasping. My other hand goes to my crotch. I feel I need to get some relief or I'll go mad and I unzip my fly. She watches me as she kisses Dennis and I stroke myself as I finger her, the rhythm synchronizing. I feel as if our pleasure is shared somehow. When I stroke my cock, Scott and Dennis moan too as if it's happening to them. It's not something I knew happened with fated mates but it turns me on even more and I lean back against the couch as I furiously rub Kate's clit until she's gasping and groaning into Dennis's mouth, shuddering her orgasm. I keep at it even as pleasure continues to thrill through her and Scott reaches into her dress to palm her breast. She's helpless and at our mercy and yet I feel as if we're the ones who have given all our power over to her.

Finally, she mumbles something I can't make out and sits up, kneeling and flopping down on her stomach over Dennis' knees, taking me in her mouth. I wasn't expecting it and I cry out, my head falling back. I stroke her hair and she looks at me while she sucks me off. Scott is palming himself, watching us, and Dennis is massaging Kate's ass, muttering how good she is. I watch him push her dress up and bite the cheeks of her ass visible around her pretty black lace panties, and all at once I'm coming. She swallows me up and I hear Scott groan as he comes in his pants. But the sight of Scott, Mr. Alpha Mission Leader, his mouth agape and his pants still bulging as he gets himself off is somehow so human and sweet and hot to me I shudder again as Kate sucks in her cheeks around me, a kind of second mini-gasm rushing through me. Kate smiles up at me and flops back on Dennis' lap, sheepishly wiping her mouth. Her lips are red and swollen and her cheeks are pink.

She's ours, I think. I don't know how it will work any more than she does. But I'm sure of it. *She's ours.*

KATE

As it turns out, waiting for what Dennis keeps calling 'the big buy at the ball' is equal parts decadent and nerve-wracking. The four of us hastily tidy up after fooling around then eat some more and chat, the smell of sex still almost stifling in the room. Scott and Dennis go to work for a while, checking the rest of the list of January's items that I gave them against their database. Meanwhile, I have to go procure a very important resource for the big soiree later, even if Scott is rolling his eyes about it.

"You're telling me, you didn't already have a dress you could wear to this thing?" He says, raising an eyebrow.

"Sure, I did," I say, still changing into a fresh top. My plan is to shop, come back and take a quick nap, and then get ready for the party. "But, I need a new one."

"You *want* a new one," Scott says.

"Miguel said I'd get reimbursed," I mutter under my breath.

"Aha!" Scott wags a finger in my face. He's standing in front of the suite door, blocking my way, and I cross my arms. "I see how it is. You just want the government to pay for your pretty dress."

"I think the government can handle it, considering I'm putting my life in danger to take this asshole down," I say, before pecking a kiss to Scott's lips. The peck turns into a proper kiss and I hum, nuzzling his throat. "You smell so good."

"Well, that's not fair."

"Take it up with Uncle Sam," I murmur, kissing him once more. "I'll be back in an hour."

"Miguel," Scott says, nodding at his pack mate. "Go with her."

"I don't need a chaperone," I say, sighing. I think I may have gotten too used to this spying life. In the beginning, I might have begged one of them to go with me, just in case.

"You absolutely do," Miguel says, putting on his jacket. "We're down to the wire here. We don't need any stupid mistakes. C'mon. Lemme play fake boyfriend."

"You can play *real* boyfriend if you're going," I say, tossing him a wink. I notice Scott and Dennis rolling their eyes and sigh. "So can the rest of you, Jesus." They pretend not to smile at that. They're ridiculous.

"How about this one?" Miguel says an hour later. He points to a mannequin wearing a dress that looks like it was designed for a particularly modest eighty-year-old (albeit a very rich one) and I snort a laugh before patting him on the shoulder. The dress shop is just down the block from the hotel and it's full of high roller types and women carrying Birkin bags. There's a level of wealth here that bowls even me over and I've seen a lot by now. There's even a kind of store butler walking around offering canapes and champagne as we shop.

"Don't try to help, sweetie," I say. "Apparently your

fashion talents don't extend past suits. Just stand there and look pretty."

It occurs to me that I might want a dress I can move in easily. Who knows if I'll have to make a run for it at some point? I feel smart for having thought of it and go with a long, slinky thing with some stretch. It has a nice slit up the side that's just a little bit sexy while making it surprisingly easy to run in. The neckline though is dramatically deep. I could get a decent cardiology exam and never take my clothes off. Hair and make-up I've got a handle on, but I buy myself some new heels with a pretty rose embroidered on the toe. They're not too high. I could run in them if need be.

"I guess you guys already have your tuxedos?" I say as the clerk rings us up, looking very excited about her commission. "It's easy for you guys."

"Hey, I mean…" Miguel clears his throat. "Sometimes the tailoring is off because we've put on a little muscle or lost some weight and we have to get it fixed."

"That's rough, buddy," I say wryly.

The moment we get to the suite, exhaustion hits me like a bullet train. I set my phone alarm for a three-hour nap and inwardly curse the guys for being shifters with better stamina. But the hotel bed is at least super comfy and I curl up under the comforter and fall asleep inside a minute.

I have two dreams when I sleep. In one, January is chasing me. He knows I betrayed him and he's out for blood and the guys are nowhere to be found. They've left me and I have to fight him off but my feet are stuck in quicksand and I'm sinking...sinking… But then that dream fades and I dream that I'm sleeping in a huge bed, an *absurdly* huge bed really. It's round and it looks like it was custom made for several people. I dream that I wake up there and the bed feels like a cloud and I'm curled up between three jaguars. They're all silky smooth and we fit together like a puzzle. And when I sigh happily as I hug them closer to me, I can feel them purring.

~

"Wake up, darlin'." Dennis the jaguar is talking to me, which is weird because I thought they couldn't talk while they were shifted. But when I reluctantly open my eyes I see Dennis smiling down at me. "You slept through your alarm."

"Shoot!"

Dennis chuckles as I jump out of bed, rubbing my eyes. "Hey, it's fine. You've got plenty of time to get ready, even factoring in an hour for hair."

"I *will* need an hour for hair," I mutter. "God..." A wave of anxiety washes over me and I spin around again to face Dennis. "Tell me we're going to be alright?"

"We're going to be alright, kid," Dennis says, kissing me softly. "Promise."

"Okay." I kiss him back; once, twice, and then take a step back. "Better stop or I'll lose that hour for my hair."

"Go primp," Dennis says, with a wave of his hand. "Even though you don't need it."

"Yeah yeah yeah."

I end up wandering into Scott's room while I'm getting dressed to ask him something and then he wanders out to get the answer from Miguel. That's when I notice that he's been inspecting the real Ares stone which is now sitting inside its safe with the door ajar. The thing is small and looks so modest. It's just a little blue rock really with a bit of a glow if you look hard enough.

The witch in me tells me to take it. I just have a *feeling* and I don't know why and it's a very dangerous choice. But on impulse, I grab the Ares stone and stick it down in my bra, the neckline of my dress so deep that it rests down by my sternum.

I don't tell any of the guys what I've done.

~

"You guys look gorgeous," I say adoringly. I'm as ready as I'll ever be in my dress. My hair is in a careful updo and my makeup is dramatic with golden shadowed wings for my eyes, because if you're not going to be dramatic when you're going to a ball with a bunch of shifter spies, then when are you really?

Miguel and Scott both puff up a little when I say that. They're both dressed to the nines in designer tuxedos, freshly shaved and cologned. Dennis on the other hand...

"What about me?" He says, smirking. He's wearing his old faded USMC jacket and a Batman t-shirt. He's the tech guy camped out in the surveillance van after all. He really doesn't need to be prettied up.

"You look gorgeous too, baby," I say, throwing my arms around him. My lipstick comes off on his mouth and he laughs, squeezing my hip. "And troublesome. Have to fix my lipstick now."

The buyer's ball is taking place at this huge place that sits on a little cliffside right over the beach. Even January, with his giant Mill Creek estate, must be jealous I think, as Scott plays driver and helps me out of the limo in front of the terra cotta colored mansion with a Cupid fountain in front of it. We're in the midst of a line of cars. Apparently, everybody who is anybody is coming to this brouhaha. Although it's safe to assume the bulk of them have no idea what their host is into, buying up a darkly magical item to help a French guy get elected president.

Miguel and I are led down a stone walkway between two

lines of date palms to a verandah that wraps around the place with a spectacular view of the ocean as it glitters in the twilight. Scott brings up the rear with George; the two heavies. As dizzying as the glamour is (I even spot a couple of movie stars in attendance), my nerves are going a little haywire. This is it. The final showdown. January just has to sell the fake and then we'll take him down. And then...and then I hope I don't just lose my guys to the next mission.

"Kate, darling!" January appears as a crowd of party goers part for him like he's Moses at the Red Sea. The ballroom is huge with marble flowers and massive chandeliers that glitter over our heads like diamonds. I tense up when I see January, like usual, but he's grinning from ear to ear, his nose a little red. I think he's had plenty to drink already. I put on my best smile and pretend to appreciate the way he's eyeing me up and down as he approaches. "Well, you look positively beatific."

"Oh, thank you, Mr. January," I say. I even give him a little spin, showing off my dress. "I saw it in a shop today and I just had to have it."

"That's how it usually goes in Monte Carlo," January says. "Listen, I'll need you later. Our patron for the evening will be purchasing that important item in a bit." He gives me a little wink and a smile. I think he's cagey for Miguel's benefit. "George has the item. I'll let you know when you're needed upstairs."

"Yes, sir," I say, still beaming.

When he's gone, I spin around and take Miguel's hand. "Must be a nice fake you guys put together."

"If we're playing our cards right, he'll never know the difference," he says quietly. "We just need the actual transaction to happen. We'd like to get January trying to purchase something the U.S. government has classified as a weapon of mass destruction *although-*"

"It's a weapon of mass destruction?" I hiss, just a little bit amused. "Really? I mean it's a stone."

"That can win any war," Miguel points out. "Shouldn't talk about it in here. You want a drink?"

"Just wine," I tell him. "Better keep my wits about me."

Miguel and I wine and dine and smile while keeping our eyes open. Dennis is in our ears and he can hear us but nothing is happening yet. Working in January's warehouse day to day as I secretly gained information about January's business and handed it off to a bunch of spies, was terrifying. This is terrifying too but in a very surreal way. When I'm at work, I can at least act like a person who's at work. But at this ball I'm also at work yet supposed to be having a good time, the transaction to come just an afterthought; an excuse for an all expenses paid trip, courtesy of my boss. But what if they want to somehow authenticate the stone before they buy? I think to myself. I did as much research into the Ares stone as I could but it's such a Holy Grail of an item that most people don't even take it seriously. I'm not sure whether there *is* a way to truly authenticate it - but on the other hand, why would you buy something for probably millions and millions of dollars if you couldn't prove it was real?

"Are you okay?" Miguel says in my ear. "You're holding my hand like you want to rip it off my body."

I let go and shake my hand out, realizing how tightly I was clenching it. "Sorry. Little tense."

"You'll get used to it," Miguel says casually.

I take a petit four from a silver platter going by and take a bite, frowning at Miguel before I swallow. "Get used to it when? In the next half hour?"

"No no, I mean, um…" He shakes his head, laughing softly to himself. "Nevermind."

"Ah, no no," I say, nudging him. "I hate it when people do

that. You can't start to say something and then stop. What is it?"

"It's just something the guys and I were talking about." He takes a sip of wine and looks around the ballroom. He nods towards the verandah. The place is huge but it's still a little crowded. I know we pass the French presidential candidate as I follow Miguel out to the marble verandah looking out on the ocean as the moon rises. Somebody who I've never seen in my life waves at me like she knows me, which I guess is the way of parties like these, and I wave back as if I know her too.

"So much better outside," I mutter as we step into the cool sea breeze. "Alright, what are you talking about then?" I look up at him expectantly.

Miguel sighs and his eyelashes flutter as he looks at me. He reaches up to run his thumb along my cheek and I can't help but smile.

We belong to each other, I think to myself.

"You have a significant amount of valuable knowledge," Miguel says abruptly. He takes a sip of wine and looks out at the ocean.

"Alright...thank you?" I nudge him again. "Want to expand on that?"

"Knowledge that would be useful to the kinds of missions we're routinely sent on," Miguel says. He looks nervous suddenly. I haven't seen him looking quite this flavor of nervous before.

Suddenly, I hear Dennis in my ear, "You're talking to her about this *now*?"

I frown at that. It sounds important. Miguel whispers, "Well, maybe now is a good time, okay? She's all liquored up."

I snort at that. "Dennis, what's he talking about?"

I picture Dennis in the van parked about a half a mile away, scratching his head and looking agitated, probably hacked into the mansion's surveillance cameras as he talks to us.

Dennis says, "It was just an idea we had-"

"Let me tell it," Miguel says.

"Well, then do it!"

"Oh my God," I mutter under my breath. "Somebody tell me *something*."

"We were thinking maybe you could join Jaguar Force," Miguel blurts out. "Maybe. Possibly. As one of the team. With us. As partners." He smiles a tight, nervous smile at that.

I feel like my heart doubles in size in my chest and I can't stop the smile that bursts across my face.

Granted, I know it's a crazy idea. Scott, Miguel, and Dennis are all three highly trained professionals with years of experience in intelligence operations. I suppose I could be of use when it comes to knowledge of the kinds of things they investigate, but I really don't know what they're thinking - imagining me as a spy, as one of them. Still, it's incredibly flattering. I feel all warm and fuzzy inside.

"You're nuts!" I say lightly. "You're completely cuckoo. All three of you."

"We are not," Miguel says firmly. "I… You know what, you should talk to Scott. It was his idea."

"Scott?" I sputter. "You're putting me on. There's no way Scott would ever approve of-"

"I'm serious," Miguel says, shrugging. "He thinks you've got a knack for this kind of work. He wants you in." He grins down at me and plays with a lock of my hair. "We all want you in, Kate."

"It's crazy," I mutter to myself. Except now I'm starting to wonder. Could I really be a spy?

"Guys, where *is* Scott?" Dennis says in my ear.

Miguel and I glance at each other and turn to look back through the French doors and into the ball that's now in full swing. I squint through the crowd of well-coiffed people in gowns and tuxedos and the servers carrying trays of drinks but I don't see Scott anywhere. Ostensibly, he's supposed to stay close since he's supposed to be my bodyguard. But he's nowhere to be seen.

"Did something happen?" I say, meaning to talk to Dennis. "What's he saying?"

"I dunno, he doesn't have an earpiece," Dennis says. "I can only talk on two channels at a time and he said you guys should have them."

Son of a bitch.

I glare at Miguel. "Did you know that?"

"He didn't want to worry you," Miguel says.

I roll my eyes. "Son of a bitch."

"Look, it's probably fine," Dennis says. "He may be tailing somebody through the party. Just keep an eye out for him and don't make any sudden moves."

"Kate!" January appears and I feel like every drop of my blood rushes down to my feet. I'm already on edge but now we can't find Scott and I don't have a good feeling about it. He rubs his beard and eyes me up and down and I bite down hard on my lip. Didn't he get enough of a look the first time? "You're needed upstairs. Fourth door on the right. The buyer would like to speak to you about the stone. Handle with kid gloves, my girl. He's a big fish."

"Oh...ah, I would love to," I say, a forced smile plastered on my face. "Except I can't find Joe? I'd like to have him with me."

"Don't worry about him, darling," January says.

"Oh, Eddie," I say smoothly. "Come with me. You can see me in action-"

"I'll take care of your paramour," January says, standing a little between us. A live jazz band is playing "Moonlight

Serenade" and the ocean is glittering and so are January's eyes as he begins to scowl. I'm pushing him too far.

I nod, smiling easily. I try to look like the cowed daughter but I really don't feel like one anymore. "Of course, I'm being silly."

"Yes, you are," January says darkly.

"I'll catch up with you in a bit," Miguel says, squeezing my arm.

"Yes..."

"Danger, Will Robinson," Dennis says in my ear. "Houston, we have a problem."

"You have any other catchphrases you want to dish out," I say under my breath, as I make my way through the crowd," or are you done?"

"I don't like this," he whispers in my ear. I want to tease but he sounds so legitimately worried.

"If I'm going to be one of your team, you're gonna have to get used to this, babe," I say.

"I'm not even used to it when it's Scott in danger," Dennis says, and I smile fondly. I love it when they cop to how much they care for each other. I love the idea that I'm stepping into a kind of family.

I smile and beam and look generally 'beatific' as I push through the crowd to the wide and twisting set of stairs at the top of which is a wide landing and a red corridor. I have to pick up my dress to make the steps, and I swallow, feeling a terrible sense of dread.

"Tell me it's going to be okay again, Dennis."

"It'll be okay, baby," Dennis mutters.

"No sign of Scott yet?"

Dennis is quiet for a few seconds and says, "No."

"Okay. Here I go." I walk with purpose up the last couple steps and down the hall to the fourth door. I knock on the broad door that has wolves and lions carved into the wood and pearl inlay. This guy, whoever he is, spares no expense. That's for sure. He'll stick some luxury wherever he can manage to shove it.

The door opens and a broadly grinning man with slicked back blonde hair beams at me. He's wearing a tux that doesn't fit very well over his portly frame. I peg him for a badly aging fifty and too much plastic surgery.

"Miss Bloom!" He says brightly, his voice oddly reedy. "Please come in. I bet you didn't think you were actually going to meet your host tonight." He grabs my hand in his and pumps it up and down. "Theodore Keeny the Third. Wonderful to meet you." He smiles again. His lips look overly plump. He's definitely had collagen. The effect is sort of comical and I have to bite back a giggle.

But really. *This* guy is the buyer? Somehow I'd gotten it into my head that the buyer must be a mysterious type. A wizard from a far away land now making his home in Monaco with his riches procured by magical means. But in the end, the answer is so freaking boring. It's just another blonde American businessman. They're like a plague.

I put on my most professional and welcome expression - cool and collected but not unfriendly. "It's lovely to meet you, Mr. Keeny. I'm so glad we can do some business today."

Keeny takes my arm like he's my escort or something, which I do not like at all. He leads me into his spacious study and I see where the conventional ends and weird begins. The place looks pretty much like how I'd imagine the study of a rich guy who secretly *wants* to be a wizard might look. He's obviously a collector of magical artifacts and anything in relation to the occult. There are a few urns and statues that I recognize from old posts on the forums that he's apparently accumulated. There are also skulls under bell jars and taxidermied creatures here and there that creep me out. There's an entire alligator on the floor by a chaise, frozen, its toothy mouth gaping open. There's also some massive *thing* draped with a black cloth in the corner by his giant mahogany desk. I shudder to think what a guy buying the Ares stone needs to cover with a black cloth, but two heavies are standing in front of it in black suits, their hands clasped in front of them.

"Is zees ze girl?" A thick French accent asks and I recognize Andre Bouchard, the candidate for the president of France, as he approaches from behind the desk. The boys showed me a picture of the guy so I was somewhat prepared but now I have to steel myself and even then, I'm sure I might be giving myself away to some degree.

There's nothing *obviously* wrong with Bouchard when you look at him. At least it's nothing you could put a finger on. But there's a vague sense of wrongness about him. He's conventionally handsome with a narrow jaw that juts a little too much and an aquiline nose and dark brown eyes. But when you look closer you see that his eyes aren't really brown and aren't really any color at all. It's as if they're somehow all the colors mixed together yet not black. They're *swirly* if you look closely enough, in a way that is not natural. They also look too deeply at you, I think now, as he grabs my hand in his. His handshake is clammy and the way his skin moves along mine, I feel as if an amphibian is slithering along my palm. I swallow, trying not to gag and step back, still smiling that forced smile.

If we somehow fail tonight, this guy will be the president of France and even if he wasn't seriously creeping me out right now on a subtle and inexplicable level, I saw his political credentials too. The guy is *evil* and he would probably seriously wreck France.

"I've 'eard so much about your charms," Bouchard says, smiling silkily.

I have to look away this time to smile back. "I'm glad I'm

spoken of so well." I put a giggle on it and play with my hair to sell it.

When there's a knock at the door, Keeny goes to answer it. It's George, with a black case that I assume contains the fake Ares stone.

It's almost over, I tell myself. *Just be cool.*

"I have Miguel looking around for Scott," Dennis says in my ear. "Still no sight of him."

January's wire information is in my phone. A long code is needed to put the transaction through so Keeny can pay January. That's it. Once Keeny types in the numbers, the transaction will be through and Scott and Miguel will come sweeping in...assuming Scott isn't dead outside or something.

My hands are clammy. My clutch purse with my phone hangs from my wrist and I surreptitiously wipe my palms on the beaded fabric.

"You want to see your prize, I expect?" I say smoothly. I gesture to George with his black case. "I think you'll be pleased."

"The keys to France are in that case," Bouchard says. His eyes practically glow and I can't help but take a step back.

"Well, I'm already pleased," Keeny says. His voice even has some New York in it. He probably lives on Fifth. I bet he has a penthouse when he's not summering in Monaco and helping fascists get elected via dark magic. "The complimentary gift your boss gifted me with is really something else. I wasn't sure about this sale, you know. Didn't believe it could be real, didn't want to get my boy, Bouchard's hopes up. But this..."

"Complimentary gift?" I mutter. I don't like the sound of that. Something about it makes me shiver.

"Oh, yes. Said he hated to part with it. But it put me right over the top."

"I wasn't aware..." I feel a little short of breath and I don't know why. "What's the complimentary gift?" I glance at George and see him smirking. That alone bothers me. George is a total psychopath. His expression rarely changes. But now he looks pleased as punch.

"Why this creature right here," Keeny says. He walks up to the big thing covered in a black cloth and yanks it off to reveal a big clear acrylic cube.

Inside the cube is Scott who is naked and human and looking very pissed off as he sits on the floor of his cage. He sees me but he doesn't give anything away other than looking pissed off.

"Ah...*oh*." I can't contain my gasp.

"Kate?" Dennis says in my ear. "What is it? Can you tell me?"

"I didn't realize," I say slowly, "that he gave you Joe. Only, he was *my* bodyguard." I laugh casually as if I'm only amused. "I guess I'll have to get a new one, huh?"

"I've always wanted a shifter for a pet," Keeny says, his eyes lighting up. "And now I've got one!"

"Oh *shit*," Dennis says.

"Right," I say, sighing just a little. "A shifter... That would make a wonderful gift. Wouldn't it?"

"Yes," Keeny says. "It absolutely does. In fact, I can shift him whenever I like. It's really a thing to behold." He glances between me and Bouchard excitedly.

I have another in a series of bad feelings and quickly say, "Oh, oh, sir! You don't need to-"

Keeny has a laptop open on his desk and he types something in and there's a low humming sound from the direction of the acrylic box just as I see Scott's mouth stretch in a silent scream and every muscle seems to clench before he suddenly shifts into jaguar form. His jaguar growls at Keeny, jumping, his paws clawing at the glass. The sight of him painfully forced to shift like that and seeing him so helpless in there makes me tear up but I try to cover, smiling through it.

"Why that's...amazing," I say, swallowing. "I mean I've seen him shift. But that's beautiful, isn't it?"

"Just so," Keeny says proudly. "Of course, he's quite dangerous in his jaguar form." I think Keeny's right. I see Scott springing on his back legs and pushing at the acrylic wall he's trapped behind with enough force to break it given half a chance. Keeny types something again and Scott trembles and shifts back collapsing on the floor. "That's why I'm keeping him human most of the time, as long as he's in there. It's only temporary. I'm going to get him a very nice habitat underground, you see, big lamps to mimic the sun and some jungle plants and things. Maybe a snake!"

"You're keeping him in human form..." I say quietly.

"Simple matter of frequencies that come up through the floor," Keeny says proudly. "One to keep him human, one to shock him into shifting. I can switch him back and forth whenever I please. Look here-"

"No no no-"

I bite down on my tongue, my eyes watering again, as Scott is shocked into jaguar form and back again. It just looks torturous and when he's back in his human form he looks pale and gaunt. He casts me one long look as he curls up in the corner, shaking. I feel like he's trying to assure *me* that things will be okay.

The thought of Scott being kept as a pet in some chintzy habitat with jungles painted on the walls *under the ground* makes me ill as does the assurance that Scott would never allow that to happen to him. Of that, I'm certain. He'd die first.

KATE

"Yes, yes. *Oui oui.*" Bouchard waves a hand. "It's a very nice keety cat. But can ve get on vis zee sale now? I vant my Ares stone."

"Yes," I say quickly, twisting my fingers together to try to calm myself. "George, why don't you show him the item?"

Everything comes down to this, I realize. I watch George approach with his black briefcase and he sets it on the desk. The fake Ares stone will hopefully be real enough to throw them off. Having seen both the real one and the fake, I *think* the fake is a good facsimile but who knows for sure? Hopefully not Bouchard, though when I look into his eyes, I feel as if he knows far too much.

The Ares stone in my bra feels like it's about to burn a hole in my chest. The plunging neckline of the dress means the bra is strapless; a barely there construction of two little cups holding me and a small blue stone in place. I still don't know if I was right to grab the thing in the first place. I just had a *feeling*. It seems like I may need to produce it at just the right time.

George sets the briefcase on the desk and pops it open,

revealing a stone identical to the one in my bra and producing a slight blue glow as it sits nestled in black velvet.

"Can you authenticate it?" Keeny says. "I'm paying an absurd amount of money for this little trinket, Bouchard. All to put you in power and put France in my wallet. I'd like to know if the damn thing is real."

"I should be able to tell if it's real," Bouchard says offhandedly. "I've seen it before."

"He what now?" Dennis says in my ear.

"You… you have?" I say, the waver in my voice potentially giving me away slightly.

"But certainly," Bouchard says. "Once it belonged to King Leopold of Belgium. I was his right-hand man. I procured the stone for him and the next thing you know, he took the Congo. But items this powerful never stay in anyone's hands for long."

"Oh...um, how old are you, sir?" I smile a little as I say it as if I'm just faintly curious.

"Over four hundred," he says with a shrug. "I look good for my age, don't I?"

"Certainly," I mutter.

Well, this isn't ideal.

Bouchard picks up the stone and holds it under a light. He grabs a magnifying glass off the desk and looks at the stone through it for an agonizing minute during which my gaze turns to Scott, brooding in his cell, perhaps biding his time. I feel like Dennis is missing something but if I say it out loud, it might give up the game… I'm sweating too much for somebody standing in a cool room wearing not much clothing and I take a deep breath.

"This is a fake," Bouchard declares.

Everyone gasps, including me.

George says, "Excuse me?" He doesn't even look rattled.

He just looks mildly surprised but he narrows his eyes at *me*. "A fake? Are you sure?"

"The true Ares stone," Bouchard says slowly, "has the tiniest, almost microscopic brass colored granules along this ridge right here." He holds the stone out to Keeny, gesturing with his fingers which I notice for the first time look a hundred years older than the rest of him. "Not many can see them. But I can. I've been authenticating such stones for years. And as I say...I've seen this one before."

"Stay cool," Dennis says softly in my ear. "Just stay cool, Kate."

I laugh a little hysterically at that and Keeny raises an eyebrow at me. "I don't understand how it could possibly be a fake."

"Don't you?" George says to me. I feel my heart jump into his throat and he whips out his phone. Presumably to speak to January. "Mr. Keeny, Mr. Bouchard, we'll take care of this. Kate, you don't move. You stay right where you are."

"George!" I say, turning up the indignation. "I don't know why you're acting like I've done something-"

"Can it," George snaps. He talks into his phone again, catching January up. He speaks quietly near the door, his eyes fixed on me as Keeny and Bouchard heatedly speak to each other in quiet murmurs. I risk a look at Scott who just shakes his head at me though I'm not entirely sure what that's supposed to mean. George slowly faces me and opens his jacket to reveal his gun. Just in case I didn't understand the threat. "Interesting information I just received. Seems your little boyfriend has the real stone. He must've swiped it from me when I wasn't looking and traded it for the fake. He was trying to score his own deal with the Ares. Little punk." George snorts a laugh at me and shakes his head. "Boy, did you get took. All he wanted from you was the Ares, girly.

Anyway, January's coming here himself with that douchebag and the *real* stone."

Dennis, I think to myself. *What is going on?*

As if reading my mind, Dennis says, "We're buying time. We got a second fake. We actually have four fakes back here in the van. Anyway, it gets Miguel here at least."

"I can't believe it," I say, summing up some tears. "I can't believe Eddie played me like that. Son of a bitch!"

"Hey, sweetheart," George says, sidling up to me, suddenly all sweetness and light.

"Men are dogs. You know...*I* always thought you were cute. You know that, right?" George waggles his eyebrows at me. It's the most human I've ever seen him and it's vaguely disgusting. It's like he's wearing a strange mask.

"Well, I'm...very upset about this," I say, sighing. I glance at Scott. "I'm a bit disappointed my *bodyguard* didn't see this coming. Wasn't that his job after all?"

"Heh. Good point," Keeny says. "He's in the doghouse now though. Er...cathouse. Ha!"

"So that signal that makes him shift," I say tiredly, rubbing my eyes as if all this is just a little wrinkle in a long day. "You send a signal from the *computer* to the cube there? And it forces him to shift? And then you shift him back? Like a *frequency?*"

Dennis says, "Jesus Christ, I'm sorry, Kate. Shit…"

"That's right," Keeny says, puffing up again. "Do you want me to show you again-"

"Oh, that's alright," I say, truly hoping he doesn't. "I was just wondering. I didn't know they made such things."

"I'm on it, I'm on it, I'm on it," Dennis mutters in my ear.

Bout time, I think to myself.

It doesn't take long before there's yet another knock on the door and January is walking in with two henchmen holding on to Miguel. January has a second briefcase and he glares at me as he sets it on the desk next to the other one. I've never seen him looking so pissed. He looks like he wants to murder me.

"You did always seem like a girl who might have shit taste in men, Kate Bloom," January says darky. "But if this isn't the real stone, I might start to think it's *you* who's playing with me."

"I swear I didn't know," I say, shrugging. "I'm *so* sorry, Mr. January." I glower at Miguel, trying to sell it. "And *he* can go die as far as I'm concerned. Lying bastard!"

"Okay okay," George says, putting up his hands. "No need to involve Mr. Keeny and Mr. Bouchard in these personal dramas."

"I don't know," Bouchard says, shrugging. "Eet's a leetle beet entertaining, no?" He smirks at me and sidles up to the second briefcase and I exchange a look with Miguel who doesn't look nearly as freaked out as I think I would in his situation. He's putting on an expression of the lout who just got caught and is maybe afraid he's about to die.

Everyone's waiting with bated breath.

"How's it looking?" I say, really speaking to Dennis.

"I got it," Dennis says in my ear. "I can make him shift when you say 'go' and kill the off switch so he can stay shifted." I glance at Miguel who nods.

"I don't know yet," Bouchard mutters, glaring through his magnifying glass at the second fake stone sitting under the light. "Mmm. No...no, it's a fake!"

"What?!" January says.

"What the hell is going on?" Keeny shouts, throwing up his hands.

January, perhaps finally realizing that his daughter/object of ogling is not his adoring servant spins around and pulls a gun from his jacket, cocks it, and point it at me.

"Kate!" January says.

"Dennis, now!" I shout.

"What?"

Our attention shifts to the cube where a shock electrifies Scott who shakes and shifts, all three hundred and fifty pounds of extra large jaguar pounding at the dinky cube that's not nearly strong enough to hold him. Keeny sputters and types away at his laptop, but he's unable to shift Scott back as he pushes at his cage and Scott is about to bust out.

"Will you kill that bitch!" Keeny shouts, pointing at me.

I hear Miguel shout and I can only gasp as January glowers and shoots his gun just as Miguel shifts and leaps at him, his great teeth bared. Everything is chaos as the jaguar they didn't know existed tackles January to the ground and Scott breaks through the cube to attack. I hear screams below and realize Dennis has likely shifted and is running to us and I'm right as I already hear him pounding up the stairs and jumping into the fray. And me...I'm shot. That terrible pressure having struck me like lightning. I fall to the ground and...there's no blood. Which is weird, I think, as I stare down at myself, Scott and Miguel taking on all the humans in the room as Dennis comes pounding in. How is there no blood? It didn't feel like getting shot really, though it did hurt.

"Oh," I say, laughing a little, jostled by the fight and running to crawl under a table. I take the Ares stone out of my bra and see it faintly scratched now, presumably by the bullet.

Of course. I had the Ares stone. I was never going to lose.

January is crawling towards me through the scramble of limbs and fur and muscle and I scurry away just as Scott's jaguar sinks his teeth into January's hip. I run to the desk and find a heavy marble paperweight, deciding that even if it means my death, I can't leave anything to chance.

"NO!" Bouchard's shriek meets the crack of the paperweight shattering the Ares stone on the desk and I smile to myself, relieved, just as I see Dennis's jaguar slam Bouchard against the wall, knocking him out.

When the fight dies down there are three jaguars and a bunch of unconscious humans and me, popping up from behind the desk with January's gun which I found on the floor. Except that now there's nobody to shoot.

"Did we win?" I say breathlessly.

Scott shifts back into a human form, unapologetically naked as a jaybird and says, "Yeah. We won. But I would really like some pants." He stalks over to a bleeding George who is not unconscious but is very much cowering in the corner and demands his pants. George happily gives them up and curls back up into a ball and I wish I had a camera.

Dennis shifts, scratches his head, and whips his phone out of his pocket. "Yes...JF code two two one. Clean-up in Monte Carlo. Follow signal. Thanks." He hangs up and pockets his phone then spins to face me. "Am I crazy or did you smash the real Ares stone a minute ago?"

"Jesus," Scott mutters. "Sachar wanted that thing intact. Plus we didn't get the sale."

"It shouldn't *be* intact," I say. "Nobody should have it. So, what...does this mean we're screwed? January gets off scot-free because we didn't get the sale?"

Miguel shifts back into human form and having heard what I said, throws his head back and laughs like it's *hilarious*. "Oh my God! Kate, no. It just means he goes away for two lifetimes instead of three."

"That's not to mention Keeny," Dennis says, rocking back and forth on his heels. "I was working on hacking his laptop, that's why I missed what he said about the signal to Scott's cage at first. I've got him on all kinds of dastardly dealings including a whole bunch of emails with Bouchard about using a dark magic WMD for the purposes of winning a presidential election. We might even have both Keeny and January on treason. Not to mention the murder of the Sewer Witch."

The January in question is currently knocked out, sprawled on his back, his mouth agape. I kick his leg and laugh down at him. "Ha! Ya big loser! Murdering scumbag son of a bitch!"

"Alright, so it's not *exactly* the mission as stated," Miguel says, shrugging. "But I think we did okay."

My ears perk up. I've just realized that I can still hear music and the noise of the crowd downstairs. "Is...the party really still going on? Has nobody noticed a jaguar was just running up the stairs? Did no one hear the fight?"

"Oh sure," Miguel says. "But stuff like that happens in Monte Carlo all the time. It's a party."

"Right." I nod and glance over at the shattered dust of the Ares stone. I did enough research to know that once broken, it's completely worthless. That makes me feel pretty good. I hope I don't get charged with treason for it. "So, that's it?"

"That's it," Scott says. He grabs my hand and gently tugs me to him. "Now, let me just do one thing…" He kisses me and I wrap my arms around him, melting into his mouth as Dennis and Miguel hoot behind us. I was afraid I was about to lose him and it was only then that I realized just how in love I am with all three of these men. If anything happened to one of them, I think it would about kill me. "Let's go home," he whispers in my ear.

SCOTT

The guys, Kate and I wait in Keeny's study for the clean-up crew; a bunch of G-men in tuxedos who look just like servers with rolling catering carts. The party is cleared out by the Monte Carlo police who think a diplomat has ordered it broken up via government contacts. It's all pretty neat and tidy, or as neat as it can be. The clean-up takes a while and Kate will undergo a lengthy debriefing back in New York, but around one in the morning, we finally head back to the hotel with what remains of the Ares stone swept into an evidence baggie and tucked into my pocket.

I reflexively want to be pretty damn pissed that Kate shattered the entire subject of our mission with a paperweight but I'm sort of impressed. I've been pretty impressed with Kate this whole time. Which is why I think she'd be a real asset to the team...and not just because I want her around all the time. Though I can't deny that is a large part of it. But I don't think that's a bad thing. It may not be something I'll be able to explain to Sachar. But the fact that we're clearly fated to be together, all four of us, I think means we're meant to function as a team. There's also the undeniable fact of fated mates which Miguel explained to me the other day...we can't just be away from Kate all the time now. We physically can't. We won't function well. We don't just want her around, we *need* her around.

I just hope Kate can understand all this. I hope it's not too overwhelming.

She's asleep on my shoulder as we pull up in front of The Hermitage and I nudge her awake, kissing her hair. We'll be flying home the next night on a red-eye, Sachar mercifully allowing us a day to relax after I mentioned how many missions we'd been on in a row. It's still not a vacation and we do need one, preferably somewhere we can go on some *good* runs. Somewhere with a jungle.

"Wake up, baby," I murmur as Kate stirs.

Dennis and I walk on either side of her, our arms around her and Miguel throws an arm around my neck as we make our way inside. I've always been close to Miguel and Dennis but since meeting Kate we all feel closer. I feel as if I've finally fully realized the extent of our group dynamic. I never would have expected a relationship like this. But in human terms, they will be my husbands as much as Kate will be my wife. Assuming Kate agrees to all this.

Upstairs Kate is like a sleepy kid. No sexy shenanigans tonight, that's for sure. I know we're all about to pass out as soon as we hit the pillow. I lead Kate into my room and the guys follow. Somehow this feels agreed upon even though none of it's been spoken aloud. Kate turns to face me, smiling fondly as I help her off with her dress and her bra and Dennis helps her off with her shoes. I absently run my knuckles down her chest, between her breasts, with no intention but to admire. She leans forward and kisses me and Dennis kisses her neck. Miguel hands her one of my t-shirts and she puts it on and takes down her hair and takes out her earrings, handing them to Miguel who sets them on the dresser. The guys and I strip down to our boxer briefs and we climb into my bed.

The bed is king size which is good, because it's got four people in it now, all snuggled under the covers. I spoon Kate, Miguel nestled behind me. She wraps her arms around Dennis. I've never slept with the guys before, other than a few times when we've fallen asleep in our shifted forms and curled up alongside each other. Yet it feels so natural, the bunch of us together in the bed. It feels like some puzzle has come together between us.

In the morning, we wake up a bit differently and I'm apparently nuzzling Miguel's neck but he only smiles sleepily at me as we all begin to stir and says, "Well, hey there, gorgeous."

"Shut up," I mumble, turning a little red.

"This is the only way to wake up in the morning," Kate murmurs. She stretches and I lean over to kiss her neck just as Dennis kisses her cheek.

"Feeling left out over here," Miguel says. Kate crawls over me to lay on top of Miguel and kisses his neck. "Better." She giggles and rolls off of him to the floor. "There's a gigantic pool downstairs and I want to try it. And I want to play roulette just to say I played roulette in Monte Carlo."

Miguel sits up and wags his eyebrows. "There's also room service brunch with mimosas and a hot tub right here."

"Ooh. Let's do that first," Kate says. She smiles brightly and rubs her tummy through my t-shirt that's swimming on her. "C'mon, boys."

"I love you," I blurt out.

I've actually never said that out loud to anybody but my parents. Everyone stares at me and now I *know* I'm turning red. I don't know *why* I have the urge to crawl out of my skin right now. I can kill a man twice my size with my bare hands or shift and rip his throat out and I can free climb solo to an impressive degree and I can break into highly secured places without anyone ever knowing but just saying the words, "I love you," has now made me want to crawl right back under the covers like a scared kid.

Kate lights up and says, "I love you too." She jumps back on the bed and Miguel groans as she crawls back over to me, pushing me down in the blankets and kissing me silly, heedless of morning breath.

"Hey, *I* love you too!" Dennis says. Kate breaks away from me and I can't help but laugh as she rolls over and kisses Dennis next.

"I love you too!" Kate says to Dennis.

"I love you too and I'm feeling left out again!" Miguel says even as he laughs. And then we're all laughing as Dennis and I help roll Kate back over to Miguel who she kisses once more before getting to her feet again.

"Coffee before mimosas," Kate says, rubbing her eyes, wandering out of the bedroom and in the direction of the kitchenette. "Who's coming?"

The day is passed leisurely. We order brunch and Kate teases me the entire time because I call it a 'girly meal'. Then I tell her how I've had brunch with two different presidents and her astonished expression makes me laugh for five minutes, but by then I'm pretty buzzed on the tiny bubbles of the mimosas. We laze around in the hot tub for a while and we don't bother with clothes; Kate drifting from lap to lap as we take turns massaging her, kissing her hot and wet and slow until we end up making love, only finally getting out when our fingers get too wrinkly.

After that, we have to contact Sachar and do a mini-debrief for a bit. January, Keeny, Bouchard, and George are in custody, and being flown to America. There's quite a hub bub with the French concerning Bouchard though, on the bright side, nobody really liked him anyway. But it's been made public that a French presidential candidate has been arrested by American officials on 'undisclosed charges'. At some point, they'll come up with an invented charge to cover up the dark magic stuff. They'll probably just say he was attempting to buy illegal weapons on the dark web from January...which is true anyway. They'll just have to get creative in naming the weapons. Kate follows the whole thing on Twitter, as the four of us lay on the beach later. She keeps reading out amusing headlines and bits and pieces of news.

"They're cleaning out the warehouse!" She shouts at one point. She's lying back on a deck chair next to us on a stretch of white sand and now she hops up and does a little dance in the orange swimsuit and sarong she bought that morning in a shop. "They taking all his tooooys!" She spins around and hoots and I can't help but grin at her.

"Are you happy, baby?" I say. She crawls up on my lap in the chair and gives me a long deep kiss and I cup her ass in my hands and squeeze so that she moans a little in my mouth as the guys egg us on.

"I am so happy right now - for *many* reasons," she says in my ear. She straddles me there on the deck chair and we make out for a while and because it's Monte Carlo nobody blinks when she moves on to Dennis and then Miguel and by the time we make our way back up to the hotel to change and go catch our flights back to New York, her lips are pink and swollen and I have to kiss her again just to taste them.

Two days later, Kate is meeting us at a temporary JF office where she's to meet Sachar and do a full debrief. I hate debriefs. They're my least favorite part of any mission. I know they're necessary but it's a tedious amount of paperwork and explanation that amounts to justifying things which, after the fact, somehow seem difficult to justify but made sense at the time.

Now, I'm sitting on a cheap plastic chair in a little white room, talking to Sachar's guy as he looks at my report on his laptop. And they don't even have any coffee. I should've brought some coffee.

"So...your informant didn't tell you she was bringing the real Ares stone along to the transaction? She just...took it?" Sachar's second in command is Rogers. He's narrowing his eyes at me. I take a long, deep breath. I've been through this dozens of times so I get a little hot under the collar about it.

"That's right," I say slowly. "And she should have told us. But if she hadn't taken it along, we might have lost. Because she was in possession of the stone at the time, she didn't get shot. And we won."

Seems simple enough to me.

"And...you've reported that you are in a romantic relationship with your informant?" Rogers looks exceptionally annoyed by this.

"Yes." There's no actual rule against it, once the mission is *over.* Of course, there is a rule about maintaining a relationship *during* the mission which is a rule we've obviously broken. But since we're copping to it and since Sachar has a lot of trust in us, I'm pretty optimistic that we won't actually be in too much trouble.

We've also all written up statements proposing that Kate be recruited to join the team on a trial basis with the understanding that we would be training her to join as a full-time member. We wrote those up on the plane to New York and emailed them so Sachar could think about it before the debrief.

I have no idea what Sachar will think of all this.

"What I'm a little confused about," Rogers says, "is that

your fellow team members of Jaguar Force also each admitted to having begun a romantic relationship with Kate Bloom."

I sit back in my seat and cross my arms, looking Rogers straight in the eye. "Yes," I say. "That is correct."

"You're...you're telling me that *all* of you are in a romantic relationship with Kate Bloom," Rogers sputters. "All three of you? At the same time?"

"Yes, that's correct."

Rogers stares at me for a seemingly endless amount of time, during which I start to imagine what it would be like to just reach over and stick my fingers in his nose and pull up.

Finally, he clears his throat and says, "Colonel Sachar has decided he...approves of the idea of Kate Bloom joining you as a member. He wasn't even angry about this relationship business." Rogers looks really peeved at that and it makes me smirk. "Something about the nature of mates and shifters, shared fated mates… I couldn't make heads or tails of it. Anyway, he said it was specific to your nature as shifters."

"Yeah. He's right," I say shrugging.

Of course. He's a shifter himself. In all our anxiety about whether our proposal would be accepted, we forgot that we were dealing with one of our own kind.

Rogers licks his lips. I can practically see smoke coming out of his ears as he taps away at his laptop, glowering. "Alright, Scott. So, you guys got a girlfriend out of this mission and a new teammate who, by the way, has *zero* experience in intelligence, much less operations. Is there anything else you'll be requiring of us today?"

"Yes."

"And what would that be, precisely?"

"We'll be needing a vacation," I say, rolling my neck and smiling at the thought of more days with Kate on the beach. "Thanks in advance."

EPILOGUE

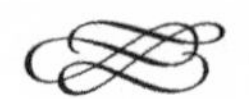

Kate

Six days later...

"I thought we were on vacation," I say, glaring at Miguel, although I can't quite help smiling. "Practicing martial arts moves is not exactly my idea of a vacation."

We're in a hotel suite that sits right on the beach in Fiji. It's even got one of those stairways that lead straight down in the water. The ocean here is so clear that I can see the glitter of the nail polish on my toes when I stand in it and look down. The sand is so white it hurts my eyes. The servers bring cocktails and shrimps and crab cakes. The place is just a five-minute drive from a jungle where the boys can run and play their hearts out like the big cats they are while I hang back and read my book on a deck chair and knock back Tequila Sunrises like a fiend. Everything here is beyond perfect.

But Miguel is trying to teach me how to flip him.

"Obviously," Miguel says. "You've never been on vacation with Scott. It often involves martial arts. Sometimes it involves jumping off cliffs. Three times its involved trips to the Emergency Room."

"Jesus Chris," I mutter. "Who have I hitched my little trailer too?"

Miguel raises an eyebrow and says, "Jaguar shifter spies."

"Oh. Right."

"C'mon," Miguel says. "Just try it one more time. Then we'll go down to the water with the guys."

Miguel comes at me and I leverage my weight like he taught me and this time he ends up on the floor with the wind knocked out of him and me on top, feeling pretty exhilarated.

"That was pretty good," he wheezes.

"You know what would be more fun than this - is if you taught me some more spells," I say, straddling him and playing with the collar of his shirt. "I'm an okay witch. I could be a better one."

Miguel catches his breath and bites his lips, smiling up at me. "Yeah. That was one of the draws for Sachar. Part of your eh...curriculum."

"Can't wait," I mutter, and grind down into Miguel until he groans and cranes his neck to kiss me.

"Fuck, Kate..."

His cock is just starting to get very interested when I hop up and take his hand, helping him to his feet. "C'mon. I want to swim."

I'm already wearing my suit; the same orange designer thing I bought in Monte Carlo and I tug him along through the airy hotel suite and out onto the deck and down the stairs into the warm, clear water.

"What took you so long!" Scott's in the water in a tiny pair of trunks that leaves little to the imagination and I can't take my eyes off him or Dennis who's leaning against him. The two of them look so cute and cozy and scalding hot together. I trot down the stairs and into the water and head straight for Dennis, laying a big kiss on him. I wrap my legs around him and Scott sandwiches us and I feel his arms around us as he kisses my neck.

I lean my head against Dennis' chest as he rubs my back. "Miguel said you always go this hard on vacations. He wouldn't let me leave until I flipped him."

"Dick!" Scott says, sticking his tongue out at Miguel. "A vacation is a vacation. Besides, it's not like we can train her in two weeks anyway."

"Yeah," Dennis says, squeezing me tight. "We'll train her on the job. It'll be great and incredibly dangerous."

"Oh good," Miguel says.

"It'll be fine," I say, and hop down to splash my way back to Miguel. "It's *fate*."

"Well, if it's fate then," he mutters before wrapping his arms around me. "The secrets of fate..."

"Hey, *I* have a secret as a matter of fact," Scott says, splashing the both of us.

"Yeah, what's that?"

"I know our next mission."

"Ooh!" I bounce on my toes. As stressful as this operation to take down January was, I think the guys are right. I think I have kind of a knack for it. I'm also hoping I can learn to deal with the anxiety of being thrown into these dangerous situations. But I have a feeling it's a little less stressful when it's not your own boss, though it will still be my own life at risk. But I trust these guys; my fated mates. I know how much we're willing to fight for each other. And I'm dedicated to living the rest of my life sharing it with theirs. I feel nothing but a delicious kind of warmth and happiness when I imagine the four of us together for as long as we're on this earth.

"What's the mission?" Miguel says, hugging me from behind as I turn in his arms.

"Vampires," Scott says. "China. Evil amulet."

"Sounds legit," Miguel says, nibbling on my earlobe. "Can't wait."

"That's your mission brief?" I say, even as I tilt my head to give Miguel better access. "China. Vampires. Amulet?"

"They're bullet points!" Scott says laughing.

"You're ridiculous," I say, and splash just as he and Dennis move in the water to wrap both me and Miguel up in their arms. "My guys are just ridiculous."

AFTERWORD

A Final Note from Jade:

I hope you enjoyed this story. Well, the good news is that there's more to come. If you want to be the first to hear about my new releases, promotions and giveaways, I urge you to join my Exclusive Reader's Club:

[Yes. Sign me up, please!]

I love supporting my readers and I want to be able to provide more to you, you can also join me on Facebook **here**.

ALSO BY JADE ALTERS

Magic & Mates

The Sharing Spell

Fated Shifter Mates :

Mated to Team Shadow

Mated to the Clan

Mated to the Pack

Mated to the Pride

In the Heat of the Pack :

Protected by the Pack

Claimed by the Pack